CHARLOTTE'S CROSSING

A novel by

Marty Thompson Arnold

Illustrations by Marty Thompson Arnold

Chapbook Press

Schuler Books
2660 28th Street SE
Grand Rapids, MI 49512
(616) 942-7330
www.schulerbooks.com

Charlotte's Crossing: a Novel

ISBN 13: 9781957169354

Library of Congress Control Number: 2023902383

Printed in the United States by Chapbook Press.

For Bruce
(1950 - 2002)

*In glorious
isolation and exotic otherness,
islands are evolutionary workshops for
Earth's most extravagant and remarkable creatures.*

PROLOGUE

In the beginning, and for 100 million years after, Earth had one large ocean with one large island. We call it Pangea. Animal life first stirred in the sea, then crawled or washed ashore, where fins and tentacles became legs, scales became fur and gills became lungs.

The animals on Pangea would be at once familiar and oddly strange to our eyes. Giant dragonflies hovered over tiny mammals that had all the charm of naked mole rats.

Earth was young and restless then. It belched and pitched and tossed Pangea until the land split apart. The pieces slid over the planet's gooey crust to the far ends of the earth.

Each fragment carried with it a portion of Pangean flora and fauna. In their new location, some species perished, but others adapted and flourished. A plant that withered in Australia grew lush in North America, while an animal that died out in Asia evolved into something unique in Africa. Eventually, each new continent found a delicate balance—with just enough plants to feed the insects and animals, and just enough small animals to keep bigger ones fed.

And the Creator looked over these seven Edens and said, "It is good."

MARCH

Skunk Cabbage   *Symplocarpus foetidus*

1

DISCOVERY

In early spring, the rusty-patch bumblebee queen emerges from winter hibernation hungry for nectar. She sets off in search of the plants she knows will provide it—cut-leaf tooth-wort, Dutchman's breeches, squirrel corn and white trout lily. She needs protein, fats and vitamins to build her strength and bolster her immune system. With luck, she'll also find pollen of the silver maple, willows, American plum and shadblow.

Thick, half-frozen raindrops slapped against the windshield of the green pick-up. It was late March in West Michigan. Charlotte turned on the wipers for the third time and cursed the miserable weather. The only thing worse than a January deep freeze lingering into February was the not-quite-neither-nor, dragged-out month of March. Her memories of glorious Michigan summers grew fuzzy by this time every year.

She drove past Chili's, Home Depot and Meijer along the ar-row-straight, five-lane commercial strip of 16th Street until it bent toward the Hawthorn River bridge at River Road. She turned left into the narrow, tree-lined lane that hugged the river's winding course.

Morning fog hung over the river, obscuring it from view. To her left were the riverfront homes of Saskawan's professionals, executives and trust fund babies. Some homes proclaimed themselves with look-at-me white pillars and putting-green lawns, while others concealed them-selves modestly behind a buffer of woods at the ends of long, winding driveways. With any luck, one of these would be Charlotte's first real client.

When she opened her business, she dreamed of creating stunning, native gardens filled with brown-eyed Susans, yellow coreopsis and showy goldenrod or shadowy woodland retreats with drifts of white Canada anemone, wild ginger, bloodroot and show-stopping trillium.

She hadn't expected to get rich, but she was confident there was a market for gardens that heal the earth and support wildlife. And, six months on, she still believed clients like that existed—but exactly where was hard to pinpoint.

She had wanted to call her business Adair Native Ecosystems, but Harp, her pragmatic fiancé, had convinced her to go with the more generic and safer Adair Natural Landscaping.

So far, all she had to show for her efforts was a flagstone path leading from her parents' back door to their bird feeder and a raised flowerbed to accommodate Gloria Grosnickle's pampered tea roses and arthritic back. That her first real job had been a bed of roses was ironic and sad, she thought. Mrs. Grosnickle, her parents' neighbor, had presented her with a catalog of disease-prone, hybrid roses whose great pompoms of petals were out of reach to hungry bees. When Charlotte suggested some native roses that could be grown without pesticides, fertilizers or fungicide, Mrs. G. had locked her arms over her ample bosom and declared, "I don't want bees anywhere near my garden."

So far, Adair Natural Landscaping had not sold one native plant.

Frozen raindrops aside, it was officially spring in Saskawan, Michigan and she, Charlotte Adair, was on her way to scout the yard of the first prospective client of the season—a Mr. Newton E. Bigelow. With any luck—any luck at all—he lived down one of these mysterious wooded lanes in a home with minimal lawn and or one that could be turned into a wildflower meadow or woodland paradise. The thought made her pulse race.

She opened her palm and re-read the address she'd written there: 2318.

"What the—?" she muttered, slowing down. All the mailboxes were odd-numbered, 2143, 2237, 2239 and on the left side. There was no room for an even-numbered house in the narrow, right-hand strip between the road and the river.

A driver behind her roared past almost clipping her bumper.

"Idiot," she muttered, demonstrating her own brand of pique.

Maybe this new prospect was a scammer. She'd gotten the email through her website, but maybe "Mr. Bigelow" was some pimply late bloomer getting a kick out of sending her on a wild goose chase. The little twerp was probably watching her right now, about to get rear-ended looking for a house that doesn't exist.

She groaned aloud. It had been a long winter and she really, really needed a paying client.

Charlotte craved the feel of warm soil crumbling in her fingers the way other people craved speed, sex or salvation. Someday, Adair Natural Landscaping would have a greenhouse where she would coax seeds into robust plants to sell to her customers. For it was Charlotte's mission in life to get Saskawan blooming with colorful native gardens teeming with pollinators, birds and wildlife.

The driver ahead swerved to avoid a tire-swallowing pothole and she followed suit. Potholes were reliable harbingers of spring in West Michigan.

Her cell phone chirped in the passenger seat.

"Hey, Mum. What's up?"

"Morning, love. I just dropped Her Majesty at school."

Her Majesty was Charlotte's twelve-year-old niece, Madelyn, better known as Mazie.

"Everything okay?"

"Oh fine. Maybe. I don't know. She's gone mute these days. Used to be a little chatterbox. She practically tripped over somebody's back-pack on her way in this morning, her nose stuck in a book. If not that, it's her phone or her iPad or her laptop. But that's not why I called. I saw Gloria Grosnickle when I was getting the mail. She still wants you to build another raised bed in her rose garden this spring. She says she hasn't heard from you."

Charlotte let out a sigh she hoped was inaudible. At the moment the garden in question was sleeping under white Styrofoam cones making her front yard look like a futuristic graveyard. "I know. It's just that I'm on my way to what could be a pretty big job and I don't want to over-commit. I'll call her. I promise."

"All right, love, but I wouldn't think you could afford to be too picky," she said, sounding as if her thirty-three-year-old daughter was a toddler refusing to eat her peas.

Charlotte strained to read the mailbox numbers through the fog. 2199, 2145, 2237.

"I'm not being picky," she said, sounding very much like a toddler. She sighed again, this time out loud. "It's just—I have a business plan. A lot of people want native gardens these days. I want to tap into that market."

"Well, I hope you're right." Her mother could have added (but did not add) for all our sakes. Charlotte's parents had inherited the Adair family farm at the north edge of town and were allowing her to live there practically rent-free as the "caretaker," but she knew better. This was her parents' compensation for being unable to help with her college tuition and student loans.

2318 whizzed by before she could react. She braked and turned around in an asphalt driveway. Her mother was right, she needed a job no matter what. Thanks for stating the obvious, Mum.

"Gotta go. I'll call Mrs. G, but I need to see this client's property first. Talk soon. Bye." She pulled off onto the shoulder next to the mailbox. Below, a steep, gravel driveway sloped down to the river's edge and continued uphill to the road again. An ancient green Mercedes was parked at the bottom.

This can't be right, she thought. The bank between the road and the river was barely wide enough for the car, let alone a house. Curiouser and curiouser.

She googled the address again. Wait. The map pin for 2318 showed the house smack in the middle of the river. She clucked in annoyance. "Newton E. Bigelow" didn't even sound like a real name.

She scrolled through her email until she found the message in question. According to his email, Mr. Bigelow was having some renovations done and the property needed to be re-landscaped. That sounded legit.

She reread carefully what she admittedly had only skimmed before. (Generally, she'd rather lose a toenail than read a set of detailed instructions.)

She opened the email again.

I'm re-landscaping my property and need the help of a professional.

A professional. Yup, that was her. B.S., cum laude, Michigan State, a bucket load of tuition debt, a decade of underpaid work experience at TipTop Landscaping, a truck payment and a startlingly enormous small-business loan. Oh, and a chronic case of insomnia and general-ized anxiety.

> I won't be home until Wednesday, but you are welcome to do
> some reconnaissance before that. The address is 2318 River Road.
> Park at the landing. You'll see a dock. Cross over on the raft.

She peered into the fog. Sure enough—a short dock jutted into the river.

> . . . Just pull on the rope. (I assure you it's less perilous than
> it appears.) Look around and let me know what you think. If
> you're still interested we can meet when I get back to town.

She rolled the truck slowly down the driveway into the foggy abyss and parked behind the Mercedes. Next to it was a small sign that read

Bigelow's Landing. Another read "Please don't walk on the water." A sense of humor was a good sign, she thought.

She flipped open the visor mirror and ran her fingers through her chin-length brown hair before remembering no one would be home.

She grabbed her shoulder bag and slipped onto the gravel below with a thud. The truck still felt several sizes too big. Apparently, a driver of hundred and twenty pounds and five-two wasn't what Ford engineers had in mind.

Yip! Yip-yip-yip!

She pivoted just in time to see the caramel-colored hind end of a small dog scrambling to put a giant cottonwood tree between himself and this unfamiliar visitor.

"Hey there, boy. What's your name?" she asked, but he had already disappeared into a burrow under the tree.

She looked around for its owner. This wasn't the kind of neighbor-hood where you'd see stray dogs or skinny, nondescript brown mutts.

She zipped her parka against the chill and stepped onto the dock. Tied to a post was a small, rectangular raft with a railing fashioned from woven branches. The effect was charming. A rope threaded through a pulley on a dock post stretched over the water and disappeared into the fog. The idea of getting on this conveyance-to-nowhere was unnerving. The river was wide and lazy here because of a hydroelectric dam about a half-mile downriver, but the water was freezing and she couldn't see the bottom.

"Looking for Mr. Bigelow?"

She followed the voice to a tall man in a floppy hat and hip waders standing knee-deep in the river.

"Yes, I am. Does he live here?"

"Across there. On the island." He pointed into the fog and chuckled. "Guess you'll have to take my word for it."

"An island?" She squinted into nothingness with no up or down, no left or right, except for the gray river carrying slabs of gray ice downstream. She let out a high, giddy laugh.

"Just pull yourself across. It's not hard."

That was two votes for risking life and limb in the name of professional development and financial gain, but she wasn't convinced.

"How far is it?"

"Not far."

She laughed again. "Are you sure it's really there?"

He smiled. "It was there yesterday."

The little dog reappeared and took up barking again—another vote for moving along.

"Is that your dog?" she called out.

"No. He's a stray. He's been living under that cottonwood most of the winter, poor fella. He's got a pretty nice burrow under there though. I bring him table scraps when I come, but he won't let me near him. I call him Speedy."

When she looked again the dog was poised, tail high, ready to defend his giant triple-trunked pillared home from this new trespasser. If he wasn't Mr. Bigelow's dog, surely this was Mr. Bigelow's land and his tree. She looked up into the bare canopy.

The cottonwood was Michigan's tallest native tree species, but was as weak as a stalk of celery and rained down dead sticks all year and produced bushels of cotton fluff each June that stuck to everything. It also started dropping dry brown leaves in mid-August. It was unpopular with homeowners, but few could afford to have these behemoths removed once they were fully grown like this one. She wouldn't recommend that Mr. Bigelow cut it. At least "Speedy" was putting this one to good use—proving her firm belief that every plant has its place.

She returned to the task at hand—risking life and limb to secure a client. The empty raft before her bucked against a loop of rope tethering it to the dock. It looked ready to snap and send her and the raft downstream and over the dam where she and it would be sucked into the turbines and ground into a meatloaf of sawdust and hamburger. She shuddered. If Mr. Bigelow lost power for a month it would serve him right.

She stepped aboard gingerly, taking a wide stance with her hip pressed tightly against the railing. The whole contraption pitched under her weight.

A wooden crate nailed to the decking seemed designed for cargo. She dropped her shoulder bag into it and freed the raft from the dock. Hand-over-hand she pulled herself ever so slowly into the icy current, managing a quick wave to the fisherman. With any luck, he would grab her by the hair as she floated by.

"Bon voyage," he called out, casting his line again.

It was actually easy, Charlotte thought, feeling her cheeks tighten into a grin. The dock she'd just left quickly disappeared into the mist. For a moment she was a lone voyager out of sight of dry land. Huck Finn, Robinson Crusoe and Marguerite de la Rocque all came to mind. It was exhilarating.

As she slid closer to her invisible destination, a gust of wind parted the fog to reveal the ghostly silhouette of a massive, disembodied stone chimney. Then, a cedar shake roof came into focus and the murky outline of an exquisite Adirondack hunting lodge.

"Whoa," she heard herself say.

Later, Charlotte would try to recall this moment—her first glimpse of the island, this house and her assumptions about its owner. But memories, she would come to learn, are so altered by what comes after that they can never be fully recaptured.

2

THE RAFT

Rivers are earth's great sculptors. Whether they meander or gush across landscapes they can change their shape and direction, refashioning the earth's surface. Along their journey to the ocean, they seek a balance between the slope of the terrain, the volume of their water and the stability of the rock and sand along their bottoms. A rush of water can bring about great upheaval, to be sure, but the presence of deeply rooted plants can calm all but the wildest rivers.

The raft bumped a second dock that was the twin of the one she'd left behind. Surely, this couldn't be Mr. Bigelow's primary residence, although he had called it his house, not his cottage, cabin or summer place.

She followed the curve of a planked walkway to a set of porch steps. The porch railing, like the raft's, was made of crisscrossed tree limbs. A pair of Adirondack chairs and a matching glider faced the river. She imagined Mr. and Mrs. Bigelow sitting there, sharing drinks before dinner and watching their children splash in the river.

To her right, the porch jutted out to make a circular seating area under a turreted shake roof with room for a table and chairs. To the left, another turret capped a semi-circular room with eight small windows giving a panoramic view of the river.

The whole effect was enchanting. If she was any judge, this house was an authentic example of late-nineteenth-century Adirondack Great Camp architecture. She half expected a bespectacled Teddy Roosevelt to open the massive front door and bellow a hearty welcome.

She pictured Mr. Bigelow and his family to be as rugged as their home. Surely, there would be a moose head above the fireplace and a gun rack in the corner. Mrs. Bigelow would play tennis and run 10Ks.

Their tanned children would play soccer and be on the high school rowing team.

All around the house was evidence of recent renovations. A wheelbarrow, a ladder and a couple of sawhorses leaned against the house. There was a lot of bare soil that needed her services. And by the looks of it, Mr. Bigelow would have the money to pay for them.

She snapped photos of the porch which begged for a bed of wild ginger and a few white trillium around the foundation. Cardinal flowers and red beebalm would lure hummingbirds and bees to the river's edge in view of the porch. Culver's root and false blue indigo could be coaxed into bloom by the sun-warmed stone chimney. A vine of native virgin's bower would make a lacy cloud of white blossoms over the porch in late summer.

But she was getting ahead of herself. First, she needed to get hired.

Behind the house she discovered a flagstone patio with a fire pit at the center and an old semi-circular stone wall that served as a bench.

She did a slow turn. There was no evidence of lawn, which was unusual in West Michigan, but an encouraging sign. She snapped a few more photos and pushed through a tangle of buckthorn trees and mentally marked them for removal.

Finally, she reached the opposite bank of the island where a few boulders near the bank riffled the water. More would help control erosion, although getting rocks to the island on the raft would be a problem.

A belted kingfisher dropped headfirst into the water from a dead elm snag and came up with a wiggling minnow. As the fog lifted, several large homes perched on a bluff behind the island came into view. Some had long flights of steps coming down to the river with docks or boathouses on the bank.

Charlotte pushed further into the woods where hickories and a few red maples hung over the water. A red-bellied woodpecker stuck its head into an old boxelder and came face-to-face with a black squirrel.

The tree was misshapen and unattractive, but she would encourage Mr. Bigelow to keep it for the wildlife.

On a rise in the middle of the island shared by the house, she walked into a spectacular grove of century-old white oaks that created the island's leafy canopy.

"Beautiful," she whispered.

She circled to the upstream point of the island on a faint path and came upon a meadow that had probably once been a lawn. She imagined it planted with native grasses and wildflowers.

But the privet and barberry shrubs had to go. She frowned at the thought and snapped a few pictures. That wouldn't be easy, but the real trick would be getting Mr. Bigelow to pay for it.

The whole island was no more than an acre but was a charming retreat for a couple with youth and means—as well as a native landscaper's dream. But a dream was all this was ever likely to be. What she envisioned was probably not what the Bigelows had in mind at all. The landscaping business, she had learned long ago, was all about doing what you could with the landowner's limited money, limited imagination and limited tolerance for Mother Nature's encroachment.

Back at the house, she knelt below the porch and picked up a clod of soil. It was heavy clay—not surprising so near the river. She was making a note of this when it started to rain.

She reached for her hood.

"Aw-aw!" said a voice above her. Then, "Oh my God!"

She looked up to see a pair of blue-white legs in red plaid boxer shorts running backwards into the porch table. At the same instant, she fell onto her backside with a loud grunt.

The man on the porch raked a pale hand through a shock of colorless hair. "I didn't see you down there!"

She scrambled to her feet, looking from his horrified face to her wet jacket. She couldn't think of one thing to say to the man who had just peed on her.

Apparently, neither could he. He held one hand over his mouth. "Did I? When I? Did I just, er, *urinate* on you?"

She held her arms out like a scarecrow.

"Apparently," she said, inspecting her sleeves (wet), clipboard (sprinkled) and shoulder bag (miraculously unscathed). She ran a hand over her hair and immediately regretted it.

The man was wrapping his bathrobe tighter and stuttering, "Here, let me . . . um . . . er. . . ." He reached over the porch railing in a vague offer of help. "Let me . . . I should . . . get something. Oh, this is unforgivable." He turned away and stifled a cough or a laugh. His mouth twitched at the corner as he watched her intently—and for longer than seemed necessary. "I'm at a complete loss to know what the proper etiquette might be following accidental urination on a stranger."

She blinked up at him. "Something to wipe off my jacket would be helpful."

As if she hadn't spoken, he said, "Not that it would be any less vulgar or shocking if we were already acquainted. I've clearly made a very poor first impression." He hesitated. "Piss poor." His mouth twitched again.

Charlotte's eyes narrowed. He seemed to be dissecting the situation and taking his own sweet time of it. He raised a long index finger. "Yes. Right. I'm going to get, um, something for this . . . situation."

"Paper towel would be good," she prompted.

"Excellent. Stay right there." He turned to leave, then spun back again. "Forgive my distraction. This might help in the meantime." He handed a neatly folded handkerchief over the railing. It was an old-fashioned white square monogrammed with the initials N.E.B.

She ran it over her hair and watched the man's white calves and enormously long feet retreat across the porch and into the house.

She was wiping her hair when he returned with a roll of paper towels, this time he was wearing a pair of buckskin moccasins. He handed her several sheets. She blotted her parka as he watched, stroking his chin.

"If you saw this scene in a movie it would be comical," he said. "Don't you think?"

She dabbed at her clipboard and her sleeve, not looking up.

"Hmm. Well. Perhaps not from where you were standing, or I think, kneeling because I didn't see you until you—. Anyway, did you know that our sense of tragedy is widely shared – even across cultures – but what we find humorous is deeply individual."

When she didn't respond, he looked crestfallen. "Yes, well, my own comedic tastes run to slapstick, which some find childish. I like Ogden

Nash poetry, for example, which many find odd. And I like ironic humor which I suppose is also a matter of personal taste."

He frowned slightly and crossed his arms. "Clearly, this incident isn't funny to you and I truly understand. But from where I was standing—." A couple of respiratory bursts escaped which caused him to cough several times into the crook of his arm. His boney shoulders pulled up tightly around a pair of purplish ears. His shoulders began to shake.

"Truly, miss, I am sorry," he said, making a fist to cover his mouth. "But I can't help but see the humor here." He seemed to expect a response.

"It's mostly on my jacket." That was all she had to offer.

He was watching her with an intensity she found unsettling.

"If you don't mind my asking, what are you up to down there in my dirt?"

Charlotte looked up. "Drying my sleeve."

"No. I mean, what are you doing here—on my island?" He cleared his throat. "Did you just happen by? Are you shipwrecked?" he asked with a chuckle.

"Me?" she asked, caught off guard. "I'm Charlotte. Charlotte Adair?"

This was followed by an awkward pause, and finally, "Well welcome, Ms. Adair." He extended his hand, hesitating long enough to show he wasn't fully committed to bodily contact. He squeezed her fingertips quickly, then tucked his hands into his pockets.

Charlotte felt her lips curl into a smile. It was *his* pee, after all.

"So, what brings you to my island so early on this foggy March morning?"

She looked up in surprise. "Adair Natural Landscaping? You asked me to take a look at your property?" She tugged at the front of her parka so he could see the logo—A.N.L. with a sprig of virgin's bower, *Clematis virginiana*, twining around the letters. He squinted to get a closer look. "Your email said you wouldn't be home until Wednesday, but that I could come out and take a look."

"Yes! I remember now. Not only am I uncouth and barbaric, but absent-minded, as well. As it turns out, I'm home early." He frowned. "I fear I've made an appalling first impression."

"Piss poor," Charlotte reminded him, smiling.

"Indeed," he said, before returning a huge, satisfied grin. "So, the least I can do is offer my facilities. I do have them—facilities, I mean. I just prefer in the morning... Oh, never mind. Would you like coffee?"

"Just the bathroom. Thank you."

Charlotte followed the gleaming beacon of Mr. Bigelow's legs into the house. The breeze lifted his wispy, cotton-candy hair that was ambiguously platinum or gray.

Mr. Bigelow was a man of sharp edges. At well over six feet, with erect posture, square shoulders, and a long, straight nose, he could be a well-preserved sixty or prematurely-aging forty-year-old, an anorexic tri-athlete, or a man who was wasting away. Either way, he looked like he'd bend in a stiff breeze.

She kicked off her rubber wellies at the door while he disappeared into another room. She was in a central room with an enormous oak dining table running up the middle and an oriental rug in rich reds and gold. She knew enough about rugs to know this one wasn't from Ikea. To her right, facing a long leather couch was a massive split stone fireplace holding up a log-beamed ceiling. The enticing semi-circular room turned out to be the kitchen with a panoramic view of the river.

Mr. Bigelow returned with a pile of thick, navy-blue bath towels. He opened a door at the opposite side of the room and flicked on the light.

"Help yourself to anything you need. You're welcome to the shower." The light caught the texture of a day's growth of colorless beard on his cheek.

"Thank you, but the sink's fine," she said.

"When you're done, we can talk about your plans for my island."

Charlotte draped her parka over the edge of a deep whirlpool tub. The room was flooded with daylight from a skylight. The new, white fixtures were a stark contrast to the rustic living area. A lone towel hung on a bar over the tub.

She scrubbed her face and hands and was toweling off her hair when her phone vibrated. It was Harp.

"Morning," she said.

"You left early. Where are you?"

"That client's property, remember? I told you last night." She sat down on the edge of the tub.

"Oh, right," he said absently. She heard him moving around the kitchen. "Is there any milk? Oh, found it. So, how's it look so far?"

"You won't believe this. It's on an island in the middle of the Hawthorn River. It's like an old hunting lodge. You'd love it."

"Sounds cool. Is he going to hire us?"

"I just met the owner, so it's too soon to tell, but he says he wants to talk—now. I thought he was out of town, so I don't even have my laptop or any notes with me. I'm not sure—."

"You'll do fine," he interrupted. "Just wing it."

"Yeah." She appreciated his faith in her, but winging it was Harp's style, not hers.

"Hey," he said, his mouth full. "I just heard it's going to be in the sixties next week. Tell him we can start right away. That'll impress him. And Charlotte, don't start lecturing him about natives. We can't be that picky."

She'd heard this all before.

"Char?"

"I know. I know. But don't count on next week. I have to do some preliminary drawings, present a budget and get a contract before I need your services."

"But my car payment is— "

"I know, Harp. I have to go. We'll talk later."

"Okay. Hurry home after. I'm bored."

"Then do a load of laundry or take the list on the fridge and go grocery shopping."

"Has this guy got any money?" he asked, chewing.

"Looks like it."

"That's what I want to hear. Anyway, good luck. And remember, the customer's always right."

She gave a begrudging "Yeah."

She pictured Harp leaning over a bowl of Cheerios and bananas with one forearm on the table. As soon as they hung up he'd check the basketball scores and go to the gym, then do something with his best friend Mike.

"I might not be home when you get here. Me and Mike might catch a movie."

"Okay, but at least put your laundry in before you go and read me the grocery list on the fridge."

"Coffee, popcorn, tomatoes, refried beans. That's it."

"Okay. See you later."

"Good luck. Get us a fat contract. Oops, was that too much unsolicited advice?"

"I'll forgive you if the laundry's done when I get home."

Harp laughed. "Love you, babe."

"You too."

3
_

HARP

_Alfred Wallace, who (with Darwin) postulated the theory of
natural selection, proposed the notion that females of a species would reject males with physical traits that might com-
promise the survival of her offspring. But in reality, evolutionary trade-offs are common. Wallace overlooked the fact
that while the peacock's outlandish tail has nearly grounded
him, the cock with the biggest tail gets the peahen. So, while
the brilliant plumage of cardinals, goldfinches and bluebirds
may catch the eye of the hawk, it catches the eye of the girl first._

The day Harper "Harp" Landis started work at TipTop
Landscaping, several female employees, and even a few male
ones, noticed how deftly he handled a Bobcat or how his biceps
flexed when he hoisted a 50-pound bag of manure onto his shoulder.
Harp's body was a natural wonder.

For almost five years at TipTop, Charlotte and Harp worked together all week and joined the rest of the crew at the bar on Friday
nights. She couldn't remember the first time they went for dinner
afterward or the first time she'd cooked dinner for him at the farmhouse. Their relationship hadn't so much blossomed as morphed un-
consciously from one thing to something more. Harp's toothbrush in
a coffee mug on the sink, her dresser overflowing with his socks and
underwear, and his dirty clothes piled next to her bed seemed to have
always been there. The day they moved an old dresser up from the basement, co-habitation was a _fait accompli._

On weekends they biked or kayaked along the Lake Michigan shore
or he went climbing or mountain biking with his buddies. On week-
nights, he played poker and softball, and darts at the bar after work.
When he got home, he watched TV or played video games until he

fell asleep on the couch. Harp's personal transmission had two gears, overdrive and park.

At TipTop, his firm handshake, winning smile and ability to chat up clients, especially female ones, endeared him to their boss, Dirk VanSlee. Dirk had thought Harp good salesman material, but when Harp realized he'd have to sit at the desk, make phone calls and learn the names of plants and their individual needs, he lost interest. Installation was where the action was, and action was what Harp Landis craved.

But after nine years at TipTop, Charlotte felt restless and pot-bound. She was tired of designing low-maintenance gardens of Russian sage and Stella d'Oro daylilies buried in vinca or an avalanche of cedar mulch. Eighteen months ago, she enrolled in an online class in entrepreneurship at the community college. After a full day's work, she spent evenings writing papers, perusing websites and watching online videos on starting a business.

Harp was supportive but chafed at the slow pace of her preparations.

"You know more than all those so-called experts, Char. If you want to open your own business, just do it."

Reluctantly, she agreed. So, the previous August she pressed her navy-blue blazer, pulled her hair into a bun and walked into the Saskawan City Bank to apply for a business loan. The day she signed the papers, Harp met her at the back door and swept her in circles around the kitchen.

"I can't wait to see the look on VanSlee's face when you quit. He's never appreciated you."

"Thanks," she said, sinking dizzily into a kitchen chair.

"Let's take some time off. We've earned it. Go camping and hiking up north." Now he was massaging her shoulders and kissing her ear.

"I'm not resigning yet."

"Why not? If I had that much money I sure wouldn't be working for TipTop."

He sat down across from her, searching her face for more symptoms of the sudden ailment she'd contracted.

"I need to get some clients first."

"Call that blonde with the cottage in Manistee. Remember? I installed her beach steps. She kept offering me gin and tonics after work," he said, with a wink. "I know she'd hire us if I was crew boss."

He reached for her hands. "You could run some ads," he said, holding up the glossy cover of *Great Lakes Living*. Or buy a billboard on the highway."

"Harp. I have a business plan. You can read it if you like." She reached into her bag for her laptop.

He ignored this. "We should get a booth at the Home and Garden Show next spring."

Besides not wanting Mr. VanSlee to know her plans yet, there were a thousand details left to work out—none of them involving billboards, booths or expensive ads.

If she was being deliberate, it was because she needed to get this right the first time. Life didn't give people like Charlotte Adair second chances.

At the end of the season, Charlotte told her boss she wouldn't be returning in the spring. Harp, she assumed, would stay on to drive a snow plow for TipTop until the landscaping season began again.

But then, in an act of love-induced lunacy, she hinted that she'd hire him as soon as she found a client. The next day he quit his job at TipTop and showed her an ad for a used Bobcat.

"Who's going to pay for this, Harp?" she snapped. "Not you. I can't believe you quit!"

Since then, he'd been moping around the house, hovering over her and occasionally calling her "boss" or "ma'am" to remind her of her flash of hubris.

Then he came home with a new snowboard.

"I got it in a pre-season sale."

"How did you pay for it?"

"My mom gave me birthday money."

"But your birthday isn't for two months. And don't you still owe her $500 for your bike?"

"Forgiving the loan was my Christmas present," he said as if that explained everything.

Actually, it explained a lot.

Late last fall she put Harp to work on the flagstone walk that her parents couldn't really afford even at the "family" rate Charlotte couldn't really afford to give them. After that, he built Gloria Grosnickle's raised rose beds, which basically involved dumping gravel, topsoil, manure and cedar chips into timber boxes. Harp was in his element but there was little profit to show for it.

Waiting for clients to call had been hard for her but torture for a man of action like Harp. It had been a long winter and she suspected he regretted his hasty decision to leave TipTop.

4

THE ISLAND

Charlotte clicked off her phone and frowned. Mr. Bigelow was waiting to hear why she should be his landscaper while she was holed up in his bathroom. This was not the scenario she imagined.

At home, on her makeshift kitchen desk was a beautiful, silvery laptop containing her painstakingly designed electronic portfolio and detailed pricing sheets. And somewhere on that same desk was a green folder marked "Initial Client Conference: Six Critical Messages" that her business instructor at Saskawan Community College had called "well organized and compelling." (At the moment she could only remember points one through four.)

She sighed at the woman in the mirror—the one in dire need of a bit of blush and mascara. The one wearing a gray hoodie with a coffee stain on the front. What was that in her hair? A burr. She pulled it out and several more on her sleeve.

Her clean, pressed khakis, casual sweater and understated gold earrings were at home too, along with most of her poise and self-confidence. What more could go wrong?

She rubbed her cheeks until they burned and drew in a long, unsteady breath. Mr. Bigelow would just have to look past her questionable grooming and thinly veiled desperation to see the talented, experienced designer she hoped was still in there somewhere.

Maybe the bizarre circumstances of this meeting would give her an edge. Didn't getting peed upon entitle her to a fair hearing of her sales pitch?—assuming she could remember Critical Messages Five and Six.

Mr. Bigelow was standing at the kitchen counter with his back to her, speaking over his shoulder. "You must have gotten an early start this morning, so I figure you could use some coffee. How do you like it? Or I could make tea."

"Coffee would be wonderful. Thanks. A little milk, if you have it."

He had changed into a pair of pressed jeans, a gray V-neck over a blue oxford shirt and a pair of brown penny loafers. Fully clothed, he wasn't unattractive, she noted.

She sat on a stool at the kitchen island while he prepared the coffee. She admired the bespoke oak cabinets and butcher-block counter tops. He either had money to burn or a great credit rating.

If he hired her as penance for the unfortunate porch incident, she'd accept without hesitation, but not without guilt. She was a businesswoman, but not a complete mercenary. Whatever his motives for hiring her, she'd make sure he didn't regret it.

She watched him grind the beans, apologizing for the noise. Maybe she should ask for a retainer, just in case he had a second mortgage. He tapped the grounds into a French press and added water from a tea kettle.

She had to admit Harp was right about one thing—she needed this job. If Mr. Bigelow wanted a garden of poison ivy and nettles, by golly that's what he'd get. Her ideals, as it turned out, were malleable when they stood between her and groceries.

He was filling a cream pitcher with real cream warmed in the microwave. He smiled as he handed her a heavy, white mug and sat down across from her. She wondered if he'd have gone to so much trouble if he knew she'd started her morning with the reheated dregs of yesterday's pot.

The smell of his aftershave wafted over—something clovey, but suitably subtle. He must have shaved while she was in the bathroom. His fine hair was parted neatly, but one lock fell over his forehead like a forelock. His chin was deeply cleft and his hollow cheeks gave his face a sculpted look. Still, the man looked like a stick figure.

He took a sip of coffee and leaned on his elbows. "Did you have a chance to look around the island?"

"Yes," she said enthusiastically. "What a great place. How long have you lived here?"

"About ten years. It was in pretty grim shape then. I did a lot of the renovation myself, but it finally got too much and I brought in professionals. I've replaced the roof, re-stained the house, replaced the windows, added the downstairs bath and a study, refinished the floors, added solar panels to the roof—" He laughed lightly. "Anyway, it's been a holy mess for a year, but it's almost done."

Charlotte laughed. "It's charming. Is it just yourself, Mr. Bigelow?"

He gave her a puzzled look—white lashes fringing the palest ice-blue eyes she'd ever seen.

"I-I mean, do you have children who will be needing a play area? A wife in need of a vegetable garden?"

"Oh. No. God no," he said, almost shuddering, then breaking into a smile. "It's just me."

She rolled the mug between her palms. "Okay. So, what do you know about the history of the island?"

His eyes swept the room. "The house was built in 1909 by a local couple who had made a fortune shipping lumber to Chicago after the Great Fire of 1871. They had a litter of kids and a mansion downtown. They wanted a summer place nearby and found this island. A farmer had been using it to keep his pigs. The island had been logged over, but some of the oaks and hickories were spared, probably to provide acorns and nuts for the pigs. The family kept the island until the Depression. There was a succession of owners after that. But by the nineties, the house was vacant. When I bought it all the windows were broken. Birds lived in the rafters and the pipes had all burst."

"Well, it looks brand new again," Charlotte said. "It's beautiful."

She got up and stood in the middle of the semi-circular kitchen with her hands in her back pockets. Through each of the eight kitchen windows was a different view of the river.

"So, you have pigs to thank for your white oaks," she said. "I bet they're at least a hundred and fifty years old. This place is unique, I'll say that. I see endless possibilities for landscaping."

"Really? I'm glad to hear it."

She looked up at the massive fireplace holding up the heavy, timbered rafters. "Adirondack Great Camp, right?"

"Correct. It's not common in Michigan, but it was popular in New England and ahead of its time because these houses used local materials, like the split river stone in the chimney. They also didn't try to clear the woods around the houses." He bowed slightly. "Forgive my lecturing, you probably already knew that."

Charlotte smiled. "No, go on."

"The floors are hickory and maple, but the banister—" He walked to the bottom of the L-shaped stairs next to the chimney and slapped the newel post, "This is black walnut. I know because I stripped off about sixteen layers of paint before I found it."

Charlotte ran her hand over the dark, oiled wood. "It was worth the trouble I think."

"Thanks. So, all that's left to do is landscaping around the house. I'm afraid whatever was there got pretty trampled by the construction crews," he said, sounding apologetic. "But they'll be done soon so you could work your magic outside this spring, if you're interested."

Her pulse quickened. She stifled the impulse to clamp Mr. Bigelow in a bear hug and yell, "Hell, yeah!" and limited herself to a warm smile and a professional nod.

"Yes. I'm very interested."

"Good. Now tell me what you learned this morning."

"Well, if you want a flower garden, you're somewhat limited by shade near the house, but the dock area and the upstream end of the island are sunny and can grow a lot of showier flowers. I'll need to know what you want and get an idea of your budget. Then, I'll make some preliminary drawings."

"I'm afraid I won't be much help. I have little in the way of opinions about plants, because I have even less knowledge of them," he said. As he brought his mug to his lips his Adam's apple bobbed up and down like a heron swallowing a fish. "I also want things as low-maintenance as possible. I'm not a gardener."

Her heart sank. If she heard "low-maintenance" one more time. Why should this guy be any different than any other client?

Calmly and without a hint of judgment, she replied, "Perhaps there are colors you prefer, or others you want to avoid?"

He nodded at the kitchen windows. "Well, there used to be a big vine with purple clusters that climbed up the porch columns and onto the roof. It was quite atmospheric. But it had to be cut to redo the roof and stain the shingles. There was also some kind of ivy but that's gone, too. It's a shame. I had a couple of trees taken out by the dock, too, so I'd like some flowers there if they're not too high maintenance."

He reached into his pocket for his cell. "I figured you'd ask, so I took some photos of gardens I like. This is the front of my office downtown."

There were clumps of Stella d'Oro daylilies, a row of Knock Out roses backed by Russian sage and fountain grass with Bradford pears behind. All the usual suspects.

He scrolled back and forth. "What do you think?"

Charlotte's gaze dropped. She could hear Harp's warning. Give the client what he wants, Charlotte. And don't start preaching about natives and invasives.

She looked up, a smile fixed on her face. "Those would be popular choices, Mr. Bigelow." Either it was suddenly hot in here or she was starting to blush. Lying, apparently, had that effect.

"Fig," he was saying.

"Fig?" she repeated. "A fig tree could grow in the house, but it wouldn't survive outside."

He laughed. "No. Fig is my name."

"Fig 's your name?" slipped out before she could stop it. "Oh, sorry, Mr. Fig. Somehow, I thought—"

He laughed. "No. My first name is Fig. It's an old nickname that stuck. My given name is Newton. Newton Ellery Bigelow, if you please. But Newton didn't last past the first grade—no big surprise there. I've been Fig ever since. Weird I know, but you'll get used to it."

She wasn't sure about that.

"Okay . . . Fig. I'll think about your plant ideas and give you my thoughts by the end of the week."

She pushed her mug to the center of the table and stood up. She heard Harp's harping again. You're running a business, not a mission. We need paying clients, now. If you browbeat them into giving up their dreams of manicured lawns and exotic plants, they'll pay someone else to do it. So long, Adair Natural Landscaping. Not to mention the owner and her fiancé who would have to beg for their old jobs at TipTop.

Harp was right. Give "Fig" what he wants and hope for a smarter client next time.

His eyes followed as she stood up, reaching for her coat and bag. Walk away, Charlotte, she warned herself. Take his order for vinca, wisteria and hosta and light out for the river. Think of that backpacking trip in Costa Rica.

He was frowning at her. "I sense you're disappointed somehow."

"Oh, no. Of course not," she said, cheerily.

The look coming from his transparent blue eyes made her feel x-rayed.

"I'll get you some drawings in a few days."

"Look, Ms. Adair—" he started in, but let the words linger there. Apparently, he was one of those people who didn't feel the need to fill awkward silences or rescue someone else when she was trying her darnedest not to say another word.

"If I knew what I wanted," he said finally, "I'd hire a gardener. You're a landscape designer, am I right? I want your professional advice." He sat back, trying to read her.

She shifted from one foot to the other. "Yes, and I'm happy to provide that."

"So, we're done here? Because I thought we were just getting started." He nodded at the stool she'd just vacated. "If you have more to say, I wish you would. Otherwise, I'm afraid you might explode right here in my kitchen."

She covered her eyes and laughed. "It's just—that my best advice isn't what clients always want to hear."

He seemed amused by this. "I'm sensing that. But I assure you it's not the case. Not only am I interested in hearing all you have to say, but I am willing to pay for the privilege." He gestured toward the stool as if he were a maître d'. "I'm told I'm a good listener and a quick learner."

She took her seat again and looked steadily at him—determined to hold his gaze. "I have lots of advice, but it may sound unorthodox. I'll share it with the understanding that it is your property and within reason, I will do what you ask of me. I would very much like your business."

He nodded. "I'm an attorney, Ms. Adair. Clients come to me all the time with crazy notions about suing their boss for not recognizing their genius, or taking their landlord to court because a red squirrel got into the attic and nested in their wedding dress. I understand their frustration, but I have a duty to give them the best legal advice I can—which isn't always what they want to hear. So, go ahead, give me your best professional advice. That's what I'm paying you for and I don't bruise easily."

"All right," she said with a firm nod. "Then let me ask you, in your vision of a newly landscaped island paradise how important are birds, bees and other wildlife?"

"They're the main reason I live here and not in a condo in town—which would be much handier, I can assure you." He looked at her through knitted eyebrows. "How do I attract wildlife? Tell me."

"With water, food sources and shelter."

He nodded slowly. "Sounds reasonable. I've got the water covered. But I expect you mean something more than a feeder and a birdhouse."

"I do."

"And the plants I suggested don't fit the bill, do they?"

"No. Not exactly."

He rubbed his hands together. "Now we're getting somewhere."

This was going well.

"So, we can choose flowers that will attract bees, right? And maybe a beehive?"

"Mm. I wouldn't suggest European honeybees unless you want to harvest their honey. Generally, they aren't as efficient or hardworking as our native bees."

Fig cocked his head. "Are there enough of them around to pollinate everything?"

"Over 460 bee species in Michigan alone. And that's only about ten percent of all native American bees."

Fig's jaw opened. "That's shocking. Where have I been?" He sized up the bearer of such rare and extraordinary news. "Not bee-watching, obviously."

Charlotte smiled at his boyish enthusiasm. "And you'll also want to consider habitat for small turtles and frogs. And, if you want to attract butterflies, moths, beetles, flies and hummingbirds—all important pollinators—you'll need to plant the flowers they depend upon."

"Like milkweed for monarchs?"

"Yes. Just like that."

He grinned. "See, I haven't been living in a cave—just on an island."

"But before you invest in new plants, we also need to get rid of some you have." She pointed through the kitchen windows toward the top of a bare red maple that arched over the river.

"Like what?"

"Invasive ones."

"I've heard of those fellows. Like the Little Prince's baobabs?"

Charlotte cocked her head and laughed. "You've lost me. The French novel?"

"*Oui. Le Petit Prince*," he said. "Have you read it?"

"In college. But in French, so it's all a bit fuzzy."

"Well, you might remember that the little prince's tiny planet was invaded by baobab trees."

"The enormous African tree?" she laughed. "I'm quite sure you don't have to worry about them here."

Fig raised a finger. "Laugh if you will, but the baobab was the worst invasive species on his planet. A real neighborhood bully."

Charlotte pressed her lips together, trying not to make light of his earnestness.

"As you may remember, the little prince lived on a tiny planet no bigger than . . . well, I'd have to say, no bigger than my island!" He smiled at the comparison and swept his long arms in an arc over his coffee cup. His voice became hushed. "He lived with his beloved rose bush. She—for "La Rose" was female—was constantly threatened by baobab seedlings that looked very much like rose sprouts, but could grow so big that their roots could crack the tiny planet to pieces. Every morning the Little Prince patrolled his planet for baobab sprouts and pulled them up to save La Rose and his planet. Are you saying we need to rid my planet of baobabs?"

Charlotte marveled at this man who made such far-flung connections.

"Yes," she replied, "metaphorically speaking. We could make a list of plants that would be at home on your, er, 'planet,' but I'm afraid we need to banish your baobabs first." She sat back and grinned. She had never expected to have such a conversation with any client—let alone her very first real one.

Fig frowned. "What kind of 'baobabs' did you find?"

She cleared her throat. "English ivy and your purple flowering vine—called wisteria by the way, and a few others."

Fig set his cup down. "You're not serious."

"Come look." She beckoned him to the kitchen windows. Outside, a maple bent over the riverbank. Its branches almost touched the water. "See that vine growing on it? That's your wisteria."

"It's not dead?"

"Hardly. But see that dead limb on the maple? The wisteria has strangled it. After it kills that tree, it'll move on to that hickory and your oaks."

He leaned over the counter to see the vine-draped tree. "Damned baobab."

"And the English ivy that was on the house is all through your woods too. This island almost certainly had pink spring beauty, lavender hepatica and white trillium at one time—all important, early flowers for pollinators—but I doubt I'll find any of those now. They've been overrun."

"Who knew what silent, existential battles were raging outside my window?" Fig crossed his arms and shook his head slowly. "Fascinating."

Fig reached for a pair of binoculars hanging on a hook by the window and trained them on the maple. "The damned thing has twined itself around the trunk about halfway up. The nerve!" He swung around and squinted intently. "So, what pray-tell should we do?"

"Well, I'll hire a crew to cut and treat them so they don't return. After that, we'll find a Michigan vine that will be really happy growing over your porch."

"Happy plants?" He grinned at the thought. "Is that a botanical term you learned at Michigan State?"

Charlotte laughed. "Not when I went there, unfortunately. We're all learning. More and more, we're learning that plants that evolved in West Michigan will put down deeper root systems than exotic ones. These roots will keep erosion in check—which is really important on an island—and they'll send up colorful blossoms that bees recognize and love. A healthy population of insects will fertilize food crops too. And, once the plants get settled, they will be beautiful to look at, beneficial to wildlife and won't ever need an ounce of fertilizer."

"Eureka!" Fig slapped the counter. "That's what I'm after—Eden before the Fall. I didn't have the words to ask. The scales have fallen from my eyes, Ms. Adair. Thanks to you."

Charlotte looked at this charming skeleton of a man who had apparently paid close attention in Sunday school. "Thank you," she said. "I think I have a good sense of what's growing here and what you want to achieve. I was just checking the soil when—when you, um, appeared on the porch." She took a drink of cold coffee to hide the smile that was spreading across her face.

Fig wagged a finger at her. "Ha! So, you do see the humor in our initial encounter. I was worried that your sense of humor was seriously underdeveloped."

Charlotte set her mug down with a bang and laughed. "The way you backed into the table—"

Fig looked at her down the length of his long nose and folded his arms across his chest, decoding her. With a firm nod, he stretched out his hand.

"Ms. Adair, I believe you and I will have a very productive working relationship."

She pumped his hand. "Thank you. And please, call me Charlotte."

5

ADAIR GIRLS

Wild morning glory, or common bindweed, can quickly take over a fallow field. Its roots secrete toxins into the soil that kill nearby plants. Its tendrils reach for any sunny place to climb, eventually shading out its neighbors. But in the end bindweed's own toxins build up in the soil and the vine poisons itself.

Charlotte texted Harp as soon as she crossed the river. Sharpen your shovel; we have a client! Home soon. Then she stopped at The Farmer's Daughter Cafe and bought a celebratory mocha cappuccino and a white-chocolate macadamia nut cookie the size of a salad plate. She had bagged her first client and an interesting one at that! She headed for home, ten over the speed limit, downing her coffee and enormous bites of chewy cookie.

She turned off the pavement of Seven Mile Road and bounced over the dirt washboard and slushy potholes that was her driveway. When it wasn't frozen, it was either muddy or kicked up dusty whirlwinds that found their way onto the kitchen table, her pillow and into her sinuses by mid-summer. Nothing a few loads of gravel wouldn't fix if she could only afford it. Maybe today was a turning point.

She stopped in front of the barn to savor the moment and the current mouthful of chocolate and nuts.

Ahead was her great-grandparents' four-square farmhouse, vintage 1924, that had been in the Adair family for four generations. The house was too big and drafty for just herself and Harp, but they paid family-rate rent and had the whole place to themselves.

She had big plans for it. Someday when she got the front pasture cleared she'd plant a nursery of young oaks, redbud, dogwood, elderberry, button bushes and row upon row of coneflowers, coreopsis, beebalm and blazing stars in all the colors of summer sunsets. She'd sell them to her clients and cut out the middleman. But so far it was just a failed experiment. Her first crop of white oak acorns came up nicely but were soon lost under a tangle of honeysuckle, multiflora rose and Norway maple seedlings. Adair Landscape Nursery—where plants go to die. She dismissed these negative thoughts with a shake of her head and another big bite of cookie.

Someday, she'd hire a crew to clear everything. Someday she'd have a greenhouse next to the barn, too, for starting young perennials.

With a promising client, that day didn't seem so far off after all.

Her parents, Mally and Ted, had inherited the farm five years before when her grandmother died. They let Charlotte move in as caretaker. Her bargain rent was their investment in Adair Landscaping. In return, she was determined to one day give the old homestead the care and attention it deserved.

The truck bounced past the barn which had been stripped long ago of red paint by time and the elements. White stenciling above the door read, Adair & Sons1955. The space after Sons was missing because when her father (son number two) was born in 1960 the "s" was shoehorned in. Despite her grandfather's grand, dynastic plan, the call of the land skipped a generation. Both her father and her uncle had left the farm for college and never returned.

Ahead stood the house which had once been the color of fresh cream with bright white trim. Now it looked friendless and unappreciated, which it surely was not. It held wonderful, fuzzy memories of shelling black walnuts on the front porch with Great-Grandpa Ray. Grandma Shirley froze the nutmeats until Christmas for her signature walnut cookies.

She parked in the gravel behind the house but didn't get out. She inhaled deeply, savoring the after-taste of white chocolate. Today could be the start of something truly momentous.

But this Fig Bigelow might be too good to be true. He might balk at the cost or the time it would take her to restore his island. It happens all the time with clients. It was too soon to count her chickens. She shook off this thought. It was also too soon to worry when she was barely halfway through the private cookie and cappuccino grand opening party for Adair Natural Landscaping.

She kicked off her wellies on the three-season back porch that doubled as a junk-slash-mudroom. Three buckets on the floor caught the snow melt that was leaking through the roof. She emptied them under the bushes beside the house.

Her cell chirped as she opened the kitchen door.

"Hello again," she said.

Her mother's long, descending "Hhhhiiii, looove," was full of meaning.

"What's wrong? Wait. Let me guess—"

"—Mazie," they said in unison.

"The girl's completely doolally."

"Doolally," Charlotte repeated as she turned the thermostat up to 66. She poured the remaining cappuccino into a mug and zapped it in the microwave.

"So, what bloody codswallop is your granddaughter up to now?" Charlotte asked. She was glad her mother couldn't see her grinning.

"You mean your niece? She blew in like a thunderstorm after school all shirty about her report card."

"Shirty? You've been on the phone with Aunt Fee again, haven't you?"

"Never mind that."

Charlotte's mother, Mally McDougal Adair, was an English ex-pat of almost forty years, but her accent got frequent tune-ups during long calls to her sister Fiona who still lived in Bristol. The result was a fresh peppering of British slang in her speech known in the Adair household as "Mallinese"—the more obscure and colorful the better.

For Mally, being English meant beans on toast on Saturday morning, sparklers on Guy Fawkes day and the firm belief that the secret to resolving marital discord, chronic depression, international terrorism or climate change starts with a perfectly brewed cup of English tea.

"So, tell me. How did my genius niece do?" Charlotte asked breaking off a bit of cookie.

"Three As, an A-minus and a C-plus—in art. *Art!* Can you believe it? Bloody hell, Charlotte! She's brilliant at art."

"Yes, she is."

Charlotte gripped her hot mug with both hands and moved to the big floor register in the front room to wait for the ancient tentacled beast in the basement to send up a fiery belch of blissful heat. She rolled the mug in her hands and shivered. One of her niece's drawings hung over the dining room sideboard in a plastic frame, a gift last Christmas. It was one of her signature mythical creatures, part rabbit, part lizard, riding a motorcycle with a long, striped scarf flapping behind.

"A C-plus? She must be crushed."

"You'd think so, wouldn't you? But that isn't why she's so cheesed off. Apparently, her art teacher is a 'daft cow' who treats seventh graders—and I quote—like 'snot-nosed knobheads.'" (British slang had a way of going viral in the Adair household.)

"No," Mally went on, "our Mazie's done a wobbler over the A-minus she got in Social Studies. She says Mr. Peebles is a fascist wanker on a witch-hunt for 'open-minded, progressives' among his students— again, I quote. She went on for a half hour, but mercifully she's stomped off to her room now."

Charlotte heard her mother release a great lungful of disgruntle- ment. She couldn't help but laugh. This was met with silence. "Sorry, Mum. It's not funny, I know."

Mally McDougal dated Ted Adair when she was a foreign exchange student at Saskawan Community College. After a year in Saskawan, Mally returned home tearfully and everyone thought that was the end of it. But they wrote to each other nearly every day, and after gradua- tion Ted took two jobs to save up for a plane ticket to Bristol. Two years later they were married. He often said with a wink that "She charmed the pants off me," which always got a playful slap from Mally.

Now approaching sixty, they were raising their only grandchild, pre-adolescent Mazie, who had a knack for turning the senior Adair household "cork up."

"I think she's depressed, Charlotte. I'm worried. She doesn't have any friends. She never goes to parties—"

"Oh, Mum," she said. "She's just a moody pre-teen" which she didn't entirely believe. Mazie was bookish and dressed without any regard for fashion, which was a recipe for a painful adolescence.

"How about if I take her this weekend, Mum? I've missed her this winter." That last part wasn't exactly true either, but her parents deserved a break.

"Really? That would be lovely."

"No problem. I love being cool Aunt Char."

Mally laughed. "Good luck with that. Oh, I have to warn you. She's dropping 'meaningless, antediluvian honorifics'— quoting again. I told her if she tried that 'Mally and Ted' bit again we'd write her out of the will." Her mother let out a meaningful puff of air. "What have we wrought, Charlotte?"

"A smart, complex kid—that's what. And endlessly entertaining, you have to admit." The "entertaining" part was bending the truth for sure.

"If you like *film noir*," Mally sniffed. "She's best taken in small doses. I would love just being her gran, you know? It's the mum part that's too bloody much. I'm overdosing on my own grandchild. Oh, dear God forgive me, that was a horrible thing to say." She sighed. "What's wrong with me today?"

"S'ok, Mum. Plan your weekend. I'll be over to pick her up after school on Friday. Tell her we'll order pizza and paint our toenails or something. I need to get some work done, so make sure she brings a book or some homework. Have some fun and try to relax a little."

"Thanks, love. Dad'll be chuffed to bits."

"Before you hang up, I have good news. I think I got my first real client today. Could be a major job."

"Brilliant! I knew it. You really know your onions."

"Whatever you say, Mum." She laughed, swallowing the last of cookie.

When Mally Adair found her daughters, thirteen-year-old Charlotte and nine-year-old Lauren, smoking behind the garage, she hauled them onto the front porch and made them smoke one cigarette after another down to the filter while she supervised. Halfway through her second one, Charlotte ran to the bathroom and threw up. She never picked up another cigarette. Lesson learned.

But nine-year-old Lauren smoked five before running into the bathroom. She came back to find her mother dumping the rest down the garbage disposal.

"Mom!" she screamed. "What are you doing? Those are *my* cigarettes!"

To Mally, this was one of the many "early signs" she had missed.

Lauren Adair had been a fussy baby, a hyperactive child and a restless teen who gravitated toward other restless teens. Charlotte had called them "Lauren's loser friends," which made her burn with shame now.

In high school, Lauren spent more time smoking cigarettes and pot in the parking lot than going to class. Rules were meaningless to her. Ted and Mally watched helplessly as Lauren drifted into a subculture of drug users, thieves and teen runaways. When the police caught her trying to fence one of the school's laptops, her parents spent a fortune on a lawyer who got her a probationary sentence and a month in rehab. They sent her to an expensive wilderness adventure camp for troubled teens in Wisconsin, but she ran away and was picked up in Chicago for shoplifting.

Then, in the fall of her junior year, Lauren became pregnant. She refused to name the father or consider either adoption or termination. Mally and Ted agreed to help with the baby if she agreed to another month in rehab. In the end, Mally and Ted pinned their last hopes and most of their savings on the idea that a baby would bring their daughter back to them. It almost happened that way.

During her pregnancy Lauren stopped using. She took a restaurant job and saved every penny for an apartment. She enrolled in a program for parenting teens and made the honor roll for the first time in her life. When the baby arrived, the Adair household began orbiting around a new little heavenly body named Madelyn McDougal Adair. *Mazie.*

Lauren seemed headed for Mother of the Year. Up at dawn to nurse Mazie and pump her breasts before pulling a full shift at the restaurant, going to night classes and studying after Mazie finally stopped crying and fell asleep. After a night interrupted by several feedings, Lauren got up and did it all over again.

When Mazie was nine months old, Lauren asked her parents to help her buy formula, explaining that fatigue had caused her milk to dry up. Then, she began sleeping through Mazie's nighttime cries. Thinking their daughter just needed the rest, Mally and Ted took turns warming bottles and rocking Mazie back to sleep.

In hindsight, alarm bells should have sounded. Lauren weaned Mazie to protect her from her own daytime hits of cocaine and nighttime doses of heroin.

Lauren's plans for her own apartment, as well as her savings account, never materialized, and by the time Mazie was two, Lauren was a full-blown addict. She would ask her parents to babysit while she went to her "study group," then send a garbled text at two in the morning that she was too tired to drive home. Eventually, she lost her restaurant job and stopped going to class. She disappeared for days at a time, only to slink home wracked with guilt and self-pity ("Mazie's better off without me") and full of empty promises. ("I'll go to Narcotics Anonymous. I'll be a better daughter. I'll be a better mother. I promise.")

Finally, after a three-day binge, Ted and Mally met her at the door with a petition of guardianship and a confirmation letter from a rehab clinic in Minnesota. Charlotte learned only later that they'd cleaned out their savings to pay for it. They were to leave at dawn to make the nine-hour drive.

Charlotte had arrived earlier that night from Michigan State to stay with Mazie while they were away. But the next morning, Mally shook Charlotte awake, "Sweetheart, have you seen Lauren? She's not in her room." She followed her mother to the kitchen.

They heard her father call out from the basement, "Oh God! Lauren! Wake up, honey! Lauren! Lauren! Mal! Charlotte! Call an ambulance!"

Charlotte dialed 911 from the basement steps as her parents bent over Lauren who lay motionless in a puddle of vomit on the old sofa, her arm dangling limply to the floor.

They tried to sit her up. Mally ran for water and splashed it on Lauren's face. She pleaded, "Lauren, sweetheart. It's time to wake up. Don't you leave us. Don't leave little Mazie. She needs her mummy, darling. We all ne-need you!"

At the sound of sirens, Charlotte rushed to the kitchen, grabbed a teething biscuit and a cold bottle from the refrigerator and ran upstairs to Mazie's room. She was standing in her crib in a sodden diaper whimpering.

"Morning, sweet pea," Charlotte said brightly. "Auntie Charlotte brought you a cookie."

Mazie reached out, working her little fingers.

Charlotte gave her the hard biscuit and lifted her to the changing table.

Thankfully, the sirens faded before the ambulance turned onto the Adair's street. But downstairs, she heard the panicked voices of her parents and the heavy tread of paramedics thundering down the basement stairs.

Charlotte took Mazie into her parents' bedroom and sat in the rocking chair facing the back of the house where Mazie wouldn't see the ambulance or neighbors who were surely milling around in their bathrobes in their front yards. This ruse seemed a pitiful, small comfort for a little girl whose world was collapsing just two floors below.

She gave Mazie her bottle and sang every song she could think of.

"The wheels on the bus go round and round, round and round."

"Roun, roun bus," Mazie sang. "Roun, roun, roun."

"All through the town."

"Aw to da tow," Mazie repeated.

Charlotte ignored the sounds coming through the ductwork. Orders being exchanged. Machines wheezing and beeping.

Then, Mally's high-pitched "No! Please! Make her breathe. Oh God! No! Please, no!

"Na-na," Mazie said, looking up at Charlotte for reassurance. "Na-na. Na-na."

Charlotte sang louder. "The babies on the bus go whaa-whaa-whaa, whaa-whaa-whaa . . . All through the town. All through . . .'"

Then, only silence. And then, the strange, unfamiliar sound of her mother's unrestrained keening. For the first time in her life, Charlotte knew terror.

Mazie looked up at Charlotte again, and so she began to sing, her voice soft and stuttering

L-lullaby, and good n-night
With roses bedight,
With lilies o'er spread
Is baby's w-wee bed.
Lay thee down now and rest,
May thy slumber be b-blessed.
Lay thee d-down now and rest,
May they slumber be blessed.

Lullaby and good night
You're thy m-mother's delight
Bright angels be . . . side
My darling abide.
Lay thee down now and rest,
May thy slumber be b-blessed.
Lay thee d-down now and rest,
May thy slu-u-um-ber be blessed.

Mazie drifted into sleep again and was spared the sound of heavy, slow steps on the basement stairs. Of the back door creaking. Of the ambulance doors closing discreetly. Of her grandfather's heavy shuffle in the kitchen. Of water filling the tea kettle. Of her Nana's quiet weeping.

But Charlotte heard every bit of it.

She lay Mazie in her crib, covered her with her yellow blanket and tucked White Bear in beside her.

"Poor little thing," she whispered. "What will become of you?"

She made the long, long journey down the stairs toward the kitchen. She lingered in the shadows of the hallway and watched her parents propping each other up at the breakfast table.

A paramedic sat in Lauren's chair speaking in hushed tones. His trespassing angered her. The incessant tick of the clock angered her too. She wanted it all to just stop. No one in this kitchen was prepared for what had just happened.

She waited for the courage to take her place in this survivors' circle. Finally, the tea kettle's urgent whistle called her forward. She filled four mugs and took her place at the table as the only child in a family she no longer recognized.

"It's not at all uncommon actually," the paramedic was saying not unkindly, as he filled in the squares of a form there on a metal clipboard. "Before entering rehab they go for one last big high. Happens more than you think."

A police officer stood guard at their kitchen door. Too late, she thought bitterly.

"The medical examiner will tell us for sure, but I suspect your daughter's heroine was laced with Fentanyl. It's a national epidemic. We see a lot of it."

This misery-loves-company approach to dealing with shell-shocked families was apparently meant to put their loss in some kind of perspective. The Adairs of Saskawan, Michigan were now a Gold Star family in America's War on Drugs and Lauren was collateral damage. Their pain was shared, common really. What was happening in their home that morning was not unusual or special, and by extrapolation, neither were they.

That was ten years ago, but since time had stopped on that morning, the passage of a decade meant nothing.

Charlotte had been twenty-three when her sister died. After the shock of it came the guilt. She had never had much sympathy for Lauren's addictions or the drama that went with it. But a decade on, every slight, every cross word, every rejection she'd visited upon her little sister was proof of her own culpability.

During the worst of her sister's addiction, she put distance between herself and her family. She stayed in East Lansing after graduation, found a part-time job as a groundskeeper on campus and waited tables. For a year, she sent her resume to dozens of landscaping firms in Minneapolis, Madison and Ann Arbor—anywhere that was more than seventy-five miles from Saskawan. The month before Lauren died, she'd had phone interviews with three companies and was about to drive to Cleveland for a face-to-face interview when she got the SOS call from her parents. They were taking Lauren to rehab. Could she babysit? Of course, she could. How could she refuse?

After Lauren died, she realized she needed to help her parents raise their orphaned grandchild. She took a job she was over-qualified for as a crew supervisor at TipTop Landscaping and moved into a cockroach-infested studio apartment above a pizza parlor downtown. She vowed to be an indispensable aunt to little Mazie.

But landscaping is exhausting work and Mazie was in daycare, then school most of the time. Months went by when she didn't see her niece except at family dinners. A walk to the playground while her parents cleaned up and the occasional Disney movie on Saturday was all she'd managed to contribute. She wasn't proud of it.

It wasn't that she never offered, but Mazie seemed bored by the usual interests of girls her age. Ted called his granddaughter "our eccentric little alien." No one in the family had broken the code to deciphering her. When she wasn't acting like a disinterested foreigner, Mazie gave the impression that she knew your deepest, darkest secrets. Thank goodness she wasn't like her mother, but she wasn't like Ted, or Mally or Charlotte either.

When Mazie turned eight and announced she didn't want a birthday party, the unsinkable Mally planned one anyway.

"Every little girl needs a birthday party," she'd told Charlotte. "She's just shy. She'll love it once the house is filled with her little mates."

But the morning of the party when Mazie saw Mally giving the house an unscheduled vacuuming she glared at her grandmother and said matter-of-factly, "I know what you're doing, Nana. Why don't you ever listen to me!"

At the party she was polite but subdued. She quietly inspected each gift in turn, thanked the giver and opened the next one with little emotion.

No one in the Adair family had any idea what was going on inside Mazie's head. How could they when she shared so little? And yet, they all felt the weight of Mazie's judgment. Charlotte herself felt Mazie knew what an inadequate big sister she had been. What would Mazie have been like if Lauren had lived, Charlotte wondered? Perhaps even more troubled and indecipherable.

To be honest, Charlotte dreaded the idea of an entire weekend with her niece.

6

THE WEEKEND

The mimosa or "sensitive plant," feeling the brush of a passing herbivore, reacts by folding its leaves and "playing dead." But after a series of gentle touches, its leaves remain open.

Over pizza on Friday night, Charlotte asked casually about Mazie's C-plus in art class.

Her niece had been silently picking mushrooms off her pizza and was adding another to the pile on her napkin before she looked up. "Mally told you to talk to me, didn't she?"

Charlotte bristled. "Mally? You mean Nana, right? Your one-and-only, loving grandmother who has provided shelter and sustenance and unconditional love since you were born? *That* Nana?"

Admittedly this was a poor opening, but Mazie didn't seem to notice.

"I've already told Nana that I don't have a problem with art—just the art teacher. I can't help it if she's a prat. She thinks it makes her a real teacher or something if she gives pop quizzes practically every other day."

"Quizzes in art? Really hard ones, huh?" she asked to demonstrate empathy. "I remember when I was your age—"

"No. Easy and stupid ones," Mazie countered. She was frowning and threatening to fire up a look known in the Adair family as Mazie's Death Ray. "I know the answers, but I can't figure out what she's asking. They're all multiple-choice."

"Is that a problem?"

"Well," she said, studying the ceiling. (If her eyes weren't boring a hole through you, they were wandering everywhere.) "All the choices are sort of right and sort of wrong. I write notes in the margins to explain how more than one answer could be partly right. They're all ambient, or ambidex—."

"Ambiguous?"

"Right, ambiguous. But she still marks them wrong. Maybe I'll rank the answers next time." Her attention wandered off for a moment; then returned. "And her true-false questions are true in certain cases, but in others they're false." She began chewing on her left thumbnail, a habit left over from when she gave up sucking her thumb at age five. "I've tried explaining that too, but she won't listen. No one ever listens to me." She folded her mushroom-stuffed napkin into quarters and placed it in the middle of her plate. "So, is that why the Big People sent me here?"

"The Big People?"

"Nana and Pop. Nana thinks I'm depressed about a stupid C+. I'm not depressed, but I'm *going* to be if everybody keeps—I don't know." She crossed her arms and slouched into her chair.

"You weren't 'sent' here. I just thought we should hang out more."

"Oh." She frowned, kicking at the leg of the table and making their glasses shake. "I'm not really a hanging-out kind of person." Then, re-membering her manners, she sat up straighter. "But thanks. You're less boring that Mal—, I mean, Nana and Pop."

"How kind of you," Charlotte said.

Mazie nodded. She didn't recognize sarcasm either, which in this case was just as well.

Next on the evening's agenda—mutual manicuring—was received with similar detachment. She inspected the row of tiny pink and red bottles on the table.

"What do polished nails say about a girl?" she asked, inspecting hers as if she'd never noticed them before that moment. "That I'm upper class and don't have to clean or dig in the dirt for a living? Or, that I want to have sex with boys? Pink nailbeds, like pink lips, are evidence of fertility, you know. But that wouldn't be interesting to a seventh-grade boy I hope. That's why I don't get it." She sighed. "But do boys even like nail polish on a girl? I doubt they notice or care. Anyway," she sighed again. "I don't actually want to have sex with any of the boys I know. So, I'll pass on the manicure, if you don't mind." She got up to take her plate to the sink. "May I go upstairs? I have reading to do."

Charlotte stared at her niece, speechless.

But in a last-ditch effort to save the evening, she said, "I have a jigsaw puzzle. Lighthouses of Michigan." She dangled this out like a limp carrot and could hear the desperation in her voice.

Mazie heard it too. She stopped in the doorway and turned around slowly, trying her level best to be polite.

"Lighthouses, huh?" she asked with a too-obvious effort at enthusiasm.

Charlotte got the box from the top of the cupboard. "Did you know Michigan has more lighthouses than any other state? See, this puzzle has fifty." This was her last shot.

Mazie looked at the box cover. "Only fifty? Because there are actually a lot more than that." Mazie must have seen the desperation in Charlotte's face because her shoulders suddenly sagged. "But okay, if you want."

Charlotte sat back, defeated. "It's okay, Maze. Go do your reading."

"Okay. Thanks for the pizza. It wasn't too bad. Maybe I'll feel like doing the puzzle tomorrow." She made her way to the doorway again but turned back. "And don't feel bad for not understanding me. I heard the Big People say that I'm like a book with a couple of chapters missing—or out of order, or something like that, so you're not the only one, Char. No one gets me. I'm used to it."

And thus endeth the Evening of Inter-Generational Female Bonding.

Charlotte stayed up late working at her desk in the kitchen, which was just a half sheet of painted plywood on two sawhorses. She studied satellite images of the island and county soil maps. She learned that most of the east side of Saskawan had been an oak and hickory forest. She also learned that on a map dated 1880, Fig's island was labeled Hog Island.

She heard Harp's Jeep rattle to a stop about ten o'clock. He shuffled into the kitchen with his tee shirt on inside out and dropped his gym bag on the floor. He planted a kiss on her temple and brushed her cheek with two-days growth of beard. "I got your text. Woo-who. Our first client. Awesome, babe."

She looked up with a triumphant smile and held it until he found her lips. "Thank you. We left you some pizza with extra mushrooms."

He leaned into the front room. "She go home already?"

"Upstairs reading."

"Reading? On a Friday night?" He opened a can of beer and looked over her shoulder at her laptop. "What kind of a job is it?"

"I'm not sure yet. Could be big."

"Big money, or big work?"

She smiled. "Both, maybe. Again, it's early days."

"Well, we won't make any money if you spend weeks doing drawings." He looked at one of her drawings and frowned, which annoyed her. "An island. He wants the whole thing landscaped?"

"No. But I think he's leaning toward a restoration. How great would that be?"

He raised an eyebrow. "Does he realize how much that would cost?"

"I haven't even figured that out."

He read the screen. "Eradication Plan. What's he got?"

"Buckthorn, wisteria, barberry, honeysuckle, privet, English ivy. I'm making a list."

He whistled. "That'll take weeks even with a Bobcat."

She grimaced. "Unless you know one that's amphibious, no Bobcat. It's an island, remember?" She clicked on the satellite map of the river.

He leaned in closer. "Wait. There's no bridge?"

She laughed. "There's a small raft with a pulley. But don't worry. I'm budgeting enough to hire a crew."

"Well, I sure can't do it all myself. I just hope this guy's pockets are bottomless. When do we start?"

"May first, I hope."

Since he'd quit his job at TipTop and March Madness was almost over, Harp was like a mustang kicking at its stall.

"I hope you know what you're doing," he said, losing interest.

She frowned. "Thanks for the vote of confidence." But she had to admit, these were her thoughts exactly.

When Mazie didn't come down for breakfast the next morning, Charlotte went up to check on her. She found her seated on the floor wrapped in a quilt with a banker's box between her legs.

"I found these comics in the back of the closet," she said without looking up. She held up a copy of *Wolverine: Death is a Man Called Tiger Shark*. "They're really, really old. Were these Great-grandpa's?"

Charlotte tried to picture her grandfather reading anything other than the *Saskawan Evening Star* or the *Farmer's Almanac*. She laughed.

"Those are mine," she said, settling onto the bed.

"Yours?" Mazie looked up then, apparently having a similar difficulty picturing her aunt reading anything but web pages.

Charlotte pulled her sweater tight around her. "I collected them when I was about your age," she said.

"When was that?"

"Let's see. About twenty years ago. But sometimes I bought vintage ones. I was going to sell them and get rich."

"Do you have Wolverine number one? That's worth at least two hundred bucks."

"I wish."

Mazie pulled out another cellophane-covered comic and laid it on a stack on the floor.

Charlotte said, "I didn't know you were into comic books."

"Generally, I think using superpowers to solve a problem is sort of cheating. You don't have to use brain power if you have magical powers. I'd rather see a comic character with super powers of deduction. These stories are predictable, but some of the old ones are interesting. Do you have *Incredible Hulk* numbers one-eighty or one-eighty-one? Even in poor condition, they could be worth hundreds."

"Those were out of my price range even back then." She turned to go back downstairs. "Let me know if you find any priceless ones."

"Do I get to keep the money?"

"If there's anything left after I buy a new furnace, paint the barn, fix the roof and plant the meadow, of course, sure."

"It's freezing in here, so I'll keep looking." Mazie picked out another comic book and set it in a pile. "And, no, I'm not hungry."

By Sunday night, she had read the entire box and cataloged them by series and in chronological order.

7

THE PROPOSAL

Flowers offer nectar to pollinators and in return get their sticky yellow pollen delivered to other flowers of their species. Some, like the primrose, flaunt their charms with big, come-hither blooms and enchanting fragrances. Others, like the delicate spring beauty, advertise their nectar with colorful striped "landing strips" on their petals. But the clever lady slipper orchid doesn't take any chances. She has a surprise for any pollinator inclined to enjoy her nectar without leaving with her pollen. When a bee enters her slipper-shaped pollen chamber, it discovers there's no room to turn around. It must exit through a tight chamber, where it gets covered in sticky yellow pollen.

The previous Christmas, Harp surprised Charlotte with a New Year's Eve trip to Ludington State Park. They snowshoed through the Lake Michigan dunes and peered into the windows of the keeper's cottage at the Big Sauble Lighthouse. They checked into a quaint Victorian bed and breakfast and had dinner at a restaurant overlooking the harbor.

When the waiter brought a bottle of sparkling wine, Charlotte said, "I'm sorry, but we didn't order this."

The waiter shot a look at Harp who dropped to one knee and grabbed Charlotte's hands.

"Char," he said, looking like he could use the Heimlich maneuver. "I mean, Charlotte Anne Adair, will you d-do me the honor of b-becoming my wife?"

She stood up so quickly that her chair toppled backward, drawing stares and murmurs from the other diners.

That's when she floated out of her body and hovered near the ceiling.

Harp was kneeling on his napkin and looking up at her the way a starving man looks at a plate of food. There was a spot of steak sauce on his upper lip and another on his tie.

Blood either rushed into her head or drained from it—she wasn't sure how it worked when you feel lightheaded and detached from reality. She closed her eyes and ran through her possible responses:

One: Oh! Wow! Harp. This is flattering beyond belief, but I haven't backpacked in Costa Rica yet, hiked the Grand Canyon or seen a wild elephant. Can I get back to you?

Two: Harp, sweetheart, I have always been of the opinion that certain decisions—like buying a house, getting a dog or getting married, for example—are best negotiated *in private*.

Or, three: Are you *outta your fucking mind*?

When she opened her eyes, Harp was holding up an open ring box and was looking up at her with a desperate, hang-dog expression that melted her. Despite the steak sauce, he looked incredibly handsome. She knew every woman in the room was thinking, Say yes! Say yes!

Life with Harp would never, ever be dull. Maybe one day they'd backpack in Costa Rica together.

She let out a squeak that must have sounded affirmative because the whole restaurant stood up and applauded. Harp pushed a ring onto her shaking finger, an awkward docking procedure that took three attempts. He stood up then and dipped her into a long kiss that gave the next table an unobstructed view of her panties. When she came up for air she felt faintly nauseous and slightly pissed off, but also somehow elated and hopeful.

She wondered how many women on the receiving end of a public proposal felt blindsided. How many Jumbotron engagements, she wondered, fouled out by the fourth quarter?

Yellow Lady's Slipper *Cypripedium parviflorum*

She covered her cheeks with her hands as the waiter righted her chair and nudged her gently into it. The ring was a small diamond, flanked by two tiny sapphires. Sparkly, perfect and much more than he could afford.

"So, did you suspect?" he whispered.

Not only could Harp not usually keep a secret, he was terrible at planning ahead and saving money.

"Not a clue," she said.

She suspected that his softball buddies, his climbing buddies, his hunting buddies, his poker buddies and his biking buddies egged him on. There was a betting pool, too. She'd put money on that. Will she, or won't she? (Later she learned he'd won most of the money in a poker game and borrowed the rest from his friend Mike and his mom.)

No, she had not seen this coming. She had always wanted to get married someday. But someday was always a couple of years off.

For much of her twenties, she'd been stuck in Saskawan, stuck in a just-okay job and stuck helping her parents with Mazie. But she still believed there was more to this life. Opening her own business was a good start. Marriage was next. It made sense.

Harp had a practical, uncomplicated view of life, which she couldn't say about herself. He was fun and generous and sexy and most importantly, he was totally in love with her. So, when he popped the question, it felt like another worthy, grown-up milestone in a life that had thus far had too few. Harp had made a bold move. She was thirty-three; it was time she did too.

8
─

THE TOUR

*By 1816, Ohio and Indiana were filling up with homesteads
and poised to achieve statehood. But just to the north, the
Territory of Michigan was largely ignored. It didn't help that
an early cartographer had stamped the words "Interminable
Swamp" across the mitten of the Lower Peninsula. So, the fed-
eral land office decided to "market" Michigan to Easterners.
They sent teams of surveyors to inventory the land and determine the location of forests, wetlands and lakes, as well
as the plant species they found. For the next forty years, these
teams recorded the diameter of a tree growing at each section
corner. They noted the agricultural potential of the soil and
the quality of the timber. In the end, the project fulfilled its
goal of attracting homesteaders and land speculators into the
Michigan wilderness. Even today, this data, called Michigan's
Natural Features Inventory is a treasure trove of information
for modern Michiganders who want to restore their land.*

"Cream, no sugar, right?" Fig said handing her a heavy white mug.
"Yes, thanks," Charlotte said, wrapping her hands around its
warmth.

It had been a week since their first meeting. This time, she wore her
pressed khakis, small gold earrings and a hint of eyeliner, mascara and
blush.

Fig sat down across from her at the huge dining table. Between
them were architectural drawings of the recent house renovations.

"You're welcome to take them if they'd be helpful."

Besides the new bathroom and study at the back of the house, he'd
replaced all the windows with authentic, wood-framed replicas. In
the semi-circular kitchen, the new oak cupboards looked like faithful

replicas of the originals. Except for the new cedar shake roof and new-ly-stained siding, the exterior remained the same.

"So, this was more of a restoration than a renovation," she observed.

"That's right. It seemed more respectful somehow."

"So, what if we take the same approach to the landscaping? I mean, return as much of the island to the way it was before the house and the pigs."

"The forest primeval?"

"Something like that. You'll want something a bit manicured near the house and along the paths, I assume, but I'd recommend plants that grew here before white settlers arrived."

"I'd like that. I'd also like a few benches where I can sit and watch the river go by."

"Yes. That's very doable."

"But other than the old oaks, how do you know what plants grew here back then?"

Charlotte said opened her laptop. "This map shows what vegetation was growing on the island before European settlement."

He looked closer. "That's remarkably detailed."

She zoomed in on the map. "This whole side of town is coded in pink, including your island, which means that it was part of an oak and hickory forest that covered thirty-three thousand acres—and that was just one, continuous forest. Most of Michigan's forests were either oak-hickory or beech-maple. But there were also bogs, marshes and wetlands. Your island is called a floodplain forest."

Fig's eyes widened. "Uh-oh. You said the F-word."

"What? No, I didn't!"

"F-L-O-O-D must never be uttered on this island." He shook his head. "Very unlucky."

Charlotte laughed. "Okay. So, has it ever 'F-ed' here?"

"Not so far." He knocked on the tabletop. "Dams control the water level pretty effectively."

"Well, the house is on a rise, but your cottonwoods, black willows, shagbark hickories and swamp white oaks wouldn't care a bit if it F-ed a bit. I'll make a list of natives that won't mind having wet feet either, like dogwoods, spicebush and trout lily or turtlehead—all very pretty."

"They grew here at one time?"

"Very likely."

"—but not wisteria," Fig said, smiling.

"Correct." She said, closing her laptop. "Let's take a walk."

He glanced out the window where a stiff wind was bending the trees and whipping the river into a froth. "Now?"

"Not if you'd rather wait—"

"No. Now is fine. Just give me a minute." He opened a hall closet while she put on her parka and started toward the door but stopped when she saw the great bundle in his arms. She watched with growing amusement as he bundled himself inside a long, puffy parka, a plaid hunter's cap with fur-lined ear flaps, a pair of fur-lined boots, a striped scarf the size of an afghan and a pair of fur-lined leather gloves.

He opened the door and bowed slightly. "After you."

She smiled. Admiral Peary had nothing on Fig Bigelow.

On the top step of the porch, he raised a gloved finger. "'I went to the woods to live deliberately,' he announced, "and . . . to see what it had to teach, and not, when I came to die, discover that I had not lived.'"

She nodded blankly.

"Thoreau said that—or some approximation of it. It seems appropriate, don't you think? This restoration project of ours could be the start of something remarkable."

Her heart responded with an extra beat. "Yes," she said. "I believe it could be."

He followed her down the steps and toward the downstream point of the island.

"We could add a path all around the island with benches at several vantage points." She pushed aside the undergrowth and pointed downstream. "You can see all the way to the bend from here."

"Yes . . . . that . . . would be perfect," he said, his breath coming out in white puffs. Although they'd only walked a few hundred steps he was winded. Her theory of the anorexic tri-athlete wasn't holding up. He was probably older than he looked.

She broke off a twig. "I'd like to get rid of this. It's privet," she said. "It was brought over from Europe in the 1950s and has escaped from yards into woodlands. Birds eat the berries in the fall and spread seeds to natural areas, which sounds like a good thing, right?"

He wagged a gloved finger at her. "Is this a trick question, right?"

She laughed. "Yes. Privet berries have little nutritional value, especially in the fall and winter when birds need it most." She tossed the twig to the ground.

"Junk food for birds."

"Exactly. Our native shrubs have evolved over eons to provide high-protein or high-fat fruit in the fall that help birds survive our cold winters or prepare them for long migrations."

"So, we must banish this foreign invader."

"And if we do," she said, bending over a patch of spindly shoots, "these maple-leaf viburnums will get the sunlight they've been missing. They'll produce fall berries that taste and smell awful to birds—"

"Wait. Birds don't like their berries? I'm confused."

Charlotte laughed. "But here's the trick. In the dead of winter—just when other food is really scarce—the taste of the berries mellows and they become an important food source."

"Ah! That Mother Nature is a clever lady," he said. His brow suddenly furrowed. "Invasive plants are a plant epidemic, aren't they?"

She tilted her head to consider this. "I hadn't thought of it quite that way, but—"

"Think about it," he said, jumping in. "Columbus brought smallpox, typhoid, syphilis and measles to the New World. The indigenous North Americans had no antibodies to fight them."

"Yes, that's a good comparison."

They walked on.

"But surely, not all foreign species are bad," he said.

"Of course not. Many European and Asian imports are perfectly well-behaved, law-abiding immigrants."

"Like what?"

"Astilbe and hostas. Japanese maples. There are dozens that I wouldn't mind using in a suburban garden—along with some good natives, too. My grandmother's Chinese peonies have been growing in front of my house for decades. Some non-natives are even beneficial. Dandelions are Eurasian, but they provide nectar for bees in the early spring when there's little else blooming."

Fig's face was creased with concern. "More people should know about this, Ms. Adair."

She smiled. "Well, one more does."

Further along the path, she pointed out another wisteria vine running along the ground thirty feet from the porch and a patch of English ivy covering the forest floor.

He sighed. "My island has been invaded by a silent menace. It's starting to depress me."

"But they don't stand a chance against the army you just hired."

"I wish I'd known this years ago," Fig said wistfully.

In a clearing next to the house she patted the trunk of a towering tree.

"What?" He crossed his arms, looking worried. "Don't tell me this is a baobab tree or some other bad actor. I know it's an oak."

"Yes, a white oak and one of our most valuable native trees."

Fig clapped his gloved hands together. "Alleluia and praise be. I was afraid you'd say I should cut it, in which case I would have to fire you."

"And I would deserve it."

Fig laughed which turned into coughing. "Sorry," he said, holding up a hand. "My cough is damned annoying, but nothing contagious. Now, tell me . . . what's so special . . . about my oaks?"

She ran her boot over a pile of acorn tops. "This tree provides food for something like 500 species of caterpillars alone and food or habitat for squirrels, turkeys, deer, quail, ducks . . . a really long list."

Fig arched backward to see into the canopy and coughed into his sleeve.

She said, "Just for comparison, you know ginkgo trees? Fan-shaped leaves?" she asked. "They're all over downtown."

He nodded.

"In China, they are nibbled by all kinds of lovely, beneficial Asian insects, but here, only 5 caterpillars can digest their leaves. It's a pretty tree but almost useless to American wildlife."

"I can't digest Chinese food either, so I feel their pain. But remind me again why I want 500 kinds of caterpillars munching on my beautiful oaks?"

"You'll never see most of them. Mrs. Chickadee will snatch about six thousand of them to feed her babies during one nesting season. So again, if you have a healthy ecosystem, leaf munching will be controlled by birds and other predators of the munchers, while bird babies get healthy and fat."

As they walked on, Fig seemed deep in thought. "So, this European buckthorn and Asian wisteria don't respect the laws of this oak and hickory ecosystem. So, there must be consequences. Death and deportation." His lips curved into a smile.

Charlotte laughed. "They didn't ask to come here."

"Perhaps we should build a wall," he said, still smiling.

"Chinese wisteria loves walls. English ivy and Asian bittersweet would scramble right over. The fault lies with humans who import them and propagate them and sell them."

Fig blew into his cupped hands. "I'm relieved, but all this talk about illegal aliens sounds suspiciously right-wing."

This wasn't the first time she'd heard this.

"Yes, but there's a fundamental difference. White, black and brown *Homo sapiens*—human beings—are all the same species. The genetic differences between a Bolivian, an African and a Norwegian are so insignificant that breeding can and does occur. The concept that all people are created equal isn't just a social ideal, it's scientific fact."

Fig nodded. "Well said."

She went on. "North American native plants aren't superior—but over eons of time, they've developed an intricate set of checks and balances that only work when all the pieces are in place. Every living thing on the planet evolved alongside a certain set of organisms it can eat and another set that eats it. It's a delicate balance that's easily upset."

"Checks and balances. The greater good. Now you're speaking my language—lawyer talk."

She bent down to point out something that looked like a wizard's cowl poking out of the ground. "See this?"

"That's got to be alien. Martian, even."

"No. It's our native skunk cabbage, one of the first plants we see in the spring. It pushes so hard through the frozen earth that it actually creates heat that melts the snow. I admire this plant, but in the UK, it's considered an invasive species."

"Ahh. So it goes both ways." Fig nodded. "I hadn't thought of that."

"Yes. The Chinese and several African countries spend millions removing the South American water hyacinth that chokes their rivers.

And the Scots hold 'rhodie-bashing' parties to remove rhododendrons from their hillsides. At the end of the day, there are no bad plants, just poorly placed ones."

He rubbed his chin thoughtfully. "I've been a complete nincompoop when it comes to plants. I won't blame you if you decide my island is too far gone."

Charlotte stood up. "I love a challenge."

He nodded slowly. "Okay. You do the hard stuff and I'll write the checks. Will that be a fair arrangement?"

"Lovely," she said.

"Let's get started soon, shall we?" He folded his arms across his chest and shivered. Her sermon had run long and even the choir was growing restless—and cold.

"Yes, absolutely. I'll get back to you in a couple of days with some drawings, a cost estimate and a contract."

They turned back toward the house, leaning into the wind. She watched him climb the steps using the porch railing for leverage.

"Thank you, Fig. You're a great listener."

He nodded without turning back. "So I've been told."

APRIL

Bloodroot *Sanguinaria canadensis*

9

RADICAL, BAD-ASS
LANDSCAPING

Most Americans can remember a frog pond before it was filled in for condos or a woods before it was a strip mall. As eyewitnesses to the destruction of wild places, Americans clamor for more "conservation." Save what's left, we say. But "what's left" amounts to just four percent of a continent that quite recently seemed endless. What's more, we've claimed the best, most fertile, flat, temperate and life-giving land for our own use. Then we've plowed, paved, bulldozed, sprayed and mowed it, making it useless to most wildlife. "What's left" are frozen peaks, remote islands, dry canyons and cliffs – places as alien to most wildlife as they are to us. In contrast, few Europeans remember wilderness. Their focus is land restoration or "re-wilding." Cemeteries are being returned to forest. Bridges are being re-purposed with trees and grasses so wildlife can cross highways safely. European bison, bear, lynx, beaver and grouse are being reintroduced into suburban landscapes. Instead of relegating wildlife to preserves, Europeans are sharing the land.

By early April, Harp had hired three men through an immigrant resettlement agency. Swahili and French-speaking brothers from the Democratic Republic of the Congo, Kiza and Martin, joined a compact, middle-aged Mexican named Hector who had just been reunited with his wife and children after six years. Under Harp's leadership, they were becoming a hard-working, focused team. Their only distraction was the little brown terrier who guarded the cottonwood tree at the landing.

The brothers named him Panya, Swahili for "mouse," while Hector called him Niñito, or "little boy." They argued endlessly about his name, what he should eat and who would take him home once they charmed him out of his burrow.

Each morning, Charlotte knew when the crew had arrived when she heard them clapping, whistling and singing to the dog. Before the raft left the landing, his bowl was overflowing with beef *frijoles* or *poulet à la Moambé*, the national dish of the D.R.C. But Speedy-Panya-Niñito didn't play favorites. His bowl was always licked clean.

"I get Panya one day," Kiza promised. "I give him a nice, warm bed."

Hector protested. "He is Chihuahua! A Mexican dog. See the ears when I talk Spanish?" He demonstrated by wiggling his fingers behind his ears and calling, "*Ven aquí, niño pequeño. Te cuidaré muy bien.*" The little dog barked, but stood his ground.

Kiza laughed. "He is Africa wild dog. He want to eat you!"

The battle for the little terrier's affections remained a draw.

One sunny afternoon Charlotte was pulling up the runners of English ivy at the side of the house when she uprooted a bloodroot plant by mistake.

"Oops! Sorry," she said, tucking the exposed tuber back into the ground.

"Why do you owe my plants an apology?" Fig asked, coming up behind her. One hand was tucked into his coat pocket and the other held a handful of mail.

"I pulled some bloodroot." She brushed the leaf litter aside to expose an intricately shaped leaf.

"Did it forgive you?"

"Absolutely," she said. "These yellow leaves will turn a healthy green now that they have more light. They were crying out for help really." She pointed to a short, white daisy-like flower. "Someday it'll spread all over the island. You'll see. I'll transplant some where you'll see them from the kitchen window next spring. It'll be quite a show."

"Lucky me." He bent for a closer look. "Where did they come from? I'm sure they weren't here last year."

"Sure they were."

"Well, apparently I wasn't listening to their cries for help."

She pushed her cap higher on her forehead and looked up at him. "They bloom for only a few days. That's why they're called spring ephemerals."

"Hmm," he said, thinking. "So it is with beauty—snowflakes, sunsets, youth. But tell me, Charlotte, why is such a pretty plant saddled with an off-putting name?"

"Bloodroot?" She held up a tuber the size of her pinky and scratched it with her fingernail. Reddish-orange sap oozed out. Fig squatted next to her for a closer look.

"Aptly named."

A bumblebee landed on a white petal nearby. They watched as it traced circles around the yellow center.

"It's looking for nectar," Fig said.

"But it won't find any."

"No?"

"Bloodroot is a clever trickster. In the early spring bees land on anything that might offer nectar. Bloodroot doesn't have to offer nectar to get pollinated."

The hopeful bee flew off to another bloodroot blossom.

"See? That flower just got pollinated without the effort of making nectar."

"Isn't that cheating?" Fig asked.

She smiled. "Like getting free flowers from your hardworking landscaper?"

"Good point."

"Besides, it takes extra effort to wake up and flower so early in the spring. Bloodroot deserves a break."

Across the river, something caused the little brown dog to bark.

Charlotte took off her gloves. "I've been meaning to ask you about that stray terrier over there."

Fig frowned. "He's been there all winter. I called the animal shelters but they can't pick him up unless he's fenced or leashed. I leave him scraps, but he's an independent character. Poor little Prince."

"Prince?" she said, laughing. "You've named him?"

"Why is that funny?"

During their second week on the island, Harp and the crew began clearing invasive privet, buckthorn and honeysuckle. Charlotte flagged them with orange tape and the crew paired up, one with loppers and the other with a brush to paint the stumps with herbicide dyed bright blue.

While the crew worked, Charlotte invited Fig to accompany her to the greenhouses at VanderLee Gardens.

"I'll show you the trees and shrubs I'm recommending."

"Oh good. I love a good field trip," he said.

That morning, Charlotte parked behind a huge brush pile that Harp was feeding into a wood chipper at the landing.

He'd also rented a flat-bottomed fishing boat with a small motor from his buddy Mike to ferry the cut brush to the chipper and take wood chips back to the island to cover the new paths. He had enjoyed the novelty at first, but his patience was wearing thin.

Charlotte found him feeding brush into the chute aimed at a tarp on the riverbank. Hector was emptying a second tarp into the boat and pushing off for the island where Martin and Kiza were loading wheelbarrows of chips from a third pile to the newly cleared path.

Harp gave her a dark look and shut down the chipper, rubbing a bloody scratch on his forearm.

"It'll take till Christmas at the rate we're going, Char! I've got Hector on full-time ferry duty." He was breathing hard with both hands on his hips. "Promise me we'll never landscape an island again."

"I can practically guarantee that," she said, trying to make light of it. She touched his arm. "Let me put some alcohol on that."

He pulled away. "It's nothing. Seriously, Char, you need to get real."

This irritated her. "Real? So, how's your bank account doing, Harp? Are those paychecks real enough for you?"

He turned away and hit a switch as the chipper roared back to life.

She headed for her truck and slammed the door shut. Across the river, Fig was rafting toward her at the unhurried pace she'd come to expect and wearing his heavy coat and twisted scarf even though the weather was mild.

As they drove toward VanderLee's she asked, "Do you mind if we take a short detour?"

"An adventure of some kind?"

"Hardly. I just want to see what the city planted in the median on 16th Street. It's more or less on the way to the nursery."

"What do you hope to see?"

"Anything but Bradford pears."

"Do you have something against Bradford? Or, just his pears?"

Charlotte smiled. "It's complicated." She hesitated. "I'll explain, but only if you have a long attention span or stop me if it's too much."

"If there is an opposite of attention deficit disorder, that's what I suffer from."

"Obsessive-compulsive disorder?"

"When something interests me, I'm like a terrier locked on to a fat, juicy ankle."

"That's a bit scary," she said with a laugh.

"So, tell me, Charlotte, what's wrong with these pears?"

She pulled into traffic. "First, some history. A variety of Asian pear trees were imported after World War I to cross with American pears that were prone to a bacterial disease called fireblight. They crossbred them successfully, but the hybrid didn't produce fruit."

"That must have been disappointing."

"At first. But the hybrid also made a lot of pretty blooms, so horticulturalists marketed it as an ornamental tree with some American-sounding names, like Bradford or Cleveland or Callery pear. It's still very popular."

"But something went wrong, right?" Fig said, his chin thrust forward in expectation.

"The tree had weak limbs. So, horticulturalists developed a hybrid with stronger limbs."

"Ah. More genetic messing around, right?"

"Exactly."

"Was Dr. Frankenstein involved?"

"I wouldn't be surprised. Anyway, pretty soon new non-fruiting, strong-limbed pear trees went on the market. Everybody was happy—for a while."

"But then . . ." Fig prompted.

"But *then*, seedlings started popping up on their own."

"Wait. I thought you said they were sterile."

"The trees produced by botanists and planted by developers *were*, but when they cross-pollinated with regular orchard pears they produce offspring that are *very* fertile."

"No!"

"Yes. And these feral pears have some really nasty new attributes."

"Like?"

"Four-inch thorns. Foul-smelling blossoms—like sweaty socks at the bottom of a gym locker. And dense growth which makes them almost impossible to get rid of."

"Demon spawn," Fig growled. "I think I saw the movie."

"These feral offspring are a huge problem down south and we're seeing outbreaks in Michigan now. Ohio has already moved to prohibit them and Indiana is considering a ban."

"Why would anyone want to plant them?"

"Because they grow fast and bloom like crazy. I saw a report on the beautification project in the 16th Street median. When I saw it included Bradford pear, I wrote a letter."

"What was the city's response?"

She shrugged. "Nothing."

"Did you tell them what you just told me?"

She nodded.

"You didn't tell me our trip would be a crusade. Did you bring picket signs? A roll of T.P? A saw? Or, are we just going to chain ourselves to the offending trees?"

Charlotte laughed. "As tempting as that sounds, I'm with an important client today. Besides, I'm hoping the city planted something else."

Charlotte drove slowly for several blocks and finally sped up.

"So, were those—?"

"Yup. At least thirty of them."

Fig frowned. "Now what?"

She shrugged and drove on in silence.

In the gravel parking lot of VanderLee Gardens, Fig wound his scarf around his neck three times before getting out. Halfway to the door, she realized he was still buttoning his coat. He followed slowly behind her into the greenhouse and down the rows of potted shrubs, nodding and asking questions as she explained the features of each species.

He leaned closer to read each plant tag and touch the raspberry-colored blossoms of the redbud. He ran his thumb over the new red and green leaves of the buttonbush. He let the crimson stems of the red-osier dogwood run through his long fingers. His body movements seemed choreographed to conserve energy, but his long fingers were unrestrained. If she didn't look away she felt she might be hypnotized by them.

"These are all native to Michigan and will bloom?"

She nodded. "This year or next."

"All right. Then let's do it."

"Great! I'll arrange for Harp to pick them up and meet you at the truck."

As always, Barb VanderLee, her friend, mentor and owner of the nursery, was behind the counter.

"Hi, Charlotte. Did you find what you needed?"

"Yes. Your shrubs are beautiful as always." She pushed her list and her credit card across the counter. "I'll send Harp to pick them up tomorrow."

Barb looked at the order and nodded. "All natives. Looks like you've got yourself a discerning client, Char."

She nodded, "That, I do."

Charlotte found Fig at a display marked Groundcovers deep in conversation with a member of the sales staff.

"Well, they're garden staples around here," she was explaining, as Fig pointed at a table of English ivy and *Vinca minor*. "They're easy to grow and thrive in our climate."

"That's rather an understatement, wouldn't you say?" he asked. "As a professional, you must know the difference between a nice, foreign plant that can handle a Michigan winter and one that escapes into natural areas and smothers native species."

The woman backed up a few steps and pointed to the outdoor display area. "We also have a native plant section. Would you like me to show you?"

"I've just come from there and ordered a number of native shrubs, as a matter of fact. But, I can't imagine why you would sell these. Years ago, someone planted this ivy all around my house and I'm having to pay good money to have it removed before it chokes out my trillium and –" He turned when he saw Charlotte. "What do you call that small white flower with the—*bloodroot*! That's it."

Charlotte smiled at the flustered woman.

Fig asked. "Do you carry wisteria, too?"

"Japanese or Chinese? They're in our vine section. I can show you."

"No, ma'am. I already have wisteria which at this moment is trying to strangle my red maple."

The woman blinked uneasily. "Perhaps you would like to talk to my manager?"

Charlotte forced a smile and looked up at Fig. "I have everything ordered. Shall we go?"

Fig ignored the question. "I was just pointing out these invasive groundcovers to—" He leaned closer to read her name tag. "—Mary. I've just been sharing with Mary that these are invasive."

Mary pursed her lips. "I believe that would be a matter of opinion."

"Is it? Well, now you're telling me something I didn't know." He looked from Charlotte to Mary and back again. "Are there experts who don't believe that an imported or genetically altered plant that spreads uncontrollably—wildly even—no pun intended—into natural areas, killing or displacing beneficial native plants, is *not* invasive? How can that be?"

Mary's vague smile seemed frozen in place. "As I said, sir—"

Charlotte stepped between Fig and the employee and smiled.

"Fig, we need to get back," Charlotte said, cocking her head toward the door.

"We could talk to the manager since Mary has offered."

At that moment, Fig seemed very much like a terrier being told to drop it!

"I'll speak to her later, Fig." Charlotte smiled at Mary. "Thanks."

Fig followed her to the truck.

"Utter piffle. That woman doesn't know anything about plants."

When Charlotte didn't reply, he grew silent.

In the truck, he turned to her. "Did I say too much?"

"No, of course not." She pulled into traffic, focusing on the road. "I ordered button bushes, redbud and dogwood. Five of each. A couple might even bloom this year if we—"

"Why didn't you want to talk to the manager?"

Charlotte pursed her lips. "That would be Barb VanderLee or her husband Hal. That's who I *was* talking to—and getting a nice discount for your shrubs—primarily because you ordered natives. The VanderLees are the biggest native growers in West Michigan. And they know as well as I do the danger of invasive plants."

"And yet they sell contraband?"

"Contraband?" She felt suddenly defensive. "The VanderLees aren't doing anything illegal."

"Really? Wait. Why aren't those plants banned like purple loosestrife? You can't buy that, can you?"

"No." She shrugged.

"Why is that?"

She wished she had an answer.

"It's . . . complicated. At least that's what I've been told. And I've been too busy planting natives to work on banning invasives." She heard her own defensiveness again. "Besides, Hal and Barb are the good guys. If they don't offer plants like vinca, their customers will go to their competitors. They have to make a living, which, by the way, so do I." She kept her eyes on the road. "I need to maintain good relationships with my suppliers in the horticultural industry, too."

"Ahhhh." He let the word lengthen into a sigh. "Of course. I'm sorry, Charlotte. I've overstepped. I thought I was being an informed consumer, but I berated the employee of a valued colleague."

"It's okay. No one's more laid-back than Barb and Hal VanderLee."

"Thanks. You are too generous with your absolution." He paused. "So, there's a rift starting to open up in your industry."

Bradford Pear *Pyrus calleryana*

"I suppose. We're a diverse group of greenhouses, tree farms, retail nurseries and even lawn care services. We're not all environmentalists—that's for sure."

"I see."

"And most invasive plant species were imported to North America by the horticultural industry itself. Over eighty percent, I've heard."

"Like?"

"Kudzu and purple loosestrife. Of course, that was a century ago and no one understood the damage they would do. Thomas Jefferson probably imported Scotch broom which is highly flammable and causing huge problems in western states. Today, we know better, and yet we still allow many invasive species to be produced and sold each year."

"Like?"

"*Vinca minor*, most honeysuckles, Bradford pear, Norway maple, barberry, teasel, privet, baby's breath, Asian bittersweet, wisteria, multiflora rose, English ivy . . ."

"Damn it, Charlotte, that isn't right!"

She hesitated before the right words came. "People still want them because they're attractive and easy to grow."

"Easy, indeed. But would they want them if they knew the harm they're doing?"

"Some wouldn't. But most gardeners don't think about the woodland or ravine over their back fence."

Fig nodded. "A few weeks ago, I would have happily planted a dozen wisteria vines." He gazed out the window, but she knew he wasn't taking in the view. "There was a time when people used leaded gas and smoked cigarettes. People resist change at first, but eventually, they demand it. People are refusing to use plastic straws. New York City banned Styrofoam cups. Kenya banned plastic bags, for God sakes! Most people *want* to do the right thing. But they have to know what that is. You have to tell them."

"Me?" She laughed. "I know too many homeowners who just want a flat, turf-covered, bug-free yard. They don't wear seatbelts or recycle their trash or wear masks during pandemics. I'm not hopeful."

"Oh, but I think you are, Charlotte. Otherwise, you'd be in another line of work. I think you believe, as I do, that people will demand change when they understand what's at stake."

Charlotte rolled her eyes. "The city ignored my letter. Trust me, people fall into a stupor when I start talking about invasive species. All I can do is inform my clients, but in the end, I have to give them what they ask for."

Fig grinned. "So far so good, right?"

"Well, you're special," she said before realizing she might have crossed a line. "An exceptional client," she corrected quickly. "Anyway, I'm not Joan of Arc. I'm nobody. I mean, *really* nobody. A one-woman landscaping company with one client. Oops," she winced. "I shouldn't have told you that."

"Well then, you're batting a thousand. Besides, I suspected I was your first client."

"You did? Why?"

"Because there are no customer reviews on your website, except one that sounded like she might be your mother."

Charlotte blushed. "All right. So, why pick a greenhorn?"

"I was impressed with your philosophy, 'Healing the Earth one yard at a time'—though I didn't fully understand it, mind you. I think you said, 'Your garden can be more than just something pretty to look at—it can be a refuge for wildlife.' That intrigued me. Also, your youth. Your sex. Your friendly face." His eyes shifted back to the road.

"Why, thank you, Mr. Bigelow."

He shrugged. "I liked the idea of helping a young woman succeed in a male dominated profession. I root for underdogs."

"Yes, well, I am that." She sighed. "But I have to ask, did you feel obligated to hire me because you peed on me?"

He threw back his head and laughed. "It was the least I could do, don't you think?" After a long pause, he added, "Look, I'm sorry I meddled back there. Beware of over-zealous converts." He opened his arms toward the sky. "Hallelujah, I've seen the light." Then, more seriously, "I'm sorry that I jeopardized a professional relationship."

"Barb VanderLee is a good friend. She would totally understand."

"Maybe, but I don't want to complicate things. You're already living under the curse of Cassandra."

Charlotte sifted through some dusty memories. "A minor Greek goddess?"

"Mortal actually. She just *looked* like a goddess. Apollo was so besotted with her that he offered her the gift of prophecy in return for her favors."

"But then she changed her mind or something?"

"Yes. So. Apollo brought down a curse that no one would believe her prophecies."

She groaned. "You're right. That's me. I know just how she felt."

"I suspect you do," he said softly. "I suspect you know exactly."

They rode through the city without saying much else until Fig saw the Common Ground Cafe. "Do you mind if we stop for coffee? If you run in, I'll pay." He handed her his credit card.

She was in line at the counter when he came in.

"Can you add a couple of pounds of medium roast? And do you mind if we drink it in here? I'm a bit chilled."

Harp would be wondering why she had been away so long, but she said, "Sure. Go save us a table."

He was leaning back with his arms crossed over his chest when she set their mugs on the table.

"So, I've been wondering, Charlotte, how did you become interested in native landscaping."

"Wow. That's a big question. I guess for me, the more I learned about how ecosystems work, the more I realized how vulnerable they are."

"But was there a pivotal moment when your life took a turn from designing rose gardens to badgering clients to go native?"

"Badgering?"

He grinned. "Coaxing, I mean."

"Educating? Enlightening."

"Yes, exactly that. I'm guessing there's a story."

She peered into her coffee and took a breath.

"Most clients have two requirements: low maintenance and beauty. The job that nearly broke me was a perennial border around a backyard pool. The homeowner wanted it colorful and absolutely maintenance-free, but she also decreed it could have no bugs. She kept saying, 'I hate bugs. I won't have them biting my children.' She wanted me to mix up a pesticide potion to douse her plants whenever her little darlings wanted to swim. It was insanity." Charlotte shook her head. "When I resisted, she called my boss and complained that I wasn't 'hearing' her concerns."

"That's bizarre," he said, nodding. "But what made you want to be a landscape designer in the first place? What made you such a radical, bad-ass native landscaping professional?"

She smiled. "Is that what you think? Well, I'm not sure."

Fig leaned toward her on his elbows. "When did you decide to push such a big boulder up that hill?"

She considered this image and laughed.

His eyes were fixed on her with such intensity that it made her squirm. He wasn't letting this go.

She looked away, toward the parking lot and the traffic beyond.

"When I was in elementary school my parents bought a lot in a new subdivision that had been a fruit farm. Ours was only the third house built, so I climbed the gnarled old trees and explored the oak and hickory woodlot along the edges. Oh, and there was a shallow pond full of frogs and turtles. I thought it was paradise.

"My friends and I built forts and teepees in the tall grass. One summer the frog chorus in the pond became almost deafening. My dad and I took flashlights and waded around in the knee-deep water for half the night just watching them. I remember exclaiming that the frogs were giving each other piggyback rides – which led to the first birds and bees talk."

When she looked up, Fig's eyes were closed.

"Sorry, that was way too much information."

"Not at all. I'm picturing the scene." He waved his hand. "Continue."

She stopped to take a sip of coffee before continuing.

"But every spring, the bulldozers came. They scraped away the grasses and wildflowers, cut down the trees and dug basements. One year, they pushed our sledding hill into the pond. My friends and I spent days rescuing frogs and turtles in buckets. My mom drove us to a nearby lake to let them go. The next night two frogs we'd missed called to each other all night long. My mom says I cried myself to sleep, but I don't remember that. Eventually, the subdivision filled up, and that was the end of it."

She gave her head a shake, surprised by the emotions that welled up.

Fig nodded. "It would be agony to watch that. And so, the seeds of Adair Natural Landscaping were planted."

"I suppose. I guess my work is redemptive."

"Are you an environmentalist who uses plants or a plant lover on an environmental crusade?"

"The former, I think. Plants are my tools. If I want butterflies, birds, food, drinkable water and breathable air, the right plants need to be growing in the right places. Maybe I should call my business Radical Bass-Ass Landscaping."

Fig laughed and pushed back his chair. "Thank you, Charlotte. I'm glad we did this field trip. I feel vivified." They got up to leave.

"Vivified? Really?" she asked as he pushed the door open.

"Enlivened. In this case, with caffeine and discourse."

She looked at him over her shoulder. "Someone gave you a Vintage Word-of-the-Day Calendar for Christmas, right?"

Fig drew up in mock indignation. "When a word dies of disuse another light goes out. Useful, old words like vivified are the endangered species of the mother tongue. You protect native plants; I protect our native language. And yet you mock me." He walked ahead to open the truck door for her. "I was an only child raised by elderly parents. I'm only forty-seven, but my soul is much older."

10

QUEEN OF THE WORLD

Charlotte was adding kibble to the dog dish by the cottonwood when a woman's voice called out to her.

"Hello! Hi." A woman with chin-length gray hair was standing at the end of her driveway with a handful of mail. "Is that your dog?"

"No. He's a stray."

"Poor thing. My grandkids leave food out for him when they visit and we put some straw in the hole for him, but we haven't been able to catch him. We named him Tramp."

That dog had more names than the King Charles, Charlotte thought, and a whole flock of guardian angels. She started to say something, but the woman was already heading up the drive.

Charlotte shook the bowl and whistled, but knew the dog would wait for her to leave before venturing out of his hole. She grabbed her bag from the truck and headed for the raft.

On the other side, she knelt on the walkway to open the packaging of a pair of new, long-handled loppers. Soon she was swearing under her breath. The tool was secured to stiff cardboard by three plastic ties, then encased in a rigid sarcophagul bubble of clear plastic. She was in the process of ruining her Swiss Army knife or slicing off a finger when Fig appeared on the porch in a white t-shirt and a pair of running pants.

"Need some help?"

"I can't get this open!" she sputtered, sitting back on her heels with a grunt. "I'm going to try gnawing it in a minute."

"Hold on." He went back inside and returned with pair of hand clippers.

She signed. "I was hoping for a stick of dynamite, but I guess these will do."

Fig chuckled, started coughing and went back inside. She heard water running at the kitchen sink.

She was still working on the plastic shell when he appeared for a third time wearing a navy V-neck sweater, jeans and moccasins and carrying two steaming mugs of coffee.

"Oh, heavenly," Charlotte said. "Give me a minute. I think I have it."

He set her mug on the top step and sat down to watch the struggle. "Ironic, don't you think?" he said.

She looked up at him.

"—needing a pair of clippers to free a pair of clippers. Makes you wonder how the very first clipper user—back at the dawn of the Clipper Age—got hers out of the package."

Charlotte laughed and groaned alternately as she gradually widened the opening in the plastic shell. "Ridiculous! This is the Fort Knox of packaging."

"Want me to take a turn?"

"Nope. I will not be defeated."

"I admire your tenacity," Fig said, contentedly. After a moment he said, "I bought a printer cartridge last week. The packaging was like a set of Russian dolls glued shut. It took me ten minutes and several tools. For my efforts, I was left with a wastebasket full of trash and a minute black cube which turned out to be the wrong size—although I can't blame the manufacturer for that."

With a satisfying snap, the last tie sprung loose. Charlotte collapsed onto the step next to Fig to drink her coffee. "You'll probably need new clippers now that I dulled these. Sorry."

"It's all part of their diabolical plan to sell more clippers. An irony, a dilemma and a conspiracy rolled into one. Life is full of them."

She sighed, savoring the coffee. "I once tried to get the city to pick up my garbage bin after a wheel came off. First, I filled it with trash and taped a note to it. They emptied the bin and left it at the side of the road. The next week I put it out empty with a big note. DISPOSE OF THIS BIN, PLEASE. But they ignored it. Then, I hacked the bin to pieces with the idea of putting it into my new bin, but of course, like the plastic bubble there, that was impossible. Finally, I backed my car over it several times. A sheriff's deputy stopped and almost arrested me for vandalism. It took several calls to the city before they got the idea."

She propped her elbows on her knees. "If I were Queen of the World, there would be a whole lot less packaging—especially plastic."

"I'd outlaw itchy shirt labels."

She said, "I'd order airlines to load passengers from back to front."

"I'd ban motorcycles without mufflers." He chuckled. "Queen of the World, eh? I like this game. Can I be King of the World?"

"Knock yourself out."

"In my kingdom, hotels wouldn't have hangers attached to the closet rod. What a nuisance they are."

"I know! And they're even worse for a short person like me."

"Do hoteliers really think we want souvenir hangers?" he asked.

"I know I don't."

"They could just use cheap plastic hangers if that's a problem."

"Plastic?" She gave him a side-eyed glance. "Have you heard anything I've said?"

"Oh, right. Recycled wire hangers then. In my kingdom that's the only kind that would be allowed."

Charlotte nodded. "And a wise king you would be."

Fig stretched his legs to their considerable length and crossed his arms. "I would ban the use of 'love you' as a valediction."

"What's a valediction?"

"The opposite of a salutation. Like goodbye, or yours truly at the end of a letter. See ya later, alligator."

"Oh, that."

"My paralegal talks to her kids about a dozen times a day—which is over-involved if you ask me, but I guess King Fig the Wise couldn't decree limited access to one's progeny without causing riots in the streets or a palace coup, so I'll let that pass."

"So, back to valedictions," she prompted.

"She's gotten into the habit of ending these calls with 'Love you!' The other day I heard her tell the court clerk, 'Yes, Tuesday, ten o'clock works for Mr. Bigelow. I'll tell him. Bye. Love you!'"

Charlotte laughed. "Oh no! Did you fire her?"

"No, but next time, it's off with her head."

"If I were queen, servers and cashiers would be thrown in the dungeon for calling me 'honey,' unless they're older than my grandma."

"Or when they use the royal we. 'Morning, hon,'" he said in a high voice, "'What are we having this morning?' And, my subjects would need a license to have children. I see way too many poorly parented children in my line of work—the collateral damage in wars between parents, between mom and her boyfriend, mom and her landlord. Kids are always caught in the crossfire."

"Do you have children yourself?"

"Me? Never. W.C. Fields and I agree, 'There's no such thing as a tough child - if you parboil them first.' "

Charlotte's jaw dropped. "That's horrible. You wouldn't think that if you had one of your own."

Fig shook his head. "I will end my days a barren bachelor." He turned to look at her. "Now, your turn again."

He was changing the subject. Perhaps she'd touched a nerve.

"Hmmm. Okay. As queen . . . I'd decree that all women's pants have real pockets."

"They don't?"

Charlotte set her coffee on the porch floor and stood up. "Look. I have, like, six pockets in these cargo pants, see? Perfect for a landscaper, right? But none of them are deep enough to keep my cell phone from falling out. Harp has a pair made by the same company with much deeper pockets. Apparently, women are supposed to carry a purse at all times or carry only a lipstick and an embroidered hanky in their teeny, tiny pockets. Again, re-DIC-ulous, and completely sexist."

Fig laughed. "What about jeans?"

"Don't get me started. Women's pockets are about half as deep as men's. I can't tell you the number of times I've dropped my phone on the ground when I'm working."

"If I were King of the World, I'd decree all of your decrees. Clothing equality for the peasants."

"Exactly." Charlotte sat down again, feeling uplifted—vivified even. "If I were Queen of the World, I'd make thee King of the World."

She cringed a little and lowered her face into her lukewarm cup.

He said, "Okay, one more. If I were King of the World, or even just mayor of Saskawan, no one would be able to grow, sell or plant invasive species in my kingdom."

"Now there's a pipe dream."

He glanced at her. "I'm serious, Charlotte. I checked the city's website. Not only are Norway maples and Bradford pears allowed, the city even recommends them to homeowners. It's shocking."

She shook her head. "It takes a lot more than that to shock me."

"City planners, park directors and arborists should know better."

"They'd tell you, Your Highness, that invasive plants save your subjects' tax dollars because they grow so well. Norway maples and Bradford pear are among the most common urban trees planted in the U.S."

"What about the growers and nursery owners and landscapers? Aren't they worried about these plant thugs?"

She shrugged. "About as much as McDonald's cares about my cholesterol or coal companies and car makers care about the air we breathe."

"But remember, all of these industries have, at times, been called to account. McDonald's has to post the calories of their meals. Car companies have to publish fuel ratings and safety data. Why isn't anyone asking Home Depot or Meijer or Walmart why they sell invasive plants? No one is calling them to task. Really Charlotte, it's time someone did."

She sighed, feeling like a deflating tire. "I know."

Harp and the crew had just pulled up across the river. She got up.

"Thanks for the coffee and the use of your clippers." She picked up the loppers. "I hope these are worth the trouble. With any luck, you'll have a nice view of the river from your firepit this evening."

Fig raised a sovereign hand. "Go forth, Queen Charlotte. Prepare my realm. If you need me, I'll be holding court inside."

11

OFFSPRING

Of the four thousand species of bees native to North America, about 90 percent lead solitary lives. Since there are no queens or androgynous drones among their species, all the females are fertile. They spend their days gathering nectar and pollen to make "bee bread" for their future offspring. Mason bee mothers often lay their eggs inside the hollow, dry stems of the previous year's plant growth. They deposit one egg on top of another with a lump of bee bread in between to sustain each tiny larva until it leaves the nursery. In a strange trick of nature, her eggs hatch in the reverse order that they were laid.

On the first Monday of spring break, the bike path on River Road was filling with kids on skateboards, bikes and scooters, shouting each other's names. It was already after nine when Charlotte drove slowly down the steep drive and parked behind Fig's Mercedes and Harp's Jeep. She could see a light in Fig's kitchen.

"We're here," Charlotte announced to her silent passenger. She had seen nothing but the tangled top of her niece's head all morning. "Maze?"

"What?" Mazie asked, not looking up from her phone.

"Wait'll you see this place. You'll love it." That last part was a mistake. The icy indifference of this twelve-year-old grew in reverse proportion to her aunt's warmth and cheerfulness.

Mazie was spending spring break with Charlotte while her grandparents joined friends in Hilton Head. When Charlotte

Mason Bee Osmia

proposed the arrangement to Fig, he had insisted Mazie would be welcome on the island.

But after another silent weekend with her niece, Charlotte was second-guessing the wisdom of her plan.

"Where are we again?" Mazie said, to demonstrate, once again, her complete disinterest, in case she hadn't made it abundantly clear. Over breakfast, she had lobbied hard to: A. Sleep in. ("It's my vacation!") and B. Stay at the house alone. ("Nana and Pop let me all the time.") Which led to a review of the terms of the Great Spring Break Agreement:

Party A (Mazie) will receive Party B's (Charlotte's) collection of "vintage" comic books and pick any PG-13 movie from Netflix every other night. In return, Party A will accompany Party B to work and perhaps assist Party B and her landscaping crew.

Charlotte sighed. "I told you, we're at Mr. Bigelow's island." At the moment, Mazie would not have been able to name which universe she was in. She'd appeared at breakfast so lost in *The Hobbit* that she tripped over the laundry basket on the kitchen floor and nearly poured orange juice onto her cereal. She'd been in Middle Earth ever since.

Charlotte opened the door of the cab and slid to the gravel below. Mazie held back the fringe of the brown curls that usually covered her eyes and squinted. "So, that's an island?" She had been listening after all. She shoved Bilbo Baggins and friends into her backpack. She was dressed in a hoodie and jeans over a tee shirt. She got out, leaving her parka on the seat.

"You'll need your jacket. It won't get above fifty today."

Mazie walked on without answering.

As tempting as it was to let her niece suffer the consequences of her short-sightedness, it was forty-four degrees and the whining she'd hear in about an hour wasn't worth the object lesson. Charlotte pushed Mazie's jacket into her own over-stuffed bag.

Mazie looked around. "So, where's the dog?"

So, she had been listening.

"He's hiding and won't come out until we're gone." Charlotte pulled a plastic container of kibble out of the truck bed. "You can fill his bowl if you want. Maybe you can make friends."

"If I catch him, I get to keep him. I'll name him Bilbo."

"Not so fast. Nana and Papa won't want a dog."

"Why not?"

"Because owning a dog is a big responsibility. If they wanted one, they'd have one by now." Charlotte zipped her parka against the brisk wind and locked the truck.

Mazie set the dish by the cottonwood but lost interest when he didn't come out. She ran to the raft where she leaped on and began rocking it violently. As Charlotte approached she pronounced the raft "sort of cool."

On the other side, Fig waved from the kitchen window.

"Is that What's-his-name?"

"Mr. Bigelow."

"I thought he was Fig or something."

"To you, he's Mr. Bigelow."

"Is he, like, a teacher or something?" Mazie said, inspecting the mechanics of the pulley system from every angle.

Charlotte stepped onto the raft just as Mazie gave the rope a yank, nearly sending her into the freezing river.

"Mazie, careful!" She grabbed for the railing.

With her usual single-mindedness, Mazie focused on the job of ferry person.

Everyone said Mazie looked more like Charlotte than her mother Lauren. They shared the same olive skin that tanned deeply in the summer, as well as small, athletic builds. Mazie was destined to have the boyish figure Charlotte had hated until her better endowed girlfriends started laying on the pounds in their thirties.

Appearances aside, it was hard to believe that this strange creature was her own flesh and blood. Mazie seemed to inhabit some alternate reality. While Charlotte was warm and gregarious, Mazie was a distant loner. Social niceties of any kind did not come naturally.

"Fig. Huh. Weird."

"Mr. Bigelow is a lawyer—"

"Even weirder for a lawyer. Does the judge call him Fig?"

"His profession has nothing to do with calling him mister. Just do it." You could never be sure if you were getting through or being tuned out. "Besides, Mr. Bigelow isn't used to children."

"Fine, because I'm not a child anyway. I'm a person."

"Don't be a stickler. A child is by definition just a young person."

Mazie's extravagant eye-roll-shrug combo was a sign of the deep apathy she'd been perfecting since the summer of her eleventh birthday.

"If I were Queen of the World," she said, "People would get to name themselves when they were twelve and if there were titles at all, they would have to be earned, like with medical doctors and knights and generals. You shouldn't get to be mister just because you're old and a man."

To her everlasting regret and by way of filling long dinner table silences, she had shared some of her Queen-of-the-World decrees with Mazie. This fed directly into her hyper-active aversion to obscure, unjust and otherwise outmoded cultural norms. In Mazie's world, hypocrites lurked behind every tree. Inequity was endemic and injustice flowed like tap water.

Queen Mazie of the World was, in fact, a terrifying prospect.

Although it was probably futile, Charlotte ventured: "It's more respectful when you don't know an adult to use a title."

"That makes no sense," she said, pulling the rope too hard. "I respect Nana and Pop, but not because they're old. I respect Gloria Grosnickle's cat but I don't call him Mr. Mordecai. He doesn't even chase chipmunks which is pretty cool for a cat. When I'm an adult—and I plan to be one when I'm old enough to drive—no one has to call me Ms. Adair." She looked over her shoulder at the landing they'd left behind. "It's about fifty feet across, I think."

"Yes. Almost exactly. But slow down so we don't crash into the dock, please. Anyway, what you want to be called is up to you, but since Mr. Bigelow is my first and only paying client, I prefer that you call him that. Got it?" She waited for an answer. "Mazie?"

"Yes, Ms. Aunt Charlotte, ma'am."

"Good, because I don't think Mr. Bigelow is overly fond of children."

Mazie shrugged. "That makes two of us."

The raft and dock collided with the thud, but this time Charlotte had a firm grip on the railing. Fig appeared on the porch.

Charlotte raised her hand in greeting and walked to the porch steps. "Good morning, Mr. Bigelow, this is my niece Madelyn. She's going to be my assistant this week."

Mazie tossed her head in an unsuccessful attempt to see through her corkscrew bangs. She adopted an erect military stance and offered an overly-stiff handshake. "I'm honored and delighted to meet you, Mr. Bigelow, sir." At least she didn't click her heels.

Fig grinned. "Well, it's very nice to meet you, Madelyn."

"It's all right if you call me Mazie. Everyone does."

"In that case, you can call me Fig. Everyone does."

"Fig," Mazie said, flashing a triumphant grin at Charlotte.

Fig rubbed his arms and backed toward the door. "Okay then, when you need to warm up or use the facilities, just knock."

In the meadow upstream from the house, Charlotte gave Mazie one end of a tape measure while she walked the perimeter and recorded the distance to the line of trees ringing the clearing.

Mazie shifted from one leg to the other. "What are we doing again?"

"We're measuring the size of this sunny area. It used to be a lawn probably, but it's going to be a small, marshy meadow full of wild-flowers—and bluebirds, if I have anything to say about it."

"We used to have a wildflower garden at my elementary school, but they mowed it down."

"Why?"

"Too maybe bees, they said."

"Were kids being stung?"

"I don't think so."

Charlotte shook her head. "People are afraid of the wrong things. I mean, I've never been stung by a bee in a garden except when I stepped on one barefoot, which was a perfectly reasonable response from the bee's perspective."

"But they're always flying around you, right?"

"Yes. But they don't pay any attention to me when they're busy gathering nectar." Charlotte took five steps to the right. "Hold the tape taut." She jotted down the measurement on her clipboard. "Honey bees—which aren't native, by the way—are only aggressive when people get too close to their hive. I mean, if you had a house full of honey you'd defend it too. But most American bees don't live in hives." She stopped to write down the next measurement.

"So, you like bees?"

"I love bees as much as I love to eat. Most of our fruits and vegetables are pollinated by bees and other insects."

Mazie ran her hand over the tops of the brown stems. "What are you going to plant here?"

"First, I'm going to wait and see what's already growing. Then I'll probably plant prairie grasses and wildflowers." Charlotte knelt to finish her notes.

"For the bees?"

Charlotte stood up. "And the butterflies, hummingbirds and beetles, too. Right now, there's nothing much for them to eat, but when I'm done, paradise . . . Just wait."

Charlotte sat in the dry grass, plotting the meadow on graph paper. When she was done, she said, "Do you know what I'd really like to see here?" she asked. "A rusty-patched bumblebee. That would be awesome."

"Why?"

"Because no one's seen one in Michigan for a long time. They used to be common."

"Because there aren't enough flowers anymore?"

"Yes. And too many pesticides."

"Aunt Charlotte?"

"Hmm?"

"Do you think there will still be bumblebees when I'm your age?"

Charlotte nodded. "I believe so, yes. They've been around just about forever. They just need good, clean water and flowers they know to survive. If I plant pink Joe Pye weed, yellow goldenrods and purple asters here, they'll find them and make lots of babies. Whether bees will survive will depend on us—my generation and yours. But we have to start now. Come on, you can help me plant some wild ginger in front of the house."

As they walked along the shaded path, Mazie asked, "We're doomed if the planet needs my generation to plan ahead. Kids my age don't plan beyond the weekend."

"You don't seem to have much faith in your generation, Mazie."

She drew her shoulders up to her ears and shivered. "I left my parka in the truck and now I'm freezing. Does that tell you anything?" She hugged herself. "Can I go get it?"

Charlotte reached into her bag and handed her the jacket.

"Oh, thank God!" She hugged it to herself and put it on. "See what I mean about planning?"

Charlotte rubbed Mazie's shoulders to warm her up. "It is the job of my generation to take care of yours until you learn these things."

"Did the Big People do that for you?"

"Yes. And they still are in some ways."

"Why? Can't you take care of yourself?"

She laughed. "What a cheeky question."

"Sorry. I just thought you'd have everything figured out by now."

Out of the mouths of babes, Charlotte thought.

They were coming to the house.

"I need to use the bathroom," Mazie said.

"Okay. Just knock on the door. I'll be working right here when you're done."

While Mazie was in the house, Charlotte carried a flat of wild ginger plants from the shed and set them on the shady side of the porch. Kiza had turned over the soil that had been trampled during the renovations. The tilled soil gave under the weight of her knees and sifted through her fingers like breadcrumbs. She would regret not wearing gloves when her hands grew cracked and dry, but at the moment, the touch of the warm earth was irresistible.

The morning light glinted off the wild ginger's velvety, heart-shaped leaves. Their glossy sheen was what she liked best about this native groundcover. She tilted the flat on its side and with the lightest pressure coaxed a cylindrical root ball into her palm. Gently, she loosened the outer roots that had wound themselves into a knot in their search for space and nutrients. Her friend Barb VanderLee had nurtured them well.

She pushed the soft earth aside with her trowel and spread the root tendrils into the surrounding soil and pressed the ginger lightly into place.

"There you go," she whispered.

She repeated this ritual twenty-four times—tip, coax, pull, dig, press. Her thoughts were so focused on this simple act of husbandry that she didn't hear the squeaky brakes of a garbage truck on River Road or feel the prick of a mosquito as it pierced the skin of her neck. Every worry, every distracting thought was momentarily displaced by her aspirations for twenty-four young plants. If time had elapsed, she was unaware of its passing.

When she was finished, she stood, hands on hips, nodding at her handiwork and picturing the hundred or more leafy ginger plants that would sprout next year. A few white turtleheads and some lady fern at the back would make a restful, shady garden for Fig to enjoy from his porch table.

Fig. She looked up at the closed screen door, remembering its significance.

Mazie!

Where was she? Probably pestering Fig with a thousand impertinent questions. She ran up the steps and tapped on the screen door.

Mazie?" she called softly. Then louder, "Mazie? Are you ready?"

"Aunt Charlotte! Quick! Come see what we found."

Mazie stood with one hand cupped over the other rocking anxiously while Fig seemed to be emptying a cabinet.

Charlotte gave him an apologetic look. "What's going on?"

"I found a bumblebee in the bathroom," Mazie said. "It's barely alive. We're going to save it."

Fig grimaced. "I opened the window after my shower last night. I'm afraid it got trapped when I closed it."

"Maybe it's that rusty kind," Mazie said. "They're really, really endangered," she added for Fig's benefit.

"Ah! Here," Fig said, handing over an empty mayonnaise jar he'd found. She flattened her hands over the opening and a lifeless, fuzzy ball tumbled in.

Mazie looked closer. "He's not moving."

Charlotte took a look. "It's probably dehydrated. Try putting a few drops of sugar water in the bottom of the jar."

"What kind is it?" Mazie demanded.

Charlotte shook her head "I'm no expert, but I doubt it's a rusty-patch, but all bumblebees need our help."

Fig offered his sugar bowl and watched as Charlotte dissolved a few grains in warm tap water in the bowl of a spoon. Then she dripped the syrupy liquid into the jar and turned the jar onto its side so the bee lay next to the sweet water. Fig gave Mazie a dishcloth and a rubber band and she set it on the sunny kitchen window sill.

"That's all we can do," Charlotte said. "We can check on it later."

Fig and Mazie leaned on their elbows at the counter, watching the jar as if it was a big-screen TV.

"It's all up to you now, mate," Mazie said.

Charlotte stood up, noticing the stiffness in her back and the dryness on her hands. "Let's go, Maze. Break's over."

Fig said, "She's welcome to do a google search for bees on my computer—if it's okay with you, Charlotte."

"Can I, pleeeease? I'll come help you as soon as I identify it." She backed up suddenly. "And as soon as I pee. I forgot about that." She ran into the bathroom.

"We were about to have some hot chocolate." Fig said. "Is that okay?"

Recalling his views on parboiled children, she shrugged. "Okay, but send her out when you've had enough."

A half-hour later, Mazie ran toward Charlotte from the edge of the meadow and skidded to a halt.

"It's a miracle!" she shouted. "He drank the sugar water and is buzzing all around in the jar. We're going to let him go, but Fig said I should get you first."

Charlotte followed Mazie to the house where Fig was seated on the porch steps holding the mayonnaise jar as if it was a bomb on a hair trigger and wearing a winter coat although it was nearly fifty.

"It's a miracle," he said, eyes wide and twinkling.

"So, I've heard," Charlotte said, smiling.

"We vivified him!"

Charlotte peered into the jar. "Pretty lively. It's probably a female, but the way. And a queen, judging by her size."

Fig grinned. "Another queen on this island? That's trouble." He leaned in. "Where shall we release Her Royal Highness?"

Mazie looked at Charlotte. "On a flower?"

"How about on the shadblow? We might find a bloom."

The three of them trudged off to find one of several small trees that the crew had planted at the water's edge.

"Bee heaven," Charlotte said.

Mazie eased the jar over the white cluster until the bee crawled onto a blossom and began exploring its lime-green center. Charlotte let out the breath she'd been holding.

"Look, it's eating," Fig said.

"Nectaring is the scientific word," Mazie corrected. "I found out that this one is *Bombus impatiens*, a common Eastern bumblebee. There are eighteen other bumblebee species in Michigan. So, we should learn their Latin names. I'm going to look for all of them."

Fig crossed his arms over his chest, looking well satisfied. "She's going to record all the species she finds on this island."

"I'll look for them every time I come. We have it all planned out."

Charlotte looked from a smiling Fig to a smiling Mazie and didn't know what to make of these two. Apparently, she would be seeing a whole lot more of her niece this summer. She shuddered at the thought.

MAY

Mayapple   Podophyllum peltatum

12

TROUBLE WITH TRIBBLES

The Starship Enterprise reaches Deep Space Station K-7 where the crew takes shore leave. At a bar, Uhuru is given a delightful furry creature called a tribble. She brings it on board as a pet, and soon it has a litter. She gives one to McCoy. It too has a litter. Spock observes, "There's something disquieting about those creatures." Soon there are tribbles all over the ship, raiding the food synthesizers and clogging the ventilation system. Spock warns that without any natural enemies they will just keep multiplying. When Captain Kirk opens a cupboard and gets buried in tribbles, he orders the crew to get them off the ship—a task that Spock predicts will take 17.9 years. But the sly Chief Engineer Scott saves the Enterprise by luring them to a nearby Klingon vessel, where he says, "They'll be no tribble at all."

May arrived eagerly, bringing kind breezes that coaxed the oaks out of their long winter dormancy. On Fig's island, a few marsh marigolds opened their butter-yellow petals along the riverbank and a patch of trout lily appeared near the dock. But with them came the interlopers—the great drifts of garlic mustard and dame's rocket which appeared without invitation, threatening to overrun the island.

For the better part of two weeks, Charlotte, Harp, Kiza, Martin and Hector bundled armloads of them, hurrying to complete the job before they dropped their seeds. Their labors uncovered striped Jack-in-the-pulpit, Mayapple umbrellas and graceful ferns that had been languishing for lack of sunlight and space.

They were cutting and treating glossy buckthorn and a nasty patch of prickly barberry when Charlotte noticed Fig watching from the path, his hands pushed deep into his pockets.

"Hey," she called out, walking toward him, and taking off her goggles and mask. "We're just finishing the purge. Next week, we can start planting. Come see what we found." She led him off the path to three small trees marked with green ribbon. "These are flowering dogwood. Poor things were starved for light. I've marked them with ribbon so the crew won't cut them. I also flagged those fiddleheads so they don't get stepped on."

Fig looked at the trampled ground.

"It'll look better by midsummer, I promise," Charlotte said.

"What does a red ribbon mean?"

"It's the mark of death," Charlotte said. "Kiza, Martin and Hector are fast learners, but they still haven't quite mastered Michigan flora."

She didn't mention that the ribbons were for Harp too, who showed more enthusiasm than judgment when it came to clearing invasives. She'd lost track of how many times she'd shown him the difference between dogwood and buckthorn. She didn't trust him not to cut a dogwood.

"I was going to suggest we order several dogwoods, but, voila!" she said.

"That's good news. Thanks." Fig nodded.

"Yeah, I'm really pleased." She started to put her mask back on.

"But I feel duty-bound to ask about the chemicals you're using.".

Charlotte dragged her sleeve across her brow and nodded. "Fair question. We're using glyphosate, or Roundup. It's a slow-acting, biodegradable herbicide. It kills just about any plant it touches, but it's safe if it's applied correctly. It's a whole lot better than the other choices."

"But what about your safety and the crews'?"

"There have been studies that say it's carcinogenic, so we use precautions." That was a hard-won battle with Harp, who complained that the mask was hot and the goggles fogged up.

"I've heard of using goats to clear brush."

"Yeah. But they'd also eat those dogwoods, your redbud, your trillium, your bloodroot—and your pant legs." She gripped a small tree and shook it. "See this? It's European buckthorn. If we just cut it, it'd send up maybe three or four new trunks. That's why we paint the stumps with glyphosate."

"Ah, the Sorcerer's Apprentice."

"Hum? From *Fantasia*?"

"Mickey Mouse borrows the wizard's hat and casts a spell to get the mop to do his work."

She nodded. "But things get out of hand." She pictured Mickey trying to stop a stampede of marching mops. "I get it. The invasive buckthorns are the mops. Cut one and dozens more appear." She laughed, remembering Fig's parable of the Little Prince's baobab trees. She'd like to get a look inside his man's brain to see how it made such far-flung connections.

"The story is actually from a Goethe poem," he said. "It was set to music by an obscure French composer, but was almost forgotten before Disney rediscovered it."

"And the takeaway is I shouldn't unleash powers I can't control. But remember, Fig, I'm the wizard, not the apprentice."

He laughed. "I believe that." He hesitated. "There's really no alternative?"

"Like digging them out? That would take months by hand and would damage the trees we're trying to save."

Fig nodded thoughtfully. "In the practice of law, we call this the Principle of Non-maleficence. When harm cannot be avoided, we are obligated to minimize it. Life doesn't always offer perfect choices." He turned back to the house. "I will leave you to your work."

She called after him. "Don't forget Dr. Frankenstein's monster. Or 'The Monkey's Paw.' Good intentions get out of hand." She read books, too.

Fig turned back to smile at her and raised one finger. "Or, 'The Trouble with Tribbles.'"

Charlotte cocked her head.

Fig smiled, flashing his straight white teeth. "*Star Trek*. Look it up."

At 7:10 the next morning, Charlotte's phone vibrated on her nightstand.

"The Big People are taking the trailer up north for Memorial Day and I really, really, really, really don't want to go!" It was Mazie.

Charlotte yawned. "Good morning to you too, sunshine."

"It's not a good morning at all. He snores and she's bringing her guitar. And tiki lights. They make me sleep on the kitchen bench. Can I stay with you and go to Fig's? Pleeeeeese!"

Charlotte sat up and rubbed her eyes. "Maybe. I need to talk to Nana. I'm not saying yes yet."

"But I have to catch the bus right now, and Nana said I shouldn't even ask you, but please say yes and don't tell her I called. Just say you missed me."

She stepped into her moccasins. "I have missed you," which, wasn't a complete lie. Fig had asked when Mazie might return.

"Call Nana right now, okay? I'll die if I have to sleep in that rolling tuna can."

"It won't be much fun here either. Harp and I are working on Saturday so we can have Monday off."

"I'll help! And maybe if there's time, I can work on my bumblebee project."

On Friday afternoon, Charlotte left Martin digging holes for button-bushes behind Fig's fire pit while she picked Mazie up after a half day of school. When they returned, he was leaning on his shovel.

"Hello, Miss Mazie," Martin said. "Welcome to return."

Mazie waved without speaking.

He shook his head, addressing Charlotte. "The earth is like a rock. I put water to make it more easy, but—" He mopped his brow and shook his head. He jabbed the tip of the shovel into the soil and came up with a small sliver of leathery earth. "How do you call this?"

Charlotte picked up a slick, gray clod. "Clay."

"I think this is not good for bushes."

"Button bushes like clay."

A small bowl was sitting on the stone bench circling the firepit. Mazie picked it up.

"Cool bowl. Did you make it?" It was perfectly round and etched with regular slashes and dimples around the edge.

Martin glanced uneasily at Charlotte. "I rest for short time at the river. I make it then."

Mazie said, "This is way better than anything we made in art class last year. How did you get it so round and smooth?"

He tapped his chest with the tips of his finger. "I am Zande. My people are very good makers of pots. You can see our pots in all the big American . . . *musée*? I don't know the English."

"Museums," Mazie said.. "Art museums. Really?"

Charlotte ran her finger along the rim. "It's beautiful, Martin."

"Oh no. Not that one. My wife makes more beautiful pots."

Mazie picked a clod from the pile and squeezed it. "I didn't know clay just comes out of the ground like this." She looked at Charlotte. "Can I have it?"

Charlotte smiled. "I'm sure Fig can spare it."

Martin went back to chipping at the hard earth while Charlotte went to the shed to get a flat of Canada anemone. When she returned, Mazie was on her haunches sorting the clods. She picked one and tried to shape it. After several minutes, she flopped down on the bench. "The clay's too hard."

"No. Is good!" Martin said. "You must—" He looked at Charlotte. "May I?"

Charlotte nodded. "Sure. Take a break."

He selected a lump of clay and dipped it into the water bucket. He knelt on the flagstones, raised his arm over his head and threw it hard against a stone. Then he dipped it in the water and slammed it down again.

"See? More soft now."

Mazie threw hers, but it missed the stone and rolled onto the grass. They both laughed. "I'm not Zande."

While Charlotte worked, she listened to the slap-slap as they synchronize their throws.

She heard Mazie say, "Yours is better."

"Here," said Martin, trading with her. "Now you make it."

Mazie worked silently while Martin continued his digging.

After a long while, Mazie said, "Martin, my pot's done."

"No not finish. Look." He picked up a twig and pressed it into the soft clay to make a pattern, then rubbed it smooth again and handed it back to Mazie. "Now you."

"Like this?" She made a row of neat slashes around the rim.

"Yes. Yes. Good. People will say, 'Ah. That is a fine pot of the Saskawan people.'"

For the rest of the afternoon, Charlotte could hear the sound of clay hitting flagstone and a shovel hitting the earth.

By the end of the day, Mazie had finished three bowls—each one smoother and rounder than the last and carefully etched on the side with "Fig" and "Martin" and the third with "Bilbo" for the little brown dog. She lined them up on the dock to dry in the sun.

"Tomorrow I'll make more so everyone can have one," she announced.

Martin nodded his approval. "Fine pots, Mazie. Very good work."

Mazie called out to Fig who had come out on the porch. "I'm going to look for bees tomorrow, too. I didn't forget."

Fig nodded. "I look forward to a full report."

13

W.I.L.H.A. WOMEN

Harp looked up from his bowl of Cheerios when Charlotte came into the kitchen wearing khakis and a lime-green cotton pullover.

"Why are you dressed up?" he asked. "I thought we were cutting buckthorn today—again."

"You are. I'll join you after my WILHA meeting."

He shrugged absently. "Okay. What time will you be done?"

"Eleven-ish," she said, picking a perfectly good piece of toast out of the sink. "What's this?"

"We're out of butter."

Charlotte opened the refrigerator and handed him the butter and the toast.

"Huh," he said, puzzling over the yellow tub. "Where'd you find it?"

"Well, since my x-ray vision is unreliable at this hour, I had to actually move the yogurt to find it." She took her bag from the hook by the back door and rooted around for her keys.

He was buttering the toast. "Is there any jam?"

"I don't know. Try using your x-ray vision this time."

He looked up. "Aren't you having breakfast?"

"No. It's a breakfast meeting." She pointed to the wall calendar hanging on the refrigerator door. "Once a month, like I told you yesterday and again a minute ago."

"Oh. Right. The Ladies Landscaping Auxiliary," he said with a chuckle that petered out when he saw her frown.

She leaned over and wiped a drop of milk off his chin with her thumb. "You're a lot to take on an empty stomach."

"I'm kidding," he said. "So, what's on the agenda?"

Charlotte suspended her hunt for keys. "Well," she said, letting her eyes sweep the ceiling. "I'll give a report on the city's non-response to my letter about planting Bradford pears. That'll take about five seconds. I'll eat a scone, maybe two and drink way too much coffee. I'll field some questions about our project at Fig's. Everyone has been pretty curious about the island. And with any luck, the county will have responded to Barb about our list of recommendations for native landscaping in the new Cross-County Linear Park. I brought a change of clothes, so I'll come to Fig's right after. I think we can finish cutting buckthorn today, but be careful not to cut the dogwoods. And make sure the crew steers clear of the south side of the house. There are lots of ferns coming up in there."

Harp looked up. "What kind of scones?"

She shook her head and laughed. "That's your take-away? Scones?"

"Bring me one?"

She plunged her hand into the bottom of her bag again and felt her keys. She slung her bag over her shoulder and opened the back door.

"What time will you be at the island?"

"*Eleven! Ish!*"

"Oh wait. I started making a sandwich, but there's no mayonnaise. Or tomatoes. Or sandwich bags." He caught her look and let his gaze drop to cereal. "Just sayin."

Charlotte set her bag down again. She took the mayonnaise jar from the refrigerator door and sent it on the counter next to a tomato she took from a bowl on the windowsill. She took a roll of wax paper from a drawer and slapped it down on the counter.

With a fist shoved into her hip, she said. "You're right. We're out of sandwich bags. Anything else, your excellency?" She tousled his thick honey-brown hair.

He looked up, still chewing. "Wha—?"

She sighed again. "While you're making yourself a sandwich, make me one, too. Okay?"

"Of course, you know I'd do anything for you, babe." He made puckery kissing noises and tugged on her wrist until she fell into his lap. "Give me a kiss that will get me through the whole day."

The Women in Landscaping and Horticulture Association, or WILHA, was founded in the late nineties to help women find work in a profession dominated by the descendants of 19th-century Dutch nurserymen.

WILHA's co-founders were Phyllis Oosterbaan, whose family had run a huge greenhouse operation for generations, and Barb VanderLee owner of VanderLee Gardens.

In the last ten years, younger members began using the group's influence as a platform to share their knowledge of native Michigan plants. This didn't sit well with Phyllis, who was strictly old-school. On the other hand, Barb VanderLee and her husband Hal sold more native plants than anyone else in the area.

In the group's e-newsletter Barb, the current president, had attached Charlotte's letter to the city, as well as a short announcement about her new island restoration job. Charlotte got congratulatory messages from several members who realized what a unique opportunity it was.

Because of her morning hunt for butter, sandwich makings and car keys, Charlotte arrived at The Farmer's Daughter Cafe almost ten minutes late. The group was gathered in a back room at tables arranged into a large rectangle. The center was set with carafes of mediocre-but-unlimited coffee, mugs, sugar, cream and plates of fresh-baked strawberry rhubarb scones.

"Hey, Charlotte's here!" Katie Clay sang out.

"Sorry I'm late," Charlotte said.

Katie pulled out the chair next to her and smiled, showing all her teeth. They had worked at TipTop together before Katie left to start a family and a backyard nursery business. She was a girlish chatterbox who saw the fun in everything.

"Take a load off," she said. "We all want to hear more about this island."

Charlotte pushed her bag under the chair and smiled at the group.

"Sure," she said, still out of breath, "but caffeine and carbs first."

Katie pushed the plate of scones and a mug of coffee her way. "It's that rustic old place on the island in the Hawthorn, right? I've kayaked by a couple of times."

"Is it true you have to cross on a raft?" someone asked.

Katie nudged her. "Out with it! We crave details."

She washed down an embarrassingly large bite of delicious scone with a gulp of coffee. "Okay. Okay. The client, Newton Bigelow, just had the house restored, so it's like new inside and out. The island is maybe two acres but has been badly neglected and there were no plantings at all around the house because of the renovations. We're still removing a lot of barberry, privet and buckthorn."

"If he's willing to pay for it, good for him," Barb said from the end of the table.

"Is it true there's no bridge to the island?" someone asked.

"Just a raft with a rope pulley," Charlotte said. "I think it's charming, but my crew isn't thrilled."

Katie said, "She means hunky Harper, her fiancé." Barb frowned and Katie quickly added, "That's what all us girls called him when we worked at TipTop. We all had a thing for Harp—but not Charlotte. She played it cool and he fell for it."

Charlotte rolled her eyes. She loved Katie, but the girl never had a thought that didn't come out of her mouth.

"Anyway," Charlotte continued, "the crew isn't complaining about their regular paychecks, that's for sure, and, I want to give VanderLee's a plug. I got a great deal on some beautiful dogwoods and redbuds." She turned to Barb. "Really, they are beautiful."

"Thanks," Barb said. "Sounds like Adair Natural Landscaping is well launched. Nice going, Charlotte."

Nods and polite applause followed.

"But I'm curious," Barb said. "How did your client become so knowledgeable about native plants?"

"I've been telling him. He's just a smart, inquisitive guy. And he can't believe most of the invasive plants we've removed are still being sold. Oh, and I should add, he's an attorney."

"Ha! That explains it," Katie said, laughing. "Before you walked in, Barb was telling us about the cross-examination he gave one of her employees."

Charlotte grimaced. "Sorry, Barb. We'd just come from 16th Street where I showed him the Bradford pears the city just put in. When he saw the vinca and English ivy, he was, well, surprised."

Barb gave a wry smile. "I can't blame him. A ban is way overdue."

"But those plants are what everybody wants," Katie added, throwing up her hands. "We were practically forbidden to use the word 'invasive' with clients at TipTop."

Barb said, "I haven't sold Bradford pears for several years now, even though people ask for them a lot, but we'd go out of business if we stopped selling vinca and English ivy."

There were murmurs of agreement around the table, but Charlotte saw the frown on Phyllis Oosterbaan's face. She suspected the city's Bradford pears were grown in her nursery.

Katie said, "At TipTop I used to order dozens of Bradford pears and truckloads of vinca and ivy for corporate clients and the big developers. Most wouldn't have even considered native alternatives."

Barb took a deep breath and blew it out. "Well, thanks for a well-crafted letter, Charlotte. Let's move on." She frowned at the paper in front of her. "For those of you who weren't here in April, we had a representative from the county parks department, John Tabor, presenting the details of their landscaping plans for their next project—and it's a big one—the new Cross-County Linear Park which will officially open next spring."

Katie said, "I'm sorry, but that guy was depressing." She sank into her chair with a drawn-out groan. "And clueless."

"As you know," Barb continued, "when the project's done early next summer, the park will run for over twenty-six miles through both the city and the county with hiking and biking paths, sculptures and landscaped gardens near downtown. It will be a real asset."

Nicky Martinez, a native plant grower, with a black and gray buzz cut and a body like a Russian shot-putter, wagged her head in disgust. "An asset to the people of Saskawan maybe, but it won't do much for the river or its wildlife. The trail will cut through some fragile habitats in the floodplain. And now they're going to replace what they've destroyed with exotic species?" She looked at her notes. "Norway maples, Bradford pears and barberry? Give me a break! How can someone work for a parks department and be so ignorant?"

Barb continued. "Good point, Nicky. I think many of us were disappointed as well. So, as many of you know, in Charlotte's thank you letter to Mr. Tabor she suggested, on behalf of this organization, several native alternatives—sugar maples to replace Norway maples, redbuds or dogwoods instead of Bradford pear and fragrant sumac instead of barberry. She included a list of growers where the county could purchase them. I hope you all got a copy in your email."

"Did Mr. Tabor respond?" Nicky asked.

Barb nodded. "I have it here. I won't read all of it." She read aloud. "'Thank you for your recommendations. We welcome citizen input. Yadda-yadda . . . our plan is to use the most reliable plants available . . .'" She sighed. "I'll pass this around. I didn't think it was worth sacrificing a tree to print copies."

"Reliable?" Katie snorted. "Now there's a hilarious understatement."

"Exactly," Nicky said, flashing a crooked smile. "You can rely on them to gallop into the woods and down the riverbank."

Charlotte nodded, "And their seeds will wash downstream into some of the bayous near Lake Michigan. It's a shame."

Barb said, "Yes, it appears their plant choices are all about expediency."

"And cost," Nicky added, "Invasive plants are cheap because they're so damn easy to grow." The letter had made its way around the table to Nicky. "Mr. Tabor says here, 'Please note that none of these species are prohibited or restricted in Michigan.'" She shook her head. "But being legal doesn't mean a plant is harmless."

"So, now what?" Katie asked.

There was an uncomfortable silence around the table.

Charlotte cleared her throat and leaned on her elbows. "Well, my client, Mr. Bigelow thinks there are grounds for a lawsuit."

Phyllis sat bolt upright. "A lawsuit? Against whom?"

Charlotte shrugged. "Importers, growers, wholesalers, retailers, consumers?"

"You'd sue a gardener for buying the wrong kind of plant?" Phyllis shot back. "That's ridiculous."

"Not individuals. But cities, counties, parks departments, highway departments, developers—"

Phyllis glared at her. "On what grounds?"

With all eyes on her, Charlotte felt her cheeks flush. "Creating green pollution. Jeopardizing the food supply. Destroying habitat. Creating a public nuisance, trafficking in harmful plants? I don't know the legalities, but I know these plants shouldn't be planted in our city and certainly not by our city."

Several members shifted uncomfortably. One looked at her watch. Another got up to leave.

Finally, Barb said, "Okay. Good discussion." She gave Charlotte a quick smile which meant, Thanks for trying. "Maybe we could send our letters to the *Evening Star* and the TV station. Pick up some media coverage. What do you all think?"

Phyllis Oosterbaan pursed her lips. "We're getting off track here. I have several letters from some talented young female designers and a couple of horticulturalists looking for work. We're supposed to be helping them find jobs."

Barb nodded. "Send them to me, Phyllis. I'll post them on our website, so everyone can have a look."

Phyllis nodded. "Let's all remember that networking for women in our profession is the mission of WILHA, not crusading against plants you don't happen to like."

An awkward silence settled over the room.

Finally, Charlotte spoke up. "I think of our recent letters to the city as advocacy and education, not crusading, Phyllis. Both were respectful and offered alternatives."

Phyllis shook her head. "I'm just not comfortable putting pressure on anybody."

"Me neither," said a young designer—either Kristin or Kirsten—who worked for one of the large landscaping firms. "My company has contracts with the city. If my boss thought I was part of this letter-writing campaign, he'd show me the door." She looked warily around the table.

Nicky eyed Charlotte, looking tired. "I'm glad you and Barb have the energy for this, but I'm afraid you're wasting your time."

Charlotte said, "We're simply proposing native alternatives to invasive trees and plants." She looked around the room, wishing someone would back her up.

It was Barb who spoke up. "Nicky, I know you try to lead your clients toward responsible choices."

"Sure I do, but I'm saying our letters are going to the wrong people. Why aren't we going after the growers of Bradford pears or the universities who graduate landscapers and horticulturalists who are so ignorant or the developers who push these plants on the public? There are plenty of guilty parties. Take your pick."

Phyllis scowled. "All the more reason for folks like us to stick to what we do best, networking and helping good women get into this business."

"But we could be doing so much more, Phyllis!" Katie said, her voice rising.

An aproned server poked her head into the room. "How are we doing in here, ladies? More coffee? Scones?"

Several members saw an escape and began getting up.

Barb closed her laptop. "Thanks, but I think we're done." She addressed the group again. "Good discussion, everyone. Let's continue this next month."

In the hallway, Katie slung an arm over Charlotte's shoulder and announced, "How did you manage to get the perfect client *and* the perfect fiancé. Do you know how much we secretly hate you?"

Charlotte laughed.

Kristin or Kirsten added. "Does he have any friends he can send my way?"

"The fiancé or the client?" Katie asked.

"Both. Either. Not picky."

Katie said in a stage whisper. "I think I have a crush on your client, too, and I'm married and never met the guy."

JUNE

Evening-Primrose Oenothera biennis

14

TRUTH AND JUSTICE

By mid-June, a path had been cleared in a loose figure-eight around the island converging at the house. Charlotte had arranged for a meeting with Fig to review their progress. He said he'd be in court all day but would meet her on the porch at five-thirty.

She sat on the top step and watched Harp pull off his tee shirt, his back rippling and glistening in the late afternoon sun. He shoved off and powered the raft across the river's corrugated surface.

A few minutes later Fig arrived, exiting his old Mercedes and reversing Harp's route at a more deliberate pace. He wore his signature Panama hat, dark sunglasses, a blue oxford cloth shirt—"light starch" she guessed—rolled to the elbow. He moved with a grace that was rare in a man, she thought.

As Fig drew closer, she felt more nervous excitement than was called for and wondered at its origin. Certainly, creating the perfect little Eden on this island was a once-in-a-lifetime opportunity. And it was she, the sole owner of Adair Natural Landscaping, that was making that happen. She needed to get it right, for herself and for Harp, as well as for this eccentric man whose vision for this island incredibly and miraculously mirrored her own. As cheesy as it sounded, this was the project of her dreams.

If only Harp felt the same. When she said she'd be staying late to meet with Fig, he'd accused her of "getting carried away," which showed how little he appreciated this opportunity and what Fig was doing to put Adair Natural Landscaping on the map.

There was no explaining these emotional butterflies otherwise—certainly not to Harp, who never wanted to rehash work at home. But these days she couldn't think of anything else to talk about and it irritated him. He'd say, "Can we please not talk shop tonight?" He had a point. Lately, she'd sit down to check Facebook, and the next thing she knew she was researching native plants for riparian ecosystems.

Of course, she found Fig really good company. He was always open to considering new ideas and even expanding the project, which Harp should be happy about. She loved Harp's boundless energy but needed to accept the natural impatience that went with it.

She wondered if Harp was jealous, which would be laughable. She wouldn't expect so much as a Christmas card from Fig once he'd paid his final invoice. In the meantime, there was no reason she shouldn't make the most of a successful collaboration.

Fig stopped midway across and lifted a hand in greeting, then stood to gaze down the river. A minute later he glided into the dock and came toward her in long, measured strides, smiling up at her. He looked exhausted.

"I hope . . . you haven't been waiting too long," he said, breathing hard and dabbing his forehead with his handkerchief.

"No. The crew just left."

He placed his hat and sunglasses on the broad arm of an Adirondack chair, lowering himself while gesturing toward its mate. "Can we sit first?"

He tilted his head back and stretched his legs out straight, crossing them at the ankle. "Thanks for staying . . . It's pleasant to find someone waiting." He rolled his head to smile at her.

"Hard day?"

"Indeed," he said, brushing pale wisps of hair off his forehead. "I've been in court all week. I work for Legal Aid. . . . We serve low-income clients . . . in civil matters."

"Did you win?"

He sighed. "If by 'win' you mean that my client—single mom with three little kids, two restraining orders against predatory ex-boyfriends and one absentee landlord who tried to double her rent—gets to stay in her rat-infested, one-bedroom firetrap for another year, then yes, justice, in her all her blind wisdom, has prevailed. Ain't life grand?"

He raised an index finger for emphasis. "But now, she won't be able to leave because the landlord we sued today probably won't give her a reference. So, it was a Pyrrhic victory, at best." He sat up slightly. "But it wasn't all bad. I gave her fifty bucks and a ride home. We stopped at McDonald's for Happy Meals."

He rubbed his temples and sighed. "Sorry for that cynical postmortem. I needed to let off steam." He looked at her and moved to get up. "Now, shall we see the work you've been doing?"

He looked even paler than usual, something that didn't seem possible. She wanted to reach over and check his forehead for fever.

"What if I just show you the pictures I took? I'm pretty knackered myself actually."

"Knackered, you say?" He looked at her with amusement.

"Sorry. One of my mum's British-isms. They creep in when I'm, well, knackered."

"Your mum's a Brit? Brilliant," Fig declared, launching into the King's English. "We can do a proper look-around tomorrow. But right now, we'll just have a bit of chin wag, shall we?"

She laughed. "You and me mum would be best mates."

"I know we would." He coughed and pulled out a monogrammed handkerchief. "Sorry again. . . Nothing contagious."

"Can I bring you a glass of water or something?"

"'Or something' sounds perfect. Let's celebrate my ignoble victory with something red and vintage. Or is that too forward and unprofessional?" He was still breathing hard.

"It would be rude—and unprofessional—to refuse my best client."

"Am I not your only client?"

"Let's not split hairs."

Fig's laugh triggered another round of coughing.

"Are you coming down with something?" she asked.

Fig waved dismissively. "It's chronic, I'm afraid. It creeps in when I'm knackered. Let me . . . get us that wine." He moved to get up but fell back.

"May I?" she asked. "I'll bring some water, too."

"Thanks, just add your bar-tending services . . . to my bill."

Charlotte rummaged around the kitchen as Fig called out instructions through the screened door.

"There's a nice Bordeaux in the sideboard cupboard. Left side. See it? Bordeaux glasses are over the sink. Corkscrew's in the drawer to the left."

She opened the sideboard. Bordeaux glasses? There were glasses of every conceivable size and shape.

She called out, "Tall skinny or big fat?"

"Pardon?"

"The wine glasses."

He laughed. "Big fat."

A moment later she pushed the door open with her hip and offered Fig water and wine from a tray.

Fig cupped the wine glass between two fingers and raised it toward hers. "To truth and justice."

"And to your health."

"Now there's a good one." Fig loosened his tie and unbuttoned the top button of his shirt. Sunlight beamed through the glass, casting a dancing red spot on his shirtfront.

She said, "And to your client."

"Yes, sweet Nanette."

"And to sweet Nanette," she repeated.

"Thank you, but it was a minor victory, even for a small-time lawyer like me."

"I bet sweet Nanette doesn't feel that way." She sipped the acrid liquid and suppressed a shudder. "Is that why you decided to become a lawyer? To help people like her?"

He tipped his head thoughtfully and stroked his chin. "My dad had his own law firm. After law school, I joined him for a while, but I hated it. I became a Legal Aid attorney mostly to annoy the old man. But, of course, I also wanted to help people like Nanette who can't afford good lawyers and are easy prey for the greedy slumlords." He sighed and took another sip. "But twenty years on and I'm not sure hauling that guy into court was what Nanette really needed."

"What does she need?"

"Better laws. In my kingdom, there'd be laws to protect her, enforced by watchdog agencies, not the courts. And no landlord would be able to double someone's rent without notice or just cause. This case should never have come to court, or if it did the landlord should risk being stripped of his license—or sent to my dungeon."

His eyes followed a brown creeper rocking up an ash tree like a child's wind-up toy, but she knew his mind was elsewhere.

"This case won't stop this landlord," he continued. "Getting hauled into court is just the cost of doing business."

Maybe it was the wine or her own fatigue, but Charlotte found herself following the fluid movement of his left hand like a cat eyeing a butterfly.

"—minor skirmish today. Tomorrow he'll just . . ."

The hand moved, palms up, fingers relaxed and unclenched. It touched his chin as he formed a thought, then opened as if to release it. "—just raise the rent on some other poor sod to cover his losses."

"That's awful," she said vaguely.

"It can be."

The other hand moved his glass in circles on the arm of his chair, sending wine up the side of the glass. The effect was hypnotic.

"Before I die . . . I'd like to change just one bad law. I'm tired of fighting the same battle . . . over and over and over." He rubbed his forehead and closed his eyes, breathing as if he'd just finished a run.

"Maybe you should run for office. Make a new law to protect sweet Nanette."

"I'm afraid that ship sailed long ago." He shifted in his chair to face her. "Never mind that. Let's talk about you. . . You can relate, I'm sure."

"I can?" she asked, feeling a bit wine-sozzled, as her mother would say.

He swept his arm in a wide arc. "You're creating this pristine oasis of native plants on my island, but there's nothing stopping the next owner from planting a truckload of Chinese wisteria and Bradford pears."

She clenched her jaw. "I can't think about that."

He opened his fingers. "Poof. All that hard work. Gone."

"I see where you're going—laws prohibiting invasive plants."

"Right. You could sue anyone in the supply chain—importers, growers, horticulturalists . . . wholesalers, retailers, or even consumers, like the city or county."

"Wouldn't you need to sue them all? I mean, if you stopped one project—say planting Bradford pears in the new Cross-County Linear Park—it wouldn't change anything in the long run."

"No, but it would get people talking—journalists, politicians, environmentalists, and, of course, the public. They'd start asking questions. Apply pressure on decision-makers. When Oliver Brown's daughter Linda was denied entrance to an all-white elementary school in Topeka, he sued his school board. The case didn't achieve its goal on its own, but it ignited the civil right movement. It happened again in 1967 when a small group of environmentalists right here in West Michigan sued nine cities to stop using DDT that killed mosquitoes, but also birds. The court rule against them, but the publicity stirred up the public and the state outlawed DDT soon after. When ordinary people get fired up, laws have a way of getting changed."

"Those are great stories, Fig, but environmentalists have been talking about regulating invasive plants for decades. Trust me, no one listens. I'm sorry to be so pessimistic. And besides, lawsuits are expensive."

His smile showed a touch of mischief. "Not if your attorney worked pro bono and was thoroughly schooled in the issue by an expert."

"What expert?" she asked, her eyes narrowing.

He grinned at her.

"Not me."

"Why not you?"

"Because. Because it would be crazy, Fig."

He turned to face her. "Hear me out, Charlotte. The way I see it, you can change the world one garden at a time for the next forty years—which would be important and no doubt satisfying—but just think what you could accomplish if you also stopped a lot of other people from filling their backyards with these aggressive plants?"

She shook her head. "Me and limelight? Not a good mix."

He nodded. "Fair enough. I'm just tossing it out there." He gestured toward their chairs. "More wine?"

When their glasses were full again, he stood, leaning back on the porch railing to face her. "In a job interview just after law school, the managing partner asked me, 'To what do you aspire, Mr. Bigelow?' The question caught me so off guard and I said something insipid like, 'I want to be a good lawyer.' I didn't get the job—but I thought a lot about the question after that. And you know what I decided? I want to make an impact. Right a wrong. So I ended up at Legal Aid. I've worked hard and helped a lot of people, but I don't know if I've made any lasting change. I think everyone should take at least one colossal risk in their life—climb a mountain no one's climbed. Even if you don't get to the top, you've blazed a trail for others."

He looked at her, his blue eyes wide with intensity and a surge of energy.

"Otherwise your life becomes one long task list—a daily surrender to life's minutiae. Wake up, shower, grab breakfast, sit in traffic, go to work. Yesterday, I spent most of the afternoon trying to unstick the O key on my keyboard. Cross off one task and two more appear." He raised one arm and dropped it. "How does anyone . . . find time to win a Nobel Prize or a MacArthur Grant? Can you tell me that? I'd like to take one, . . . big winner-take-all gamble. Zero in on one important thing. . . To hell with everything else."

His eyes followed a pair of kingbirds diving for insects above the water.

"We all have dormant muscles . . . we never use." He was getting out of breath again. "We could . . . do so much more . . . Don't you think?"

"Yes. Yes, of course," she said, although she didn't know what. This was a Fig she didn't know. Instead of measured thoughts artfully stitched together, his words tumbled over one other.

"At some point, Charlotte . . . you have to decide how you want to be remembered—what will be your . . . your legacy."

Did he mean his, hers or both?

"I—I don't know, Fig. I think we should, of course, go after our dreams, but I don't know if I can right now. Maybe in a couple of years."

He ran his hand through his hair and sat down again. She wondered if he was annoyed with her.

"Please don't get me wrong, Fig. I respect the idea—the *ideal*. I do. But I've just opened this business. I still have student loans. I need to maintain good relationships with growers and green businesses to be successful. I can't start accusing my suppliers of—I can't just—"

He gave a nod of resignation and rested his head on the back of the chair. "I know. I'm sorry. I'm sure I sound . . . absolutely mad."

"No. No, Fig. Not at all."

He rolled his head to look at her and smiled. "You're right. It's not the right time for you." She saw the old weariness creep back in. He let out a low chuckle. "Besides, worrying about one's legacy is pretty self-serving."

"No. A lawsuit like that would be beneficial to every living thing."

He rolled his head toward her and smiled. "Do you ever think about yours?"

"My legacy? Sure." She smiled. "It's on my task list for 2050."

He let out a little hm-hm-hm riff of amusement and closed his eyes. When he opened them again he said, "I didn't mean to imply that building your business isn't important, Charlotte. You've found a worthwhile profession. I admire that."

"Thank you. But you should take heart, too. Your victory today might not change the law, but it changed Nanette's life and her kids."

He was peering into his wine glass again with one eye closed.

"Are you seeing the future in there? Dorothy and Toto on a bike, perhaps?"

"In the wine?" He laughed. "I see a slightly opaque, full-bodied Bordeaux."

"I see a pretty red liquid."

"I noticed a grimace when you took your first sip."

"Sorry. I'm used to white."

Fig set his glass on the arm of his chair to swirl it until the wine reached the rim of the glass. "Try this."

She practiced until her circles matched his. "Why are we doing this? I've always wondered."

"We're aerating."

"Um, why?"

"The motion creates tiny bubbles which dissipate the bitter gases and releases the aroma. It's part of the wine experience."

"'The wine 'experience,'" she repeated, smiling.

"Don't laugh until you try it."

She took a sip.

"Better?"

'Hmmm. Yes, but if you paid more than ten bucks for the bottle, you should have saved it for a classier guest. I'm hopelessly low-brow when it comes to wine, but I am a plant snob—just to even things out.

I bet you didn't know that plant roots need to be aerated, too. In nature, insects and worms fluff up the soil to allow air to get to the roots."

"If I can learn to appreciate bloodroot and marsh marigolds, you can learn to appreciate a fine wine. "

"I will try my best."

He raised his glass again. "First, use your eyes. Enjoy what you see. What color would you call it?"

"Somewhere between *Monarda didyma* and *Lobelia cardinalis*. Irresistible. I also like that comes all the way from France with the picture of a chateau on the label."

"Good start. Now, smell it as you might enjoy a – what?"

"Black cohosh, milkweed, Queen of the Prairie?"

"You're catching on."

She inhaled deeply, feeling giddy. "Loamy," she said, "with ecotones of wild clover and Culver's root."

"Okay. Do you know how oak timber smells when it's newly cut?"

"I think so."

"Concentrating now, take the wine into your mouth and hold it there without swallowing. Can you taste that this wine was aged in oak barrels?"

She swallowed. "I can, actually. The swirling makes a difference too. It's lost its bite. Thanks for the lesson."

Fig crossed his legs and leaned toward her. "The quality of the conversation and one's companion also enhances the experience. Don't you think?"

Her eyes met his and lingered there. She dropped her gaze and thought about the spaghetti dinner Harp was making for her.

Fig lifted his chin. "Of course, sound is another sense that comes into play while enjoying a fine vintage."

Charlotte yawned theatrically and glanced at an imaginary watch. "You don't say."

"But I do say. It's well documented that a full-bodied Bordeaux pairs well with the Baroque composers: Bach, Scarlatti, Telemann. While whites are enhanced by large-scale operas of Bizet, Wagner and the like."

Charlotte blinked. "Seriously?"

One corner of his mouth curled up, creasing his cheek. "Why, I know a little claret that enhanced a Beethoven piano sonata at least sevenfold, maybe eight."

Charlotte backhanded his shoulder. "That's complete bullshit."

Fig wagged a long finger at her and laughed. "But I had you going. Besides, I don't want this happy hour to end." Fig's blue eyes, translucent as beach glass, lingered again on hers. An awkward silence dropped like a rock between them.

"Would you like to show me your work on the path now?"

She sighed. "I really need to be getting home. Tomorrow?"

"Yes. Of course, but let me walk you to the raft." He started to get up.

"No, don't get up. Thank you for the wine." She paused, then added just to put the conversation back into its proper context, "And I don't think I have thanked you enough for this opportunity. For the work, I mean."

"Nonsense. I should be paying extra for your tutelage."

"Harp says I'm preachy." She felt duty-bound to mention her fiancée.

"Tell Harp that as someone who has just joined the choir I find your sermons uplifting."

"Thanks. I have enjoyed your wine-appreciation sermon as well."

He nodded. "You and Harp have a fine evening. We can walk that path tomorrow—by then my vim and vigor will have returned from wherever they have gone."

15

AIR-HEADS AND NITWITS

The next afternoon while Harp and the crew cut brush at the edges of the meadow, Charlotte squatted over a flat of Canada anemone near the back patio, humming to herself and enjoying the sun's warmth on her back.

Fig called to her from his study window. "I could use a break. How about that tour?"

"Sure. Give me a minute." She peeled off her gloves and was rinsing her hands in the river when he came around the house with two tumblers of iced tea.

She took off her hat and swiped her forehead with her sleeve. "You're spoiling me, Fig. And this better not have whiskey in it. I have a lot of work to finish today."

He handed her the frosty glass. "No, and no whiskey-appreciation sermon either."

"You may have spoiled me forever for cheap wine. I'll need a lot more clients to stock my wine cellar—if I had a wine cellar."

"Thanks for humoring me."

"Come on, then. I have a habitat-appreciation sermon all rehearsed. We begin this way." With a flourish, she gestured toward a new clearing at the riverbank.

"Nice!" Fig said. "I can see my neighbor's wildflowers from here. They bloom every May. This is the best year yet."

"I bet," she said.

"What are they called?"

"Dame's rocket."

"Stunning, don't you think?"

She sighed.

"What?" he asked. "What could possibly be wrong with six shades of lavender? Don't tell me they're invasive. I don't want to hear it."

"I wish they weren't."

Fig looked crestfallen. "Shouldn't there be an exception made for such beauty?"

She considered his question. "Bradford pears are pretty. And tribbles are cute, I understand." She smiled up at him. "I looked it up."

"So you have." His smile faded. "But in nature, isn't beauty enough?"

She considered this. "Is it enough in our human community? Shouldn't every individual contribute?"

Fig considered this with tightly folded arms and a deep frown. "I'm picturing fashionably-dressed air-heads and nitwits loitering against every lamppost."

"Shocking," she said, laughing.

"So, you're saying that plants should be useful as well attractive."

"We don't have to choose between beauty and utility. Some plants have it all."

"Beauty and brains," Fig said.

"Exactly. Black-eyed Susans and coneflowers – or any number of our native perennials are just as colorful as dame's rocket, but they also offer edible seeds, leaves or roots for insects and other wildlife. And with so few wild places left in North America, we shouldn't fill up our precious garden space with air-heads and nitwits."

Fig sighed. "You've just spoiled that view of my neighbor's yard."

"Ignorance was bliss, wasn't it?"

They continued along the path.

She pointed at a clump of bushes. "Here. This will lift your spirits. These red osier dogwoods will spread all along the bank, too. They'll be good cover for ducks and frogs and other wildlife, too. Maybe even river otters."

"Otters? Are they included in the price, or will you bill them separately?"

She caught the gleam in his eye. "That could be a lucrative sideline business—pairs of otters, choruses of frogs and rows and rows of turtles to sun themselves on your logs every afternoon. A package deal."

Fig whistled. "Wouldn't that be something?"

Charlotte pick up a stick and tossed it off the path. "I'd love to raise endangered animals to release into the habitats I create. I love plants, of course—their variety, their function, their secret lives and their beauty, but it's their role in sheltering and sustaining wildlife that really makes my heart sing. But for now, you'll just have to settle for my if-you-build-it-they-will-come approach."

"I can't wait forever, you know."

"We're playing the long game here."

Fig pushed his hands into his pockets and sighed.

At the northernmost point of the island, the trail became spongy and smelled of new woodchips. There, the crew had cleared another opening that looked directly downriver. The sun glinted off the surface and lit up the undersides of the leaves.

"What a peaceful place," he said.

"You can see all the way to the river bend but you can't see your neighbors. We can put a bench here if you want."

"I'd like that. Thank you."

They turned back toward the house.

"You really are an optimist aren't you?" he said. "Planting saplings you may never see as mature trees. Banking on the next generation to carry on. Banking on the future. I just—"

She looked up, waiting for him to finish, just as his voice dropped away.

"Thank you, Charlotte. What you are doing here and with your life, it's . . . noble."

She felt an unexpected sting in her eyes. "Thank you," she whispered, unable to make eye contact.

They walked slowly toward the house.

"Otters," he said finally. "Now that would be the frosting on the cake. Do you really think that's possible?"

"Harp saw a pair about ten miles up the river when he was kayaking a few summers ago. It's not impossible."

"Hmm. Just knowing they might come someday—that's—well, that's really something."

"Thanks for listening to everything I go on about."

He pulled himself slowly up the porch steps. "You sound surprised. You may think I'm not listening, but I am."

She smiled. She never doubted Fig was listening, not for a moment.

That night over dinner Charlotte mused to Harp, "I never see anyone visit the island. Maybe Fig's in a long-distance relationship. Do you think he has a girlfriend or an ex-wife somewhere?"

"A boyfriend maybe," Harp said.

She dropped her ham sandwich. "You think he's gay?"

Harp shrugged. "He's a natty dresser and has one of those fancy coffee makers. And his house is always clean. I have pretty good gaydar." A piece of tomato dropped into his soup and splattered the front of his tee shirt. He stretched the front and licked it off.

"Not to stereotype or anything," she said, scowling. "I think you're wrong. He could just as easily be between relationships or divorced. I think he's lonely out there on the island all by himself."

"He's fine with it," said Harp, who specialized in definitive answers.

She looked at Harp's shirtfront. "Being a slob isn't a sign of virility, by the way."

He wiped his chin on his sleeve.

"And showering after work wouldn't make me think you were gay, either." She meant this to come off as good-natured ribbing, but she heard the edge in her voice as clearly as he did.

He surrendered with a casual shrug. Typical. Harp lobbed opinions like tennis balls to see if they were in-bounds. If not, he quickly conceded. She supposed this could be a good thing in a marriage, but sometimes she itched for a full-on debate.

Like now.

"You don't like Fig?" she asked.

"Fig?" He tipped his head to the side, stalling. "He's a bit of a relic. Those blue Oxford shirts and that old Mercedes?" He eyed her over a spoonful of soup. "But you like him." A smile spread across his face. They were going to spar after all.

She lifted her chin. "I admire him. He's smart and well-read . . . curious, too." *Which you aren't,* she was tempted to say.

"Yeah?" Harp was watchful. "What about? What do you talk about?"

Now, he was curious. "Work." Which was mostly true. "Work mostly," she slipped in. "He's gotten pretty interested in native plants. He told me about the history of the Sorcerer's Apprentice story. Turns out Disney – ."

"I thought you said you talk about plants—mostly."

"We do." Charlotte leaned back and grinned. "You're jealous."

He parried. "No way."

She advanced. "Yes, you are."

He threw his balled-up napkin into his soup bowl and got up. "I'm going to watch some TV." He took a beer from the fridge and disappeared into the front room.

It was far too easy to turn tables on Harp.

The next afternoon, Harp stood by the truck with his hands on his hips while Charlotte looked over the perennials she'd sent him to pick up.

"I know you like VanderLee's," he said, "but I was at Walmart getting a new shovel handle and noticed they had fall clematis on sale. Nice and compact and half what VanderLee's is asking."

She lifted the pot to inspect the tag and gave a loud grunt. "This isn't what I told you to buy, Harp."

He turned over the tag. "Yeah, it is. See? 'Fall clematis.'"

"This is *Clematis terniflora*. Native to Asia and very aggressive here. In a couple of years, it would be smothering the redbud and the dogwood we just planted. I ordered *Clematis virginiana*, the native vine. Big difference." She leaned against the bumper and rubbed her eyes. "How many times have we talked about this, Harp?"

He took off his cap and scratched his head. "You just said autumn clematis. I can't remember the Latin."

"Which is why I wrote it down for you. Check the list I gave you." She closed the back of the truck. "These have to go back and then please go to VanderLee's and ask for Barb. She'll help." She walked off toward the dock. "Or, read the damn labels!"

He threw his gloves in the back of the truck. "Yes, ma'am."

She watched him drive off, throwing gravel as he accelerated up the drive.

Was this an honest mistake, or a challenge? The worst thing was, she'd obsess about this until she was angrier at herself than at Harp.

At the downstream end of the island in the new clearings, Harp had fashioned a fallen hickory tree into a log bench. He had sliced off the top with the chainsaw to create a flat seat.

Charlotte was trimming back more of the undergrowth when Fig came down the path carrying two glasses of iced tea.

"A log bench," he said. "Very nice."

She took off her hat and ran her fingers through her damp hair.

"Harp just finished it," she said. "We'll install a regular one if you tell me what you'd like. But temporarily—"

"Let's give it a try."

He eased himself down to catch his breath and ran his hand over the level surface. "I think this is perfect. It'll be m'thinkin' log." He gazed at the receding river. "I must thank Harp for this. He's a good worker."

"He is." She sipped her tea and nodded.

"So, is he the lucky fellow who gave you that diamond?" He pointed to her engagement ring with a gesture resembling DaVinci's hand of God.

She nodded. "Last New Year's Eve. Yeah."

"When's the big day?"

"We haven't—I'm not sure. I think we're both still adjusting to the idea."

His brow furrowed slightly. "Doesn't an engagement usually imply the intent to wed?"

She picked at the dirt under her nail. "We just haven't set a date." In fact, neither of them had even broached the subject of a wedding in months.

"Well, there's no statute of limitations on engagements, I suppose," Fig said, giving her an out.

Silence settled between them. Fig had pushed open a door. It was time to turn the tables.

"So, Mr. Bigelow, is there perhaps a hot lawyer out there?" she asked, carefully avoiding gender pronouns.

"Oh, I'm sure there is."

"Really?" Her face probably betrayed more surprise than she intended.

He chuckled. "Oh, you mean a hot lawyer for me? There very well may be, but I haven't yet made her acquaintance."

Charlotte grinned into her iced tea.

Fig hadn't stopped laughing. He raised his forearms in an open V. "I know it's shocking that a handsome dude such as myself should still be, shall we say, singing solo. I haven't always been such a sorry old recluse, you know. I have a long history of relationships with women—but alas, all with sad endings."

"Have you given up on love?"

"On matters of the heart, I suppose you could say I'm unenthusiastic. In my experience, one person usually wants another who doesn't want him or her. I have been on both ends of that and I don't recommend either." His legs stretched endlessly before him and crossed at the ankles.

"So, you've never been married?"

"No, thank God. Just a couple of close calls."

"You don't want to get married?"

"I don't see the point if you don't want kids. In both cases, my refusal to procreate was a deal-breaker. How about you? Do you want children?"

"Sure. Of course." She thought of Mazie. "Maybe. It depends on the child."

"What about Harp?"

"We haven't really discussed it yet."

Fig threw up his hands in exasperation. "Again, with the not talking."

"We talk," she said a trifle defensively. "There's no hurry. There's the business and helping my parents with Mazie. That's more than enough right now."

His voice softened. "Where are Mazie's parents, if you don't mind me asking?"

"My younger sister Lauren—her mom—died when she was a toddler. We don't know who the father is."

"How tragic."

"It was. Is. I try to help." She didn't feel like going into the Lauren story, so she deflected. "Why don't you want kids?"

"I was an only child born to older parents, so I wasn't around other children much. Kids are fine as long as they aren't tired, hungry, spitting up or smelling funny which narrows my tolerance to about ten minutes."

She considered this. "I haven't thought about having children like I should, I suppose. My sister obviously didn't. She was seventeen when she got pregnant." She looked at the river but felt his gaze.

"Did you like being a child?" he asked.

She laughed. "I thought the topic was landscaping." She pointed at the riverbank. "Did I point out the log we rolled into the river for the turtles to sun themselves on?" Another section of the hickory log jutted about three feet into the water.

"I didn't enjoy being a child," he said. "Grown-ups always seemed to be having way more fun. I liked being with them, or by myself. I was weird and insufferable, I'm sure." He looked at her again, "You?"

Did she like being a child? No one had ever asked her that. She had been a horrible big sister, that much was clear.

"I don't know," she said with a long sigh. "I've never thought about it." Fig had a way of finding locks and rattling them. It was unsettling. Time to change the subject. She said, "This island is beautiful, but it must get lonely here sometimes."

Two could play the prying game.

"Ah," he said. "You regard my lack of personal attachments as pitiable."

"No, not at all." This was only a small lie.

"You think I'm lonely because you have found love and someone to marry —despite lack of a wedding date or plans for progeny." One eyebrow was lifted and full of meaning. "That could be significant, wouldn't you agree?"

"I don't know," she admitted, sighing again. She sounded shallow and thoughtless. She sat on her hands and swung her feet.

"You're doing a great deal of sighing." He lifted his chin to study her. "What is it you don't know?"

"Why you ask such loaded questions." She looked into the bottom of her empty glass. "Are you sure there isn't truth serum in this?"

He was waiting for a response.

"It's just——" She stopped mid-sigh and started over. "Harp and I are different in a lot of ways. He doesn't worry about anything—except whether the Cubs will ever win the pennant. I admire that in the abstract, but in real time I want to throttle him sometimes." She laughed, but it came out shrill and nervous. "He's probably assuming we'll have enough kids to field a baseball team, which is probably why he's never brought it up. He's an in-the-moment guy. He'll live to be a hundred and I'll bust an artery next week worrying about dame's rocket and tree-eating wisteria. But—" she stopped.

His eyes pulled on her.

She shook her head. She'd been drawn into a conversation she was uncomfortable with. One that was layered with blurred meaning.

She stood up. "I need to get some plants in the ground today. Do you mind if we head back?"

On the way to the house she pointed out the button bushes she'd planted along the bank. Near the porch, she showed him new shoots on the virgin's bower vine that were already twining around the railing.

"This was a near disaster though," she said, letting a tendril slip through her fingers. "I sent Harp to the growers and he came back with the invasive version of this vine. After working with me for years, he still doesn't get this whole 'native plant thing,'" she said, drawing air quotes. "He's a smart guy and hardworking, but this—" she swept her hand to indicate the island, "this is just another job to him. I can't demand more of him, but wish he shared some of my passion for native landscaping."

Fig had been watching her through an intense squint. "He's a man of action. D'Artagnan of the Three Musketeers. Married life will be a great adventure I suspect."

She nodded but felt exposed. She'd said too much.

"I really need to get back to work. Thanks for the tea." She thrust her empty glass into his hand too quickly.

He blinked and took a step back. "I apologize, Charlotte," he said. "I didn't mean to pry." He turned to go up the steps.

She called after him. "It's just—Harp has a lot of skills I didn't mention." She said to his back. "He's done awesome work on this project—and . . . and I love him."

He turned to smile at her. "Yes. I should hope so."

She headed for the meadow to find Harp, feeling suddenly out of sorts.

As May ended, something quiet and heavy settled between Charlotte and Harp, and Charlotte and Fig. She'd put both of them on the defensive and regretted it.

Harp was as impatient with the pace of work on the island as ever and looking for shortcuts. When she stood her ground he backed off, which only made her feel like a bully. Their disagreements usually ended with him changing the subject to the Cub's chances of making it to the division finals. She found herself answering "uh-huh" without really listening.

As for Fig, she'd revealed way more than she should have to a client, then blamed him for being nosy, which was completely unfair and unprofessional. She needed to be more careful.

One night, after she'd stayed late to discuss next steps with Fig—keeping everything on topic—she found Harp in the kitchen mixing crackers into a bowl of canned soup.

He looked at the clock. It was almost seven. "I hope you're charging this guy overtime."

Charlotte dropped her bag on the floor and pulled off her wellies. "That's hard to say, Harp. But I do know that for what he's paying us he deserves to understand what we're doing. And he's interested. I just talked him into spending an extra $300 for shrubs at the landing. We're not offering standard landscaping services and Fig's agreed to a bigger project because I'm taking the time to explain it to him." Her voice rose and she was too tired to control it. "Besides, we'll need his review on our website. It's a good use of my time."

There was a pile of dirty dishes by the sink. She busied herself with scraping two-day-old garbage into the compost bucket.

"As long as that's all it is."

She dropped the spatula. "What's that supposed to mean?"

"It means I think you just like spending time with the guy."

"We have a good working relationship." She shrugged. "Not everything is about sex, you know," immediately regretting opening that door.

"Geez, Charlotte." He let his spoon drop and glared at her. "I wasn't accusing you of sleeping with him. The guy's practically old enough to be your father."

"No, he's not. He's forty-seven."

"Really? Well, he lives like a hermit and looks like he's at death's door."

She turned back to the sink. "Nice, Harp."

She was filling the wash pan when she felt his hands on her shoulders.

"Sorry. That was a crap thing to say. Fig's an okay guy." She felt him sigh. "But goddamn that island. That river. That tiny-ass raft. I'm sick of hauling everything in wheelbarrows instead of a Bobcat. It's beginning to feel like a death march. Mike wanted to bike this Saturday but I'm just too beat, so I guess I'm feeling cranky. And I miss you." He kissed her neck.

She turned to slip her arms around his waist. "I'll be home tomorrow on time. Promise. Just remember, we couldn't ask for a better client."

He nuzzled her ear and said in a low voice. "Well Fig's got the hots for you, that's obvious."

Charlotte pushed him away. "Don't be ridiculous." She grabbed her purse from the hook by the back door and stopped. She didn't want to storm out. "You need anything at the store?"

"Beer maybe. Want me to come?"

"No. Thanks. I just need . . . some stuff." She had no idea what, other than to be somewhere that wasn't here.

He gave her his lonely puppy look that used to melt her, but now just brought a stab of angry guilt.

"Don't be pissed at me," he said.

She shook her head to dislodge some heavy, anxiety-provoking thing that had wedged itself between her shoulder blades. "I'm not. I'm just tired."

She let the screen door slam and walked into the night.

They used to do everything together. A trip to the store was like date night. He would take three-point shots across the produce and hit the cart every time. What do you want to eat this week, she'd ask? Bagels or English muffins? Chicken or fish? How about spaghetti? What do you think? What do you like? What do you think? It had been ages since they'd asked each other that.

She was afraid she was leaving him behind when they were supposed to be walking side-by-side.

And then there was Fig, whose words could be so magical when they weren't finding some soft, vulnerable spot to dissect.

She had done nothing wrong, but she knew she wasn't doing right by Harp either. He had every right to question her. She would apologize later and promise Harp that her meetings with Fig would be shorter and less frequent. And, she would promise herself that there would be no long, philosophical discussions or conversation that didn't involve plants or landscaping. And no more fat glasses of bitter old wine.

16

ISLAND GIRL

If plants dropped all of their seeds directly on the ground, their offspring would have to fight for space. So, plant parents have clever strategies for scattering their offspring. Maple trees equip their seeds with tiny propellers. Cottonwoods send their seeds aloft on wind-borne fluff. The pretty orange jewelweed clasps her seeds so tightly that when a passerby brushes against them, seeds explode in a wide arc. Fall hikers know well the Velcro-like seeds of avens and beggar-ticks that hitch rides on pant-legs and socks, but few realize the valuable service they're providing to these species.

The following week, Hurricane George sucked great gulps of moisture from the Gulf of Mexico and wrung itself out over the Great Lakes. The deluge lasted two solid weeks until the Hawthorn River threatened to spill over its banks. Charlotte was happy to let Harp take a couple of days off to go to a Cub's doubleheader in slightly less sodden St. Louis.

Charlotte spent the week updating her website. She was sorting through new photos of the island when her phone chimed.

"Hey, Mum."

Mally let out a long sigh. "Sorry to call—I know this is probably an interruption—but it was either this or infanticide."

"Mazie-cide again? That should be a word."

There was a long silence.

"What?"

Mally plunged in. "A few months ago, I found a middle-school science camp at Sas U. Kids stay in the dorms for a week in June and use the labs and go on field trips. There's even a boat trip on Lake Michigan on a research vessel. I showed it to Mazie and she was keen on the idea."

"Sounds perfect."

"So, I returned the application and paid a hefty deposit and made hotel reservations for Dad and me on Mackinac Island for the week."

"Okaaaaay. What's the catch?"

"She's refusing to go. I'm so bloody angry I can't see straight."

"Why doesn't she want to go?"

"It's suddenly become Stupid Camp, which could mean anything. Anyway, we're at loggerheads—again."

"And you can't get your deposit back or change your reservations?"

"Non-refundable and non-refundable. But it's not just the money, Charlotte, or even our v-vacation. It's j—just— No matter what I do, everything with Mazie goes pear-shaped!"

There was a sniffle on the other end. And finally, a high-pitched "I keep thinking. I mean, what if—" and another long pause.

Charlotte knew very well what. "Mom. No."

"I can't even say it." She yanked in a huge breath and held it until it came out in a sudden burst. "I can't do this again, not if things end like they did with Lauren."

"I'm coming over."

"No, no. Really, I'm fine."

"I'll be there in ten."

A blue light flickered in the window of Mazie's bedroom. Her niece's obsession with technology was another flash point in the Adair household.

Charlotte ran up the porch steps, instinctively avoiding the third tread that had been rotted through for years. A pot of pink geraniums partially covered the hole.

Mally was waiting on the wicker love seat, a glass of wine in each hand, looking beleaguered.

"I hope one of those is for me," Charlotte said, giving her mother an air kiss and sitting down next to her.

"'Tis, indeed. Dad's at the baseball game tonight with Carl, our new neighbor. They've become good mates. He's got a daughter Mazie's age, but of course, Mazie wasn't interested in going. She's holed up in her room, never to come out if we make her go to Stupid Camp. I tell you, I'm at sixes and sevens."

"Mum. Listen to me. Mazie may be difficult, but she's is nothing, I repeat nothing like Lauren."

"Maybe not. If she was like either of you girls I think I'd feel more confident about this child-rearing do-over God has given me—without my permission, I might add." She sighed. "But Mazie isn't like either of you. I never know where things stand. Charlotte, honestly, if she goes off the rails I don't know if your dad and I will sur—." Her voice broke again. "I don't know if we'll make it."

"She'll be fine. She's a smart kid. Brilliant even," Charlotte said.

"She's a know-it-all."

"But funny."

"She's sarcastic."

"But honest and insightful. She's her own person, Mum."

"I know, and I love her to bits, but I never know what she—my own granddaughter—or daughter, really—is thinking—ever. I just don't get her. I was so excited to find this camp," she continued. "I mean, I knew better than to try Girl Scout camp again." She laughed. "The only thing she liked was quiet hour. She wrote some pretty interesting letters home, listing the shortcomings of the camp. The counselor who reeked of cigarette smoke, the kid who ate a live frog, the green slime

Jewelweed *Impatiens capensis*

floating in the lake, the giant mosquitoes, even the excessive pulp level of the orange juice."

Charlotte laughed. "That's our Mazie."

The street lights came on. Somewhere a basketball bounced and a kid shouted, "Shoot it! Shoot!"

At Mazie's age, she rode her bike in endless circles with a whole gang of neighborhood kids every night after dinner. Her mother was right. Mazie wasn't like anyone else in the Adair family.

"When are you and Dad going to Mackinac Island?"

"Right after school gets out." Mally turned to Charlotte. "Do you know what else Mazie said the other day? She said, 'No one ever even tries to understand me, Nana.' I admit, we don't understand her, but God knows we try." She shook her head. "I'm tempted to stuff her in a duffel and drop her at Stupid Camp anyway."

"Let me talk to Harp and my client. I'll see if we can take her for the week."

"Oh, honey. You can't. You have to work. I wasn't asking that."

"Give me a few days to figure things out. Don't cancel your reservations yet."

Harp had no objection to the plan, although this was based on his general how-hard-could-it-be attitude toward any challenge. And despite Fig's previous W.C. Field assessment of children, he was surprisingly enthusiastic about having Mazie on the island again.

"She can continue cataloging my bumblebees," he pointed out.

Charlotte smiled. "I wouldn't count on it. But I promise she won't pester you this time."

"She made those bowls last time," he reminded her. "If you ignore her, she'll find something of interest to occupy herself. When I was a boy, I had hours and hours to myself. It was quite energizing."

"I thought you were weird and insufferable?"

"I still am, but after forty they call it eccentric—at least to my face."

"I can't just let a 12-year-old run wild."

"This is an island. What's the worst that could happen?"

Charlotte laughed. "I have no idea, but I suspect we'll find out. Thank you, Fig."

On the last afternoon of the last week of Mazie's last day of seventh grade, her parents dropped her off at the farm.

Mazie shuffled through the back door and dropped a giant gym bag at Charlotte's feet.

"Big Ted stuffed me in the back seat with all their stuff. My foot is, like, crushed and Mally made me bring crap I don't even need."

Charlotte's mother entered the kitchen rolling a huge orange suitcase.

Mazie raised her eyebrows at Charlotte.

"Holy cow, Mum!" Charlotte said, taking the handle. "Is there a cow in here?"

"Just some art supplies, a beach towel, books, her pillow, White Bear," her mother panted and gave Charlotte a hug.

Mazie shot Mally the death ray and muttered, "I don't sleep with White Bear anymore." She dropped into a kitchen chair and propped her chin on her hands.

Mally ignored her. "Don't let her spend all day in her room and she's got a limit of two hours of screen time."

Ted came into the kitchen carrying a grocery bag. "Here's stuff from our fridge for you girls."

Mazie rolled her eyes again.

Mally tousled her granddaughter's unruly curls. "If you keep doing that, your eyeballs'll get stuck and it'll serve you right."

Ted bent over and nuzzled Mazie's cheek with his whiskers. "I need goodbye hugs from both m'girls." He cupped her face between his huge palms and planted a loud, sloppy kiss on the bridge of her nose.

"Ew! Get away, old geezer." She pushed him away, giggling.

"Be good, poppet," he said. "And try not to be a royal pain in yer wee ass this week, Madelyn."

Mazie made a show of wiping her nose with her shirt sleeve.

"We'll be fine," Charlotte promised, giving him a hug. "Have fun, you two."

Mally clapped her hands together. "Brilliant. We'll see you both in a week. Call us if you need anything. Anything at all! Thank you, darling." She gave Charlotte a hug and whispered, "Good luck."

An hour later, Charlotte was browning onions and ground turkey for spaghetti sauce when Mazie wandered into the kitchen.

"All unpacked?"

Mazie leaned over the skillet. "What the hell is that? The hamburger's gray."

"It's turkey."

She sniffed it with deep suspicion. "Do I have to eat it?"

Charlotte shrugged. "The alternative is peanut butter."

"We could order pizza."

"No. It's turkey spaghetti or peanut butter."

"When do we eat? My blood sugar is plummeting."

Charlotte gave her a slice of carrot. "A half-hour—less if you go pick us some greens from the garden."

"But I'm hungry *now*."

"Have a Saltine." She nodded toward the pantry cupboard.

Mazie rummaged around and found the box. "So, where's your imaginary boyfriend tonight?"

Charlotte frowned. "Harper, my actual fiancé, is at the gym. He's going out with some guys after, so we're having a girls' night in."

"Is he cute? I forgot what he looks like."

Mally and Ted hosted an engagement dinner for them last winter and always invited him to family gatherings, but Harp was impatient with long dinners and made excuses not to go. Charlotte ignored Mazie's impertinence.

"So, do I get to pick out my own outfit?" Mazie went on, stuffing crackers into her mouth and blowing crumbs into the air.

"For dinner?"

"No! For your wedding, duh. You and Mystery Man."

"Why are you asking?" Charlotte got a pepper out of the refrigerator.

"My friend Cullen was an assistant groomsmaid at his sister's wedding."

"Groomsman."

"Whatever. That seems kind of sexist, or someone who brushes a horse. I'll wear a dress if you want me to, as long as it isn't pink and doesn't have a lot of frilly shit."

"Mazie. Where are you picking up this language?" This was a rhetorical question. Ted Adair was a fount of colorful profanity that her mother was still trying to eradicate.

"Social studies," Mazie said. "Cussing as Cultural Competency. Brand new unit. Required curriculum."

Charlotte stopped what she was doing and gawked at her niece. "What?"

"Ha! You believed me for a second."

"Very funny, Maze." She slid the peppers into the pan of onions. "You're spending too much time with Pop when Nana's not around."

"That's not my fault."

"Well, he raised me too and I don't talk like a sailor on shore leave."

Mazie laughed and crumbs flew out like dandelion fluff. "Pop really gets going when the Tigers lose. I know swear words even A.J. Curtis hasn't heard and his dad owns a bar. I have a list. Do you want to see?"

"No, thank you. And I'd appreciate it if you didn't use those words in my house—and definitely not on the island. Here, fill this pan with water almost to the top."

Mazie turned on the faucet. "Technically, I don't have to follow your house rules because this isn't really your house and you're not actually a real adult."

"Well, you're not actually a real child."

Mazie took a bow. "Thank you! Finally, somebody noticed." She popped another carrot in her mouth, adding, "Carrots aren't filling enough to really count as a snack." She stuffed a whole cracker into her mouth. "And no high heels either."

"Back to the wedding again? No more crackers." Charlotte covered the water and turned on the burner.

"Heels ruin your entire spinal alignment. You realize that, right?"

Charlotte lifted one bare foot. "Do you see me wearing heels?" She nodded toward a row of Nikes, her wellies and two pairs of sensible Clarks and a pair of knock-off Crocs under the coat rack at the back door.

"When?" Mazie wasn't giving up.

"When what?"

"When's the wedding?"

"We haven't chosen a date."

"Why? You've been engaged a long time."

"Not *that* long," she said, feeling irritated. "We're just getting used to the idea of being engaged."

She turned to leave. "Okay. Good."

"What? Wait. Good? What's 'good?' Come back here, missy." Had her parents said something? "Why is not setting a date 'good'?"

Mazie backed into the doorway, her shoulders pulled up, looking cornered.

"Tell me," Charlotte said, poking at her with the sharp end of a carrot.

Mazie rolled her head back to look at the ceiling. "Nana says she likes being with Pop more than anybody. She says that's what makes you know you should get married. And Pop says Nana makes him happy most of the time, too."

"And?"

She rolled her eyes again. Charlotte let her squirm in the silence.

"It's just that . . . Nana's worried you and Harp aren't happy."

Charlotte turned back to the sink and whacked the carrot with her knife. "Of course, we're happy."

The truth was she was annoyed with Harp for making other plans tonight. She'd planned a full evening of model domesticity that Mazie would then describe in detail to her parents.

Mazie was leaning against the door jamb watching.

"Go." Charlotte said, "Those salad greens won't pick themselves."

"But you and Harp don't really hang out," Mazie said. "And you never bring him over anymore."

Charlotte set down the knife. "Honey, we work together all day. We don't need to be together all evening to be happy. We have our own lives. There are different kinds of love, Mazie."

"Are there kinds of love that don't really make you happy?"

Charlotte dropped her knife and pointed at the kitchen door. "Skedaddle, you! And take some scissors. Be sure you cut the leaves so you don't pull up the whole plant. *Now!* Please."

"Okay. Okay. Keep your wig on."

The next morning, Mazie was seated behind a stack of cereal boxes that propped up a book when Charlotte came into the kitchen.

"Is there any milk milk?" Mazie asked without looking up.

"Milk milk?"

"This almond crap tastes like birdbath water."

Charlotte put a hand on her hip. "Have you been drinking out of the birdbath again?" She would not let Mazie push her buttons today.

Mazie's eyes narrowed. "That was a joke, right?"

"Never mind. We can stop at the store later, but for now, you'll just have to suffer—in silence."

Mazie sighed deeply and rested her chin on her palm. "Well, if *I* were Queen of the World . . ."

"You mean princess. *I'm* queen. Don't forget that." Charlotte sat down across from her.

Mazie's on-going fascination with Charlotte's Queen of the World fantasy was fueled by her hyper-sensitivity to defects in everything and shortcomings everywhere, as well as her firm conviction that what was fundamentally wrong with the world was that Madelyn McDougal Adair had not been put in charge.

"Why can't I be a queen?"

"You need to be at least eighteen and have a royal license. Besides, having two queens always ends badly."

Mazie grunted—momentarily caught without a retort. Then she rallied. "I bet there've been lots of teen queens."

"I doubt that. But just for the sake of argument, what would you decree?"

"Two things. First, nut milk should taste like nuts. When they do stuff to the almonds or the cashews or whatever, what do they do with the nut flavor?"

Charlotte nodded. "Excellent question. You're a natural, my royal niece."

"And second, if I were Queen of the World—"

"A-hum."

"I mean, princess. Teachers wouldn't be allowed to give Ds."

"Really? Why not?"

"Because you should either understand the stuff or have to take the class over. And, there would also be no ribbons just for participation. That's soooooo lame."

Charlotte wasn't sure how far she'd get debating the merits of below-average grades for below-average minds. Or, for students like herself, for whom credit in high school physics was needed for college and for whom a D was a gift and all she could muster.

After breakfast, Charlotte sent Mazie to brush her teeth and get ready to go to the island. As she was printing out some of her designs, Mazie appeared in the doorway with her open iPad and announced, "You were wrong. Mary Stuart became Queen of Scotland when she was six days old."

Then she turned on her heel and headed back upstairs.

Charlotte called after her. "And how did that work out for her?"

A minute later Mazie reappeared. "Gross! It took, like, three chops to get her whole head off. Then, when the executioner picked up her head by the hair her wig fell off and her head rolled away. Her real hair was this scraggly gray fuzz. Gross! Queen Elizabeth was bad-ass."

"Like I said, two queens are never a good idea." Charlotte grabbed Mazie's parka and pushed her out the door. "Now remember, you're only a princess and I'm your bad-ass queen. Help me load the truck or it's off with your head."

By midweek, Mazie's arms were cross-hatched with scratches and dotted with mosquito bites. A new batch of freckles was scattered like confetti across her nose and cheeks.

Charlotte and Mazie had joined Harp, Kiza, Martin and Hector for lunch in the oak clearing north of the house when Kiza called out to them from the woods.

"Come and see what I have found," he said. The group gathered in a semi-circle around a small mound of dirt, their sandwiches in hand. Kiza brushed the dirt off a boulder the size of a beach ball. "Maybe we use. Yes? Look. Many, many more."

"This is a good discovery, Kiza," Charlotte said, looking at Harp.

Harp pushed one with his foot. "Some have been split. They're probably left over from the foundation."

"They've been buried here for, like, a hundred years," Mazie said, brushing off another. "Here's a really big one."

By the end of the day, Kiza had uncovered about fifty boulders—a fortune in landscaping materials and a lucky find on a small, inaccessible island.

Meanwhile, Mazie helped Charlotte stake out two areas near the house where the rocks would help stabilize the riverbank and provide cover for minnows, frogs and turtles and moisture-loving plants. One boulder was way too heavy to lift, so Harp went to the hardware store for a couple of wood fence posts to use as rollers.

Charlotte and Mazie went to Fig's shed to get a crowbar and a half sheet of plywood.

"Cool! A Hobbit house!" Mazie declared, opening one of the heavy arched doors.

Harp had rearranged things to accommodate their chainsaws, weed whackers and hand tools. The other side was filled with castoffs from previous owners.

Mazie waded in. "Wow. This is some cool shit, I mean stuff, in here. Look, there's kayaks." Two yellow kayaks looked like they hadn't been in the water for a long time.

Charlotte found the crowbar and told Mazie to follow her with the plywood. When Harp returned with the fence posts, the crew had dug out the largest boulder.

"Ready?" Harp asked. "Where's the plywood?"

Charlotte looked around. "Mazie has it. Mazie!" she called out. She sighed. "Just a minute."

She found Mazie on the dock dangling her feet in the water and swinging a butterfly net overhead.

"Mazie, where's the plywood?"

"I forgot," she said as if this was explanation enough. "Look what I found in the shed. Fig said I could have it, as long as I give him" –she slowed her words to quote him exactly—"frequent daily updates on the insects I find on his island. He wants me to make a list."

Charlotte sighed. "Well, Harp wants that plywood."

Mazie was taking practice swings in the air and watching the net fill with air.

Charlotte slapped a mosquito on her arm. "You can take that mosquito off your list." She shaded her eyes against the afternoon sun. "Looks like the netting is ripped. If you bring it home I'll mend it."

"That's okay. Fig's going to. I was going to ask if I can take a break and help."

Charlotte put a hand on her hip. "You can't take a break from a break, Maze. Now go take that plywood to Harp."

"After my break?"

"Now. The crew's waiting."

"Okaaaay."

Mazie shuffled off to the shed while Charlotte rinsed her hands in the river.

Mazie reappeared later with a badminton racket and a shuttlecock. "Oh, I almost forgot. Fig made lemonade. He says he wants a Frequent Daily Update ASAB.

"You mean, ASA*P*, 'as soon as possible.'" She arched her back and grunted. "A break actually sounds good."

On the way to the house she said, "Boy, Fig really likes his Frequent Daily Updates."

Charlotte smiled. "Yup, FDUs ASAP."

"Does he get to order them? I thought you were a queen."

"On this island, he's the boss. I'm more of a figurehead kind of queen."

"I don't see why there even have to *be* bosses."

"So hard-working crews don't have to wait and wait for plywood."

Just then, Harp came striding down the path, "Mazie? Where's that plywood?"

"Uh-oh," Mazie gasped, running back to the shed.

Fig was seated at the porch table with three glasses of lemonade in front of him. He motioned them up.

"Come join me?"

"Perfect," Charlotte said, sitting beside him in front of an elaborate lacquered Chinese box. "The family jewels?"

Fig laughed. "My mother's sewing box. I believe we'll find everything we need to mend Mazie's net."

Mazie came up the steps out of breath.

"Mission accomplished?" Charlotte lifted her chin.

Mazie nodded and sat down on Fig's other side.

"There's a needle and thread in there," Fig said, taking a long swallow of his lemonade.

"I don't know how to sew." She pushed the box and net toward Charlotte.

Fig pushed it back. "Then it's the perfect time to learn." He reached into the box. "This, my dear, is a needle."

Mazie rolled her eyes. "I know what a needle is."

"Then you've got a head start," he said. "Now pick out some good, strong thread. There are some monster bugs on my island and we can't have them breaching the net and evading our research."

Mazie rummaged through the box. "This thread looks strong."

"Cut a piece of thread about this long," he said, holding his hands apart. "Now find the eye of the needle."

Mazie shut one eye and jabbed the thread at the needle repeatedly. Finally, she pushed the whole project toward Charlotte. "You do it."

Fig folded his hands in his lap. "The net belongs to you, Mazie. This is an opportunity to learn a new skill so you can take care of it."

Mazie frowned, but took up the thread again.

Fig leaned in, taking great interest in the journey of the thread through the eye of the needle.

"By George, you've got it. Now make a couple of little stitches to attach the thread. Just like that. Now pull the edges together. Repeat, repeat, repeat."

After a few seconds, Mazie screwed up her face. "It looks messy."

Charlotte examined the seam. "It's fine, Maze."

"Function before form, mademoiselle," Fig said. "Your only goal is a serviceable bug net. Style and artistry are irrelevant in this case."

Mazie worked her tongue along her lips with each stitch while Fig turned his attention to Charlotte. He asked about the discovery of the boulder pile, ignoring Mazie's clucks, sighs and theatrical moans.

Finally, she announced, "Look. One hole mended."

"Not bad," he said, leaning over to inspect her work. "I see you've been working hard this week, Mazie, but I'm surprised you gave up science camp for this."

"Trust me, it would have been really stupid." She sat cross-legged on the chair bent over her work.

"Stupid. Really?" Fig looked surprised. "Then I guess it's good you didn't go."

"Nana didn't think so."

"Well, she should have asked you before she paid all that money and planned a vacation with your granddad."

Mazie shot a look at Charlotte but didn't respond.

"If it were me," Fig said. "I would have asked you."

Mazie mumbled something.

Fig leaned closer, cupping his ear. "Hmm?"

She shot him a death ray. "I said, she did ask me, but I changed my mind."

"You changed your mind. I see. Then it was a good thing she didn't mind losing all her deposit money and almost forfeiting her vacation."

Mazie opened her eyes wide. "Oh, she was mad all right. Really mad. Ouch! I pricked my finger." She shook her hand and stuck her finger in her mouth. She glared at Fig. "I have a right to change my mind."

"A right? Ah, well, rights are important." Fig mulled this over. "So, your grandma really had no choice—being that changing one's mind is one of those inalienable rights. I guess it's understandable if camp was going to be stupid."

Charlotte was watching this exchange as if Alex Rodriquez was at bat with bases loaded.

"I would have hated that camp!" Mazie protested with the conviction of the guilty.

Fig shifted again to face Charlotte. "So, Ms. Adair. Asserting my inalienable right to change my mind I won't be paying you for your work last week."

"Is that so, Mr. Bigelow?" Charlotte said, doing her best imitation of Mazie's death ray. She sucked in her breath. "Have you forgotten our contract? If you change your mind now, I will take you to court. The judge will make you pay me. I guess I won't be planting the shrubs you already paid me for."

Fig sat back, slack-jawed. "But that's not fair! I have a right to change my mind. I believe it's in the Constitution. Right, Mazie?"

Mazie stood up. "Okay, you guys! Just quit it!" She pounded down the steps and headed for the dock.

Fig winced. "Too much?"

She laughed. "Heck no! That was fun. Let's do it again soon."

Fig watched Mazie get on the raft. "No. I interfered again, just like I did at the plant store and when I grilled you about your engagement." He shook his head and started to get up.

She reached for his arm. "Leave her. She needed to hear that, and better from you than me or my parents."

He frowned, deep in thought. "It was a bloody cross-examination."

Charlotte laughed. "You can't help yourself."

Mazie stopped in the middle of the river and sat down.

"Thanks for taking an interest in her." She looked at him sideways. "I thought you didn't like kids."

"Is she a kid? I hadn't noticed."

Charlotte laughed. "She'd love to hear you say that. She can't wait to grow up."

"I was the same way." After a pause, he said, "She's a bit different, I grant you that, but I get her."

She nodded slowly. "Yes. Of course you do."

"Why is that?"

"Because she's a younger, female, more hormonal version of yourself. I just realized that."

His face broke into a wide grin. "You think so? No wonder I like her."

Mazie was on her back now, with one arm draped across her face.

"The other night she started in about the wedding and why Harp and I haven't set a date and what she wanted and didn't want to wear and whether she's going to be my assistant 'bridesman,' or some-such thing. It was a proper Fig-style cross-examination."

Fig slapped his knee. "That's my girl! You're right. Two peas." He crossed his arms, looking extraordinarily pleased.

After a pause, he turned to her, "Maybe she could work off her debt this summer. What do you think?"

"Here? With me?"

"You and Harp could use the help, right? I don't mind a little extra cost and although I can't believe I'm saying this, I enjoy having her around."

"I don't know," Charlotte said, remembering the plywood.

Mazie got off the raft and shuffled slowly up the walk kicking a pine cone into the woods. She stopped below the porch railing to pull back her bangs to look up at them.

"I've thought about what you said and I'm going to pay Nana back. Every penny. But –." She screwed her face into a deep grimace. "What if I already spent all my Christmas money and my allowance?"

Charlotte looked at Fig, "Well if you're really serious about this, I guess I could put you on Harp's crew. You'll have to work really hard. Say, four hours a day—with no complaining and one break. You'd be free to read or work on your bug collection in the afternoon."

"It's not a collection; it's a study. And it's bugs and insects and maybe spiders, I haven't decided."

"Nevertheless, you should have enough money by Labor Day to pay Nana back. If it's okay with Fig."

Mazie clasped her hands under her chin. "Can I, Mr. Bigelow? Please? I'll work really hard."

He reached over the railing to shake her hand. "Deal, Ms. Adair."

Charlotte added, "You'll have to be dressed and ready to go by 8:30. Monday through Friday."

"But it's summer vacation."

"It's summer, but not a vacation anymore," Charlotte said.

"Okay."

Fig said, "And one more thing, Mazie. If we agree on this today, none of us can change our minds. Got it?"

"Got it."

Charlotte said, "Go see if Harp needs anything. I'll be along in a minute."

Mazie tore down the path, yelling, "Harp! Martin! Kiza! Hector!"

Charlotte sighed. "You're a wise man, Fig Bigelow, but an interfering butt-insky."

Fig nodded. "You are so welcome."

The next morning Charlotte was cleaning the kitchen when Mazie shuffled in dressed in the jeans, tee-shirt, long-sleeved shirt and athletic shoes they'd picked out that night before.

"Morning, Maze. Ready for some on-the-job training today?"

"Sure," she said, absently pouring cereal into a bowl at the counter. "What's up?"

"I'm afraid to tell you."

"Why?"

"You'll say no."

Charlotte hung the skillet on its hook over the sink. "Then you have your answer."

Mazie grabbed Charlotte's hands, swinging them awkwardly—apparently toying with the idea of a hug, but changing her mind.

"I really, really, *really* want to catch Bilbo this summer, I mean, Speedy-Panya-Tramp-Prince-Bilbo. Can I, please, Auntie Charlotte? Let me at least try."

The "Auntie Charlotte" may have been gilding the lily.

"Honey, we've all tried. He's just too wild."

"But I know how to do it. It'll take, like, two minutes every morning and a little bit more on the day I catch him. I have it all planned out."

"And if you catch him?"

She shrugged. "I'll take him home."

Charlotte dropped a handful of spoons into the drawer. "No. No. Absolutely not. You know Nana doesn't want a dog. You may not even ask them. Is that clear?" She squeezed Mazie's shoulder. "Do I have your word? Otherwise, you can't even try to catch him."

"Okay! Okay, but couldn't you and Harp keep him? He'd love living here."

"He'd be here by himself all day, honey. That's no life for a little dog. If you catch him—and that's a big if—I promise we'll find him a good home, but he's just not ever going to be Bilbo Adair. Are we clear?"

"Okaaaay," she huffed in exasperation.

Charlotte took the opportunity to steal a hug.

17

W.I.L.H.A. - JUNE

At the June meeting of the Women in Landscaping and Horticulture Association, Katie Clay sat down next to Charlotte and cocked her head toward the far end of the table.

"Look. Barbie's joining our sorority," Katie whispered, her eyes full of mischief.

Phyllis Oosterbaan was chatting with a slim, fortyish woman with frosted blond hair and ten perfectly manicured crimson nails.

Charlotte rolled her eyes.

At the other end of the table, Barb VanderLee, began tapping her coffee mug with a spoon. The room came to order.

"Good morning. Let's get started, but keep the coffee and scones going around. We have a visitor this morning. This is Elena Lewis. Welcome, Elena. Tell us about yourself."

"Thank you, Barb. I'm pleased to be here. I'm from the Lansing area but am exploring professional opportunities on this side of the state. I've worked in the horticultural industry quite holistically—combining traditional horticulture with emerging markets. My core competencies are data mining, actionable analytics and market realignment but I'd like to take a deep dive—double-click, if you will—into the native plant arena, which is really all about customer personalization. Basically, I want to increase my bandwidth in an industry that is reinventing itself."

Katie scribbled on her napkin and slid it toward Charlotte. *What the F-!?!* Charlotte ignored her.

Elena continued. "This is really a case of sustainability meets profit as native species become a key touchpoint of the customer journey. As you all know, native plants are optimal, next-gen products. And because of that, I hear you're the go-to gals in West Michigan. And by the way, I think these little, local consortia create great synergy." She wrapped her red nails around her water bottle and smiled at her audience.

Barb seemed struck dumb. "Well. Okay. . . um . . . So, you are looking for work in this area, Elena?"

"I'm doing private consulting at the moment. My research has convinced me that Saskawan is ripe for expansion among qualified early adopters."

Katie scribbled again, *Business school dropout?*

Charlotte took a large bite of scone to keep a straight face and avoided looking at Katie. But she had to admit that Elena's coiffed hair, gold earrings, and white linen blouse looked like they'd never been near a bag of composted cow manure.

Barb nodded. "Okay. Let's keep our ears to the ground for consulting opportunities. Again, welcome." She took a deep breath. "Moving on, Charlotte Adair, our secretary, has something to show us.

Charlotte turned her laptop to face the group. "I want to show some photos I took at South Middle School last week." She clicked the track pad. "This first shot is the front entrance showing six mature Bradford pears that according to a plaque were a gift from the class of 2001. That would make them about twenty-five years old." There were a few murmurs around the table. She moved to the next photo. "And here's the woods behind the school. When I attended there eons ago, there was a nature trail through the woods with white pines, dogwoods, maples, redbuds and oaks."

"I used to smoke back there," Katie added.

"But, now—" She clicked on a shot of a roped-off area and a sign reading, Danger Keep Out. "The whole woods is choked with the wild offspring of those Bradford pears. Unlike their parents —" She clicked to a close-up of a branch. "—the feral offspring have thorns." She showed a close-up of her own finger pointing at a four-inch thorn.

Murmurs turned to nods and sighs of concern.

"And finally, here's Arcadia Elementary, Central High and the district administration building on Tyler Street—all landscaped with Bradford pears."

"Looks like the district can't get enough of them," Katie said.

Barb added, "All these schools are adjacent to parks or wooded areas that are vulnerable to infestation."

Nicky said, "The district has no idea what they're doing."

Charlotte closed her laptop and looked around the room. "Then I suggest we tell them."

"Heck yeah," Katie said. "It's a teachable moment for teachers."

"I'm happy to draft a letter," Charlotte said, looking at Barb. "If there's support for it." She knew she was stirring things up with Phyllis who was looking perpetually peeved again. "The district might be more responsive than the city was."

There were a few nods around the table.

Nicky leaned forward with her hands gripping her coffee mug and her shoulders shrugged up to her ears. "I know I said last month that I wasn't enthused about this letter writing, but my only real objection is that it doesn't go far enough. But since it's the only tool we have, you have my support."

Charlotte smiled. "Thanks, Nicky. I appreciate the vote of confidence."

Nicky flashed a smile. "I said you have my support, not my confidence."

"Baby steps," Katie offered.

"Shall we take a vote, Barb?" Charlotte asked.

"Excuse me!" Phyllis raised both her hands, palms forward, eyes closed—the picture of forbearance. "I was under the impression, Madam President, that we were going to discuss this today. Rabble-rousing isn't the mission of this organization. We're way off course."

"How do the rest of you feel?" Barb asked.

Katie looked straight at Phyllis. "What good is knowing all this if we just keep it to ourselves?"

Kelly, a young landscape designer, spoke up. "Most people have no idea the damage these trees are doing. Educators might listen."

Phyllis tented her fingers in front of her face and sighed dramatically. "Let me explain something. It's the job of three state departments—Agriculture, Natural Resources and Environmental Quality, to determine what's invasive and what's not. There's a specific and very thorough process that every plant has to go through before they decide whether to take it off the market. We can't just jump up and declare a plant invasive. Bradford pear, Norway maple and barberry and most of the others you're going on about are not prohibited in this state.

Period." She jabbed her finger into the table. "Until they are, I say, stay out of it!"

"Wait, Phyllis," Nicky said. "When was the last time these agencies actually took a plant off the market?"

Phyllis shrugged.

Charlotte said, "Twenty-twelve. Autumn olive was the last."

Barb's expression revealed nothing. "Is there a question in anyone's mind here—based on your own observations and what you have read in the literature—that Bradford pear, Norway maple or barberry—are invasive plants in this state?"

Nicky said, "All three are a scourge."

"Barberries are a favorite food of mice that carry Lyme disease," Katie added.

Nicky went on. "And the thorns on those Bradford pear hybrids can puncture the tires of heavy equipment. And they're spreading fast across the US and into Michigan. The sooner we act the better."

"Asian bittersweet is just as bad," Katie said. "It's strangling hundred-year-old oaks all along the Hawthorn River as we speak."

Charlotte said, "My crew just spent a week eradicating wisteria, privet, buckthorn and exotic honeysuckle on the island where I'm working. I'd add any of those to a banned list."

Barb looked around the table, "I think we—this organization, our industry and our state—have a big problem. So, does this organization want to help raise public awareness about invasive species that are marketed and sold in Michigan, or stay silent?"

A young woman named Olivia whose eye had been on her cell screen for most of the meeting finally raised her hand. "Excuse me," she said, "I think we should speak out, but—" She continued scrolling her cell with her thumb. "Sorry, I'm looking for something that might help. Give me a second."

Olivia had joined the group a few months earlier after graduating from Michigan State with an environmental science degree. She was still looking for a job.

"When I was at MSU," she said, "I wrote a research paper about invasive plants in the Midwest. Each state has the power to ban harmful plants within its boundaries. I have those state lists—somewhere in my phone."

"Ban? In what way?" Phyllis asked.

"They can't be imported, propagated, distributed, sold and in some cases, you can't even possess them. But I was surprised when I compared Michigan to our neighbors. I mean, you'd expect lists to be a little different, but Michigan is an outlier. Oh, here. Found it," Olivia said, looking at her screen. She leaned on her elbows and read from her screen. "Multiflora rose is illegal in Wisconsin and Ohio—but not in Michigan. Asian bittersweet is illegal in Wisconsin, Ohio and Indiana—but not in Michigan. And, barberry and several species of non-native honeysuckle are banned in all four of our neighbors, Wisconsin, Illinois, Indiana and Illinois—but still legal in Michigan."

"What about Bradford pear?" Charlotte asked.

"It's still legal in all the Great Lake states, except Ohio which banned it this year. The species is clearly on the move from the southeast US and, as Charlotte showed us, it's already here. Today would be the best time to ban it; yesterday would have been better. South Carolina has an active eradication program. Pittsburgh has outlawed it and Fayetteville, Arkansas offers a bounty on them."

"Why isn't Michigan doing anything?" Charlotte asked.

"That's what I wanted to find out," Olivia said. "But no one could give me an answer—at least not one that made any sense."

Elena raised her hand. "I believe I can shed light on this," she said, tucking a blonde lock behind her ear. "Michigan does its due diligence in every case. It conducts a risk analysis to identify optimal management approaches for the species in question. Such careful analysis and implementation is quite labor intensive."

Nicky coughed. "You can say that again. To get a plant banned in this state requires a 'weed risk assessment' which is ridiculously complicated, expensive and time consuming. You have to do a complete literature review, do detailed field surveys and present your findings to two separate commissions. It can take years and thousands of dollars. And in the end, there's no guarantee of success, so it's a huge gamble."

"Nicky's right," said Portia, a woman in her fifties who headed up a land restoration non-profit. "And the state doesn't initiate assessments. Citizen groups and NGOs like mine have to. But we don't have the resources. If you ask me, this isn't 'due diligence' we're seeing, it's obstruction. I can't prove it, but I know it."

Charlotte dug into her bag and produced a small spiral-bound book. "I know a lot of you own this book—*A Field Identification Guide to Invasive Plants of Michigan's Natural Communities.* I use it all the time. It was published in 2015 by Michigan State University Extension and funded by the departments of Natural Resources and Environmental Quality and a who's who of environmental groups." She paged through the booklet and held up a photo page of Morrow's Honeysuckle. "It lists forty plants as invasive with photos of each.

"How many of those are banned in Michigan?" Barb asked.

"Five," Charlotte said.

"Out of forty?" Katie said. "Pitiful."

Charlotte said, "The five are giant hogweed, Japanese knotweed, phragmites, autumn olive and purple loosestrife.

"Not Asian bittersweet?" Katie said, shaking her head.

Olivia read from her cell. "It's banned in all neighboring states, but not here."

"Why would these state agencies help fund this guide, but not ban them?" Katie asked.

Charlotte said, "I think it's because they know they'd get pushback from the horticultural industry."

"It's all about profits," Nicky said. "Apparently, no plant is invasive if someone somewhere is making money off it."

Barb looked uncomfortable. "Thank you, Charlotte and Olivia for your research. Now, let's—"

"Excuse me, Barb," Elena said, clicking her fingernails on the table. "I'd like to respond." She looked around the table, her lips curled, but her eyes were cold. "I really do appreciate that these exotic plants are a pain point for some of you, but paradigm shifts within any industry are extremely time intensive. I know everyone around this table gives a thousand percent, but please remember, there's a lot at stake here."

"For whom—?" Nicky asked.

"Some around this table, I expect," Elena said. "I know Phyllis grows some of the plants you've named. A lot of you landscapers get requests for them, too, because they grow reliably and are relatively inexpensive."

Olivia looked around the table. "That's what I kept hearing during my research. Some of the horticulturalists I interviewed said our neighboring states are recklessly banning harmless plants. But the more I know, the less I believe that. Neither did my professor. She said my conclusions were incomplete, and I have to admit she was right. I didn't get an A, but the research has stuck with me, which is one reason I want to work with native plants."

There was a thoughtful silence before Katie exploded. "Our state agencies are acting like a bunch of firemen studying a house while it burns to the ground."

Portia, who had been staring into her coffee mug, looked up. "I understand that this is shocking news to some of you. But it isn't to me. I'd love to make the state move faster, but I don't pick fights I can't win. David and Goliath is a lovely story, but that's all it is."

"I don't want a fight, Portia," Charlotte said. "That's why I think a respectful letter makes sense. If we can't shut down the supply of invasive plants from the horticultural industry, maybe we can reduce the demand. School districts might be a good start."

Nicky shrugged. "Elena said we're the experts. We should speak up."

Elena gave Nicky a patronizing smile. "I did say you were experts, but I also think we're fortunate that our state takes a thorough, science-driven approach to assessing plants. The state shouldn't rely on the casual observations of a few well-meaning tree-huggers."

"Really?" Portia said, leaning in to make eye contact. "Because from where I sit, the state's so-called 'science-driven' approach looks more like evasion. They're so afraid of opposition from the horticultural industry, that they've designed a process that's guaranteed to fail."

"I agree, Portia," Charlotte said. "But why doesn't the state want these plants off its roadsides and out of its state parks and forests? They must know there's a problem."

"I had the same question," Olivia said. "But couldn't get anyone to give me a satisfying answer."

The room broke into several side conversations before Barb tapped her coffee cup. "Okay, everyone. We all have a full workday ahead. Good discussion this month. If there are no more comments—"

"Wait," Katie said. "Are we going to send a letter to the school district or not?"

"A lawsuit sounds tempting," Nicky said with a half-smile. "But I'll settle for one of Charlotte's nice, respectful letters."

Portia raised her hand. "I move that we send a letter to the school district stating our case for removing Bradford pears—but let's add barberry to the list. We don't need Lyme ticks in our schoolyards. That should get parents' attention."

"I second," Katie said quickly. "And I vote yes."

Eighteen hands went up. Phyllis and three others voted no. The Saskawan Public Schools would get a letter.

On the way out, Katie threaded her arm through Charlotte's and whispered, "Nice going, rabble rouser." She looked over her shoulder before adding, "I think most of them only voted to send the letter so you wouldn't make them join your lawsuit."

Charlotte grimaced. "I'm not starting a lawsuit."

"Why not? Making pencil pushers squirm in their cubicles? What could be more fun?"

"I have a business to run, but I'll tell Fig he's got a plaintiff."

"Fig?"

"My client. The lawyer."

"Fig? That's your client's name?"

"Well, it's Newton Bigelow actually."

"Fig Newton. Get it. Love it!"

Katie was still grinning when Elena brushed past them toward a shiny, white BMW that stood out among the muddy trucks and banged-up minivans in the parking lot.

Katie lowered her voice. "I don't think I'd have the balls to speak my mind quite so bluntly if I was a visitor."

"You? Oh, you definitely would." Charlotte said, laughing as she watched Elena drive off with her ear to her phone. "But I agree, she's got some nerve."

Charlotte was climbing into her truck when she noticed a slip of paper tucked under her windshield wiper. A handwritten note read,

> Elena isn't who she says she is.
> It's not the state; it's the MHA.

That night, Charlotte scoured Facebook and LinkedIn but found no Elena Lewis.

Later that day, when she dropped off an invoice at Fig's door, she told him about the WILHA meeting and their mystery visitor.

Fig scowled intently. "Interesting. You've apparently ruffled somebody's feathers."

"If she shows up next month, I'll take down her license plate."

"Hmm. I'd be glad to do some checking. Would you mind?"

"Be my guest. But if she's a spy—" She laughed suddenly. "I can't believe I just said that. A spy in quiet little Saskawan. Anyway, she might not be using her real name."

"Don't underestimate my Doc Watson skills, Sherlock. I'll let you know if I find her."

When Ted and Mally returned from their trip, Charlotte drove Mazie home. After Mazie bounced up the front steps and into the house, Charlotte explained her plan to have Mazie work for her.

"I've got plenty of room at the farm and she can come home as often as she wants."

Her parents reacted with a mixture of suspicion and disbelief.

"Is this your idea?" her mother whispered.

Ted gave a sidelong smile. "She blackmailing you?"

She laughed. "No, Dad. She's not a bad little assistant – given the right guidance."

"Hot damn and knock me over with a feather!" Ted said, grabbing his wife around the waist. "How much do we owe you, Charlotte?"

Charlotte lifted her chin. "My services are beyond price, Dad. But I won't turn down any dinner invitations."

"We'll make it happen, right Mal?"

Mally smiled. "We'll miss her, but—" she giggled and grinned up at Ted. "You know. We really need a break."

As Charlotte backed out of the driveway, she heard her father say. "What say you, Mally? Chicago next week? Or the Detroit Institute of Art? Maybe a Tiger game?"

Charlotte called out. "Oh, by the way, no matter what Mazie says, you're not getting a dog."

She left her parents standing in the driveway, one smiling and the other scratching his bald spot.

JULY

Red Beebalm *Monarda didyma*

18

ONE GIANT LEAP

Before moving a plant from the greenhouse or windowsill into the garden, it is wise to withhold fertilizer and water to condition it to outdoor life. Next, a period of "hardening off" is advised. This means gradually preparing it for the garden by setting it in a sheltered area outside for a few days. Anything that helps the plant adjust to its new environment will reward the gardener in the long run.

On Monday morning, instead of leaving Speedy-Panya-Tramp-Prince-Bilbo's dish by the cottonwood, Mazie moved it closer to the landing dock. On Tuesday, and Wednesday, she inched it even closer but left only a half ration of kibble. On Thursday, she left another half ration.

Kiza looked worried. "Why Panya not have so much food to eat?"

"You'll see," Mazie said with a smug grin.

On Friday, when Mazie and Charlotte arrived, the tall fisherman waved at them from the river.

"Any progress with Speedy?"

"I'm catching him today," Mazie announced. "You can watch from there."

"Wouldn't miss it."

The dog barked at them, but as usual, didn't venture out from his cottonwood fortress. Mazie retrieved the empty dish and shook the bag before pouring kibble into the bowl. The hungry dog went silent and dropped onto his belly, his ears pricked at attention.

"Mm. Look at this, Bilbo. Breakfast. Yum!" she said.

His eyes locked onto the dish as she walked backward toward the dock, dropping a trail of kibble along the way. Then she set the full bowl on the raft.

"Okay, let's go."

The fisherman tipped his hat. "Good luck, ladies."

Charlotte waved as she joined Mazie on the raft.

"I don't get it," she said to Mazie as they floated across. "Why are you bringing the dish to the island?"

Mazie lifted her chin. "You'll see."

Harp, Kiza, Martin and Hector were carrying flats of wild ginger and pale purple coneflower to the shed when they arrived.

"So, what's the plan?" Harp asked, looking at the dish. "You're going to make the little guy swim for his breakfast?"

Charlotte looked at Mazie. "You know he's not big enough to swim against this current, right?"

Mazie replied with a withering look. "Of course."

Kiza said, "Ah! I think I know." He said something to Martin in Swahili who nodded in agreement.

Mazie turned to Harp. "For my plan to succeed, I need to stay by the dock for a while. Can I, pleeeeease, Harp?" She picked up a flat and followed him toward the shed. "I'll work extra time after lunch. Okay?"

Harp gave her a doubtful sideways glance but didn't reply.

"I'll drag five bundles of brush to the dock."

Harp set the flat in the shade behind the shed. "Seven."

"Six and I'll bake brownies for you guys tomorrow."

Harp extended his hand. "Deal."

Fig had been watching the unfolding drama from the porch. He called out. "I've made coffee for everyone. Come take a break."

When they were all seated around the porch table, Fig set out a carafe of coffee, mugs, cream, sugar and a plate of chocolate biscotti.

Meanwhile, Mazie took a sandwich bag of sliced turkey and cheese from her pocket and mixed it with the kibble in the dog's bowl.

Charlotte nudged Harp. "That's why you couldn't find the turkey this morning."

"Told you," he said.

Kiza rummaged through his backpack. "Mademoiselle, please to wait," he called out. From a plastic tub, he pulled out a chunk of chicken. Martin and Hector followed suit, adding meaty tidbits of beef and roasted vegetables to the overflowing bowl.

Fig nodded. "International fusion dog cuisine. Lucky pup."

When the bowl was thoroughly mixed, Mazie announced. "Okay. For this to work, we need to be really quiet."

"*Bahati njema*, miss," Martin said. "God brings a good luck day to you."

Kiza joined it. "*Bon chance, mademoiselle!*"

Hector lifted his mug. "*Buena suerte, senorita!*"

Fig chimed in, "Oodgay ucklay!"

"Okay okay!" Mazie said, laughing. "Now everybody hush!"

They all watched as she knelt on the dock and set the bowl on the raft.

Fig passed around the biscotti and pantomimed dipping the sweet, crisp biscuits into the hot coffee. Soon, Kiza, Martin and Hector were sipping and dipping with their eyes trained on the unfolding drama in the river.

Charlotte leaned closer to Fig and whispered, "Did you have a hand in this?"

He shook his head. "This is all Mazie." Then he added, "Although she did ask permission to bring him to live on the island."

"And you said yes?"

He shrugged. "He'll be safe here for now."

Charlotte caught Harp watching them and moved to sit next to him.

Kneeling at the end of the dock, Mazie pulled the rope and sent the raft with its cargo of one meaty dog feast slowly into the river toward the landing. As it drew closer, the Dog-With-Five-Names came out of his borrow and sniffed the air. Mazie stopped the raft a foot short of the landing.

Further down the bank, the tall fisherman stopped casting his line.

Then, a motorcycle sped by sending the dog back into his hole under the cottonwood. The spectators on Fig's porch groaned in unison as the fisherman raised an arm in disappointment.

After several minutes, the dog ventured out again but dove back into hiding when two skateboarders rolled by, and again when a garbage truck stopped to pick up bins. When a firetruck sped by, sirens screaming, he stayed in his burrow for ten long minutes.

"This is unbearable," Charlotte whispered, squeezing Harp's shoulder. "Come on, Speedy-Panya, whatever your name is!"

Finally, the traffic was quiet and the dog appeared once again following his nose to the end of the landing dock where he seemed to see his bowl for the first time. He peered into the watery gap between the landing and the raft and sat down. Then he turned three circles and sat down again to think things over. He tipped his head left and right to judge the distance, taking into consideration the width of the gap compared to the size of his body and the level of his hunger.

He barked at the stubborn, unmoving raft in frustration. Then, he backed up and turned more circles as if winding himself up. He crouched onto his haunches and shot forward, runnung pell-mell the full length of the landing. At the last moment, he flung himself into the air, his short brown legs extended fore and aft. His body traveled in a perfect arc and landed less than a muzzle-length from a most delectable breakfast.

When his audience on the porch began to cheer Mazie signaled for silence.

From her place on the island dock, she pulled the rope taut again and eased the raft slowly into the current. By the time the dog finished eating, the raft was halfway across. He spun around to look back at the receding riverbank, pacing nervously. The raft closed in on the island dock. When he saw Mazie, he retreated to the far side of the raft. Seconds before the raft bumped the dock, he leaped several times his body length into the water, scrambled up the bank and disappeared into the woods.

Harp, Hector, Kiza and Martin whooped, punched the air and high-fived. Across the river, the tall fisherman waved his hat in the air.

"Genius," Fig said under his breath. "She's a genius."

"Nice job, kid!" Hark shouted.

"*Brava, señorita!*" Hector said.

Mazie took a bow.

As they left the porch, Hector elbowed Kiza, "See? He like enchilada."

"No, no. *Fumbwa*," Kiza protested.

Charlotte smiled at Fig, "Thanks for the coffee and biscotti."

"My pleasure. I wouldn't have missed this drama for anything," Fig said, loading up a tray with empty mugs.

Mazie ran up the steps. "If you're going to keep him, he needs a shorter name. All those hyphens will give him serious identity issues."

"So, Bilbo, then," Fig said.

She thought for a minute. "No. You should name him. Besides, I like the name you gave him."

"Prince?"

"Yeah, I mean if you're king of this island, he's the prince now, right?"

And Prince he was.

Prince spent his first night on the island behind a stack of firewood next to the shed. In the morning he watched as the thin, white man set his dish on the ground. Each morning since then, his dish was in a new place. He followed his nose to find it.

This wasn't a bad place. And the way the man moved didn't frighten him. Sometimes the man hardly moved an inch, but repeated, "Good boy, Prince. Good boy" in a low, soothing voice.

Just when the dog was beginning to think life couldn't get any better, he woke to the scent of fresh meat. He discovered a pink morsel in the grass right beside the woodpile. A few steps away was another and another. He followed the trail of deliciousness to some steps. The aroma drew him up and to the feet of the quiet man.

Prince sat down to watch the man, cocking his head and sniffing the air. Hoping the man might have more meat, but the man didn't seem to notice a hungry little brown dog.

He sniffed the air and the edges of the porch . . . under the chair. He cocked his head to the right. The man didn't see him.

He whined, Hello. He wagged. He whined, Hey!

The scent was so close his tongue tingled. He needed that meat. He took a step closer.

There it was. A big, juicy chunk in the man's dangling fingers. He stretched his neck as far as it would go. It was soooo lovely. He stretched his body and stretched his tongue, but he couldn't reach it. He licked his muzzle.

He turned in a circle. He wagged. He smiled. He panted. He stood on his hind legs. Clearly, the man didn't see him. Finally, he took several steps backward.

"*Yip! Yip! Yip!*"

The man turned his head and smiled back. "Hello there, Prince." He opened his fingers and offered the meat.

Prince pulled back his lips and eased it from between the man's fingers and swallowed it whole.

Wonder of wonders, another piece appeared! He wolfed it down.

He was anticipating another when his ears filled with the dreaded wailing of a noise-making beast. It was coming fast. He dashed around the porch looking for a hiding place. The thing came closer, screaming louder. There wasn't time to get to the woodpile. He froze. It was almost upon him!

Suddenly, he reared back and flung himself into the air, hiding his face where he landed.

"You don't like sirens, I see," the pale man said, letting Prince burrow under his arm. "That makes two of us."

Fig's lap is where Prince spent the rest of that morning and every other morning—and many evenings—for the rest of that summer.

When Mazie and Charlotte arrived, Prince was standing on Fig's lap, whipping Fig's face with his tail.

"Oh my God!" Mazie shouted, running toward the porch. When Fig raised his hand, she slowed to a walk and whispered, "How did you get him to do that?"

"Patience and finesse," Fig said, grinning like the Cheshire Cat, "and meat."

With each new day, Prince found new ways to demonstrate his love for Fig while asserting his own authority over the island. When the raft approached, Prince barked to proclaim it. If he judged the occupants to be friendly, he turned pirouettes on the dock. Fig called this his "song and dance." When the raft came within a few feet of the dock Prince leaped aboard to escort their guests to the dock.

The crew shared their lunches with him until Fig pointed out Prince's growing pot belly. After that, Martin bought him a red collar and Harp returned from the hardware store with a bright red dog raincoat.

"They had a big display by the checkout," he explained with a sheepish shrug. "He'll look dapper in it."

After cashing her first paycheck, Mazie showed up with a Prince-sized, fur-lined igloo. She set it on the porch where Charlotte and Fig were going over plans for the back patio and coaxed Prince into it. He turned around three times and lay down.

"Look! He likes it," she said. She pulled a handful of bills out of her pocket. "Can you keep this money for me, Aunt Charlotte? If I spend any more, I won't have enough to pay Nana back."

When Charlotte held out her hand, Fig asked, "Don't you trust yourself, Mazie?"

Mazie laughed. "Not exactly."

"I would have thought that the person who devised such a clever plan to catch a stray dog and then executed it so expertly would be able to resist spending money belonging to her grandmother—if she was determined to do so."

"I am determined. I just—I don't know."

She bit the inside of her cheek and slowly pocketed the money again. "I guess so."

Charlotte got up and brushed Mazie's bangs from her forehead. "Come on. We have a lot of work to do today and you need some more paychecks."

19

BEN'S KITE

Within hours of hatching, wood duck chicks fling themselves out of their treetop nests, bounce a few times in the soft leaf litter below and march off in the direction of their mother's calls. Any newborn that can stand, walk and sometimes run shortly after birth is called "precocial." These include foals, fawns, ducklings and turkeys. But "altricial" babies like robins, kangaroos, owls, cats, dogs and humans are born wholly dependent upon their doting parents for several weeks or, as in the case of some humans, for decades.

A few days later Charlotte waited in the Adirondack chair next to Fig while Mazie went inside to use the bathroom. When she came out, she declared, "Wow, Fig, you sure have a lot of pills. What are they for?"

"Mazie," Charlotte said sharply. "People's medicine cabinets are private."

She glanced at Fig. "Sorry."

"They're for my cough and to help my breathing mostly," Fig said.

"Do they help?"

"I think so, yes."

"You still cough a lot."

He nodded.

"Would your pills help me? If I had a cough?"

Charlotte sat up. "You didn't take any, did you?"

"Of course not. I'd never do that. I was just wondering."

"Those medicines were prescribed by my doctors," Fig said. "The dosage varies for each person."

"You mean, like how tall they are?"

"Or how old or how heavy or what other medicines they take—lots of considerations."

"Well, there are sure a lot of bottles in there." She swung a leg over the railing and leaned back against the post. "My friend A.J. says if you take cough medicine when you don't have a cough, you'll get a cough. Is that true?"

Charlotte suspected her niece was trying to stall so she didn't have to help Harp cut brush in the meadow.

Fig looked up at Mazie. "I very much doubt that."

"Well, what would happen if someone took someone else's pills?"

Charlotte sat up, irritated now. "Why are you asking this?" she said. "Go find Harp and give him a hand."

Fig looked calmly at Charlotte. "I'd like to answer her question, if you don't mind."

Charlotte folded her arms. She didn't like where this was going.

Fig was looking intently at Mazie. "I don't know exactly what would happen, but it wouldn't be good. If they're for a tall person like me and, say, a smaller person like you took them instead, there could be all kinds of problems."

"Like what?"

"Headache, racing heart, dizziness, vomiting."

Mazie wrinkled her nose.

"Your ears could fall off," he added.

Mazie rolled her eyes. "Right."

"My point is, I don't know what would happen. A lot of drugs are helpful in the right doses and for the right condition, but in the higher doses or if you don't need them, they can damage your stomach lining, your kidneys or your liver, make your heart fibrillate, or even stop—permanently."

"That's probably what happened to my mom when she overdosed. But I guess I'll never know since no one ever talks about her when I'm around." She shot a defiant look at Charlotte.

Charlotte felt blood rush to her head. Mazie was curious about her mom and this was a challenge.

"We can talk about this at home," Charlotte said, keeping her voice even.

Fig glanced at Charlotte before saying, "I'd like to hear about your mom, Mazie. If that's all right with your aunt."

Charlotte bit her lip. "My sister—Lauren—died of a drug overdose when Mazie was a baby."

Mazie's eyes dropped to her lap. "I don't remember her and I don't know who my father is. That's about all I know."

"I'm so sorry for you and your family, Mazie."

Mazie's voice rose. "No one ever even says her name. Whenever my grandparents are talking about her and I walk in the room, they change the subject." She turned to face the river. "It makes her—I don't know—deader."

"Come here, sweetie," Charlotte said, reaching for her wrist to pull her onto her lap. This was a gamble. Mazie might curl up like a kitten or stiffen like a block of ice. This time, Mazie slumped against her shoulder.

"Sweetheart. I know it feels like it happened a long, long time ago, but to Nana and Pop and me, it feels like yesterday. It hurts so much that it's hard to talk about. But you're right. We do need to talk and we will. I promise."

"You're just saying that. Is everyone afraid it's hereditary or something? That I'm going to be an addict like her?"

Fig was watching intently.

"No! No, of course not," Charlotte said. "But to be honest, Mazie. All grown-ups are afraid that the kids they love will take drugs." She was buying time. Hoping some pearl of wisdom would come to her. She wasn't prepared. She turned to face her niece. "When you get into your teens somebody—maybe an older student—will probably offer you some pills and tell you they're fun or will make you feel silly or happy."

"You mean high."

"Yeah. High." Charlotte frowned, feeling out of her depth. "It might be hard to say no."

Mazie snorted in disgust. "No, it wouldn't. I'm not that stupid. I'd never take drugs."

Charlotte floundered. "But—but what if they said, 'If you take these, you can be in our club, or come to our party?'"

Mazie cocked her head at an angle that asked, What do you take me for? "You mean cave to peer pressure? Trust me, I wouldn't."

"Great," Charlotte said, patting Mazie's knee and heaving a sigh of relief. "What a wise girl you are, Maze. Now. Let's get back to work." She started to get up.

Fig crossed one leg over the other. He was frowning. "May I weigh in, Charlotte?"

She shrugged.

"Mazie. I believe you are immune to peer pressure in the way most people think of it. And that's excellent."

Mazie nodded smugly.

"But before we bring this discussion to a close, can you tell me who's the smartest, coolest boy in your science class?"

"A.J. Definitely A.J."

"So, what if you're taking, say, chemistry in a couple of years and A.J., who is your lab partner now, invites you to go see *Star Wars Thirteen*."

"There isn't a *Star Wars Thirteen*."

Fig laughed. "Trust me, there will be. He has two tickets to a secret, private premier, an uncut, underground version that he got from his cousin's friend's neighbor who plays tennis with the film editor."

Mazie sat up. "That would be so cool!"

"I know. And as the top chemistry student in the whole school, A.J.'s distilled a special formulation that makes you see the ocean moon of Kef Bir in the Endor system in 3D without the dorky glasses. The formula is top secret of course, but he invites you to experience it with him."

Mazie gave Fig an open-mouthed stare. "No glasses? Do you think there could ever be something like that?"

"Mazie!" Charlotte grabbed Mazie's knee and shook it, then turned on Fig with a horrified stare.

He shrugged. "That's a different kind of peer pressure, Mazie. Taking that formula would be really, really dangerous and—" He leaned forward until he'd locked onto Mazie's eyes. "—and utterly STUPID." He sat back and frowned. "Any pill or medicine—or a top-secret formulation made by the smartest guy you know—needs to undergo years of testing and retesting before it's safe for human use, otherwise it could irreparably damage your brain and your body."

Mazie dropped her chin and mumbled, "Yeah."

Fig continued. "You readily agree, Mazie, that taking drugs to be cool is stupid. But do you also see that it's just as dangerous to take drugs out of curiosity or as part of an unauthorized science experiment?" He raked his finger through his hair and sighed gravely. "Do you understand what I'm saying?"

Mazie nodded.

He continued. "When I was in school I always wanted to be the best student. I wanted to know everything and learn it faster than my classmates. So, one night before a really important law exam I took a pill to stay awake—just over-the-counter stuff. But when that wasn't enough, I took two. I studied all night and when I went to class I was so shaky and exhausted I didn't do very well. After that, I was never tempted to use drugs again. My point is, Mazie, we're all vulnerable."

He turned to Charlotte. "Mazie and I are curious to find out what's just beyond the horizon, but we're not very good at following rules we don't fully understand or agree with."

Mazie wrinkled her nose. "But being curious is good."

"Not if it leads you into danger," Charlotte said.

Mazie chewed on her thumbnail.

Fig said, "Ben Franklin wanted to demonstrate that lightning was static electricity, so he rigged a kite and flew it into a storm cloud, which was dangerous enough, but then he touched the metal key he'd attached to the string. Zap! In his drive to discover new things, he put himself in real danger. Just think," he said, nudging Mazie. "If he'd been electrocuted then, we might all be wearing red coats and saying *brilliant* and *bloody hell* all the time."

Mazie threw back her head and laughed. "Nana would love that."

For a while they sat quietly, absorbing all that had been said.

Finally, Fig said, "When I was about six, I made a parachute out of a bed sheet and jumped off the garage roof because I was convinced I'd float to the ground." He wiggled his left foot. "This ankle still aches sometimes. Another time, I burned a hole in my mother's tablecloth with a magnifying glass. She was not pleased."

"Mazie tried to screw a ketchup bottle into a lamp socket to see if it would light up," Charlotte said, poking Mazie in the ribs.

Mazie giggled. "I did?"

Charlotte hugged Mazie while mouthing a silent, thank you, to Fig over her shoulder.

Mazie got up to stretch. "So, the moral of your story—your stories—is that no one's too smart to do stupid stuff. Even me."

He smiled. "Even you. And remember, it's good to learn from our mistakes, but it's a lot less painful to learn from other people's."

"Like my mom's," Mazie said.

'Yes," Charlotte whispered. "And you know what? If your mom was here today, I know she'd tell you the same thing."

"Can I ask you stuff about my mom? I can't ask Nana. It just makes her cry."

"Of course. It will make me cry too, but don't let that stop you." Charlotte sighed and got to her feet. "Off you go. Back to the meadow."

Fig said, "Just remember, Mazie, people like us are born watchers. That's how we learn. If you keep your eyes open and think things through step-by-step, you'll live to be a hundred."

"Like you?"

He smiled. "One can only hope."

When Mazie had disappeared down the path, Charlotte turned to Fig with wide eyes. "That was intense. She doesn't usually engage like that. She's so hard to reach and quick to judge."

Fig's frowned. "She can spot ambiguity, injustice and hypocrisy a mile away. I suppose this makes her seem a bit contrary—disrespectful even. But she's just trying to make sense of a world that's full of contradictions."

On the drive home, Mazie tested Charlotte's promise.

"Aunt Charlotte, what do you think my mom would be doing if she hadn't died?"

"Being proud of her daughter, I know that," Charlotte said. "And I think she'd be running some sort of business—a café, maybe."

"Like the Farmer's Daughter?"

"Yeah, like that. It'd be called Lauren's Table and you'd help out after school and in the summers. She was a smart cookie."

"Then why did she take drugs?"

Charlotte shook her head. "I don't know. A lot of the kids she used with are just fine today, but once she got started, she just couldn't stop. Maybe there was a gene involved."

She regretted this immediately.

Mazie leaned her forehead against the window and retreated into herself. "I knew it," she moaned. "I'm doomed."

"No. No, honey, I didn't mean—. You're not doomed. You're not your mom. She didn't like school like you do. I think she just kind of gave up. We all loved her and we adore you, but you're not like her at all. She wanted excitement more than anything. She was reckless. You're observant and careful. You'll choose your path carefully. You won't let bad things happen."

Mazie gnawed on her thumbnail.

"I mean it, Maze. Realizing that drug addiction is real is like knowing there are hazards in the road. Knowledge is like armor." She swerved around a deep pothole and laughed. "Case in point. Pretty skillful, that maneuver, eh?"

Mazie wasn't going to smile. "I wish my mom'd had a friend like Fig."

Charlotte's eyes begin to sting. "He would have liked your mum." Honestly, she wasn't sure about that, but maybe. "After she died, all of us, Nana, Pop and me, we kept wondering what we could have done to stop her—to save her. I think we still do sometimes. Nana regrets that she didn't send her to a boarding school or to rehab sooner. Pop regrets that he let her quit soccer and Girl Scouts."

"And you?"

"Me?" She felt a lump form in her throat. "I—I could have been a better sister."

"Were you mean to her?"

"Sometimes. When she was little and wanted to play with me and I pushed her away. When she started taking drugs and skipping school, I was really angry at her. I was ashamed when my classmates called her a druggie. There are a lot of things I should have done."

"Me too."

"You? You were just a baby."

Mazie's chin began to quiver. "I cried too much."

"Oh honey, no! You were a wonderful, sweet little girl!"

Charlotte turned on her blinker and turned into a side street. She turned off the engine and pulled Mazie into her arms. "Come here, sweetie. Tell me what you're thinking."

"N-nana says I c-cried a-all n-night."

"Of course, you did, because that's what babies do."

"But I made my mom tired and that's when she s-started using again. I heard Nana and Pop talking. It was m-my f-fault. She should n-never have h-had me!"

"Whoa, whoa, Maze." Charlotte gripped her shoulders tightly. "Look at me." Mazie raised her eyes. Her lashes were clumped into wet spikes. "You, my darling, were absolutely, positively the very, very best thing that ever happened to your mum. She said so a million times. She was in a very dark place before you came along. It was because of you— only because of you—that she got clean and went back to school and got a job. She was clean for a whole year. It was really, really hard for her, but she loved you that much. She wanted to go to rehab because of you."

"But she never made it."

Charlotte wiped Mazie's cheek with her thumbs. "Your mom stayed on this earth longer because she wanted to be your mom more than anything. Don't ever doubt that. Ever, ever. Promise?"

Mazie nodded.

Charlotte reached into the glove compartment and handed Mazie a napkin.

"You know what?" she said, starting up the engine. "There's nothing that excites my sweet tooth more than a good cry. How about we stop at The Farmer's Daughter for two ginormous peanut butter cookies? We'll even eat them before dinner."

By mid-July, Mazie had become fully freckled and half feral. She was seldom without her bug net and mayonnaise jar. She often forgot her cell phone and used her iPad only to identify insects.

"Left untreated, boredom is a kind of liberation," Fig pointed out to Charlotte on a midsummer morning. "Look at her."

And true to her word, she helped the crew or Charlotte until noon, then roamed the island until it was time to go home. Prince orbited her like a dependable little moon, running ahead, then circling back to hurry her along and keeping her in his sights at all times.

Fig took a keen interest in Mazie's insect obsession.

"Look at her," he kept saying. "The bugs line up to be counted when they see her coming. I'm certain I didn't have this many before she arrived."

He bought her a field notebook and a clipboard to record her findings and lent her his magnifying glass. During her free afternoons, Mazie found many reasons to knock on Fig's screen door and regale him with her newest discovery. At first, Charlotte put this down to Fig's extraordinary kindness and patience but soon came to realize he truly shared Mazie's fascination for six-legged creatures.

One hot afternoon, Charlotte and Mazie ate their sandwiches on the dock with their feet dangling into the cool water.

"You'll be thirteen soon," Charlotte pointed out. "Any plans? Wishes?"

"I don't want a party if that's what you're hinting at."

"I'm not planning one if that's what you're hinting at. But there must be something you'd like. A new bug net maybe?" Charlotte suggested.

Mazie dipped the net into the water and caught something, examined it and let it go. "No. This one's fine." She sighed then. "I can't think of anything I want except to find a Wood-Nymph, *Eudryas grata*. It's a beautiful moth. I don't know how it gets such beautiful black and white wings when the caterpillar looks like a pile of bird poop."

"Look here!" Charlotte said, pointing to a white blob on a dock board. "I found one. Happy Birthday!"

"That *is* bird poop." Mazie laughed, splashing water on Charlotte.

"Hey!" Charlotte said, splashing back. Mazie lost her balance and grabbed Charlotte's arm as she fell, pulling Charlotte into the river with her. They came up sputtering and laughing.

Their squeals brought the crew to the river. Harp kicked off his boots and ran down the walk to cannonball off the raft. Kiza, Martin and Hector followed, shouting their delight in several languages. Fig soon appeared on the porch with a pile of towels.

Mazie discovered a cardinal nesting in the eaves of the porch. For several weeks after, the porch became off-limits. She made signs:

QUIET ZONE!
Don't slam this door!!!!
2 3 4! eggs!
1, 2, 3, 4 chicks!

While the chicks grew their pinkish feathers, FDUs—Frequent Daily Updates—were relocated to Fig's thinkin' log. One day Mazie showed him two spiders she was trying to identify.

Fig studied the captives at the bottom of the jar. "I've never seen anything like these."

"Me neither!" Mazie fumed. "My new app gave me three different guesses—but none are right. I've looked in every book and every website." She puffed out her cheeks. "Maybe I should just stick to insects."

"They must be a really rare species," Charlotte offered.

"Or you've discovered a new one entirely," Fig said. "*Acrachnid mazeii*, they'll call it."

"It would be *Araneae*. But Michigan has, like, 500 kinds of spiders. Too many to ever learn." She sighed theatrically. "Do you think that if I live long enough I can know everything about insects and spiders?"

"Impossible," Fig said. "Knowledge is expanding faster than any one person can learn it. That's one of the best things about living in the twenty-first century, I think," Fig said. "Besides, if you knew everything, then what would you do?"

For once, Mazie didn't have an answer. "I guess that would be pretty boring. But, remember, you said nothing is boring except the person who is bored."

"That's because, thank goodness, there's always something new to learn."

Mazie grinned. "So, I'll never run out of things to learn."

"I should think not, but if you keep trying, oh what an interesting and wonderful life you will have led."

One day was so cloudy that dusk arrived prematurely to the island. Charlotte was pushing the wheelbarrow back to the shed for the night and Harp, Hector, Martin and Kiza were putting their tools away when Mazie came out of the undergrowth completely winded.

"Look what I caught!"

The men wiped their brows and stretched their aching backs as she passed the bug jar among them. They nodded at the black beetles inside, showing just enough interest to be polite, but not enough to encourage a long, detailed lecture that would delay their trip home to dinner and their families.

"I found them in the tall grass along the bank," she was saying. "Do you have them in Africa and Mexico?"

Hector looked closer and scratched his head. "I don't know."

"Most people call them fireflies or lightning bugs because their bodies light up."

"Ah! *Luciérnagas? Si!*" Hector nodded. "Yes. We have. Very beautiful in the night."

Kiza nodded. "They are in Congo, too."

Mazie ran toward the porch to shout at Fig through the screened door.

Charlotte called after her. "Mazie, don't bother him. We need to go."

Fig had been working from home lately and didn't discourage Mazie's interruptions nearly enough in Charlotte's opinion.

"I'm not bothered," he said, coming onto the porch in jeans and another blue oxford shirt rolled above the elbow. "What captives have you got there?"

Mazie thrust her jar above her head like a trophy. "Fireflies! But they aren't flies at all. They're bioluminescent beetles. That's why you should call them *Lampyridae*. And I'm going to let them go."

"I did not know fireflies were beetles," he said.

"Really?" Mazie squinted up through her bangs. "I thought you would know that."

"I'm flattered, but there's a lot I don't know." He bent low to peer through the glass with a solemn frown. "Rather disappointing in the looks department, don't you think?"

"Why?"

"I thought they'd look more like Tinker Bell." Then he brightened. "Wait. That one definitely has a green dress and a wand."

Mazie rolled her eyes. "Ha-ha. People believe all kinds of stupid stuff about insects." She peered into the jar again. "Did you know every insect has just one Latin name used by entomologists all over the world? I bet you didn't know that either."

"Now there's where you're wrong. I learned that when I was about your age."

"Well, I bet you didn't know you have a Latin name too. *Ficus* is the genus of the fig tree."

"Really? Fascinating," he said.

Mazie shrugged. "Yes, and '*Lampein*' is Greek for 'shine,' like a lamp. We should all stay until it's dark and watch them light up."

Behind her, Harp and the crew were hurrying toward the raft.

Harp waved to Charlotte as he pushed off from the dock. "Don't wait dinner. I have a softball game."

Fig took a seat on the top step of the porch while Mazie continued her lecture. "There's stuff inside their abdomens and tails that give off light when they combine."

"Bioluminescence, like you said. I know about that too."

"Right. Then you do know a few things about bugs." She hesitated before continuing. "If you were my age, we might be friends."

"I thought we were friends already."

"Yeah, I guess." Mazie sank heavily onto the top step next to Fig as if her thoughts were too weighty to allow more activity. "It's kind of weird, you know." She shrugged. "My generation is mostly being raised by neurotic Millennials younger than you, while I'm being raised by Baby Boomers. And I'm spending my entire summer hanging out with people old enough to be my parents." She sighed. "When I'm with kids my age, I feel like a time traveler sometimes."

Fig nodded. "My parents were old enough to be my grandparents, so I think I know what you mean."

"Did you have any friends in middle school?"

"Yes," he said slowly. "But I felt like a spectator, not a participant."

Mazie set the jar down and stared at Fig in complete amazement. "I know! Exactly!"

"Like I said, Maze, we're two peas."

Charlotte slung her bag over her shoulder. "Come on, kiddo. Get a wiggle on."

"Can't we stay until my *Lampyridae* light up?"

Fig smiled. "Great idea. I have enough chicken salad for three and I'd love to watch the firefl—I mean *Lampyridae* light up." He raised his eyebrows and tipped his head to one side. "Harp won't home for dinner."

"Can we, Aunt Charlotte? Pleeeease?"

"We need get home," she said reflexively.

Fig cleared his throat and said in a stern, gravelly voice, "Ms. Adair, I believe your FDU is several days overdue."

"We had one day before yesterday."

"Be that as it may, Ms. Adair, FDUs are ATCD."

"What's that?"

"—at the customer's discretion. I guess you missed the fine print."

Charlotte laughed. "I should have had a lawyer look at it."

Fig got up and gestured toward the Adirondack chairs. "Come. Sit. We'll have an FDU ATCD ASAP, very business-like, but with chicken salad."

"All right. Can I help?"

"Just sit. Mazie can help me inside."

A few minutes later the three of them were eating chicken salad and watermelon at the porch table.

When Mazie and Prince left in search of more fireflies, Fig brought out two glasses of white wine.

"I know you prefer white."

"As long as it's cheap too," she said. "I can't take the pressure of another bottle you've been saving."

As the sky darkened and the three imprisoned *Lampyridae* began twinkling in their jar, Mazie took them to the dock and released them.

Charlotte said, "I've wanted to thank you for that talk you had with Mazie about drugs. I never thought about it quite that way. My family beats ourselves up fairly regularly for my sister's death. You made me realize how complex people's motivations are."

Fig nodded. "Stoics think they can control their use with their superior willpower. Thrill seekers are attracted to the danger. Depressives medicate themselves. But people like Mazie and I think we're too smart to become addicted. It was curiosity and hubris, not peer pressure, that drove me to do risky things when I was young."

"Like parachuting off garage roofs and taking uppers?"

"Exactly. Stupidity knows no bounds."

"What else did you do?"

Fig drummed his fingers on the arm of the chair as he thought. "Back in college, I asked a woman friend of mine to test my hypothesis that sex without an emotional attachment between consenting adults could still be satisfying."

"And?"

"Inconclusive."

"Because?"

"When I pronounced our experiment a success, she burst into tears and confessed that she'd had feelings for me all along and hoped I'd develop some for her. I was annoyed at her deceit at first. What an arrogant prick I was. Later, I realized my 'research' had really hurt her. So, that taught me to be a lot more careful with people's feelings."

After a long pause, Charlotte nodded.

"A penny for your thoughts," he said.

She shook her head.

"Regretting a one-night stand?"

She gave a wan smile. "No. Not that."

"But regretting, nevertheless."

"Mazie thinks her mom overdosed because she was a fussy baby."

Fig blew out a long breath. "Poor kid. Guilt's a slow poison."

Charlotte set down her glass. "It was a delicious dinner, Fig. Thank you. I need to get her home."

"Are you all right, Charlotte?"

"I'm fine."

20

THE IMPOSTOR

Bees and plants have an understanding. Says the flower to the bee, "I will give you my sweet nectar." Says the bee to the flower, "I will carry your pollen." But some plants don't play by the rules. A Puerto Rican bee orchid looks and smells so much like a female bee that the male bee inadvertently pollinates the flower during "mating." A hungry wasp can be fooled into pollinating a flower that smells like cabbage—expecting to find a tasty caterpillar there—but it will find none. The red trillium emits the odor of rotten meat that tricks a fly into laying her eggs among its petals. The fly's offspring go hungry, but the trillium gets pollinated.

Fig called to Charlotte from the edge of the meadow. "If you have a minute, I think I found your mystery woman."

"Elena Lewis?" Charlotte patted the last showy goldenrod into place and followed him toward the house. "She's the wife of a Russian oligarch, right? Plotting to invade our country using Eurasian plants."

Fig laughed. "Well. I couldn't find an Elena Lewis," he said, "unless she lives in a nursing facility in Albuquerque or owns a nail salon named Elena's Beauty Bar in Spokane. So, I dug around in the Michigan Horticultural Association website—the industry trade and lobbying group—wholesale growers, retail nurseries, landscapers."

"I looked there first," Charlotte said. "They don't publish their membership list."

"I know, but I found something else."

In Fig's study, Elena smiled up at them from his laptop screen, holding a golf club and wearing a very short skirt and a baseball cap.

"That's her!" Charlotte said.

"Actually, that's Elena Scott playing in an MHA foursome at a golf outing for the children's hospital. "I found her when I searched by just her first name. I also found this."

He brought up the staff directory. "Elena L. Scott's an MHA employee working in Lansing."

Charlotte leaned against the desk. "She said she was consulting. Maybe she left recently and the website hasn't been updated."

"She probably didn't want you to know who she was. When I called the number, her voice message said she was out of the office, but would return messages. I didn't leave one."

Charlotte glared at Elena's face. "Did she mention she was out increasing her bandwidth?"

"Bandwidth?"

She shook her head. "Never mind. Thank you, Fig. It's odd that the MHA wanted to send someone to our meeting, but it's shocking that she came undercover."

He shut the laptop and walked her to the porch.

"This is my fault," she said, putting her gloves on. "I scared somebody when I mentioned that my lawyer-client said there are grounds for a lawsuit. One of our members must have alerted the MHA. I'm guessing Phyllis Oosterbaan. Her family runs a huge wholesale greenhouse operation. She's feeling threatened."

"She wanted the MHA to see what you're up to."

"I guess."

He pushed his hands into his pockets and looked past her. "I've been rethinking this lawsuit."

"Really?" she asked, surprised by the prick of disappointment she felt. She had enjoyed discussing legal strategies with him, even if they were only hypothetical. "What changed your mind?"

"I haven't changed my mind about the need for a lawsuit—just about suing the State of Michigan—which they richly deserve. But after some digging into case law, I suspect that would take years."

Charlotte smiled. "I suppose. But are you in a hurry?"

Fig looked down at his shoes. "I suppose I am."

She laughed. "You? In a hurry?"

He shrugged. "One hates to be too predictable."

"One does, does one?" she said, still smiling.

At the July meeting of WILHA., Elena walked in with Phyllis Oosterbaan, Charlotte noted. This time she wore skinny jeans and a sporty red blouse fitted loosely over a revealing camisole. Paired with teal cowboy boots, Elena looked ready for line dancing at a country bar.

Charlotte was enjoying this mental image immensely when Katie sat down. "What's so funny?"

"Nothing." Charlotte pursed her lips.

"You were laughing."

"I was not."

"Were too."

"Shh."

Barb VanderLee opened the meeting by thanking Charlotte for her letter to the Saskawan Public Schools, noting that there had been no response to their concerns about the number of Bradford pears and barberry bushes planted in schoolyards across the city.

Katie pushed a slip of paper toward Charlotte. *Wow! Boots and boobs! Did Cowgirl Barbie ride in on her pink pony?*

Charlotte gave Katie her best imitation of Mazie's death ray but barely managed to keep a straight face.

At the end of the table, Barb was saying. ". . . hope all of you felt heard last month. Before we begin, I want to add a personal note. I'm very concerned about the state's slowness in banning plants that are so clearly damaging. I also understand what's at stake for those of us who make a living selling invasives to customers who demand them— including my own store. But I want to say publicly that VanderLee Gardens would stop selling any harmful plant today if my competitors would do the same." She glanced quickly at Phyllis. "That's why the state should act. That's all."

Charlotte raised her hand, turning to Olivia. "I'd like to thank Olivia again for sharing her college research with us last month. You deserved an A on that research paper. You discovered how slow Michigan has been to ban invasive plants compared to our neighbors. I've been thinking a lot about what you told us."

Elena listened to this stone-faced.

Olivia smiled. "Thanks. I actually want to add something that might be significant. May I?"

Barb said, "Yes, of course."

"After I graduated, I got an internship at Mid-Michigan Land Preservation Partners. They had a grant to do an inventory of invasive species in several counties with the idea of prioritizing them for a Weed Risk Assessment."

Portia put down her coffee. "You mean to get them banned?"

"Right. But before we got started, our director pulled the plug. We were stunned. The rumor was that someone had threatened to sue us, but no one knew who—at least not officially."

"And unofficially?" Portia asked.

"Everybody figured it was the horticultural lobby."

"The MHA?" Katie asked.

Phyllis whispered something to Elena, who shook her head. They were hopeless at spying, Charlotte thought.

"I don't doubt it," Portia was saying. "Their members expect the MHA to protect their profits—ecosystems be damned."

Charlotte looked toward Barb. "I did a bit of research about the MHA this month. I'd like to share it."

Barb nodded.

Charlotte said, "The MHA has lobbyists in Lansing to keep legislators informed on issues related to the industry, but also apparently to keep them in line. I suspect that if a legislator gets too interested in banning barberries or Bradford pears he or she might find their opponent's campaign chests greatly enhanced in the next election."

Barb frowned. "I don't know, Charlotte. I've been a member of the MHA for decades. The idea that they would threaten environmental groups with lawsuits or intimidate legislators is hard to believe. Let's not jump to conclusions."

There were murmurs of agreement around the table.

Elena leaned forward, tenting her manicured fingers. "Ladies, let me unpack this for you. All of us who value our jobs in this industry must insist on a vigorous, peer-reviewed process based in science. We can't allow a few zealots to cast out plants with high ROIs, i.e. 'return on investment.' Our livelihood depends on a robust horticultural industry. I applaud the MHA for partnering with state agencies to look out for our interests."

Charlotte started to respond, but Nicky beat her to it.

"Sure. Maybe some members are getting rich selling invasive plants, but it sure isn't me. I have too many scruples for that. The actual 'ROI' of these exotic plants is the destruction of habitats, decimation of pollinators and, ultimately, the collapse of the food web. The cost is incalculable and frankly terrifying." Nicky jabbed her finger at Elena. "You want science? That's science."

Elena smiled. "You misunderstand me, Nicky. The MHA is on your—our—side. To be successful, we must pull together. Hyper-local, fringe groups can't be allowed to threaten the livelihood of thousands of hardworking Michiganders. It's in the best interest of the majority—."

"Stop there, Elena. I've heard enough," Charlotte said, opening her laptop. Barb looked shocked at Charlotte's interruption. "I'm sorry, Barb. I'll explain. Since our last meeting, I've learned something about our guest." She turned toward Elena. "I wonder if you could remind us again of your last name?"

Phyllis cheeks turned from pink to blotchy purple. The woman had no poker face whatsoever.

Elena blinked several times. "Lewis," she said.

"Then how do you explain this?" Charlotte asked, pivoting her laptop so it faced the group. Elena's face smiled back at them.

"I believe this is you, Elena Scott, Vice-President of Marketing and Community Relations at the Michigan Horticultural Association."

Barb's eyes widened. "Is this true, Elena?"

The whole group stared.

Elena shrugged. "Lewis is my maiden name."

"You came here to *spy* on us? For the MHA?" Barb asked.

Elena's expression hardened. "I don't answer to you." She reached for her bag and stood up.

"Hold on," Barb said. "You can't just waltz out of here now. I have more to say to you."

Nicky, who had been seated by the door, moved into the doorway, crossing her arms like a bouncer. Elena rolled her eyes, but she didn't move.

Barb closed her eyes and sighed before she spoke. "I think I speak for all of us when I say that any woman who works in our industry, including you, is welcome here at WILHA. However, there is and will always be an understanding that we are women of goodwill, offering our mutual support—and, damn it, that we are who we say we are!"

No one moved.

Finally, Portia spoke. "I'm curious, Elena. The 'fringe group' you spoke of that is threatening the livelihood of thousands is us? I wasn't aware we had such influence."

Elena pressed her lips together, eyeing the door and probably calculating whether she could take Nicky down. Nicky reached slowly into her back pocket, took out her wallet and produced her green and gold MHA membership card.

"When you get back to the office, Elena, do me a favor. Give this to your boss." Then she ripped the card to shreds and dropped the pieces into Elena's bag.

"We're well rid of you." Elena scoffed. Then, with a toss of her blonde hair, she turned to face the table. "You, my friends, are like flies on a bull elephant. But a word to the wise, if you continue down this path, you will find more roadblocks than you ever imagined. You ladies are way out of your league."

Nicky took a step closer. "Was that a threat?"

Charlotte held her breath.

"Let's just say, it doesn't pay to pick a fight with the MHA." Elena forced a smile. "Consider that some friendly advice." Then she elbowed past Nicky and disappeared down the hall.

As the sound of her boots receded, the room erupted with a mixture of anger and excited chatter. A few members followed her, Charlotte noticed, including Phyllis.

Barb called the meeting back to order.

Portia shook her head, chuckling. "Okay, *now* I'm shocked. The MHA actually sent a spy! What made you suspect her, Charlotte?"

"When I got to my car last month, I found this note on my windshield." She passed it around to *tsks* and looks of incredulity.

Barb smiled. "I guess our letters haven't been entirely ignored. Would anyone like to claim authorship of Charlotte's note?"

Olivia raised her hand. "It was me. Back when I was writing my research paper, I called the MHA to get a statement. The woman called herself Elena. She pretty much told me what she told us today. I remembered that name."

Katie couldn't contain herself. "Just think, guys, the MHA sent in a plant. An invasive plant! Ha! They're scared— of little old us."

Charlotte spent that afternoon planting lady ferns under a trio of new dogwoods by the back patio while giving Fig a detailed rundown of the drama at the WILHA meeting. He listened from the stone bench, one leg draped over the other stroking his chin, his foot juddering with irritation.

"Corporate espionage. That's pretty aggressive," he said.

"You should have heard her, Fig. She was so arrogant!"

"Your letters are making the MHA nervous."

"And I think Phyllis Oosterbaan invited her. Their greenhouse sells a ton of popular invasives and they supply both the city and the county. I suspect Phyllis complained to Elena who decided to see for herself. I can't imagine why the MHA feels we're a threat."

"They're vulnerable," Fig said. "They know most of your members advise clients not to buy some of the horticultural industry's most profitable products."

"I suppose. Native growers are getting a bigger share of the market these days—although I can't believe it's significant. She called us flies on a bull elephant and she's right. We're not much competition for juggernauts like Oosterbaan Greenhouses."

Fig's eyebrows shot up. "Big organizations with lawyers on retainer like to nip even little upstarts in the bud—so to speak. At the very least, Elena wanted to make sure you heard the industry's position."

Charlotte sighed. "She made it clear that the MHA would be watching us."

Fig took so long to respond that she thought he hadn't been listening. Finally, he said, "That might work in our favor. They know that consumers have concerns, like your member who runs the non-profit."

"Portia."

"She has a board of directors, employees and donors who wield influence and could embarrass the MHA. Elena's worried you and WILHA are just the tip of the iceberg."

"Maybe, but Portia feels vulnerable too. She says Davids don't slay Goliaths in the twenty-first century. And Nicky, another member, said she wasn't going to fight a battle she couldn't win, but then today she looked ready to head-butt Elena." Charlotte smiled at the memory.

"And you've said Barb VanderLee would like an excuse to stop selling invasives."

Charlotte stood up and brushed off her knees. "So, maybe the MHA *should* be nervous. They've been pulling strings for too long."

"But they haven't broken any laws—unless they're blackmailing bureaucrats or offering legislators bribes in dark alleys—which I doubt. If we haul them into court they'd send in a dozen lawyers and lobbyists to drown us in paperwork. Our case would be an uphill slog. No fun at all." He crossed his arms and sighed.

Charlotte rolled her eyes. "Fun? I should introduce you to my friend Katie. She's up for anything."

Fig seemed lost in thought. "They'd argue that lobbying is free speech. That they're just protecting their members. It would be hard to prove that any campaign contributions to state legislators are meant to discourage the Ag Department from outlawing invasive species or that Ag's lack of action is the result of MHA lobbying."

"Objection, your honor. That calls for speculation," Charlotte said.

"Exactly. They'd say they had nothing to do with the infamous Weed Risk Assessment. But if we looked closely, I bet we'd find the MHA's dirty fingerprints all over it."

She sat down next to him and took off her gloves. "So, doesn't that leave us with the demand side of the equation? I mean, maybe should we go after the city or county or the school district? Stop them from planting invasive species."

"Maybe."

"The way I see it," she continued, "the MHA answers only to its members, but schools answer to parents and cities have to answer to taxpayers and voters who might be more sympathetic to environmental concerns. It's the ear of regular citizens we're after, right?" She tilted her head back and sighed. She didn't know whether her fatigue was physical or mental.

She watched a pair of blue jays fly overhead and disappear into the tree canopy.

"I mean, people really care about the woods near their home and the nature trail behind their child's school, the trails where they bike or walk the dog. We have to convince them that city and county landscaping practices are threatening those places with thorny pear trees and bushes harboring Lyme ticks."

When she looked up, Fig's face had softened into a smile. "Nice opening, counselor. You think like a lawyer."

Charlotte laughed. "Then why do I feel like I'm losing my case—"

He looked puzzled. "What case is that?"

"—the one where I argue that I can't be your plaintiff."

"So, are you reconsidering?"

"No. I'll support you behind the scenes, but I can't put my name to a suit. I can't risk my business."

"I know." Fig drummed his fingers on his knee. "But after Ms. Lewis' stunt today, do you think any other members of your group might be interested?"

She wrinkled her nose. "I don't know. It's one thing to confront a spy, it's another to actually sue someone."

He picked up an acorn top and tossed it into the fire pit. "You're probably right."

Charlotte felt a prick of guilt. She enjoy discussing a hypothetical case with him, but it got his hopes up each time and then she dashed them again.

He interlaced his fingers behind his head and stretched to his full length. "You exposed a spy today. I wish I'd been there."

"You should have heard Barb VanderLee. 'We are women of goodwill—and, damn it, we are who we say we are!' And Nicky, blocking the doorway, ripping her membership card to shreds. They're my heroes."

"But you blew her cover."

"And you found her," she reminded him. "Yeah, the whole thing was a rush. We're all totally bad-ass!"

21

THE SWING

On the morning of Mazie's thirteenth birthday Prince and Fig met the raft wearing matching red bow ties and foil party hats.

"Ahoy there, birthday girl!" Fig shouted.

Mazie zapped Charlotte with her death ray. "I said I didn't want a party."

"I know nothing about this, honest," Charlotte said through a toothy grin. "But be polite, Maze, or I swear I'll throw you overboard right now."

At a hand signal from Fig, Prince rose up on his hind legs, turned three pirouettes, yipped twice and leaped into Mazie's arms, giving her face a thorough washing.

Mazie beamed. "You learned a new trick. Good boy. But your hat looks ridiculous."

"All the cool islanders are wearing them these days," Fig said, strapping one on Mazie and handing one to Charlotte.

"Now turn around," he said, gripping her shoulders.

"Do I have to bark too?" Mazie said, cringing.

"Hold still." He tied his handkerchief over her eyes.

"Ow. Are you trying to blind me?" she sputtered, trying unsuccessfully to hold a frown. "You know I hate surprises."

"I know nothing of the kind. In fact, your aunt told me 'Mazie adores surprises. Can't get enough of them.'"

"I didn't say that, Mazie. Honestly," Charlotte protested. "This is a surprise to me too."

Fig rubbed his hands together. "What kind of a birthday would it be without surprises?" He pushed her up the walk. "Off you go."

Kiza, Martin and Hector appeared at the corner of the house, laughing and elbowing each other.

"Is that the crew? Is everyone gawking at me or what?"

"I don't see anyone. Do you, Aunt Charlotte?"

"See who?" Charlotte said.

"I hear you, Kiza!" Mazie called out. "This is so lame."

In the clearing under the oaks, Charlotte was surprised to see Harp standing on a small platform about ten feet off the ground attached by a set of straps to the biggest of the island's white oaks. Harp grinned as he held on to two ropes as thick as Charlotte's wrists that were threaded through the ends of a wooden seat. She traced the ropes upward until they disappeared into the leafy canopy. Her mouth dropped open. The tallest swing she'd ever seen had somehow appeared in the clearing since yesterday.

Fig guided Mazie to the bottom of the ladder and loosened her blindfold so she could just see her feet.

"Climb on up. Harp's at the top."

"The top of what?"

"This very sturdy ladder." Harp said from above her, "Give me your hand."

"You're making me walk the plank?" she whined. "What did I ever do to you, Ficus?"

"Plenty," Fig said. "Up you go. Hup, two, three!"

Mazie felt her way slowly from one rung to the next. "You're trying to kill me, aren't you? Do you know any good lawyers? Because this is child abuse!"

Charlotte stepped closer to Fig and whispered, "When did you do this?"

"The crew did some moonlighting after you left. Harp's a skilled climber, as you know, and Kiza and Martin are naturals. Hector not so much, but he made the seat. Double overtime was on the table, but they all refused. Nice fellows, these."

"Harp said he was going climbing last night, but I never imagined he meant a tree," Charlotte said.

Mazie squealed as Harp pulled her from the last rung onto the small platform where he held her by her shoulders. She pulled off the blindfold and looked down.

"Holy crap! You're trying to murder me!"

Harp slipped the wooden seat under her.

"A swing? Are you kidding? I'm thirteen!"

Fig stepped back and pulled Charlotte out of the way.

Harp guided Mazie's hands to the ropes. "This swing could hold a baby elephant," he said. "Just hang on and you'll be safe. Ready?"

"Oh, m'God. Oh, m'God. Oh m'God . . ." Mazie chanted.

Fig hugged his shoulders, looking like he might burst with happiness. "No screaming allowed," he called up.

"I'm not a screamer," Mazie said.

Harp said, "Ready! Set! GO!"

Mazie dropped from the platform and flew in an arc that covered half the island. She almost disappeared into the canopy, mouth agape in a banshee scream before swinging back toward earth.

From the edge of the clearing, Kiza, Martin and Hector clapped and whooped. Prince tried to catch the swing but ended up just running in circles.

When the swing finally came to rest, Mazie dropped to her knees, panting. "Oh, m'God! Oh, m'God! That was so awesome!" She jumped up and ran to the bottom of the ladder. "You have to try it, Harp. But no screaming. Right Fig?"

After Harp let loose a Tarzan yodel, Kiza and Martin each took a turn. Their screams made Mazie collapse with laughter. But Hector refused to budge and Fig reminded everyone that he was "not built for flying" and needed to remain alive to sign their checks.

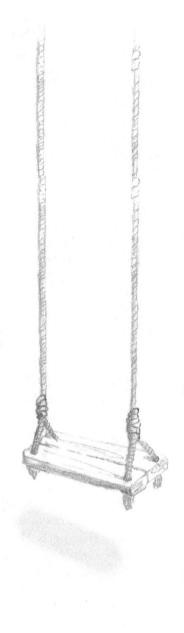

Then, everyone ganged up on Charlotte. Mazie claimed her screams were the loudest of all.

After chocolate cake and mint chip ice cream on the porch and the crew went to work, Fig brought out a pile of wrapped gifts for Mazie.

"What's all this?" Charlotte said, feigning disapproval. "You're spoiling her, Fig."

"I'm merely guiding her development. And besides, I have selfish motives. Dig in, Maze."

Inside, there was a heavy scrapbook with acetate page covers. "I'd like you to make me a scrapbook of all the insects you find on the island with labels for reference. Would you do that?"

"Where will I get the pictures?"

"Open the next package." Inside were two ink cartridges and a package of photo paper.

"You can print them here from your phone."

That night Charlotte thanked Harp for helping build the swing. "She loved it. And she's hard to please."

Harp shrugged. "What could I say? Fig paid us overtime," which she knew wasn't true.

22

A SECOND LOOK

The inability to distinguish red from green is a common form of color blindness. But many people with normal eyesight are said to be "green blind." They may live near woodlands filled with dozens of trees, shrubs, grasses, forbs and sedges, but they see only "woods." All vegetation is the same in their eyes. No wonder they derive so little joy from nature. Fortunately, green blindness is highly preventable. Given the right guidance, the human eye can learn to see the great diversity that Mother Nature offers. The experience can be eye-opening.

Fig came and went from the island on an unpredictable schedule. Charlotte watched him make his way across the river. Never in a hurry. Taking his own time. Often pausing in the middle to admire the view before taking up the rope again.

On weekdays, he was invariably dressed in a blue Oxford shirt (lightly starched and expertly pressed), creased gray trousers, a red or blue tie, polished wingtips with a navy or gray blazer folded over one arm. This was accessorized with a rather battered leather briefcase. She began to think of this as Look #1, Preppy Lawyer.

Look #2: Preppy Weekender included jeans that looked pressed, another blue Oxford shirt (rolled to the elbows) and a pair of polished loafers, often with no socks. When he appeared in Look #2, she assumed he was working from home.

One morning near the end of July Preppy Lawyer Fig appeared on the porch, but with a suitcase.

"Going somewhere?" she asked, coming from the shed.

He looked up from his phone. "Minnesota. But you can reach me on my cell if you have any questions. I'll be back in a few days."

"I have a few errands I can do near the airport. How about a lift?"

"I'll just call an Uber. Anyway, I'm taking the train. I'm not a flyer."

"I'll drop you at the station then."

"Now there's an offer I won't refuse."

She took off her gloves and joined him on the raft.

The fly fisherman was casting his line in graceful arcs from his usual spot near the landing. He waved. "Morning, Fig."

"Morning, Ronner. What's biting?"

He lifted a good-sized fish from a bucket. "Steelhead. Seven pounds. When I get it smoked I'll bring some over."

"I look forward to it."

In the truck, Fig put his suitcase between his feet and draped his coat over his knees.

"So, which is it? Fear of flying, or love of rail travel?"

"The former. When I was working for a real law firm, I flew a lot. But I was on the verge of panic all the time."

"How awful."

"I very nearly get religion at twenty-five thousand feet. I seek redemption. I humbly ask forgiveness for every transgression. I bargain with God, Jesus, the Buddha and the ancestors to deliver me from my imminent demise."

"Your prayers were answered," Charlotte pointed out.

"Perhaps, but something tells me the deities have begun to question the sincerity of my promises."

"Promises?"

"Opening an orphanage in Bangladesh. Selling my car and buying a bike. Becoming vegan. Curing cancer. Reversing climate change. The usual stuff." He grinned sheepishly. "So, my near-term strategy is to keep both feet on the ground."

After a pause, he continued. "Two things of note happened on my way home yesterday. On my walk to the parking garage, I saw city workers planting trees along the sidewalk. I asked them what kind they were and they said Norway maple. When I questioned their choice, they literally shrugged and said I could call the city. Honestly, Charlotte, I think I might do that. It's one thing to ignore invasive trees that are already here, it's another to plant more."

"The nerve of them!" she said, smiling. "And the second thing?"

"I'll show you. Turn here." Charlotte followed his directions to the First Presbyterian Church.

He said, "See how the entire front is planted with blazing star and purple coneflower and grasses."

"It's beautiful. A member of my WILHA group, Nicky Martinez, designed it. She supervised volunteers from the church to put it in about three years ago."

"You knew about this?" he said, looking crestfallen. "I've driven by dozens of times and never noticed it until yesterday. Isn't that odd?"

"Ah! Your reprogramming is complete." She gave her eyebrows a malevolent wiggle as she pulled back into traffic. "You won't need a Vulcan mind meld after all."

Fig laughed. "I prefer to think I've been enlightened." After another long, thoughtful pause, he said, "I've been doing more research." He saw her cringe. "What?"

"About a lawsuit again?"

He raised his hands and looked heavenward. "I can't help myself. It's my destiny."

"Uh-huh."

"People don't understand the threat of invasive plants."

She rolled her eyes. "Tell me about it."

"Well, first of all, we'd need to—"

"No. No," she laughed. "I don't literally want you to tell me about it." She pointed at her face. "See my eyes? Rolling. Rolling."

He crossed his arms over his chest. "Am I not paying you handsomely to listen to my needs? I've just spent good money for the eradication services of Adair Natural Landscaping and I don't want more marauding baobabs, or whatever, floating down the Hawthorn River and invading my island kingdom. I am merely protecting my considerable investment."

He had a point.

"So, am I your client, or are you my client?" she asked.

"I'll admit the water has become murky in that regard."

"And what did you say about paying me to listen to you? Would you pay me to let you sue someone on my behalf?"

"Fair question. I'm certainly not paying you enough to afford my legal services, so if you remain intransigent and I get desperate enough, who knows?" He caught her worried look and touched her wrist. "Charlotte. In all seriousness, I would never pressure you into anything that would jeopardize you financially."

This was comforting—as was the brief touch of his hand—very comforting indeed, but a lawsuit was still a crazy idea. "Thanks, but I can't afford to make enemies either. I'm sorry, Fig."

He raised a hand in surrender. "Okay. But you can still help with strategy, right?"

"Sure. I love that part."

He rubbed his hands together. "Okay. Hear me out."

She sighed. "Don't you have a train to catch?"

He glanced at his phone. "In fifteen minutes." He leaned closer. "You and I—the strategy team—need to make a list of species recognized by credible groups as invasive—the undisputed terrorists of the plant world—that are still being propagated and sold in Michigan. And, it would help our case if they are already illegal in at least one other Midwest state."

"That's easy." She pushed her bag toward him. "Feel around for a little spiral notebook."

Fig pulled out her copy of a *Field Identification Guide to Invasive Plants in Michigan's Natural Communities.*

"In the front, I wrote a list of the ones that are popular landscaping plants."

He ran his finger down her list.

"The starred ones are illegal in at least one neighboring state."

He read, "Barberry, oriental bittersweet and multiflora rose and amur honeysuckle, Bell's honeysuckle—actually two . . . no, *five* kinds of honeysuckle. Good God, Charlotte," his mouth dropping. "This is exactly what we need."

She smiled. "I think Bradford pear will be added if they ever publish another edition. It's spreading from the southeast."

"I'd argue that they're a public nuisance—like a belching smokestack or a death metal band who practices all night in the house next door." Fig tapped a finger on his temple. "Now, if I only had a plaintiff."

"Poor you," she said, pushing out her lower lip.

"Mark my word," he said. "I'll find one."

She turned into the Amtrak station and parked. Fig draped his coat over his arm, smoothed out a wrinkle and patted the breast pocket, checking for his ticket. Just a few weeks ago she had thought him gaunt and frankly odd-looking. How had she overlooked how elegantly he moved, or the laugh lines creasing his cheeks or his sculpted jawline?

He opened his door and put one foot on the pavement. Then he leaned toward her with a warm half-smile.

"Goodbye Charlotte," he said.

She gripped the steering wheel, afraid if she didn't she would reach for him. "Have a nice trip, Fig."

"I'll be back in a few days. I can't be sure when." He scanned the station before turning back to her. As usual, he was in no hurry. He pointed at the entrance. "Look there. See how they've planted black-eyed Susans around the door and that other little yellow fellow—the one you planted in the meadow?"

"Coreopsis."

"I noticed them as soon as we pulled up. A year ago, I wouldn't have given them a second look. Isn't it interesting the way we ascribe beauty to what we value? Or perhaps we value what we understand—when we know the full truth of something."

Had he read her thoughts?

When she didn't answer, he asked, "You don't agree, Charlotte?"

She nodded, thinking how much she wanted to kiss his cheek and tell him how nice he looked in his Panama hat.

"Yes, Fig. I know exactly what you mean."

He closed the door, smiled at her through the open window and lifted his hat. "I'll see you in a few days."

She watched him stride across the parking lot. At the station door, he bent to touch a yellow petal.

Back at the landing she boarded the raft. In the middle of the river, she stopped to look back. Her life split here, at this cool, silvery frontier. Behind her was the landing, Harp, the farm and the entire known world. Ahead lay the uncharted territory of the island—and of the man himself. Two lives strung together by a thin rope and a tiny raft.

AUGUST

Cardinal Flower *Lobelia cardinalis*

23

MAROONED, DAY ONE

*"I understand how a flower and a bee might slowly become,
either simultaneously or one after the other, modified
and adapted in the most perfect manner to each other.
— Charles Darwin, 1859*

During the first week of August, the remnants of a second gulf hurricane—Juanita—spun up the Mississippi and came to rest over Michigan. Though work on the island came to a halt, the restoration of Fig's island was nearly done . This troubled Charlotte greatly since she still had no new clients lined up.

While Fig was in Minneapolis, Charlotte created a budget for her tree nursery in front of the farmhouse. She even drove by Gloria Grosnickle's to see if she'd added the other raised rose bed she wanted. The woman was in her front yard happily sprinkling powered poison on her roses, bees, caterpillars and any other six or eight-legged creature that happened by. Charlotte hit the accelerator before Gloria could flag her down. She'd rather starve.

In the meantime, she designed two additional seating areas she hoped Fig might be enticed to add along his new path, although he seemed to be perfectly happy with his simple thinkin' log.

After a week at her desk, she had a serious case of claustrophobia. Surely the new plantings along the swollen riverbank deserved an inspection. Mazie was upstairs reading. Harp was watching YouTube videos about inflatable kayaks.

"I'm going to the island," Charlotte announced.

"Is Fig back?" Harp asked.

"No. I just want to make sure everything's still above water."

"Careful. There's another storm coming."

She gave him a kiss. "I won't be long."

Mazie came halfway down the stairs still in her pajamas and carrying the Ray Bradbury book Fig had loaned her.

"Can I come?"

"Sure, but Fig's not back."

"Oh. Never mind."

"I'll be back in an hour, two at most."

Mazie was shuffling back upstairs.

"Don't burn the house down," Charlotte called out.

"Aw gees!" Mazie said. "You spoil all my fun!"

The raft was slick and Charlotte struggled to keep her footing as the swollen river pulled on the raft. A gust of wind lifted the branches of the maple near the house as distant thunder rolled in from Lake Michigan.

A light glowed in Fig's kitchen. Apparently, he was home early. She had no reason to knock on the door or even to say hello. There was no Frequent Daily Update to deliver. She'd do a quick inspection and be on her way.

When she reached the island, rain began pelting her parka. Fig wasn't in the kitchen, but when she passed the open door, she could hear him coughing somewhere in the house.

She headed toward the thinkin' log where spikes of great blue lobelia had come into bloom near the water's edge. The morning gloom only enhanced their vibrant lavender-blue spikes and rain-glossed leaves. The blue-flag iris and cardinal flowers she'd planted were holding their own too. The new boulders along the bank had done their job.

She continued along the path. Behind the house, she checked the dogwoods which had taken full advantage of their daily drenching by growing several new sprigs.

When the wind died down and she heard Fig coughing again. It sounded desperate. On the pretense of inspecting the elderberries, she squatted below the window of his study to listen. He was gasping for breath.

She ran to the front porch. Prince barked through the screen.

"Fig?" she called out. "Are you okay?"

He was doubled over on the couch. He lifted his hand and motioned her in.

She pushed the door open and headed to the kitchen. "I'll get you some water."

His face was ashen and his hair was matted to his forehead. He was unshaven and wearing the same plaid bathrobe he'd worn the day they met.

He gave a halfhearted nod between coughs. "Sorry. I've caught . . . a bug. . . and not the. . . beneficial . . . pollinator kind. . . ." He pointed at the kitchen. "Coffee's . . . in the carafe."

His lips were blue.

She handed him the water. "Fig. You *really* don't look good. Can I call your doctor? Or drive you to the ER?"

He shook his head and took a drink.

"But your color. Are you cold? Can I get you a blanket? I could start a fire in the grate."

He exhaled and managed not to cough. "I'm okay now. But coffee would help."

She headed back to the kitchen. When he thought she wasn't looking, he pinched the bridge of his nose and squeezed his eyes shut.

When she handed him a mug, he gestured toward the other end of the couch. She perched on the arm, not wanting to appear too forward. Prince had curled up next to him.

A clap of thunder shook the room and Prince crawled onto Fig's lap.

"Where's your coffee? Can you sit for a while?"

She poured herself a cup and settled on the opposite end of the leather couch.

His breathing had eased. "So, Ms. Adair. What are you up to on this soggy morning?"

"Making sure the island hadn't washed away and all my hard work with it. I'm happy to report that those boulders have stabilized your bank nicely." She eyed him over the rim of her mug. "So, you don't want to see your doctor?"

Fig shook his head. "Naw, he's sick of me."

"You probably picked up something at your conference. Is that why you're home early? Law conferences must be exhausting. Landscaping conferences make my head spin. And hotel rooms are crawling with germs."

Fig coughed several times and shook his head.

"I could have you at the hospital in fifteen minutes," she offered once again.

Outside the wind bent the branches of the big cottonwood at the landing and blew leaves across the river. It would be a dangerous crossing.

"Charlotte," he said with a touch of impatience. "I never said I was going to a law conference."

Her thoughts raced back to what he'd told her on the way to the train station, then jumped ahead. He'd gone to visit his girlfriend—the Swedish belle of the Twin Cities. Good for you, she'd say. He deserved a partner like she had.

"Sorry," she said off-handedly. "I misunderstood. Did you have a nice visit?"

Ignoring her question, he rubbed his eyes and took a sip of water. "I might have said I was going 'for' a conference." He coughed again. "In Minnesota . . . not Minneapolis. My conference was at the Mayo Clinic. And it wasn't my first."

The rain hammered the roof and the wind buffeted the trees along the riverbank like seaweed at high tide.

"Oh," she said.

He rolled his head back and stared up at the ceiling for a long time before he spoke again.

"Charlotte," he said finally, and with such weary resignation that she wanted desperately to hold his hand. "About ten years ago, I got a respiratory infection I couldn't shake. Eventually, it turned into pneumonia. I was in the hospital for a month. Ever since, I catch every damn virus that goes around. And, the thing is, Charlotte, I've never really recovered."

He still hadn't looked at her.

Warmth rose up her neck and spread into her cheeks. The edges of the room lost focus.

"What did they tell you?"

"What my doctors here keep saying—that my lungs are shot." He glanced at her and drew in a deep breath that ended in another spasm of coughing. "And because my lungs . . . don't pump enough oxygen . . . my heart has been damaged, too."

The walls, the floor and the whole planet warped and she struggled to remain upright.

"I'm so, so sorry, Fig," was all she could think of to say.

"I've known this for a while now, Charlotte. My doctors sent me to Mayo hoping they were wrong, but alas." He gave a low, sardonic chuckle.

"What are they going to do? Is—Is there an operation? A transplant?"

"It would have to be a heart-lung transplant. Do you know how rare and difficult they are?" He rolled his head toward her slowly, as if it took all his strength. "So, no. There's nothing anyone can do. That's the reality, Charlotte."

His eyes circled the room. "I remodeled this house, so it's accessible—well, more accessible—for when—" His voice trailed off. "I can move a bed into the study. I want to stay here as long as I can." He stroked Prince's ears. "At least Prince and I have our very own little planet for the duration."

She looked down at her hands, clutched in her lap and felt her own breath catch behind a painful knob in her chest. She felt paralyzed by the weight of what he had told her.

He offered his hand to her, palm up. She curled her finger around it and felt his cool fingertips.

"I'm so sorry to burden you with this, Charlotte."

"No, I'm glad you told me. I—I want to help. How can I help?"

He nodded toward the stairs. "You can bring me my oxygen pump. It's upstairs by my bed. Those steps look like Mount Everest right now."

She stood in the doorway of Fig's bedroom. Her presence felt like a breach of Fig's private world—the king-sized bed neatly made with a duvet in navy and green plaid, a small television on the dresser top, a stack of books on the nightstand, a blazer folded over the back of a chair, his polished loafers side-by-side under the ottoman.

My lungs don't pump enough oxygen, he'd said.

My heart is damaged, too.

On the floor next to the bed was a wastebasket-sized machine with a row of control buttons and a coil of tubing. She hated how it looked there, disturbing the peace of this room, this island, this man's life. She hated what it meant.

She picked it up and coiled the tubing in her hand.

There's nothing anyone can do. That's the reality, Charlotte.

She carried it downstairs and watched with growing horror as he fixed the tubing into his nostrils, eying her self-consciously.

"Does it help?" she asked, not knowing where to look. She wanted to touch his hand again, but that moment had passed.

He nodded but didn't let his eyes meet hers.

As his landscaper, she should excuse herself and go home, but he shouldn't be alone. "Can I fix you some lunch before I go?"

"Only if you join me. You shouldn't be on the raft with a storm coming."

From the kitchen window, she watched the double-trunked cottonwood, Prince's old home, whipping its top branches over the foamy river.

I never really recovered, he'd said.

An uprooted tree floated by, barely missing the raft.

There's nothing anyone can do. There's nothing anyone can do!

She filled a glass and watched its contents tremble in her hand. She leaned against the sink.

Nothing anyone can do. Nothing. Nothing. Nothing! NOTHING!

She walked quickly into the bathroom and muffled her sobs with a hand towel. She should have known. His slow movements. His pale skin. The chronic coughing. The shortness of breath. All those days he worked from home.

How could this happen in the 21st century? Forty-seven wasn't old.

She splashed cold water on her face and tried smiling into the mirror. But her bloodshot eyes and shaking hands didn't lie. She sighed. She cared more about this man than she dared to admit and had no idea what to do next.

She took three long breaths and opened the bathroom door.

Fig was resting on the couch with one arm bent over his face and the other around Prince. His breathing was steady now.

She tip-toed into the kitchen and searched the refrigerator and cabinets. She heated two bowls of roasted red pepper and tomato soup and arranged their plates with red grapes, a few slices of Provolone cheese and crusty French bread—a whole different class of lunch than she'd find in her own kitchen. She arranged a tray and turned to find Fig standing behind her at the edge of the kitchen.

She busied herself at the counter to hide her face.

"Feeling better?" she asked.

"Much. Oxygen's terrific stuff. Completely underrated by ordinary Earthlings."

"I heated some soup," she said, still with her back to him.

She felt his warmth behind her.

"Charlotte?"

She lifted the tray and pivoted away. "Shall we eat on the couch or the table?"

"Charlotte," he said again.

"I could build a fire. That might be nice."

"Please. Stop a minute."

She set the tray on the counter again. She folded their napkins into rectangles, then refolded them into triangles and tucked them under the soup spoons. "Would you like more water?" She opened the cupboard to reach for another glass.

"I'm sorry. I shouldn't have told you," he said.

"No. I'm glad you did. It's just that –." She shook her head and her voice trailed off. She dabbed at the tears that wouldn't stop.

Fig said, "I don't usually tell people, but for some reason, I don't know, I wanted you to know. It was selfish of me. Your work here is almost done. You and Harp have your lives to plan and a business to run. Forgive me. I wish I could take it back."

Her lips pulled back into a taut grimace and her hands flew up to cover her face.

She felt his hands on her shoulders, turning her around and pressing her cheek to his chest. She let out a god-awful sob.

She was mortified. She should be apologizing to him, instead of making a sloppy mess on his bathrobe. Making everything about herself. Making him feel guilty for causing her pain.

She wanted to evaporate. She wanted to flee into that other world where people in their forties didn't die.

But outside a storm raged. And truthfully, despite everything, she wanted most of all to be right here, on this island, with this man. She listened to his heart thump and his lungs fill with air. She wanted to stay just like this forever.

But he released her then and stepped away to lean against the counter and study her face with great concern. "I shouldn't have sprung this on you. It's just that—that you've come to mean a great deal to me."

She wiped her face and nodded, but this intimacy had left her tongue-tied.

"I hope this doesn't ruin our friendship," he said. "I'm still your favorite client, right?"

She nodded, but his reference to their professional relationship surprised her. They were quickly falling back into their assigned roles. At the end of the summer, he'd give her a handshake and a check and she'd never see him again.

The door that had opened a crack was quickly closing. There wasn't time to hold back.

She looked up at him. "Fig? I need to tell you. I think . . . I think I'm fa—"

A blinding flash and a deafening boom rattled the windows. The hair on Charlotte's arms stood up. Prince dove under the coffee table and Fig and Charlotte rushed to the windows.

Across the river, a loud WONGGGGG resonated like a giant bass string. A ball of blue light at the top of the electric pole at the landing rained blue and orange sparks onto Charlotte's truck.

A series of loud cracks followed as Prince's old cottonwood tree began listing slowly in their direction. In one final spasm, the trunk hit the water sending up a massive crash and a plume of water. Seconds later its top branches lay quivering at the foot of Fig's porch.

"Holy shit!" Fig said, rushing for the door.

"Wait! I'll go."

She pulled on her wellies and ran down the steps. The tree lay across the rope pulley, pinning the raft. Across the river, a power line lay across her truck with its severed end dangling into the water.

They were standed.

She jogged around the island and found no further damage. By the time she reached the house again, the rain was tapering off as the storm moved east.

The fresh air had done her good. Here she was, stranded with a man who might succumb at any moment, but she was grateful for the chance just to be with him. She had been looking for excuses to be near him all summer—she had to admit that. And now, an opportunity had presented itself. She'd make the most of it.

She ran up the steps, kicked off her wellies and announced, "We're shipwrecked. Marooned!" She even managed a believable laugh. She flicked the light switch up and down. "And we're definitely off the grid."

Fig smiled from the couch where he was comforting Prince. "And you find this amusing?"

"Don't you? I love storms. Mother Nature just reminded us who's boss. She's ordering us to stay put, by the way. The raft's pinned down and there's a power line in the river. So, you're stuck with me. We better have that soup while it's still warm. It may be our last hot meal for a while."

Charlotte was proud of this sanguine soliloquy.

They sat with trays on their knees at opposite ends of the couch.

Fig was saying, ". . . and I have a well, but without electricity, the pump won't work, but I keep jugs of water in the backs of the cupboards for occasions like this. We bring in buckets from the river for flushing or I can offer you any number of nice, private trees."

"Do you have dibs on the front porch?"

He smiled. "I can assure you I am fully reformed in that regard—at least with guests in the house."

After lunch, Fig and Prince dozed on the couch while Charlotte cleaned up using a jug of water she found behind the cereal boxes. Then she sat on the porch watching water dripped from the eaves like strings of glass beads.

She called Harp who was on the treadmill at the gym.

"You're kidding! All the way across the river?" he asked, breathing hard with his healthy lungs. "You're lucky it didn't hit the house."

"So anyway, I'm stuck here. Would you mind dropping Mazie at my parents' tonight? And report Fig's address to the power company."

"Sure, but it might take them a while. Power's out all over the place. I'll get Mike's boat again and come get you."

"There's a live wire over my truck and in the river."

"I'll figure something out."

"Harp," she spoke his name softly. "Don't risk it. I'm fine for now."

"You can't stay there, Char."

Her throat clenched, robbing her of speech and common sense.

"What? What's going on?"

The words caught. "I—I, um, found out that Fig's um—sick. Really sick. He shouldn't stay here alone."

"Really? How sick?"

There was silence on the line. She could tell that he'd stopped running.

"It's his heart. And lungs." Her voice rose, sharp and thin. "There's nothing —. He's just really, um, weak."

"He's, like, going to die?"

"I just can't leave right now, and it's too dangerous for you to come. Just call the power company. Please, Harp."

She heard him sigh. "Sure. Whatever you want."

"Harp. Don't be mad."

He took a deep breath and held it for a long time. "I'm not," he exhaled. "Just think about me once in a while."

"I will. I do."

"I love you, Char."

"I love you, too."

She sank onto the porch step and watched the river roll on and on, knowing as rivers do, the way to the ocean. She, on the other hand, had absolutely no clue where she was headed or what was around the next bend.

By early evening Fig had regained some of his strength and despite her protests prepared chicken for the grill and peach halves glazed with balsamic vinegar and honey and lightly toasted slices of French bread. Domestic chores had a calming effect on Charlotte. She wiped off the patio chairs and set two places at the table on the flagstone patio behind the house.

Fig watched over the grill while Charlotte gathered sunflowers and a few early asters from the meadow and arranged them in a vase. She stripped the yellow-orange petals from a sunflower and popped one into her mouth, offering another to Fig.

"Do you know these to be edible, or are we test subjects?"

"Go on," she laughed. "They won't kill you," realizing too late what she'd said. "Sorry. I didn't mean—sorry."

He nibbled a petal. "Not bad. A bit of a kick."

"The stalks taste like celery and you can roast the roots too. Pretty handy when you're a castaway, don't you think?" She sprinkled the rest on the grilling peach halves.

Fig said, "So what other sustenance can my island offer?"

"Let's see. You've got three new elderberry bushes for jam or wine, but not for at least another year." A year. How long did Fig have she wondered? She cringed at the thought.

"That's it?"

"Let's see. There are loads of fox grapes in the woods, too. We could stuff the young leaves with dried spicebush berries this fall, but personally, I'd save these for soap. They'd make an awesome aftershave."

"I won't need that when my beard is down to my waist."

"Good point."

He set their plates on the table and pulled out her chair with a flourish. "Madam?"

"This looks wonderful. Thank you."

She watch him take a perfectly toasted slice of French bread between the tips of his long fingers and drizzled warm, herbed olive oil to the edges.

"The stegosaurus had a second brain near its tail. Did you know that?" she mused. This got a polite nod.

"My dino facts are a bit rusty. Relevance?" he asked, looking up.

"Your hands. They're very—um—" She ran through several options: supple, nimble, lithe, flowing, even sexy, before settling on, "—graceful."

"Graceful?" he laughed. He opened his hands and turned them over as if he'd never seen them before. "On a macho guy such as myself?"

"I think a second brain controls them."

"So, if we have to live off the land, you can forage while I grow a beard down to my knees," he said, changing the subject.

She smiled. "There will be hickory nuts. I still remember the taste. We gathered them in the woods near my elementary school. We'd crack them with the heels of our shoes and dig out the nut meat. Have you ever sucked the nectar out of a violet? I was always tasting things—which was probably foolish, but I was a big fan of Swiss Family Robinson. And I love islands." She inhaled the clean summer air and took in her surroundings. "I like their loneliness and their survival challenges."

She shook her head suddenly. "Sorry. I didn't mean . . . That was inappropriate."

He put down his fork and sighed. "Go on," he said, circling his fork. "What other plant resources do I have?"

She sat back, but the thought of Fig's fragile heart and frail lungs pushed out all others. He was waiting.

"Let's see . . . Edible landscaping is a separate field really. I've always been more interested in what's edible for wildlife. Hmm. You can make a citrusy beverage out of sumac berries if you add a whole lot of sugar. And they make a good dye, too."

"We could tap the maple trees for syrup," he offered.

"True. We could make jam from mayapple fruit too. Bloodroot, goldenrod and elderberry also make good dyes."

"We'll be ragged, but not faded. That's comforting."

Charlotte laughed. "A lot of plants have medicinal properties, too. Traditional healers knew that willow bark eases pain, which led to the production of aspirin."

"We don't respect the wisdom of our ancestors enough, do we?"

"No, but they weren't always right. Have you heard of the doctrine of signatures."

"What's that?"

"At one time, both Christianity and Islam taught that God designed plants to resemble the part of the body they were meant to heal."

"That would be useful. Like what?"

"Like hepatica, a tiny spring flower that probably grows somewhere on this island. It was used to treat the liver ailments because its leaves are liver-shaped."

"Thus *hepa-*, Latin for 'liver'. Fascinating."

"They also thought brown-eyed Susans could treat eye problems and milkweed sap was good for breastfeeding mothers. It seems silly now, but they were desperate for cures . . ." She stopped again.

My lungs are shot. There's nothing they can do.

She was hopeless.

She held up a chunk of her peach, forcing a smile. "So, what do you think of the sunflower garnish?"

"Not bad. But you realize, don't you, that we're eating a plant you just sold me. I'll expect an adjustment to my next invoice."

She popped a petal into her mouth and grinned. "But I'll be including an up-charge for edible plants. Which, by the way, I'd recommend to any client who can be marooned on his own property."

After a pause, Fig put down his fork and looked at her. "I'm sorry you're marooned too, Charlotte."

"Don't be. I love it here."

He shook his head. "I've drawn you into my unfortunate life. I didn't want to. I—I didn't want you to feel—How should I say this?—obligated in any way. Besides, there's nothing to be done."

She leaned her elbows on the table. "But there must be *something*. Maybe you could get a second opinion? I mean what about—?"

"Charlotte." He lifted a hand to stop her. "There's no medical trial, no alternative therapy, acupuncture, vitamin supplement, bio-feedback, meditation, snake oil . . . I've tried them all, and more. Some of them probably even helped." His voice dropped to a whisper. "My doctors are rather surprised I'm still here."

She shook off a strong urge to lay her head down on the table and sob.

"But medical science is developing new treatments all the time! I mean, what if—?"

"If there were, my phone would be ringing right now. Doctors in several states are consulting on my case."

"Doctors can be wrong."

"Regrettably, about a dozen cardiac, thoracic and pulmonary specialists are in complete agreement about my crappy heart and shitty lungs and the probable length of my life." His lips curved into a smile, but his eyes didn't follow. "As the saying goes, I'm living on borrowed time."

Charlotte looked into her lap and shook her head. "I don't mean to put you on the defensive."

"I know," he said softly. "But you see, I have moved past the point of desperate optimism. My hope now is that you can get there too—and quickly, because, believe me, it's a much better place to be." He reached across the table and took her hand. "You need to move past this, Charlotte. We're almost to the end of our contract. I'll miss your FDUs, but it's time you moved on to other clients and started planning that wedding."

Hepatica *Hepatica nobilis*

He was giving her an out. Pushing her back into her easy life with hunky Harp. And he was right, of course. She and Harp would marry and spend their lives building their business, backpacking, kayaking and biking. Their healthy young bodies moving together, making a baby or two. Sharing a long future together.

A memory pushed at her suddenly, of a day more than a decade ago when she found a bottle of Ativan under the seat of Mally's car, the one Lauren drove to work.

Charlotte shook the bottle in Lauren's face. Where'd you get these? They were prescribed to a Stacy Knapp. Who is she?

That's none of your business.

How *could* you, Lauren? You have a daughter! How could you do this to her?

They're legal, she'd said.

But they're not *yours!*

Just leave me alone, she'd said.

Oh, I'd love to, Lauren, but who's going to take care of Mazie when you're strung out? Or dead?

Just fuck off.

Gladly, she'd said. And that's exactly what she did.

Charlotte looked at the man seated across the table from her.

She was older now, and stronger somehow. She wouldn't turn away from trouble and heartache this time. Not if Fig would have her.

"When my work here is done here, I'd like to stay in touch," she said.

Fig paused before speaking. "It won't drive a wedge between you and Harp?"

"No. It won't," she said, at least she hoped it wouldn't.

He fingered his glass, thinking. "I have one rule though."

She smiled. "Okay."

"I'm serious," he said, sighing. "It's quite simple and goes like this: From you, my dear friend Charlotte—I need joy. Only joy. Radical, bad-ass, joy."

"Joy?"

"Yes. At long last and with great effort, I have accepted my illness and impending death because not doing so was killing me all the same."

Charlotte started to speak, but he raised a finger to stop her.

"To wallow, to chase charlatans hawking snake oil would be to waste time and energy, which are both in short supply and therefore precious to me. If you focus on my death, or even on my illness—twist every conversation to avoid every reference to it or worry that some plant won't bear fruit until after I'm gone—then I can't enjoy the limited time I have left. If I need a caregiver, I'll hire one. So, Charlotte, if we are going to be friends, my illness can't be part of the equation. Understood?"

Charlotte nodded sheepishly. Then she tilted her head up and bit her lip. "But I just have to say, if I were Queen of the World . . . "

"I know." He smiled. "Duly noted."

24

MAROONED, DAY TWO

If a homeowner has a sunny spot for one new tree, she would do well to choose an oak. Beloved for its stature, longevity and great strength, few Americans know that a single oak provides food and shelter for over four thousand different species of wildlife—more than any other tree in the world. But this common tree is now imperiled. Michigan's oaks faced their first trial after the Chicago fire of 1871, when Michigan felled its vast forests to rebuild the Windy City. By 1910, much of Michigan was a stubbled wasteland. Thankfully, century-old oaks are again plentiful, but they may be the last. Each year, the burgeoning deer population strips the forest floor of acorns and oak seedlings, while fire suppression policies have left forests so overgrown that young oaks aren't getting the sunlight they need. When the old oaks die, there will be few to take their place. Yes, a young oak tree would be a splendid addition to any yard.

Charlotte washed their dishes in the river and rinsed them with water heated on the grill. When Fig came into the kitchen to dry them she slid onto a stool to watch him. He leaned against the counter facing her, his legs crossed at the ankles, polishing each dish and utensil as if it was made of sterling and crystal.

"I like living off the grid, don't you?" he mused.

She nodded. "Who needs stupid old electricity anyway?"

"Yeah," he growled, "alternating current is for sissies."

"But wait." She sat up straight. "What about your oxygen pump."

"I have tanks that don't need power." He looked at her worried face and sighed. "I also have a gasoline generator, but it sounds like a jet engine run by howler monkeys."

She stood up. "Can you show me the tanks? With joy, the radical bad-ass kind, of course. Come on. It'll be so fun!"

He closed the cupboard and sighed again. "More wine?"

Charlotte stood her ground. "You know, Mr. Bigelow, I have rules, too. Prerequisites for delivering that joy you ordered. For example, I need information about these oxygen tanks."

"You're skatin' on thin ice there, missy, but fair enough." He led her to the hallway closet. Inside were shelves of linens, light bulbs, vases, rolls of wrapping paper and water jugs. On the floor were three tanks.

"Behind these shelves is a bomb shelter and a panic room."

"You're kidding."

Fig laughed. "Yes, I am. But I'm prepared for just about every other eventuality."

She bent over the tanks. "Show me how these work."

He adjusted the valves until she heard the hiss of oxygen.

"See," he said. "Days and days of lovely oxygen. I have a portable model too, but I'm much too fashion-forward to wear it in public."

He dropped his gaze in a defeated, self-conscious way that she'd never seen before and never wanted to see again.

"Thanks," she said, shrugging it off. "If you could see how it improves your color, you'd use it more often. You look good right now."

That night, they sat side-by-side in the Adirondack chairs until river and sky merged into seamless blue. A half dozen bats came out of their hiding places to chase mosquitoes. Prince slept through all of this on Charlotte's lap.

She sighed. "This is heaven."

"Pretty close, I reckon," Fig said, stirring out of his own reverie. "I've been contemplating the afterlife lately."

He was smiling to himself. She wondered if he was testing her.

"Really?" she asked.

"When I was about Mazie's age, I created quite a brouhaha by refusing to join my parent's church with the other middle schoolers. My father, Deacon Bigelow as he was called, was mortified, but I think my mother was proud of her free-thinking son."

"Why didn't you want to join?"

"We parted ways over the afterlife. The idea of spending eternity with my Sunday school teachers had no appeal. Sunday school hour already felt like eternity." He laughed. "And besides, what could be better than *this* life? It's not perfect, but perfect would be boring, don't you think? So anyway, I'm considering reincarnation."

"Considering? Do you think Saint Peter will ask, 'Well, Newton, what's your pleasure? Heaven or back to earth as a sea slug? Your call, dude.'"

"A choice would be nice. Maybe there's a lotto tumbler and you pick a ball. It makes about as much sense as anything I ever heard in church."

There was an obvious third choice, which Charlotte wasn't going to bring up. Anyway, Fig, of all people, would never be going there.

He was still talking. ". . . 're-embodiment' or re-creation. There's a good bit of empirical evidence for it."

"For reincarnation?"

Fig gazed into the mist. "Sure. Mother Nature recycles everything."

"Except plastics. We really threw her a curve ball there."

"Anyway, so you see, nothing really dies. Not one atom is lost. After I die, my molecules will be rearranged and reused. That's fact; not faith."

"But without self-awareness, what's the appeal?" She wasn't ready to put a positive spin on death and decay.

Near the river's edge, a pair of mallards dabbled in the reeds looking for dinner.

"Do you think those ducks are any worse off for not remembering they were once a blade of grass or a woodchuck?"

"Or a Potawatomi chief? Or a tomato? I don't know. Maybe not."

"Consciousness of past lives would be nice. Think how much wiser and more empathetic we'd be. But it's enough for me to know that my atoms are immortal. And that this sorry excuse for a body might get an upgrade."

"Okay. I get that." How could she deny him this small comfort?

"In a former life, I think I could fly," he said. "I may have been an eagle or an albatross."

"But you're terrified of flying."

"Only when I'm awake apparently. I dream of flying all the time and it never frightens me. I think I could have been a pilot."

"In a past life?"

He laughed. "As a career choice."

"That makes absolutely no sense."

"When I dissect it closely, as I have on way too many occasions at thirty thousand feet, I realize I'm only afraid of being flown. I like to be in control."

"I didn't know that about you."

"You're a captive on my island, aren't you?" He flashed her a creepy smile.

"You made the cottonwood fall on the raft?"

He wound one long leg around the other and shrugged. "I may have been warned by an arborist that it might fall, but a little dog was living under it at the time." He stroked Prince's ears.

Charlotte smiled. "And here I was blaming Zeus and his lightning bolt." She glanced sideways. "So, you don't mind having me here?"

"If I have to be stranded on a desert island, I'm glad it's with you."

"Desert? After all my beautiful landscaping?"

"Okay, lush island paradise."

"Good save."

They sat for a long time without speaking. Prince woke up, stretched and trotted off toward the meadow.

"Nature is my church," Charlotte said finally. "When I'm working outside, I'm completely absorbed and at peace. I'm receptive to bird songs, the splash of a fish in the river, the buzz of a bee. Nature is where I experience awe. That's religion for me."

"Awe?"

"Wonder. Inspiration. Feeling that I'm a part of something much greater than myself. Helping to restore a woodland or a prairie makes me feel whole and purposeful. It's an act of redemption and, I guess, worship. For me, helping a plant grow is a prayerful act."

"You spend many hours on your knees."

She smiled. "Yes. That, too. Some would call me an atheist, but I don't think of myself as a non-believer at all."

"If beauty—or awe, as you say—is part of religion, religious naturalists have the advantage, I should think. And nature brings you peace. That's important too."

"It doesn't always. When I see people destroying my holy places I get really angry. This isn't a harmless, tree-hugging kind of religion. In fact," she said, smiling. "I belong to the evangelical wing. I try my best to bring people around to my way of thinking."

"Yes, I've noticed," he said. "Most people spend their lives searching for what you've already found, Charlotte." He turned to face her, leaning his chin on his hand. "So, what's your ideal landscaping project? A cabin in a virgin forest? A cottage on a dune overlooking Lake Michigan?"

"Neither. We need to stop pushing further into the wilderness. There's too little of it left. Thou shalt bring wilderness back to your yard—That's a commandment. In this century landscaping needs to be an act of restoration and redemption. I don't want to help someone grow tulips on a dune. I'd rather restore land that's been used and abused. Redeem it, so to speak."

"Like this island." Fig nodded.

"Yes. Like that."

The first star sent out a tentative twinkle just as the first mosquito found her ankle. Prince returned from his nightly rounds and whined to go inside.

While Fig read by candlelight on the couch, Charlotte browsed his bookshelves and found a well-worn copy of an Isaac Asimov book. She tried reading by candlelight but soon dozed off. She awoke to Fig setting a stack of linens on the coffee table. She yawned and sat up.

"Here are some sheets and towels, a tee shirt and some shorts for you to sleep in. I'm sorry I don't have a guest room or a shower or a working toilet or electricity." He laughed. "I'm an appalling host."

"And no chocolates on my pillow, I see." She waved him off. "I'll manage."

He started up the stairs but turned to look at her. "I wouldn't have blamed you if you swam for shore. But thanks for staying."

"I hope you feel better in the morning."

She saw his shoulders sag and knew she'd said the wrong thing.

"I'm still not sure I should have told you," he said, glancing down at the oxygen tank he was carrying. "But under the circumstances, you'd have figured it out."

"Does it help?"

"What? The oxygen?"

"Telling someone. Telling me. Does it lift . . . I don't know . . . the weight of it?"

"Yes and no. It creates a different kind of weight. I've added to your worries. I regret that."

"It's painful, but I'm glad you told me. It feels good when a friend confides something important."

He hesitated before nodding, then slowly climbed the stairs. Prince was waiting at the top.

"Goodnight, Charlotte."

"Goodnight, Fig."

But sleep wouldn't come. Every thought of Fig, and there were many, felt like a jab in the gut. She thought about calling Harp but texted him goodnight instead.

At 11:20 Prince whined to go out again and she followed him out. The moon cast a blue glow over the river. She trailed him to the oak grove and sat on the swing while he followed a scent into the undergrowth.

Fig wanted only joy from her. Radical, bad-ass joy. The one thing she wasn't sure she could manage. But if she wanted to remain in his life, she would need to figure it out.

And Harp? How could she navigate these turbulent new waters between Harp and Fig?

Prince nuzzled her knee. She lifted him up and held him as they swung together in a lazy arc. Across the river, a car chased its headlights along River Road.

She set Prince down and turned on her phone. There were five messages from her parents. The last one said, "Call us, please."

Ted answered immediately. "Hey, sweetie. Harp said you're stuck on that island. We were worried." He covered the receiver and said a muffled, "Charlotte."

"Sorry, Dad. I need to save my battery."

"You okay?"

"Fine."

"Kinda up shit's creek without a paddle though." He chuckled.

"Or a raft," she added. "But Fig's got cupboards full of food."

There was long pause. "Harp said Fig's ill."

"I hope he didn't tell Mazie. I forgot to tell him not to."

"He didn't. But she'll be gutted. It's been Fig-this or Fig-that all summer."

"I know."

"You can't keep this from her, honey. If it's serious."

"I know, Dad. Just not yet."

"Harp said you and Fig have become good friends. He didn't sound too pleased. Wait. Your mum wants to say something."

"Hi, love," Mally said. "I wanted to tell you that Mazie paid me back *every cent* of her camp deposit today. I'm chuffed to bits. Dad and I both got a bit misty-eyed, truth be told." She paused. "Oh yes, you did, Ted," she said, laughing. "Anyway, she told us she's been working all summer to pay us back. You've been a good influence, sweetheart."

"You should thank Fig. Those two are thick as thieves." She paused. "He gets her, you know, in a way I never have." Her voice seized in her throat and she had to pause. "They're so alike. So, there's hope for her yet." Charlotte laughed then. "She's worked hard, mostly to please him."

"Well, thank him for us, won't you? Here's Dad again."

"Got everything you need, honey? Clean water? Clean underwear? Condoms?"

She could hear her mother say, "Ted!"

"Well, it sounds to me like there's more to this than—"

"Well, there's *not*, Dad."

He laughed. "Okay, sweet thing. We'll keep buggin' the power company."

"Hug Mazie for me, if she'll let you. Bye."

Charlotte tilted her head back and followed the ropes till they disappeared into the dark leaf canopy. A long sigh became a yawn, but the entire day wouldn't stop replaying itself.

You've come to mean a great deal to me . . . living on borrowed time . . . I need joy from you . . . my illness can't be part of the equation. I never recovered. . . living on borrowed time.

She spun the swing, twisting the ropes until her toes came off the ground. She let go, letting it spin faster and faster, then reversing.

A terminal illness would put you at war with your own body, she thought. Hurling toward a cliff without brakes.

The swing came to rest, leaving her nauseous and frightened. She staggered into the house and collapsed onto the couch.

Soon, she was lying on the raft between Fig and Mazie, letting the current carry them in lazy circles around and around the island. Then faster and faster until a whirlpool pulled them into its airless vortex.

She woke up covered in sweat to the staccato hack of Fig's coughing. It was still dark outside. She got up to stand barefoot at the bottom of the stairs until he was quiet again.

The sound of rain woke her. She rubbed her eyes and sat up. The sight of Fig's living room at dawn sparked the same mix of euphoria and sudden dread she'd felt all day yesterday. How was it possible to feel joy and fear, hope and dread—simultaneously and in equal proportion—without cracking down the middle?

She hadn't cried so hard since the day Lauren died. It was as if she had been cast in a drama where only the Act III Scene 3 had been written with everything else just improv. But what if in Act II there was a miracle? Fig cured, with a ruddy complexion and robust body. Well then, the end would just have to be revised.

A spasm of coughing came from upstairs. Act III was unalterable, he insisted. Hope was as foolish as her parents' denials that Lauren was using. Fig had been clear— hope was a cruel distraction. He was right, of course. And yet—

Yesterday, she had made a bold calculation—that the joy of remaining in Fig's life would outweigh the pain of losing him later. She hugged her knees to her chest and breathed slowly, determined not to give in to emotion.

How long would he put up with her lapses into hopefulness? Did she have the strength to stand by him and not collapse into him like she had yesterday? How could she possibly bring him joy? She now understood that living every day as if it was your last is horribly exhausting.

And then there was Harp. Dear, simple Harp. How could she make him understand why she needed to stand by Fig? She looked at the diamond on her finger. The man attached to it felt more and more like a stranger. A boy really. A sweet, beautiful, energetic boy, but a boy nonetheless.

How long could she continue like this, knowing what she knew and feeling what she felt? And what, pray tell, *was* she feeling anyway? At the moment nothing was clear. She massaged her aching temples.

Coffee! Coffee was the answer.

She filled the tea kettle from a jug on the counter. The noise brought Prince downstairs. He pushed his empty bowl with his nose until it hit the back of her foot. Then he whined up at her.

"Subtle," she said, filling his dish with kibble.

She put on her parka and went outside to fire up the grill, which Fig had rolled under the eaves. The blinds in Fig's window were closed. Back in the kitchen, she poured the water through a coffee filter into the carafe. When the coffee was done, she poured herself a cup, took cream from the dark refrigerator and sniffed it before adding it to her coffee. She let Prince out and stood on the porch surveying the downed cottonwood. The trunk looked almost wide enough to crawl across if she got desperate enough and if there wasn't a live wire electrifying the river.

A wave of luscious, caffeinated euphoria lifted her up and she inhaled a great breath of August morning. She had no desire to go anywhere.

Prince sniffed the edges of the new, leafy bridge. Did he recognize his winter home?

The rain had let up, so she sat on the dock to watch two map turtles sleeping on a limb of the half-submerged cottonwood. Since they obviously weren't electrocuted, she took off her shoes and waded into the cool water. She splashed her face and dried it with her shirt.

A third, smaller turtle climbed up and seeing the limb fully occupied crawled onto the back of the largest turtle.

Where the current ran under the downed tree, a turquoise damsel fly was caught in an eddy. She scooped it up and let its wings dry out on her knee. After several minutes it darted off. A fish was not going to have a damsel fly breakfast on this morning.

Three of the cardinal flowers she'd planted between boulders were showing the first signs of growth, but they wouldn't bloom for another year. She should tell Fig to watch for hummingbirds—the flower's favored pollinator. Her heart dropped with the realization that Fig might not be around to see them bloom next year. She looked at the house with its new landscaping. She had designed it for Fig to enjoy for decades. But what was the point now?

She frowned at the cardinal flowers, mere suggestions of the tall red-spiked flower they'd be next summer.

"Bloom, damn-it!"

Perhaps VanderLee's would have some in bloom. Fig deserved that. This landscaping job had a new urgency. A deadline. A *deadline*. Bile rose in her throat and she wanted to scream.

She had advised Fig to adopt a long view. To choose hearty, long-lived natives that needed time to mature but would give back beauty and pleasure for years to come. If only she'd known. Never once had he demanded "instant bloom" as so many clients do.

She lay on her back on the dock. It was too early to process all these thoughts. When Fig came downstairs, she would be cheerful and in-the-moment. But not yet. Not with damsel flies drowning in eddies and cardinal flowers blooming too late.

She heard a splash. The biggest turtle had shifted, sending its young piggybacker into the river. Charlotte caught herself smiling.

When Fig came downstairs, she would hold fast to her long view—that we don't plant oaks for ourselves, but for our children's children. This island might be freed of invasive species and planted with natives, but it would take time for it to fully heal and restore itself. But it *would* happen. Fig believed this as wholeheartedly as she did.

Across the river a man in a trench coat walked around her truck, picking his way through the debris.

"Morning!" he called out.

It was the tall fisherman, Ronner.

She cupped her hands. "Watch out for the wire!"

He lifted a hand and backed up. "You okay over there?"

"Yes. Fine."

"I can get my boat."

"No thanks."

"Call if you change your mind."

He waved again and walked back up the driveway. She went inside to start breakfast.

When Fig came downstairs, she had two plates of scrambled eggs with chopped kale, marjoram and flakes of Parmesan served with slightly charred English muffins.

He slipped onto a kitchen stool across from her. She poured his coffee and seconds for herself.

"Were you comfortable on the couch?" he asked.

"Yes. Thanks."

She told him about Mazie's repayment of her camp deposit. "My parents asked me to thank you, especially for the lesson that went with it."

"She worked hard for it," he said. There was a long silence before he added, "By the way, breakfast is delicious."

He was probably sensing—well, he probably *knew*—that every cell in her body was screaming for a blow-by-blow replay of yesterday's discussion. She wanted a review of every test result, every diagnosis by every doctor he'd ever consulted. She demanded a recount!

Instead, she described the rescue of the damsel fly, the pile of turtles and her exchange with the fisherman. Gradually, her monologue petered out and she picked at her food. When she looked up, his pale blue eyes were watchful.

She smiled. "The couch was fine, thanks."

He smiled. "I thought we were discussing turtles."

She put down her fork. "Oh. Right. Sorry."

She got up to clear the table. "So, what's on the schedule today? Food foraging? Soap making? Raiding a beehive for candle wax? We could tie-dye a few of your tee shirts with sumac juice? What'll it be?"

Fig laughed at this, but soon it led to a bout of coughing.

"Sorry," he said, getting up. "That sounds fun, but I have some deadlines that can't wait and without WIFI it's going to be slow going, but don't let me keep you from all that nature fun."

"Actually, I have work to do too."

Fig and Prince went into his study while Charlotte settled in at the porch table, emptying her bag and weighing down her papers with her coffee mug and a citronella candle.

Fig's next invoice was going to be a big one. But how could she send an invoice to someone with mountains of medical bills? She was pretty sure Legal Aid attorneys didn't get rich. Charlotte gnawed at her thumbnail until it start to bleed. She should offer to stop the project. Maybe she could just come over on the weekends and finish up on her own time. The problem was, she had no other clients and four employees to pay.

Mid-morning, Fig brought out two mugs of fresh coffee.

"Time for a break," he announced.

She cleared a space for him at the table.

"Good. Can we talk?" she asked.

His face fell. "In my experience, conversations that start with those three words usually end badly, but please speak your mind."

She fingered the paper in front of her. "I was working on your invoice. But I just need to say, um, that I'll understand if you can't—or don't want to—finish the project. We can scale it back, or suspend it. Whatever you say. I'll understand. I don't want—"

Fig held up a hand.

"Charlotte. First of all, I planned this project months ago despite my prognosis. I didn't learn anything new at Mayo this week. I've been planning this renovation for a long time. I needed a first-floor bathroom, a solid walkway and a better heating system. One thing led to another and then . . . you came along."

"But the expense."

"Let me see." He looked at the invoice and handed it back to her. "This is what we agreed on, Charlotte."

He went back into the house and returned with a checkbook. "Have you been stewing about this all morning?"

"No," she lied, "but thank you." She folded the check and tucked it into her bag. "For your information, I also updated this drawing of the meadow. If I don't get things recorded, I'll forget where I planted things." She ran her finger over a kidney-shaped area shaded in pencil.

"Yesterday, I found this area of New England asters. They'll be five feet tall and the most gorgeous shade of periwinkle with yellow centers. And you have a lot of little bluestem prairie grass too—about the best native for the site. And the New York ironweed I found will be very tall and very purple and very beautiful."

"And very free," he pointed out. "See? Your services are a bargain."

"I can divide them if you'd like more and we can try some other wildflowers. I'd like to plant lavender hyssop, too. The blossoms smell like black jellybeans."

"Hmm," he murmured, but his gaze was elsewhere.

"Sorry. I'm talking too much."

"No." He gave a deep sigh. "I'm just distracted. These eviction cases are tedious and without a working computer, I'm spinning my wheels."

And a terminal prognosis probably wasn't helping, she thought.

Fig was drumming his fingers on the table and frowning.

"What else?" she asked.

He closed his eyes. "I think I'm losing interest in Legal Aid cases."

"Really? Why?"

"I'm at . . . a crossroads, of sorts." He raked his hand through his hair and squinted at her. "When I first got sick, my doctors offered me hope. But as I got weaker, there were more and more 'ifs' in the prognosis. It became harder and harder to remain hopeful. I felt suspended between life and death. But finally, my doctors had to admit that my death is inevitable. This was strangely liberating. Certainty can be a kind of comfort." He gave a rueful laugh. "But now, oddly perhaps, fear of death has been replaced by a new restlessness." He eyed her with a flicker of uncertainly. "My worst fear isn't dying, Charlotte, it's living a life unfinished."

He spread his fingers on the tabletop and nodded. "I know how I want to spend the time I have left. As ridiculous as this will sound, it seems I've found my inspiration—my muse, so to speak."

"Your muse?"

One corner of his mouth lifted. "Yup. I found her kneeling in my flowerbed last spring."

In the seconds before Fig spoke again, three questions came to mind.

1. Was Fig in love with her?

2. Did she want him to be?

3. Why had she forgotten to call Harp this morning?

Fig was still talking. "—to leave this island—this world—a healthier place. I want to use my legal skills to stop the spread of harmful, alien plants. I want to encourage North Americans to be better stewards of the land we seem so bent on destroying.

"I don't have a defendant or even a plaintiff yet, but Charlotte, because of what you've taught me, I *know* I can do this. You've inspired me." He looked at her. "I may be on the ropes, but I know I've got another round in me."

She rolled her head against the chair back, mortified by her romantic fantasies and perplexed by what he just said. He wasn't in love with her, he was playing the sick card to lure her into a lawsuit.

And because she'd cry if she didn't, she came back with, "Oh, you're good, Fig Bigelow. Is this how you sway jurors?"

He winced. "What? No. I—I didn't mean *you'd* be my plaintiff. I'm sorry. I wasn't trying to manipulate you. Strike that. The jury will disregard that last statement. ."

She shook her head. "I don't really think that."

"No. You're right. I'm sliding into self-pity."

"Fig." She felt awful now. She wanted so much to cover his hand with hers. "I didn't mean to make light of it. You just caught me off guard."

"I know. But please, just hear me out." He stood up and leaned against the porch railing, his arms folded tightly across his chest. The gears were cranking again. "I only meant that I want to bring this case. There's no time for a protracted lawsuit, first because of my health, but also because these plant prohibitions are long overdue.." He grinned at her. "Who better to make the case for urgency than yours truly?"

"Maybe. But it won't be easy." Charlotte propped her chin on her hand and frowned. "The state's been dragging its feet on banning plants for decades. And because most people don't understand, they don't care. The epidemic of invasive species and habitat degradation, like climate change and global warming, are such enormous, slow-moving disasters that we don't notice them any more than a fish notices the ocean it's swimming in."

"Well said! I can use that."

"I'll add a nickel to your bill."

"But our problem is that the courts don't have the power to stop a glacier from melting or an invasive plant from crowding out a native one. A better first step would be to identify a *specific*, intentional act of someone selling, propagating or planting harmful plant species. Then we could petition the court to stop it with a temporary restraining order, also called a 'T.R.O.'"

"I thought restraining orders were for abusive ex-boyfriends and creepy stalkers."

"They're for a lot more than that. Suppose the Lumpy Concrete Company was doing repairs on the dam downriver and you found out that they were using inferior cement that would crack open and flood the town below. You'd want the court to stop the work immediately, right?"

"Yes, but do courts ever work quickly?"

"TROs are all about speed. They're an emergency order by a judge to preserve the status quo—in this case, to halt work on the dam. But it's only temporary."

"How temporary?"

"A few weeks maybe. It's meant to be a Band-Aid, not a cure."

"Then what good is it?"

"Well, it stops Lumpy Concrete from doing further damage while you gather evidence to convince the judge to stop them permanently."

"How do you get a TRO?"

"You write to a judge, citing plenty of convincing evidence, of course."

"But wouldn't Lumpy Concrete's attorneys tie everything up in court?"

"Not for a TRO. In fact, Lumpy Concrete might not even know you were asking for a TRO. If the court agrees that there's an imminent danger to the villagers, it would order the work stopped."

"And the peasants are saved. Whoopee!"

"Temporarily. Later, there would be a hearing and Lumpy Concrete would get their day in court."

"How much later?"

"That depends—enough time for their attorneys to build their defense or prove they've fixed the problem. After the court has heard from both sides, work on the dam could resume or the court could order the work stopped permanently."

"So, in the case of invasive species, we'd need to catch someone in the act of planting them so we can stop them." Charlotte rose to her feet. "Since I have no idea how to do that, so I'm going to forage for lunch."

After tuna and dandelion green sandwiches on the porch, Fig returned to his study while Charlotte leafed through a stack of architectural magazines she found by the fireplace and browsed a huge coffee table book on the Civil War. Finally, she picked up Sunday's issue of the *Saskawan Evening Star*. She didn't know anyone who still got a newspaper delivered, but then again she didn't know many old souls like Fig Bigelow.

On page three she found a short article with the headline, "Plant-a-Palooza Set for Cross-County Linear Park."

She stood in the study door. "You won't believe our luck, Fig. Twenty-six miles of invasive trees, shrubs and groundcovers are going to be planted across Saskawan County in October."

Fig skimmed the article. "The park boosters are looking for volunteers to help plant, but it doesn't say whether the plants are invasives."

"Trust me, a lot of them are. A guy from the county parks talked to my WILHA group last spring. Their plans include a lot of nasty invasives, I can assure you. And look who's donating them?" She pointed to the end of the article. "The Michigan Horticultural Association."

Fig nodded, rubbing his chin.

"Should we ask the court to stop the MHA from donating the plants or stop the city and county from planting them?"

"We can ask whatever we want."

She frowned. "But it's only eight weeks away. Isn't it too late?"

"Not at all. An impending event creates the urgency we need to ask for a restraining order. It might only buy us a few weeks, but if it's granted, planting would be delayed until after a hearing. That would take a few months more."

Her eyes widened. "Winter would delay planting anyway, so even a short delay would delay planting until spring."

Fig nodded. "Any delay buys us time to think of something else. Now, all I need is a plaintiff."

Charlotte leaned against the doorway. "All right," she said.

"All right, what?"

"I'll be your plaintiff."

"Really? Don't toy with me. I have a weak heart." His face softened into a broad grin.

"With one stipulation," she said. "I can't do this alone. You need to find other plaintiffs."

"Fair enough. Any come to mind?"

"A few WILHA members have been asking to see the island. What if I invite them for a tour and you can tell them about this restlessness of yours?"

He closed his eyes and whispered, "Thank you."

That night, Fig went upstairs early again, leaving Charlotte to wander the darkening house and second-guess her decision. Harp was going to freak out when she told him. He would say she should be finding new clients. He was right. What was she thinking?

Sleep was impossible—again.

In the bathroom, she brushed her teeth with a finger-full of toothpaste and frowned at her oily hair and sweaty body. She undressed, found a bottle of shampoo, wrapped herself in a towel and headed barefoot to the riverbank, swatting mosquitoes along the way. She hung her towel on a branch and waded into the chilly water. On the count of three, she dove into the current and came up with a gasp. She floated on her back, letting the cool water envelop her. In the stillness above, fireflies danced among their sister stars.

25

MAROONED, DAY THREE

*When the bright yellow flowers of the compass plant first open,
they are arranged randomly on stalks that can reach twelve
feet. But within a few weeks, the flowers re-orient themselves
to face east and west. Early travelers relied on this tall plant
to guide them through America's vast, uncharted prairies.*

Charlotte awoke to Prince's staccato yipping, a low mechanical hum and shouting in the distance.

Through the screened door she watched a motorcade of utility trucks arriving at the landing. She returned to the couch, covered her head with the sheet and slept until Fig came down the stairs.

"What was Prince going on about?"

"D'know. Squirrel?" She tried to ignore the incessant beeping of heavy equipment closing in on the cottonwood wreckage.

She opened one eye. Fig was at the window. "That looks more like the power company than a squirrel, but I could be wrong."

She got up to stand next to him, wrapped in the sheet. "We still have plenty of food, you know. It's a pity to waste it."

Fig looked down at her, amused. "I'm not going to banish you when the electricity goes back on. I like having you here."

She walked to the kitchen, following her hunger. The clock on the stove was stalled at 11:43 while the microwave had somehow achieved 11:46.

"What if we're in a time warp?" she asked, with a wild-eyed look. "Over there, it could be 2040, or 1940. Or, what if I leave and when I come back your house is just an old ruin or was never even built? What then, huh?"

"What if there's no island even?" Fig's eyebrows were wiggled up and down. "But it couldn't be 2040 or they would have rescued us with jet packs by now. We're way overdue for those, in my opinion."

"Totally."

They were both smiling.

"The raft might be too damaged to use," he pointed out.

"True. "

"There's no need to rush off."

She thought of Harp, but still she said, "Nope. No rush."

He filled the teapot with water. "You better to stay put until we're sure. That would be the most prudent course of action." He headed for the grill on the back patio. "I'll start the coffee."

"I'll bring the oatmeal."

They spent the rest of the day on the porch watching rain fall on their slow-motion rescue. She wanted to talk about life, friendship and the future. Of thoughts unexpressed. Instead, they discussed the lunch menu, the best sites for a pair of wren houses and whether a bench should replace Fig's thinkin' log.

At lunch, Fig said, "Yesterday you expressed concern about the cost of this landscaping project and my medical bills on a Legal Aid attorney's salary. Right?"

She nodded.

"So, you're probably wondering how I can represent you pro bono. Right?"

"Kinda. Yeah."

He inhaled and sat back. "Then, I should share some highly classified intel. Are you ready?"

"As long as it's not bad news."

He squirmed a little. "I don't rely completely on the chicken feed they pay me at Legal Aid. You can finish landscaping the island and my checks won't bounce. Promise. And I can represent you pro bono in our lawsuit and still pay my medical bills. And if we lose, I'll be able to cover any court costs."

"Court costs?" She gave him a worried look.

"The legal system has a way of punishing those who get too big for their breeches."

"Like me?"

"Just tell the judge, 'My lawyer made me do it.'"

"And that would be the truth."

By late afternoon the cottonwood had been sliced and diced and hauled away. The raft, which had been underwater for two days, escaped with only a broken railing and a coat of slime. Even the rope was still threaded through the posts. Fig tugged and pushed on every connection and pronounced the raft seaworthy.

"I'll get Harp to fix the railing this week," Charlotte said, feeling a stab of guilt at the mention of his name. "I should go now. I really do need to check on things at home and change clothes. If I don't get a real shower soon, I'll sprout mushrooms—not that I didn't enjoy bathing in the river with the mosquitoes."

When the last truck drove off, the rain let up and the lights came on, Fig walked Charlotte to the dock.

"Thank you, Fig. These last two days have been—" She cast around for the right words. "—in a category by themselves."

"In a good way, I hope." His eyes held on to hers until a flush of emotion made her turn away.

"I hope I haven't twisted your arm on this lawsuit idea. It might be temporary insanity—or permanent, if I'm honest. So, if you change your mind when—" He looked at her truck parked across the river. "—when you get back to the real world, I'll understand."

"Thanks. "

"I do think it's a worthy endeavor. But to be honest, I've also been thinking—quite selfishly— about how quiet it will be around here

Compass Plant *Silphium laciniatum*

with everyone gone and Mazie back in school." His voice trailed off and she saw him swallow hard.

She didn't know what to say.

"And something else," he said. "I've been putting some thought into your religion."

"My religion?"

"Something strange has happened to me this summer. I want to know the name of every damn leaf and twig and flower. I want to know what bird is singing and what the song means. I want to know which flowers each kind of bee prefers. I want to know what trees say when they talk to one another. I want the backstory." He pushed his hands deep into his pockets and squinted into the distance. "I suspect this is what a religious awakening must feel like."

Charlotte felt her eyes begin to sting. Was he telling her goodbye or asking her to stay? She waited a long time before deciding how to reply.

"I, and Mazie, too—both of us—will miss this place. Mazie'd move here if she could. Anyway," she added, "Adair Natural Landscaping has a few projects to finish up before we're done here."

"Good," he said, reaching for the broken railing and gripping her elbow as she stepped on. "Be careful going across," he said, testing the post one more time.

"Thanks for the hospitality, Fig. I enjoyed it."

"Me too." He nodded, glancing down at his loafers.

The raft slid lightly across the river's steel-gray surface as the rope worn smooth by Fig's hands ran through her fingers. In the middle, she turned to wave at the still, unmoving figure growing smaller in the distance.

Ahead, her truck waited, miraculously unscathed, its bed filled with the tools of her trade. Ahead, too, was the farm and Harp and a future yet undefined.

A blue heron lifted up soundlessly from the shore and headed toward the river bend where the opposite banks came together in a convincing optical illusion.

Charlotte's truck rolled slowly down the long driveway toward the farmhouse. The storm had left deep ruts in the gravel. Were there more honeysuckle bushes sprouting in the old pasture? Was the sag at the corner of the porch getting worse?

It had only been two days. And yet nothing about the farm looked completely familiar to her. And yet, her time with Fig felt like something she had only imagined. Part nightmare; part fantasy.

At present, she felt suspended between this farm and the island. Not here and not there, but in a void between them. Between Fig and Harp. Nothing fit. Nothing was right.

Harp sounded relieved when she'd called him from the landing. He said he'd start dinner and open some wine.

On the drive home, she'd worked herself up to a state of high anxiety again. She didn't know what to make of things with Fig. Male-female friendships were like that.

She had often wondered how clandestine love affairs began. In her experience, such things didn't "just happen" like they do in movies or romance novels—clutched in a fevered, bodice-ripping embrace or tumbling into the nearest heart-shaped bed. That was too much spontaneity for someone who spent years planning ecosystems that take decades to mature.

And why had her thoughts wandered there?

She parked the truck at the kitchen door, closed her eyes and inhaled deeply. It was good to be home. Good to be with Harp and his simple needs, healthy body and limitless future. He opened the kitchen door and greeted her with a long, slow kiss.

"God, I missed you," he said, handing her a glass of wine. "There's a hot bubble bath ready upstairs. Take your time. I'll hold dinner until you're ready."

"Thank you."

But fifteen minutes later, submerged up to her chin, the flashbacks kept coming. The crash of the cottonwood. Harp's growing impatience. Fig's shocking disclosure. Her promise to be his plaintiff.

The flash forwards were worse. Fig staggering, gasping for air or clutching his chest as he sank to his knees, all *alone*.

She submerged herself until her own lungs demanded air and came up gasping. How could she continue her own life, knowing what she knew?

Harp came into the bathroom and held a towel for her. He dried her shoulders and her hair. He took her hand, leading her toward the bedroom.

"I'm starving," she said, brightly. "Is dinner ready?"

By the end of dinner, they were arguing.

"Okay! I'll fix the raft. But *you* don't need to go," Harp said. "The crew and I can handle whatever he needs done, but you need to find some new clients. That's all, I'm saying. We'll lose the crew if you don't."

"It's not that easy in August. Most people are tired of their gardens and aren't thinking about spring projects yet."

"It feels like you're stalling."

"I'm *not* stalling!"

But he was right. She'd never find another client like Fig. Hell, she never *wanted* another client but Fig—which was a ridiculous and completely silly notion.

She sighed. "As soon as I write up a maintenance plan for Fig, we're done at the island."

Harp pushed back from the table. "A maintenance plan? I mean how's he going to maintain anything if—? Never mind." He shook his head. "But, you know what I don't get? If the guy's so sick, why did he even want all that expensive landscaping in the first place?"

Charlotte swirled the wine in her glass. "To leave the island better than he found it? To leave a legacy?"

"Like a shrine or something? Geez."

She hated Harp just then. She had planned to tell him about the TRO, but he would never understand. She stood up and moved to her desk. "I have work to do before bed," she said. "I'll do the dishes in the morning."

She heard him crack another beer, shuffle toward the living room and turn on the TV. She'd ruined the romantic homecoming he'd planned. She hated herself even more.

At 2:00 a.m., when Harp finally came to bed she was still staring at the crack in the ceiling. Guilt and confusion are as effective as caffeine, she thought bitterly. She really did love Harp and cared deeply about Fig, but didn't know how to be with either of them.

At 3:00 a.m. she went to the kitchen to fix a cup of tea. She opened her laptop. By three-thirty, she'd finished her email.

TO: Barb, Katie, Nicky and Portia,
From: Charlotte
Subject: An invitation
BCC: Newton Bigelow

[CONFIDENTIAL TO YOU]
I'm contacting you as respected colleagues and friends who share my concerns about the proliferation of invasive plants in West Michigan. As I mentioned last May, my client and friend Newton ("Fig") Bigelow, an attorney with considerable trial experience, believes that legal action against the city and county is warranted and might ultimately succeed in stopping the installation of harmful species at the "Plant-a-Palooza" planned for the new Cross-County Linear Park on October 8. He is offering his services pro bono. I have agreed to be a plaintiff in the lawsuit with the stipulation that there be others.

Our initial strategy will be to ask the court for a Temporary Restraining Order, or TRO, to stop this event. Meanwhile, we'd apply pressure through the media to raise public concern. A TRO is meant to be a quick, temporary solution to give us more time to prepare for a full hearing.

Fig and I both feel there is enough evidence for a strong case, but we still need a group of well-respected plaintiffs. I can't think of a better team that the four of you.

If you would like to learn more, please meet with us on Wednesday, August 20th, 6:00 p.m. at Fig's home for drinks, a brief tour and to discuss the case.

For reasons I'm sure you understand, any information about this case must remain completely confidential.

Please let me know your plans. I've attached a map to the island.

Yours, Charlotte

26

THE WILLFUL HEART

Beech-maple forests are common in West Michigan. Where maples thrive, beeches often grow nearby. This partnership has lasted for eons. Understandings have been reached. Compromises made. Sunlight, water and soil shared. But maple remains maple, and beech remains beech.

Wednesday night dinners at Mally and Ted's became routine after Mazie came to stay with Charlotte that summer. The week after the cottonwood fell, Ted grilled hamburgers and sweetcorn and Mally served salad made from her own tomatoes and cucumbers. After dinner, Mazie disappeared into the backyard to assess the firefly population while Ted loaded the dishwasher.

Mally poured two glasses of wine and led Charlotte onto the front porch.

"So, where's Harp these days?"

"He had a softball game tonight. City League. I should be there, cheering in the stands, but I'd rather be here."

Mally lifted her chin. "Is everything okay?"

Charlotte sighed. "Long dinners and conversation bore him silly." She gazed into her glass. "But to be honest, things are a bit tense."

She stammered through a condensed version of her summer, her disappointment with Harp and her confusing friendship with Fig. "When I say it out loud it sounds silly and melodramatic."

"No, it doesn't," Mally said, wrinkling her forehead. "But I have no wisdom to offer. Poor Fig. Is that really his name? Sounds like Harp has a right to be a bit green-eyed though. How can he compete with a man who's so ill?"

"I've neglected Harp horribly."

"Is Fig's condition really terminal?"

Charlotte nodded, keeping a tight rein on her emotions.

"Does being Fig's friend make you happy or break your heart?"

"Both? Part of me wanted to run away when he told me about his prognosis, but I love, um, just love being with him. He's so smart and —I don't know—fascinating."

"Too bad you can't put Fig's brain in Harp's body!" Ted said, coming through the screen door with a dishtowel over his shoulder.

"Ted!" Mally frowned. "What a thing to say."

Charlotte patted the cushion next to her. Her father sat down, slipping an arm around her shoulders.

"I just don't want your heart broken and ruining things with Harp."

"I don't want that either, Dad, but I can't turn my back on Fig. He doesn't have family or anyone really."

Ted frowned. "But you've only known him for, what, four or five months? You've got no obligation to him, honey, if he's lookin' for a nurse."

"That's not it," she said, bristling. "He kept his condition from me as long as he could. He's not asking for anything."

"Well it sounds like you're gettin' stretched in two directions," Ted said, rubbing her shoulder.

Mally sighed. "The heart is a willful thing, Charlotte. I know that much. But Dad's right about one thing. If Harp can't accept this friendship, you could be heading for a world of hurt."

Charlotte sagged against her father's shoulder. "I know. I know."

A week after her stay on the island, Hurricane Juanita finally wrung herself out and slipped quietly into the north Atlantic. Charlotte, Mazie, Harp and the crew returned to the island to finish their work.

Harp was wary, though Charlotte tried to reassure him by going with him to the climbing gym and joining the old TipTop crew at the bar on Friday night.

He needn't have worried, since Fig was apparently avoiding her. When she arrived in the morning, his Mercedes was gone and the driveway was still empty when she left for home.

She had forwarded him the email invitations to Barb, Portia, Nicky and Katie as well as their RSVPs, but he responded with only a terse, "Thanks, Charlotte. I'll get back to you soon."

She hadn't expected a dozen roses after their time together, but the disappearing act hurt. Maybe he'd changed his mind about the lawsuit or regretted taking her into his confidence. Well, so be it. She never wanted to be his plaintiff anyway, although he'd done one hell-of-a job of convincing her she did.

Even Mazie sensed something was off. She'd been wandering aimlessly around the island all week.

"Where's Fig lately?" she asked, finding Charlotte laying brick around the patio. "I found a new beetle and a couple of—."

"Just leave him alone, Maze," Charlotte snapped. "He's busy."

Mazie seemed to wilt in place. "Did he say I was annoying him or something?"

"No. Not that." Charlotte sat on her heels and sighed. "Sorry, honey. He's probably in court or something."

It was she, Charlotte, who had annoyed him. When the cottonwood fell and he told her everything, she reacted with too much emotion. He had probably sensed her ambivalence about Harp, too, and now he was distancing himself, being a gentleman. She could easily hate him for that.

Just before lunch that Friday, Mazie came around the house, shouting, "Aunt Charlotte, Fig's coming!"

Charlotte placed another brick into Fig's expanding patio.

"Ok," she said without enthusiasm.

"I'm going to show him this." Mazie held out her phone, showing a photo of a handsome black and red dragonfly. "He was on the thinkin' log—the dragonfly, not Fig. I'm still trying to identify it and Fig has the book I need."

"Give him ten minutes in the house before you knock on the door. Then just three soft taps. If he doesn't answer he's probably resting or working in his study. And be back here in twenty minutes. I'm timing you. I need more bricks."

A few minutes later, Fig came out with Mazie and Prince running ahead.

"Hey there," he said, his hands pushed casually into his pockets. He looked at the patio. "Nice. Very nice."

She looked up, but didn't allow herself to smile. "Harp's bringing more bricks over on Monday and we'll get it finished."

He nodded.

Charlotte said, "Maze, get your gloves on and bring me as many bricks as you can carry in the wheelbarrow, but don't overload it or you'll dump everything."

"Okay, but first I need to finish identifying—"

Charlotte frowned. "Break's over."

Mazie sauntered off, scuffing her feet against the gravel.

Fig squinted into the sun. "I'm sorry I've been out of touch. It's been a hell of a week."

She pulled another brick from the stack.

He took a step closer. "I've been reading a lot of cases and have a rough outline for the TRO and a workable timeline and an agenda for our meeting with your WILHA group. I was hoping you'd have time to talk later today."

Any woman with an ounce of self-respect would have said, Gee, I'm totally slammed right now. I'll get back to you when I can fit you in.

"Five thirty?" she asked.

Under protest, Mazie left the island with Harp and the crew that night, while Charlotte joined Fig on the Adirondack chairs.

He handed her a glass of wine and raised his. "To our landscaper-client relationship turned client-lawyer relationship."

"Indeed," she said without much enthusiasm. He didn't seem to notice.

He crossed one leg over the other. "You called my bluff, you know."

"Your bluff? About the lawsuit? I thought it was what you wanted."

He sighed. "It was – and is."

"But you're having second thoughts?"

"Second . . . thirds, maybe fourths by now. But mostly I just needed this week to . . . rearrange things."

"Like?"

He swallowed before speaking. "Like my career. I resigned from Legal Aid."

Charlotte sat up. "What? Why?"

"Our case will be a private legal matter. Legal Aid doesn't look kindly upon moonlighting." He brushed dog hair from his pant leg. "It's better this way. I can devote more time to our case."

She didn't know what to make of this.

He gave a quick, sideways glance. "I need to prioritize things." He sat for a few minutes, letting this sink in, she supposed. Then suddenly he chuckled.

"I had a private talk with my assistant. I know I complained about her phone etiquette, but she's a good woman—a good *Christian* woman she'd say. She's known me too long to overlook the changes in my health. So, when I called her into my office to tell her I was leaving, I wasn't surprised when she said she'd pray for me. I thanked her and started to see her out. But then, she did the damnedest thing, Charlotte. She reached across my desk and took my hands. Then she closed her eyes and prayed for me. Right there. Out loud. In my office."

"What did she say?"

He took a quick breath. "Well, she asked God to watch over my body, comfort my spirit and give me acceptance of what can't be changed. She asked that my fears be calmed and something about experiencing the healing power of love. She prayed for laughter, too, which surprised me. For a Sunday school dropout, I was really touched."

"That's beautiful."

Fig rubbed the tops of his thighs, working up to something. "So, the first item on our agenda this evening is the meeting with your colleagues next week. I'm thinking you can give them a tour, then we'll have drinks and hor d'oeuvres here on the porch while you and I outline our strategy. Do you think they'll sign on?"

"I don't know. They're curious, but apprehensive too. Let's not get our hopes up."

He nodded, but his eyes had extra shine. "Thank you for coming this far with me, Charlotte. I know I've been a pushy so-and-so."

She smiled. "I won't argue with that."

Fig rolled his head back and let his lids droop, smiling serenely. "You won't regret this, Charlotte. I promise."

Then suddenly he pitched forward, coughing uncontrollably. "Sorry," he said into his handkerchief.

"Can I get you some water?"

He shook his head. "It'll . . . pass." But the coughing turned to wheezing and then gasping. She resisted the urge to slap him on the back, offer him oxygen or a trip to the ER.

When the episode finally passed, he was completely winded. With closed eyes he said, "One day . . . you realize . . . that the planet . . . isn't going . . . to slow its orbit because . . . you need more time." He coughed again. "I know what . . . you're thinking. . . But what's the point of caution now?"

"Will you feel this way if we don't get our TRO or if you—? " She couldn't finish.

"—if I die trying? Yes, unequivocally. Let me burn bright and streak to Earth like a meteorite. I don't want to just sputter and grow dim. My sights are set . . . on a different point on the horizon now . . . something other . . . than my own demise. I can't tell you . . . what powerful medicine . . . that is, Charlotte, dear Charlotte. No matter what happens . . . or when . . . please remember that. This time. . . this work. . . this collaboration . . . is how I want to spend the time I have left."

His words came easier now. It was she who was speechless.

"If I'm honest," he continued, "this case is a long shot. But every argument we make will help the next plaintiff and the next—that's the way the law often works."

She struggled to keep up. "But stopping one volunteer event won't change the way plants are regulated."

"Maybe not, but we'll enlighten one judge with our data and heartfelt, ironclad arguments about the scourge of invasive species. We'll work to change the public's hearts and minds so justice can prevail."

"Easy-peasy," she said, with a smile that took effort.

"Like I always say, if you're willing to fail—and make a total ass of yourself—you can achieve something brilliant."

"I've never heard you say that."

"Well, I'm going to from now on." He raised his glass again. "Here's to tilting at windmills. To giving it all we got, or die trying."

She squinted at him. "Please, no gallows humor."

"Like, what did one casket say to the other casket? Is that you coffin?'"

"Wow. I haven't heard that one since fourth grade."

"It's a classic."

"*You're* a classic, Fig Newton Bigelow," she said, shaking her head.

After a long silence, he said, "The day you know death is at the door, is the day you begin to ask why you were given this life. You've thrown me a lifeline, Charlotte." Then he whispered, "Thank you."

"Aunt Charlotte!" Mazie shouted from the edge of the meadow the next morning. "I need your phone. ASAP! There are bumblebees all over that turtle flower and I think I can get a good picture."

"The white turtlehead?" Charlotte straightened up from her weeding, her arms full of mare's tail and thistle. She arched her stiff back and grunted.

"Come look! ASAP!"

Sometimes she regretted Mazie's expanding vocabulary. She dropped her bundle in the grass and followed her niece. The sight of two Adairs rushing behind the house brought Fig to the window of his study. "Where's the fire?"

Mazie ran backward a few steps cupping her hands and shouting. "Fig! Come on! Bumbleheads on the turtle bees!"

Fig caught up to them on the shady north end of the island, winded and smiling. Charlotte was pointing her phone at a white flower.

"Turtle bees? Do they have shells?"

Mazie slapped her forehead and laughed. "I meant *bumblebees* on the *turtleheads!* Look, Fig. Only bumblebees are strong enough to get inside."

Fig folded himself into a low squat.

"See? Each flower has two petals, one above the other like a turtle's mouth. Now watch."

A fat bumblebee landed on the lower lip of the blossom and butted its head against the opening like a linebacker at the offensive line. Pushing with its back legs and head, it pried the petals open and disappeared inside.

"Wow. Look at that," Fig said, amazed.

"Regular bees aren't strong enough to get inside. Did you get a picture, Aunt Charlotte?"

"Got it," she said.

"That's fascinating, Mazie."

Charlotte stood up and handed Mazie her phone. "Looks like the turtleheads are happy here. There are more by the dock, Mazie, but don't you dare drop my cell in the river."

Fig and Mazie weren't listening. With their heads almost touching they whispered words of encouragement or praise for the next bee's triumph.

Charlotte shook her head and turned back toward the other end of the island leaving these two exotic creatures to marvel at the world around them.

Turtlehead *Chelone glabra*

27

TRIANGLE

After their Wednesday night family night dinner, Charlotte and Mally retired to the porch again.

"So, you're really taking out a restraining order against the city?" Mally asked.

Charlotte gave a wide-eyed nod. "And the county! Can you believe it?"

"And Fig isn't going to charge you? I don't know what to think, Charlotte. Does he think you'll win?"

She shrugged. "He thinks there's a good chance. But he wants this so badly, Mum. I couldn't say no—even though I see how it drains him."

"And how are you handling the . . . the reality of his illness?"

Mally's posture—legs and forearms crossed—and her intense, probing look had a Pavlovian effect on Charlotte. *Fine*, was not an answer that would satisfy her mother.

Charlotte puffed out her cheeks and exhaled slowly. "Honestly, I don't know if I'm helping him or killing him."

Mally reached for her daughter's hand. "If life has purpose, that means the world to someone facing the end of life."

Charlotte nodded. "We're recruiting more plaintiffs and outlining our case. It is meaningful work and he loves it, but he fights for every breath."

Mally frowned.

"What?" Charlotte asked.

"Fig is taking up a lot of space in your life. What about Harp?"

"They say the heart has many chambers."

"Meaning?"

"Meaning I love Harp, but I care a lot about Fig, too. Completely different. Completely separate."

"And Harp's okay with this?"

She tilted her head. "He tries to be."

"It's hard to compete for attention with a man who's dying."

Charlotte rolled her head back. "I know."

After a long pause, Mally said, "You and Harp have a future." And after another long pause, she asked, "But you and Fig? I think your devotion to him can only be one thing."

Charlotte could only shake her head again. "We care about each other very deeply, but it's different. I can't explain it."

Mally dropped her chin. "Yes, well whatever it is, it certainly defies description."

Truth be told, something heavy and ill-fitting had been wedging itself between Charlotte and Harp for weeks. He wasn't happy about her involvement in the lawsuit. Not happy at all. They argued endlessly about why she was letting herself be "manipulated" by Fig and distracted from finding new clients for her business.

When she came home late from Fig's for the third day in a row, Harp was kneeling in the driveway changing the tire on his bike. He didn't move to get up.

"Another late night, eh?" He looked up. "Do you want to tell me what's going on?"

"We're outlining the agenda for our meeting with the four WILHA members who are coming to the island in a few days, but we got it done."

"I mean with you and me. Or, should I say, you and me and Fig?"

"I don't know what you mean." She was stalling. She knew exactly what he meant.

"Sure you do." He worked the pump to fill the inner tube. "We've been dancing around in a weird love triangle all summer."

"Love triangle? It's a lawsuit, not—. Come on, Harp!"

He stood up slowly, wiping his hands on a rag and locking eyes on her. "I didn't want to see it, but now . . . Well, it just seems suspicious."

"Suspicious! There's nothing—"

"Oh, come on, Char. Be honest with me. Be honest with yourself for once. This isn't just about some lawsuit."

She backed away from him and watched his face fall. His look of defeat made her feel sick.

"It's obvious you have feelings for the guy, Char. Everyone can see that but you."

"Of course I have feelings, but as a friend and a colleague. That's all."

He threw his head back and laughed bitterly. "What's sad is that I think you actually believe the crap you're saying. I swear you're even more clueless than I've been all these months. Wake up!"

And so there it was. Harp was holding up a mirror to her and wasn't going to let her look away. She felt her mouth grow dry.

"Please, Charlotte. It shouldn't be this hard to love me. I should never have proposed. I made our relationship into something it wasn't meant to be. All this—whatever you and Fig are doing—it hurts. I know you're trying hard to keep it professional with him, but you've made our engagement a goddamn joke." He threw the rag on the ground and put his hands on his hip. "I can't do this anymore."

She took a step backward and covered her forehead with her hand. "I've been a terrible fiancée. I'm so sorry, Harp. And I won't deny I have feelings for Fig, but I'm not sure what they are."

She covered her face and wept. She felt his hands fall lightly on her shoulders. She didn't deserve this kindness. She looked up at him. "I haven't been unfaithful. I want you to know that."

"There's more than one way to—." He shook his head, holding back. Then he nodded. "I know."

They walked together into the kitchen where he washed his hands at the sink. The clock ticked. The refrigerator hummed. She didn't know what to say or do.

He laid the towel next to the sink and turned to her. "I don't see a future for us anymore, Charlotte. But what makes me really sad is that Fig can't give you one either. The road he's taking you down is a dead end." He squeezed his eyes shut and shook his head. "Sorry. That came out wrong."

"I know. You're right. But I can't turn my back on him. I don't expect you to understand."

Harp rubbed his eyes. "No, I *do* understand. Fig's a pretty great guy. That's hard for me to admit. And he should have someone beside him with what he's facing. I see that. I just hate that it has to be you."

Charlotte let go of a long, shuddering breath. "This would be easier if you told me to go to hell and storm out."

He shrugged and smiled a little.

"I'll miss being your fiancée, Harp." She slipped the ring from her finger and pressed it into his palm and closed his hand around it. "It was always fun."

He nodded and backed toward the living room. "I'll probably stay at Mike's until I figure things out."

"Will I see you Monday?"

"We're going fishing next week. The crew can handle everything that's left."

"Okay. Sure."

He went upstairs and came down with a full duffel bag.

"I'll come by tomorrow to clear out the rest of my stuff."

As the door swung closed behind him, she said "I'm so sorry, Harp," but so softly he didn't hear.

The next evening, his bike and kayak were gone and his key was under the mat.

Fig spent the following week at Legal Aid, handing over his cases to co-workers and cleaning out his office. With Harp gone, Charlotte arranged for Hector, who had just bought a used SUV, to drive himself, Martin and Kiza to and from the island.

Mazie and Mally spent Wednesday getting haircuts and shopping for school clothes while Charlotte and the crew planted a dozen junipers at the edges of the meadow. After the crew went home, she was pushing the wheelbarrow toward the shed when Fig arrived.

"I saw the crew leaving. Is Harp taking time off?"

Charlotte took off her gloves. "You could say that." She wiggled her ringless finger. "We ended things a few days ago."

Fig stepped back. "I'm surprised—and really sorry. Are you all right?"

"It should have ended months ago—or never started in the first place. But it was painful."

Fig hesitated, considering something. "Would a big glass of water with a wine chaser be therapeutic? You look a bit haggard."

"Haggard? Just what a newly single girl wants to hear. But yes. I'd love both of those in that order."

She followed him up the porch steps and sank into a chair while he went inside.

When he returned with a tray of glasses, he said, "I've been told I'm a world-class listener."

She took a long drink of the water before speaking. "Harp ended it, actually. But it's all for the best. I wasn't being honest with him—or myself, really."

Fig's expression was full of interest.

"He became, I don't know, I guess . . . resentful."

"Of what?"

She folded one leg under her to face him, considering just how candid she dared to be. Later, she would always wonder what made her say what she said next—whether it was fatigue or resignation or despair or just plain foolishness. She couldn't blame the wine that sat untouched on the arm of the chair.

"Of you, actually. Of the time I spent here. Of FDUs and TROs." She laughed to make light of it. "I didn't mean for it to be . . . that way, but—." She shrugged and took her first sip. "Whatever. I don't know."

The ball had been officially served and had bounced barely in bounds on Fig's side of the net. She took a big gulp to keep her mouth occupied.

Fig hadn't moved, but his pale blue eyes darted over every feature of her face. Why wasn't he saying anything?

She stood up suddenly to stand at the railing and give him time to consider whether to return the serve or call it out-of-bounds.

The far bank was sandwiched between blue river and bluer sky. How she loved this place. How she would miss it . . . and him if—. How she longed to feel his warmth behind her again. Arms encircling her as they had the day of the storm.

But Fig wasn't responding and this vacuum of silence threatened to suck words from her. Finally, she addressed the river, "So, anyway, I'm kind of at loose ends."

Apparently, her words had struck him dumb. Damn him.

She yammered on. "Harp quit and moved out last weekend. I can't blame him."

With her back to him she couldn't tell what effect if any, her words were having. She knew her own face was flushed from the exertion of the day, from the first effects of the wine and from her own emotional nakedness.

Still no word from Mr. Bigelow. Double damn the man!

Finally, she heard him get up and felt his radiant warmth beside her at the porch railing. She looked up.

"Charlotte," he said breathing her name slowly, softly. He leaned onto his forearms and lowered his forehead into his hands. He drew in a long, irregular breath. "I need to say something to you and I don't want you to misunderstand."

He rubbed his eyes as if they hurt. "I'm not sure what happened this summer. I may be reading things all wrong. But I'm—I'm going to crawl out on a very long, very shaky limb anyway." He took her glass from her hand and set it down. Then took her hands in his so they were facing each other.

"I care a great deal for you. I regret that I have been unable to conceal that, though God knows I've tried." He shook his head, looking over her shoulder. "But this can't—. The timing of it—." She felt the pressure on her hands. "You must see, nothing can happen between us."

She pulled her hands back as if she'd touched a hot stove and stepped back.

"Charlotte. Please. Just listen." He reached for her shoulders, but she shrugged him off. She felt so ashamed and exposed.

"The truth is, I'm using oxygen more and more. You must know what that means."

In an instant the porch, the island, the universe warped into something grotesque and unrecognizable. Her peripheral vision blurred. Her thoughts unspooled into a tangled heap. She gripped the railing to remain upright.

"I'm so sorry, Charlotte. I care about you too much to—"

"Stop there. I *know* how sick you are. That's why we should be together. Even if it's just for a few months or even a week. I don't care."

And there it was—her deepest secret, her most private longing laid bare. Now that she'd said it, she knew it was the truth.

His eyes glistened. "No. It's too late for us."

His words landed like blows. Tears were beyond her control now—everything on this earth was apparently beyond her control.

He pulled her to him and into the same gentle embrace that had weakened her knees the day of the storm.

"You deserve a full life, Charlotte—a long, normal life with someone who can share all of it. I can't give you that. Please, you must see that we can't start a relationship now." Then, he stepped back and whispered, "You need to go now—back to your life." Wearily, he bent down and lifted her bag onto her shoulder and wiped her cheeks with the soft skin of his knuckles.

"Please, Fig."

"No." He folded his arms across his chest, pulling his shoulders up. "There's—There's nothing more to say."

A sob worked its way up from her chest and into her throat and erupted. "But what about the lawsuit?" She sobbed. "Without me . . . You need me," She couldn't finish what sounded so desperate and manipulative.

He shook his head, "Please, leave before—. Please, Charlotte." He looked at the raft. "Just go."

She ran down the steps and didn't look back until she reached her truck. And when she did, he was gone. He was gone.

Mally took one look at Charlotte's red-rimmed eyes and said, "I'll put the kettle on." Charlotte sank into a kitchen chair and hugged her knees to her chest.

"I know you're a coffee drinker, but trust me, tea's what you need," she said, looking over her shoulder. "So, Harp upped sticks?"

She nodded. Everything she wanted to say was stuck behind an enormous lump in her throat.

"Oh, I'm so sorry, love." She set a box of Kleenex and a plate of McVitie's Digestives on the table. "So the wedding's off?"

Charlotte nodded. "Sorry, Mum."

"Oh gosh. Don't be sorry on *my* account. Although I had my eye on a peach fascinator—with black feathers, like the Princess of Wales waers, you know. A real show-stopper." She fluttered her eyelashes and laughed. "Oh, honey, you know I'm not one of those mums who lives for her daughter's wedding day."

The electric tea kettle hissed and whooshed to a crescendo. Just as it was threatening to lift off, it shut down.

With her back turned, Mally sighed. "I'm a bit relieved if I'm honest."

"You are?" Charlotte squeaked.

Mally poured boiling water into the Spode teapot, swirled it and emptied it down the drain. Then she filled it again and added loose tea from a tin and covered the pot with a crocheted tea cozy. She sat down across from Charlotte.

"I think you would have outgrown Harp eventually, if you haven't already." Mally cocked one eyebrow and watched her daughter's reaction. "Especially if there's a more mature man to compare him to?"

Charlotte propped her chin on her knee to stop it from quivering. "Yeah, I suppose." She still didn't trust her voice.

Mally poured milk into the bottom of two matching Spode teacups and then the steeped tea. "It's just so tragic that a young man like Fig is so ill. I'm glad you have the lawsuit to take your mind off of Harp."

Charlotte pulled in a shaky breath and blew her nose, "Not now."

"So what is it then?" Mally set her cup down and searched Charlotte's face. "Oh, love. Those tears aren't for Harp, are they?"

Charlotte swallowed hard. "W—When I told Fig a-about H-Harp and me, and how jealous Harp was, he s-sent me a-away."

Mally reached across the table for Charlotte's hand.

"So, it's Fig who's broken your heart, isn't it?"

Charlotte shrugged as her face crumpled. "I don't know."

"Well, it's as plain as the tears on your face."

TO: Barb, Katie, Nicky and Portia,
SUBJECT: Our Meeting
BCC: Newton Bigelow

Dear Barb, Katie, Nicky and Portia,
I'm so sorry, but I find I am unable to join you at the meeting
with Newton Bigelow. If you are interested in joining the lawsuit,
please contact him directly. I wish you all the best of luck.

Sincerely,
Charlotte

FROM: Portia Easter
SUBJECT: Our meeting

Dear Charlotte,
I don't know what to make of your cancellation. You don't owe
me an explanation if your decision is personal, but if you have
doubts about Mr. Bigelow's ability to represent us, I would appreciate knowing that before I take the matter to my board.

I hope all is well with you and I look forward to seeing you again soon.

Portia

TO: Portia Easter
SUBJECT: Our meeting

Dear Portia,
I have complete faith in Mr. Bigelow's legal abilities and I hope
you join the suit. He will represent you brilliantly. You are
welcome to forward this email to Barb, Katie and Nicky.

Your friend,
Charlotte

TO: Charlotte Adair
FROM: Katie Clay

What's up, girl? Call me!

Love,
Katie

The day after the meeting with Fig, Katie called Charlotte.

"What's going on?"

"Nothing really. How did the meeting go?"

"Great! What a beautiful place and such a nice man. He didn't explain why you weren't there, but of course, we were all wondering." She lowered her voice to a conspiratorial whisper. "Did he hit on you or something?"

Charlotte almost laughed. "No, not that." She paused. "But I guess you could say I hit on him, which was monumentally stupid."

"Really?" She paused to take this in. "But what about Hunky Harp?" Charlotte suspected Katie was mentally undressing Harp and Fig and trying to make sense of this.

She gave Katie an abridged version of her summer with Fig, leaving out his grim prognosis.

"So, when we started working on the lawsuit, Harp got jealous and broke up with me. I had hoped Fig would be happy to hear that, but he wasn't." Her voice trailed off. "God, it all sounds so sordid." She didn't want to talk about it. "The important thing is there's a strong case to be made, Fig needs plaintiffs and you'd be great. Are you going to sign on?"

"I'm thinking about it. He asked us all to tell him how invasive plant species affect our businesses. I guess financial loss gives us the right to sue or something. But darn it, Charlotte, I'm so disappointed you won't be part of it."

"Thanks, but it's for the best."

In the waning days of summer, Mazie moved back to Mally and Ted's. She took half of Charlotte's comic collection with her and left the other half to read when she visited the farm. She complained about not seeing Fig but didn't question Charlotte's explanation that the work on the island was coming to an end.

Meanwhile, Charlotte avoided the island as much as possible and when Fig's Mercedes was parked at the landing she steered clear.

The initial hurt and humiliation gradually solidified into righteous indignation. If Fig didn't want her, she certainly wasn't going to pine over him.

At the end of a long week of successful avoidance, Charlotte was helping the crew load trash and equipment into her truck.

Hector had just tossed a stack of plastic pots into the back when he turned to her. "Why you not come to Fig's now?"

"I'm looking for new clients."

Hector eyed her skeptically. "You not marry Harp and you don't talk to Fig neither?"

She looked away. "It's . . . complicated."

Martin dropped a coil of hose into the truck bed. "What is 'complicated'?"

"*Deficil. Complicado*," Hector offered.

"Ah, *compliquée*," Martin nodded solemnly. "Everything is *compliquée* with a man and a woman."

Kiza laughed. "Or a woman and two mans."

Charlotte rolled her eyes. "Just load the truck."

SEPTEMBER

Sandhill Crane Grus canadensis

28

THE SLEEPOVER

In the world of bees, not all species have the ability to sting, and of those that do, only females have stingers, which are also used to lay eggs. While solitary species rarely sting, hive-dwelling bees will go to great lengths to defend queen and colony. An intruder nearing the hive triggers an alarm response followed by a painful injection of venom, which can be deadly for some victims.

September arrived in the morning mist that settled over the Hawthorn River. The scarlet fruit of the river's eponymous tree rippened into a feast for flocks of robins and cedar waxwings. Sun-tinged maples turned a hundred shades of orange and pink. The leaves of the cottonwood curled and fell, skittering across Fig's dock or sailing downriver like tiny regattas.

After leaving the crew with instructions for the day, Charlotte was choosing a cantaloupe at a small farmer's market nearby. She turn at the sound of her name.

"Charlotte? I thought it was you! I'm Heather Kohn. Remember me? We were in school together. I'm Heather Geller now."

Charlotte mentally morphed this petite, blond woman back into a teenager before nodding. "Yes. Of course. Nice to see you, Heather. Do you live on this side of town?"

"Yeah, on the river. How about you?"

"No. I've been working nearby. Landscaping at a house on the river actually. On the island. Do you know it?"

"Sure. We go by there on our boat all the time. I hear the guy's kind of a hermit." She wrinkled her nose. "What's he like?"

"He's an attorney. Definitely not a hermit," she added. Did a quiet, contemplative life qualify Fig as a hermit?

Behind her, a younger, even blonder version of Heather leaned against the dairy case texting.

"This must be your daughter," Charlotte said. "She looks just like you."

"This is Alison. I think she's in your niece's class. Mandy, right?"

"Mazie," Charlotte corrected.

"You know Mazie Adair, right, honey?" Heather asked her daughter, who returned a shrug.

"Sort of. She was in my science class last year." She managed a half-hearted smile before dropping her focus back to her phone.

Heather leaned closer, touched Charlotte's wrist and lowered her voice. "I was sooooooo sorry to hear about your sister. I know it's been ages and I should have sent a note, but we were in the middle of building the house. What a process that was! It's just a little ways upstream from the island. We've got a great view. You should come by sometime. Anyways, I heard Mindy lives with your parents. That has to be hard."

"Actually, Mazie worked for me this summer."

"So, are you married? Any kids?"

Charlotte shook her head and put a melon into her basket, hoping to curtail the conversation.

"Really?" Heather said, looking let down, but then brightened. "Ali says your niece is some kind of genius."

Alison did a quick head-shake-eye-roll-tsk combo before replying. "I never said *genius*, Mom."

Heather returned an identical head-shake-eye-roll-tsk. "Studious. Brainy. What-*ever*."

Charlotte nodded. "We're proud of her."

"Well of *course*, you are! And you *should* be." Heather said, reaching for Charlotte's wrist and giving it a firm squeeze. "All those brains will pay off someday, but it can be hard to be the brainy type in middle school."

Charlotte smiled stiffly and promised to tell Mazie she'd met Alison before hurrying to the checkout.

She was surprised three days later when Mazie showed her a pink envelope addressed in calligraphy. It was an invitation to Alison Geller's thirteenth birthday party and "Boathouse Sleepover" to be held the Saturday before Labor Day. Mazie handled the card as if it might be booby-trapped.

"I don't know why she's inviting me. We haven't said two words since, like, fourth grade. I don't even *like* her." Mazie sniffed the letter and made a face.

Charlotte imagined the conversation in the Geller household on the subject of charity toward the poor, motherless, too-smart-for-her-own good Adair girl. Expensive bribes probably sealed the deal.

"You don't have to go, Maze."

But to Charlotte's surprise, Mazie was curious.

"It will be a cross-cultural experience," she announced with a shrug. "Maybe I'll figure out what goes on in the twisted minds of normal teenage girls."

"*You're* normal, honey."

Mazie coughed. "Please don't insult me, Aunt Charlotte."

A little after five, Charlotte and Mazie pulled into the Geller's brick driveway and stopped in front of their three-stall garage. The house sat on the bluff overlooking the river just a few hundred yards upstream from the island. It was enormous. Heather, who had grown up in a modest Saskawan neighborhood, was letting the world know she'd married up.

Mazie sat ramrod straight in the passenger seat with a wrapped gift on her knees. She made no move to get out.

When they'd gone shopping the day before, Mazie had picked out a star locater kit for Alison.

"Look. It includes star maps for both the Northern and Southern hemispheres with over a thousand stars shown and the brightest ones identified by name."

"Does Alison like astronomy?" Charlotte asked.

"No, but she got a D in science last year, so it's time she learned."

With some artful coaching, for which she was quite proud, Charlotte steered Mazie toward a bestselling young adult novel that Mazie admitted was "not totally insipid."

"So you'll be sleeping in a boathouse, eh?" Charlotte said to her passenger. "That sounds pretty fun."

This got a dubious, "Hmm," a tilt of the head and, "Actually, I'm more interested to see what Alison and her clones *do* at sleepovers."

It seemed Mazie would be gathering data on juvenile female *Homo-sapiens* as well as insects.

"Well, I hope you have some fun, too," Charlotte said. "Join in."

Another hmm was followed by, "Well, they better not try to put my hand in warm water when I'm asleep."

"Why would they do that?"

"To make me pee my sleeping bag. It's the oldest trick in the book, but according to the Internet it's just a myth, so I'm not that worried."

Charlotte didn't believe any of this bravado. "I'll be home all night. Call me if you need me."

"I won't."

Heather came out of the house then, pushing Alison ahead of her and waving. Trailing behind was an entourage of five leggy, mostly blonde, girls each wearing shockingly short cut-offs and cropped tee shirts. Mazie was right, they did look like clones. Two of them were whispering behind cupped hands. The rest ignored the new arrival.

Mazie slid out of the car with her backpack and the gift-wrapped book. She pulled her sleeping bag and pillow out of the back and stood in front of the truck.

"What should I do with my stuff?" she asked, getting down to business. Pleasantries still didn't come naturally, but they didn't seem to for the other girls either.

Heather nudged her daughter forward. "Help Mandy carry her stuff, honey." She turned on a smile. "Welcome, honey. I'll take the gift. Such pretty wrapping. We'll open them after the barbecue when we cut the cake. It's chocolate. Do you like chocolate?"

"It's Mazie," Mazie said, deadpan.

"Oh, that's right," Heather said. "Alison, girls, show Mazie where you'll be sleeping." She motioned to Charlotte. "Come on. I'll show you around."

Charlotte followed Heather down several flights of steps behind the house that ended at a boathouse with a flat roof. Half the roof was a screened-in room with chairs and a ping-pong table covered with backpacks and sleeping bags. The other half was an open deck with hammocks, more patio furniture and an outdoor kitchen already strewn with bags of chips and popcorn. Next to the boathouse, jutting into the river was a dock and a rowboat.

Inside the boathouse was a pontoon boat.

"My husband will take the girls for a ride in the pontoon later unless it rains," Heather said, looking up at the gathering clouds. "At least the weather will keep them inside tonight. But don't worry, we'll be keeping an eye on them."

Inside the screened area, six girls were bending over someone's phone as Mazie painstakingly unpacked her gear and arranged things on the table. When she pulled out her bug jar, Charlotte felt the sudden urge to grab Mazie and head home.

Heather was squeezing her wrist again. "Come on. I'll make us martinis and we can rehash old times."

"Thanks, Heather, but I should go. Call me if anything—I mean, if you need to—for anything," Charlotte stuttered.

Heather's radar for weakness followed Charlotte's distracted gaze to Mazie standing outside the tight circle of girls, gnawing on her thumbnail. Heather tilted her head and rubbed Charlotte's shoulder. "Char, don't you worry about Mandy. She'll be just fine."

Charlotte resisted the urge to shove Heather into the river.

She was folding laundry at the kitchen table when her phone rang.

"Char, it's Heather. I'm sorry to call and it's probably nothing but—" She heard throat clearing.

"But *what*?"

"It's just that the girls and I . . . We've looked everywhere, but we can't find Mindy. Is she prone to wandering off? Her phone and all her stuff is still here, so I'm sure she hasn't gone far."

Her truck hit ninety on the expressway and shaved six minutes off her usual commute to Fig's side of town. On the phone, Heather had said she'd heard screams ("Just teen girl squealing, really.") coming from the boathouse and went to investigate.

"Mattie was wading in the river with that net and jar and was scaring the girls with something she found in the water. The next thing we knew she was gone. No one saw her leave."

Charlotte called Mazie's cell from the truck but got her voicemail.

"Where are you? We're all worried. I'm on my way to Alison's now. Call me *now*!"

When Charlotte arrived at the Geller's, the other girls were loitering in the kitchen in a loose huddle, hugging themselves, each other and whispering as if Mazie's waterlogged body had already been dragged from the river.

Charlotte glared at the girls. "Tell me what happened—*now!*" Heads shook, shoulders shrugged, eyes wandered to the coffered ceiling or dropped to the floor. "None of you saw her leave? I don't believe that."

Several girls glanced at Alison.

Charlotte said, "Alison? Look at me."

The little tyrant lifted her chin and wrinkled her nose in disgust. "*I* don't know where she is. She didn't want to hang with us. She just wanted to catch bugs."

"Alison!" her mother warned. "Don't be rude. Tell us exactly what happened."

Alison sighed. "How would *I* know? She just *left*. She's probably home by now."

"We live miles from here," Charlotte snapped. "She wouldn't do that."

Alison twisted a lock of her hair and shifted from one foot to the other. "She was going on and on about knowing that old guy who lives on the island." She looked quickly at the other girls, challenging them to contradict her.

Another girl nodded. "Yeah. She was acting kinda weird."

Charlotte flew out the door and down the step with Heather at her heels. It was starting to drizzle.

"I'm sure Mandy's just hiding somewhere, Char. You know how emotional girls can be."

"Mazie!" Charlotte hissed. "Her name is Mazie, damn it, Heather. M-A-Z-I-E!"

From the stairs, she cupped her hands and shouted her name as thunder rumbled overhead. She ran down the steps to the boathouse and shouted again, searching the riverbank for any sign of her. The rain began in earnest and the wind came up.

Charlotte pointed to the dock. "Wait! Where's the rowboat that was here?"

Heather shook her head. "I-I don't know." She looked ready to cry.

"It's a good thing you were keeping an eye on things, Heather!" She brought her hand to her forehead, ready to panic. "Is there another boat I could use?"

"Just the pontoon, but my husband has the key. He's on his way home. He'll be here in about twenty minutes. He can take you out. We'll find her. Don't worry."

"I can't wait twenty minutes!"

She ran angrily up the steps, dialing Fig. Maybe Mazie took the rowboat to the island. Maybe she was already at Fig's safe and sound.

The phone rang three times. "You've reached Newton Bigelow. Please leave . . ."

She jumped into the truck and made for the island.

The Mercedes was parked at the landing and the raft was moored at the island. But if Fig was at home, why hadn't he picked up? And if Mazie decided to row to the island, why wasn't the rowboat at the dock? Maybe she landed at the other side of the island.

She pulled the raft to the landing, cursing the wasted minutes. Meanwhile, the wind was whipping up white caps and the temperature was dropping. She jumped onto the raft and jerked the rope hard, making the raft speed through the water.

Several feet from the dock, she leaped over the gap, shouting. "*Mazie! Fig!*"

Prince came out of the woods jumping on her and barking frantically. Something wasn't right. She ran to the back of the island, hoping to find the rowboat pulled up, but the bank and the river were deserted. She yelled through cupped hands. "*Mazie! Fig!*"

She ran back to the house and let herself in. In the study, Fig's oxygen machine whirred next to his desk and the screen was lit up. His phone lay next to the screen. She ran upstair. His bed was empty. She ran back outside.

In the oak grove, the shed doors stood open and one of the kayaks was missing. Maybe Mazie had stopped at the island and invited Fig to join her. But why was Prince still here? Mazie would have insisted—. And Fig wouldn't have taken a kayak out now, unless—.

The rain came down in earnest now. She dragged the second kayak to the riverbank and had one foot in before remembering the paddle. She pulled the kayak back onto the bank, cursing her stupidity and ran back to the shed. When she returned Prince was standing in the kayak.

"No. Get out!"

She waded into the chilly water, tossed Prince onto the bank and pushed off, ignoring his high-pitched yipping. Just as she cleared the point of the island she heard a splash. Prince was paddling madly toward her but was being swept away by the racing current.

"Prince!" She paddled hard and caught up with him, then scooped him up. He shook himself, nearly swamping them.

"Sit down!"

She had lost so much time. Her breath came in shallow pants and blood pumped painfully through her temples. She needed help. She reached into her pocket for her phone but found it empty. She'd left it on the seat of the truck. She was hopeless.

Meanwhile, the wind and the river swept the kayak toward the dam just a half mile away. Above her, a crack of thunder split the sky and the shoreline soon vanished behind billowing curtains of rain. How would she ever find them now?

She leaned hard into the paddle with Prince wedged between her knees. She had no idea if Mazie knew how to row a boat, but surely, she would bump the shore before she got to the dam or Fig would catch up to her—unless the strain was too much for his heart or they were both stuck by lightning or they were swept into the spillway.

"*Fig! Mazie!*"

She shook off panic. Paralysis was not an option. Prince licked her chin.

"I know. I know, Prince. We'll find them."

Ahead, another island divided the river. She paddled into the east channel looking for any signs of a rowboat or a yellow kayak carrying the two people she loved most in this world.

To her right, the east bank rose so steeply above the river that few homes on that side had docks, or even steps down to the river as the Gellers did. Even if Mazie got to shore there, it would be a long climb up to get help. And Fig could never —. Her heart sank.

Below the second island, the river widened and slowed, queuing up to plunge over the dam. In good weather there would be other boaters and fishermen here, but tonight the river was empty. She spun the kayak in a circle searching the densely wooded banks. Should she paddle back upstream and search the other side of the second island? Should she find a house and ask for help? She wiped her face and tried to bring the shore into focus through the rain.

Ahead, red and white buoys were strung like beads across the width of the river to warn boaters away from the dam. If Fig and Mazie weren't here, maybe they had already been rescued and were warm and dry somewhere. But where were the rowboat and Fig's kayak?

Then she saw it, barely visible through the downpour, Fig's empty kayak bobbing at the top of the spillway. There was only one possibility—Mazie had gone over the dam and Fig had gone after her.

She let out an anguished cry that was downed out by a million raindrops. Her stomach heaved.

Prince let out a string of frantic yelps and pivoted to face the eastern shore. His front paws followed the rim of the kayak as his hind claws sunk into her thighs.

"Stop it!" she yelled, pushing him down.

He raised his muzzle and howled.

"What *is* it?" She spun the kayak, but saw nothing but empty river and a wall of trees. Prince was barking so hard now that he lost his footing and he nearly fell overboard.

"What do you see, boy?"

She grabbed him around the belly and leaned forward. Following his nose, she paddled toward the bank. As they drew closer an overhanging limb bobbed up and down. She laid into the paddle.

Prince stood motionless. The tree bobbed again. Then an arm emerged from the foliage, waving in a broad arc. Mazie's arm.

"Mazie!" Charlotte screamed.

"Over here!" She was balanced on the limb and riding it up and down.

"Charlotte!" She heard her muffled voice. "Over here!"

"Prince! You found her." Prince's tail whacked her in the face.

But where was Fig? With each stroke, her heart leaped at the sight of Mazie and fell when Fig didn't appear.

Closer now, the rowboat came into view. Fig pulled himself to a partial stand and waved.

A moment later, Charlotte's kayak bumped the side of the rowboat and catapulted Prince into Fig's arms.

Charlotte grabbed Mazie and pulled her into a bear hug.

"Thank God! Are you hurt?" She held Mazie at arm's length to look for signs of injury then hugged her again.

Prince covered Fig's face with kisses in an unbridled display of dog joy.

"Prince spotted you first," she said. "He led us here."

"Attaboy, Prince," Fig said.

Mazie rubbed him all over. "Good boy!"

Charlotte frowned. "Are you really okay?"

"We're fine, Aunt Charlotte, but pretty cold," she said, looking at Fig.

Charlotte took off her parka and wrapped it around Fig's hunched shoulders and lifted Prince into his arms. "Here boy. Keep him warm."

"I'm fine. I'm fine," Fig said through blue lips and chattering teeth. He pointed to the top of the bank. "Apparently, someone called 911."

Two paramedics in orange vests were making their way slowly down the steep bank with a rescue sled attached to a winch.

Fig sighed. "This will be undignified."

Charlotte smiled. "Think of it as a hero's welcome."

On the slow ascent, Fig complained that he could have climbed up on his own with a couple of rests. In the ambulance, one of the paramedics listen to Fig's heart and lungs and frowned. "I'd like a doctor to take a look at you, Mr. Bigelow"

"Thank you, but a ride home, a hot shower and dry clothes are all I need."

"I hear pretty clear signs of—."

"I have medication and everything I need at home."

"He's a lawyer. Can you tell?" Charlotte said, rolling her eyes.

"You his wife?"

"Me? Nope. Just the landscaper." She looked away. Now that Fig was safe, she was pissed again.

"Are you willing to stay with him for a few hours?"

She glanced at Fig and watched his eyes drop to the floor.

"Sure. No problem."

The second paramedic called out from the driver's seat. "Just got a call from a guy named Geller who says he's out looking for this young lady in his boat." He looked at Mazie in the rear-view mirror. "He said you took the rowboat from his house just before the storm? That's pretty dangerous so close to the dam, especially in a storm."

"But—." Mazie's chin started to quiver. "I'm sorry."

Charlotte hugged her again. "It's okay, sweetheart. We're just glad you're safe."

Mazie whispered, "Aunt Charlotte, please don't tell Nana and Pop what happened. Okay?"

"Well, we don't need to call them tonight."

When they reached the landing, the driver pulled out a clipboard and asked for the full story. Fig explained that he was at home in his study when he heard Mazie calling for him.

"I ran outside and saw her coming down the river in a rowboat. She was trying to get to the island, but only had one oar. I waded out to catch her, but I wasn't able to reach her in time."

He swallowed his emotions before he spoke again. "By the time I got my kayak in the water, she was pretty far ahead."

Mazie said, "But just before the dam, he caught up with me and jumped into the rowboat."

"Between her oar and my paddle, we made it to shore just before the storm hit."

Mazie went on. "But the bank was so steep and slippery we couldn't make it up. Then we saw Charlotte in the other kayak. That's when I waved and Prince saw me."

"What happened to the other oar, Mazie?" Charlotte asked.

"I—I don't know." Mazie said, biting into her thumbnail. "I must have dropped it."

"Well, you're both very lucky you didn't go over the spillway," the paramedic said. "And you say the dog spotted you first? What's his name?"

"Prince," they said in unison.

The paramedic took a small, red pin out of a compartment and fastened it to Prince's collar. It said Super Hero in gold lettering.

"Good job, Prince," he said. "You're one of the big dogs today."

29

AFTERMATH

Traditional healers in Uganda use soil to treat many ailments. Recently, neuroscientists in England exposed mice to common soil bacteria. They found that their test subjects were able to navigate a complex maze faster, with fewer signs of anxiety. Soil bacteria, they found, also increases brain serotonin levels and may boost the immune system. Scientists are optimistic about soil's value in the treatment of allergies, cancer, skin diseases and tuberculosis. But none of this news to gardeners, who have long appreciated the curative powers of good old garden dirt.

When the ambulance left the landing, Charlotte retrieved her phone from the truck and joined Mazie and Fig on the raft. It was going to be a long, awkward evening, she thought. But this whole terrifying incident only proved what she already knew—that she and Fig needed each other and Mazie needed both of them.

Fig went upstairs and came back with two pairs of dry sweatpants, sweatshirts and socks for them. Then he took a long shower while Charlotte put their wet clothes into the dryer, turned on the heat, made a pot of honeyed tea and got a fire going in the grate. Afterward, the three of them sat on the couch under a pile of blankets with Mazie sandwiched in the middle.

Charlotte's phone rang. It was Heather Geller. She sighed. "I can't deal with that woman right now."

Fig held out his hand, "May I?" He took the phone into his study and shut the door behind him. She was too exhausted to protest.

She reached for Mazie's hand. "Do you realize how dangerous it was to take that rowboat out by yourself?"

Mazie rested her head against the sofa back. "I know. But I couldn't stay at that stupid sleepover a minute longer. I just couldn't! The music was loud and all they did was talk about the boys they like and the girls they hate. They're a bunch of petty narcissists. The whole time, I felt like a poseur. We played truth or dare and I told them I made out with a boy at my cousin's cottage this summer."

"What cousin? What cottage? What boy?"

Mazie closed her eyes. "Exactly."

"Oh, honey."

"I don't know why I made that up."

Fig came back and sat down again.

"Anyway," Mazie continued, "I wanted to see what kind of insects were in that part of the river." She brightened. "So, I got into the rowboat, just to look into the water. I found some cool caddis flies." She looked at Fig for approval.

He nodded, watching as she formed each word.

"Then what?" he asked, almost in a whisper.

She bit her lip. "Well, then, I-I wanted to explore the river—just, you know, float around a little, but I forgot one of the oars. I was going to go back, but sort of, you know, got caught in the current. So," she shrugged her shoulders and let them drop. "I figured I'd just float down here for a visit. It's been quite a while, you know."

Charlotte and Fig exchanged looks over Mazie's head.

"Mazie," Fig said. "Is that all?"

She covered her head with the blanket. "That's all I remember."

"Okay, sweetie," Charlotte said. "The main thing is you're all right."

From under the blanket came a small, teary voice. "Nana and Pop will go ape shit."

Charlotte kissed her through the blanket. "Let's not worry about that tonight."

Fig went into the kitchen and opened the refrigerator.

"I have mushroom and cheese ravioli in the freezer and everything for a Caesar salad," he announced.

"Thanks," Charlotte said, "but we're really not hungry."

"I'm starving!" Mazie protested. "And we promised we'd stay here for a few hours. Besides, I haven't seen Fig in forever."

When Charlotte got up to tend the fire, she caught him watching her so fixedly that she wondered if he could see through her. She was surprised he was still vertical after the strain of the rescue.

"And your clothes aren't dry," he added, "and I'd like to see that Mazie's okay." He was playing his ace.

She sighed. "Okay. Go sit with Mazie. I'll make dinner."

She would not be pulled into his gravitational field again.

After dinner, she cleaned up the kitchen while Fig and Mazie retreated to his study to find her something to read. Charlotte knew he was trying as hard as she was not to be alone together.

She could hear them talking.

"Look. *Plumbing for Dummies*," Mazie was saying. "Pop has an old book like this about computers, but he still keeps losing his emails and forgetting to save his work, so either he can't read or he's dumber than the average dummy. Hey look. You can buy a book on personal finance, auto repair, even football. You'd never have to be ignorant about anything. They could make a bundle on *Eighth Grade for Dummies*."

She heard him chuckle and say something she couldn't make out.

"Everybody tells me I'm really smart, but in middle school the stupid kids think they're smart and the smart kids get treated like we don't know anything. Everything's sort of turned around."

Charlotte moved nearer the door where she heard Fig say, "Maybe that's because the smart kids understand how hard it is to know anything for sure."

"And the dumb kids think they know everything, but they don't," Mazie added.

"It's called 'blissful ignorance.' Lewis Carroll wrote a book called *Alice, Through the Looking Glass*, about a topsy-turvy world where nothing makes sense."

"I bet Alice was in eighth grade. Anyway, that's middle school for you." There was a long silence. "But it still seems like everybody else knows more about being an eighth grader than I ever will."

"I very much doubt that," Fig said. "—having been a pretty confused eighth grader myself."

"You're saying that just to make me feel better."

"They used to call me Casper, which I really didn't appreciate."

"The Friendly Ghost? Kind of appropriate, you have to admit."

"Oh, you think so?" She heard Mazie giggle, then there was silence for a long time.

"Did they ever call you Ficus?"

"Nope. Just you."

Charlotte returned to the couch and gradually dozed off.

She woke again to Mazie's angry voice.

"I *hate* those girls! They started calling me Creepy-crawly Mazie, because I showed them the caddis flies I found. So what if I like bugs and lots of stuff they don't, like stars and computers and books and birds? What's wrong with that?"

"Absolutely nothing," Fig was saying.

"They were just as loud and mean and obnoxious as I thought they'd be. I gave them a chance. I *tried* to get to know them, you know? I *tried*."

"That was very mature, Maze." There was a pause. "So, what would you want to learn about being an eighth grader? After all, I, Casper the Friendly Ghost, lived to tell about it."

There was another giggle, a pause and a big sigh from Mazie.

"Let's see. Chapter One: How to Act Like Everybody Else." Mazie's voice was animated now and Charlotte pictured her pacing around Fig's study.

"Chapter Two: Conversation Topics to Avoid, like insects. Chapter Three: What Not to Wear. I don't actually want to *be* a cool girl—I just want to *look* like one so they'll leave me alone. It would be nice to be normal and invisible."

"Too late, you're already normal—but definitively not invisible."

"Just ordinary then."

"Ordinary? I don't know. That's dangerously close to average."

"Then maybe just invisible between 8:40 a.m. and 3:20 p.m., Monday through Friday, late August to mid-June, excluding vacations." Charlotte could hear the smile in Mazie's voice. "Life would be sooooo much easier."

"I'm afraid invisibility is out of the question for someone as extraordinary as you, Madelyn McDougal Adair."

Charlotte dozed off again, waking to a light tap on her shoulder. Fig stood over her looking grim.

She sat up. "What's wrong?"

"I made up the sofa in my study for Mazie. I hope that's okay. She's exhausted and still pretty upset. She's reading now, but won't be awake for long I suspect. Please, don't take her home tonight, Charlotte. She's been through a lot."

"What's going on?"

"I'm going over to the Geller's."

She sat up. "What? Why?" She glanced at the clock in the kitchen. "Now? It's almost eleven."

"They'll be up." He sat down next to her and rubbed his face with his hands. "Mazie told me that the rowboat was tied to the dock. She got in it to look for insects in the river, but the other girls started teasing her. When Mazie splashed at them, Alison untied the boat, grabbed one of the oars and pushed the boat into the river."

Charlotte rose to her knees. "What? Oh, my God, Fig!"

"There were never two oars in that boat."

"Mazie told you this?"

"With a little coaxing." He moved slowly toward the door. "I'm going over to have a chat with the Gellers while the girls are still there. That party needs a good crashing." He held an envelope.

"What's that?"

He held it for her to see. The return address read "Newton Ellery Bigelow, Attorney at Law"

Charlotte looked up at him. "What's it say?"

"It suggests some things they need to think about. I won't be long. Promise me you'll be here when I get back."

She sighed. "All right."

Mazie was reading a paperback with Prince on her stomach. She looked up at Charlotte.

"Time to turn out the light, Maze. You've had a long day."

"Aunt Charlotte?"

"Hmm?"

"Did Fig tell you what happened?"

"Yes. But I wish you had told me. Did you think I'd be mad?"

"No. It's just so embarrassing. Those girls are bullies. I'd rather not talk about it."

"Not tonight at least."

Mazie closed her book and looked away, setting her jaw at an angle that showed resolve. "Why does Fig have to use oxygen to breathe?"

Charlotte pulled the sheet up to Mazie's chin. She felt Mazie eyes on her but couldn't meet them. "You know. Because of his lung condition."

Mazie chewed her thumb nail. "When I was in the boat, I yelled for him when I was almost at the island. I kept screaming his name, over and over. I knew about the dam. I was so scared. I didn't know what else to do." A tear rolled down her cheek.

"He ran into the water when he saw me—with his shoes on and everything. He tried to grab the rowboat but he couldn't get there in time." She wiped her eyes with the sheet. "He shouldn't have gotten into the kayak. He's not strong enough. I was headed . . . right . . . right for the dam. Then I grabbed one of those red balls on a rope."

"A buoy."

"Yeah, and he just *followed* me." She covered her face with her hands. "He grabbed hold of the boat and climbed in with me. Then he paddled really hard to get us to shore. I tried to help with my oar, but he did everything. He was shaking and his mouth was all blue and I knew he was really, really tired. And when we got to the bank I thought he was going to – I don't know. I've never been so scared."

Charlotte pulled Mazie into a hug. "I know. We were all scared. Even Prince. But we're all safe now."

"I should have done more! I should have jumped out of the boat at the Geller's, or at the island. I should have swum to shore. I don't know why I didn't. I didn't know wh-what to do."

"Shhh. Shhh. It's all over now."

Charlotte wiped Mazie's cheeks with her thumbs and kissed her forehead.

"We'll talk more about this tomorrow if you want. You'll feel better then, you'll see."

"But every time I close my eyes—"

"Turn over, sweetie. I'll give you a backrub."

Mazie hesitated, but rolled slowly onto her stomach.

When Mazie's breathing was deep and steady, Charlotte kissed her again and inhaled her sweet, familiar scent.

Under this tangle of curls, as familiar as her own, the woman Mazie would be was coming into focus. Not a perfectionist like her aunt or a thrill-seeker like her mother, but a fiercely determined and independent young woman.

She sat down in Fig's desk chair to watched Mazie sleep. Exhaustion and youth were a godsend at times like these, she thought. Her own troubled thoughts, careening and crashing against each other, would disturb her sleep for weeks.

By the glow of Fig's screensaver, Charlotte searched Fig's shelves for a book to distract herself. She fingered the bindings. *The World of Matisse, The Jerusalem Bible, The Poisonwood Bible, The Complete Works of Shakespeare* were shelved next to the *Complete Works of Ogden Nash* and a collection of Calvin and Hobbes. Their owner certainly had eclectic tastes.

Over the desk was a framed quote by Jorge Luis Borges that read, "I have always imagined that Paradise will be a kind of library." His reading glasses were folded into their case, a gel pen was clipped to the top of a legal pad. Spotless as usual, even at the end of a long, traumatic day.

She missed him so.

On the top sheet in neat, angular printing he'd written, "Strategy: alternative plants." And "Planting phases," with Oct. 8 underlined twice. "TRO/ Sept. 26" was also underlined twice.

When she touched the keyboard, the screen lit up with an email from Portia. She couldn't help but see.

From: Portia Easter
Subject: TRO

Dear Mr. Bigelow,
My apologies for this delay getting back to you. I needed to discuss things with my board.

Thank you for hosting us last week. Charlotte has done wonders with your island and it will only get better over the years. I'm sorry she wasn't there to give us a tour, but you were an able substitute. And thank you, too, for explaining things so well about the TRO. It is all very intriguing.

Charlotte felt a prick of jealousy. Fig had moved on. Her better self understood, of course. Their star-crossed relationship should not stand in the way of truth and justice. But still.

She eased herself into Fig chair and read on.

The short answer to your question is that invasive species have done a great deal of harm to my organization. But I know you want the long answer, so here it is.

The Land Restoration Trust (LRT) was founded 1978 as the Land Reserve Trust. Its mission then was to acquire unspoiled forests, prairies, oak savannas, dunes and wetlands that once covered most of West Michigan. The idea was to protect them from development.

But that has now changed. The properties we acquire now are old farms, industrial sites, golf courses and in one case, a sealed landfill. Each site poses unique challenges, but they all have one thing in common—they're choked with invasive plants.

So now, instead of protecting healthy ecosystems, we're treating sick ones. With this new reality, we changed our name to the Land Restoration Trust. We are the PETA of ecosystems.

Ironically, some of the worst invasives—exotic honeysuckle, multiflora rose, Asian bittersweet, baby's breath, teasel, euonymus, vinca minor and privet—are still sold at nearly every local nursery or on the Internet. This is a great frustration.

And now, we have the wild strain of Bradford or "Callery" pear which is relatively new in the state, but has all the hallmarks of being the next kudzu. I'm at a loss to understand why our city and county—or state, for that matter—are blind to the warning signs and deaf to pleas from organizations like mine.

The cost of restoring abused land is exponentially more than safeguarding a pristine forest or dune.

I estimate that at least half of the LRT's resources go to removing aggressive plants—over and over again. Our annual expenses are roughly $1,200,000, so you can do the math. Herbicides are expensive, the labor involved is intense and dangerous to those who apply them.

On top of that, donors prefer us to acquire an unspoiled dune at Lake Michigan instead of restoring an old factory site. So I can add "lost donations" to the associated costs of invasive plants.

You can imagine our frustration, after spending months eradicating acres of invasives along the Saskawan River at two sites, to learn that the city and county plan to plant more directly upstream.

I blame everyone, but some more than others. Years ago, huge numbers of exotic plants were brought to North America in ignorance and without intent to harm. But today we know better. Horticulturalists, nursery owners and others who traffic in these plants know better. The city and the county know better. This shouldn't still be happening.

I want to thank you, Mr. Bigelow, for offering your services pro bono. We absolutely could not consider signing on as plaintiffs if that weren't the case.

I will also arrange a meeting for you with my board president. She will be very interested to hear your thoughts.

Sincerely,

Portia Easter
Executive Director

Charlotte propped her chin on her palm and frowned. Portia would be a better plaintiff anyway. She sent the screen into sleep mode and noticed a lime green folder labeled "CA" next to the keyboard. Her initials? She started to open it, but caught herself. It was one thing to read a screen. Another to open a closed file.

The corner of one sheet stuck out far enough that she could easily pull it out with her fingers. She stopped herself again. Now she was just being nosy. She called upon her x-ray vision and her powers of ESP to see what might be inside, but got nothing. Damn! She had worked hard with Fig to build this case. He couldn't have done it without her. She should be part of it.

She stood up to search the shelves for a book again—but none of the titles were nearly as interesting as what might be inside that green folder. Her eyes darted from the book shelf to the folder. Shelf, folder, shelf, folder . . .

This was insane. *She* was insane. She looked over at Mazie and Prince. They were snoring in unison.

One of the over-sized art books on the top shelf might provide a distraction for an adult behaving like Curious George.

The Art of Nicolaes Maes was just out of reach. She rose to her tip-toes and stretched with her left hand while balancing with her right hand on the desk. The green folder slipped closer to the edge.

She sat down in Fig's chair, feeling the shape of his body in its contours. She shook off all thought of him and paged lazily through the color plates. Maes, she learned, was a student of Rembrandt, and an apt one, in her opinion. The paintings were shadowy domestic scenes of women at their chores—plucking fowl, scaling fish, spinning, or reading a leather-bound Bible by the light of a cradle. One painting, of a young servant girl standing behind an open door, caught her eye. The girl looked directly at the viewer with a finger to her lips as she eavesdropped on her master and mistress.

Charlotte took this as a sign and eyed the green folder again, now cantilevered precariously over the edge of the desk.

She got up and opened the window all the way. She crossed the living room and opened the front door to let the breeze blow through the house. When she returned to the study, the file was still on the desk. She frowned.

Mazie's bangs lifted in the breeze. She got an extra blanket from the hall closet and shook it hard to open it. A sticky note above the laptop fluttered, but the green file stood its ground, damn it anyway. She covered Mazie and kissed her forehead.

Fig wouldn't even mind if she looked. He'd left it right there—with her initials on it even. She'd already read Portia's letter, so she was already a snoopy busybody. In for a penny, in for a . . .

But still.

She sat down and fingered the edge of the mystery paper.

Prince woke up, yawning, and came over to see what he was missing. She patted her thighs and he jumped onto her lap.

"What's in there, Princey?" she whispered, looking him in the eye. "What is it, huh?"

He licked her nose and she scratched the soft fur behind his ears.

"You were such a brave boy today. Yes, you were." She kissed him on the forehead. "You deserve a treat." This word he knew.

She carried him to the kitchen, feeling his tail smack against her back as she neared the treat drawer. She took several and set him down in the doorway of the study.

"Sit," she whispered. She put a treat on the floor just out of reach, a second on Fig's chair, and the last on the corner of the green folder over the floor. She stepped back. "Okay. Go."

Prince vacuumed up the first treat without chewing, which seemed to defeat the purpose of a treat. Then he leapt to the chair for the second and put two paws on the desk for the third. The green file slid to the floor. Two sheets of paper fluttered out, landing face up as luck would have it.

"Oh, no! Look what you did." She laughed softly and gave Prince one more treat. "Now I have to pick up this mess."

She knelt on the floor and read a printed email from Katie.

Hi Fig,

Thanks for a nice time on your island. You have a really awesome place. You were smart to hire Charlotte. She's the best!

Thanks for telling us all about the lawsuit. I'm really interested, but I have to convince my husband (Donny) that I won't end up in jail or stuck with court costs. Don't worry. I can be very convincing!

Anyway, I'll try to answer your question about how invasive plants have hurt our family business . . .

Donnie and I are just busy parents trying to make a living and be home as much as we can with our sons. He has a screen-printing business in our garage and I have a native tree and shrub business on our five-acre farm. I learned all about plants when I worked in sales at TipTop, but I never realized that in the native plant business you have to fight invasives all the time.

Our property is next to a subdivision where they planted barberry bushes along the back of the property maybe fifteen years ago. Now they're all through our woods. We spend a weekend each spring clearing the seedlings with heavy gloves because of the prickers. It's horrible work, especially knowing they'll be back and that they attract the mice that carry Lyme ticks. Why does the county want to plant more of them?

And another thing. A really good customer called me this year to say the native button bushes I'd sold her had either died or didn't bloom. It turned out, her neighbor's barberry hedge had choked them out. I offered her some replacements (even though it wasn't my fault) and explained that she really needed to get rid of those barberries, but I think I've lost a good customer.

A bigger problem for us native growers is that a lot of home-owners actually WANT invasive plants because they spread so fast!

I don't know if anyone knows how the problem of deer relates to all this. Deer generally don't like exotic vegetation like Bradford pears and barberry. They'd rather eat my young oaks, serviceberry and dogwoods. Every time the city plants another "deer resistant" invasive plant, it forces deer into my nursery where they eat everything in sight. That's not right!

The city and county might say that a lot of non-native species, like ginkgo, do no harm. Maybe, but they take up valuable space where an oak, hickory or maple could be doing so much more for wildlife. There's so little space left in this world. We need to use it better.

I always tell my customers that a tree or a shrub can be so much more than something pretty to look at. Plants should offer food and shelter for wildlife, too!

I guess when I write down all the bad things about invasive plants, I have to say they're a major pain in the you-know-what. I hope this helps.

Katherine (Katie) Clay
Owner,
My Big Backyard Native Plant Nursery

The second sheet was a short email from Nicky Martinez.

Dear Mr. Bigelow,
Whenever I find invasive species on a client's property, I have to charge up to thirty percent more to clean up a site first. But many clients balk at that. Often, I have to eat the expense or they'll just call a competitor who'll Bobcat everything even though the invasives will come up from their roots in just a couple of years.

If a client had a bunch of junk cars on their property they wouldn't complain about the clean-up costs, but they don't understand that there are junk plants, too.

At least a quarter of my profits are eaten up by these eradication projects that I can't really bill for and another 10% for jobs I've probably lost.

I wouldn't complain so much if my competitors in the horticultural industry were in the same boat. But a lot of them are benefiting from my losses. I wish we could sue the state's watchdog agencies too for not banning these plants years ago. They say they "cooperate" with the horticultural industry—meaning the MHA, of course, but in reality they're caving to pressure. It's a clear conflict of interest, if you ask me.

So, about the lawsuit, I don't see a down side. Count me in!

Nicky Martinez
Martinez Landscape Design

Charlotte returned the papers to their green folder. Fig had his plaintiffs. He didn't need her. Like Harp, he'd moved on.

Prince was asleep again. This time in the bend of Mazie's knees. Charlotte went to the hallway to remove her clothes from the dryer and change into them. Then she made herself a cup of tea and took it onto the porch. When Fig returned she'd wake Mazie and head home.

The Mercedes rolled slowly down the driveway and stopped behind her truck. She watched Fig's silhouette step onto the raft and pull with that slow rhythm she'd once thought graceful but now knew was all he could manage. One day soon, she thought, he wouldn't be able to do even that.

He came up the walk and stopped at the steps to catch his breath. It must hurt to breathe that hard, she thought.

"She asleep?" he asked.

She nodded but couldn't help asking, "How'd it go?" She didn't want to start a long discussion but was curious.

"All right, I think."

She waited for more.

He pulled himself up the steps, his breath wheezy, his fatigue unmistakable

"I offered them some . . . legal advice . . . pro bono," he added with a wry smile.

"Hmm." She couldn't look him in the eye.

. "I . . . suggested . . . that if they didn't get their daughter into therapy . . . she might end up in the juvenile . . . justice system."

"And you could expedite the process?"

"I believe I left that impression . . . Yes." He gestured toward the chair next to hers. "Mind if I sit?"

Charlotte shifted to get up. "I need to get Mazie home."

"Not yet . . . please?" He didn't give a reason. "Let's just sit for a while."

She didn't say yes, but she didn't move.

He pointed at the darkening river, "Did you know . . . fireflies use their light to attract a mate . . . or an easy meal?"

Was this a metaphor for what teen girls do to each other or what Fig did to her? She felt wounded and resentful. She wished she had a sarcastic retort, but she was too tired to come up with one.

He said, "Mazie told me that. I kind of wish . . . she hadn't." After a long pause, he added, "I think there are more fireflies than usual. Don't you? They're probably celebrating that the president of the Firefly Fan Club is safe."

She turned to face him and moved again to stand up. "Before I go, I want to thank you again. You saved Mazie's life today—and risked your own. It was brave—incredibly brave—under the circumstances."

"Not at all. Not brave. It just needed doing."

"Well, there was a lot at stake." She shivered, remembering it. "And it wasn't just Mazie's life you saved, but my parents' too. I haven't had the courage to call them tonight. Just the idea that—" Her voice rose and trailed off. "If they lost her, too, I don't think they'd recover." She swallowed hard.

"How long has it been since you lost your sister?"

"Over ten years."

"How painful that must have been."

"It still is."

"I can't imagine how hard that would be."

"The loss is something you carry everywhere, all the time. Stuck like a burr. Lauren's chair at the kitchen table. Her empty bedroom. Her Christmas stocking. She's always around the edges, but my parents can't acknowledge it. They—"

She stopped. What was she doing? He was drawing her in again. He had sent her away. *Just go*, he'd said.

Just go. That's exactly what she should be doing.

But over the river the Milky Way shone like a star-spangled banner. Crickets sang their love songs and fireflies choreographed novel constellations.

But she was still furious with Fig.

But this might be the last time she'd sit on his porch, or see the river so blue or feel the warmth of his arm inches from hers. It would be so damned easy to let go of her anger.

But he'd said, *Just go.*

She stood up quickly, before she lost her resolve.

"Anyway, Mr. Bigelow, thank you again for what you did today."

He reached toward her, but stopped short. "Please stay. Charlotte. Don't wake Mazie. I'd like to see her when she wakes up. I'll make up the couch for you."

"No. No, I can't."

"I'll beg if it will change your mind," he said, getting to his feet with surprising energy. "Don't move. I have a new wine for us to try."

But there was no "us."

"I can't," she said again, but too softly and too late. He was already through the door.

She sat down again and pulled her knees up. Her anger, which was her only armor, was failing.

He returned and as he handed her the glass, his fingers brushed hers, sending a volt of longing up into her solar plexus. She would regret this.

Later and forever after that, she would remember that first swallow of wine as a kind of holy communion.

"It's from Northern Italy," he was saying. "What do you think? Not too pricey, so be honest."

"Nice," she said, though it wasn't the wine. And because she needed to say something more, she said, "So, will there be a gunfight at high noon between you and Mr. Geller?"

"The Gellers are just lucky I oppose gun ownership. The world would be better off without the Geller clan."

"They don't deserve all the blame. I should never have let Mazie go to that party. He mother and I were classmates all through school. Believe me, the apple hasn't fallen far from that tree."

"Well, that little apple of theirs is rotten. Mazie's refusal to join Alison's gang nearly got her killed, Charlotte. And her parents just stood there and made excuses. The father called it 'teenage high jinx.' I wanted to punch him in the nose."

Charlotte smiled into her wine glass.

"What? You think I wouldn't?"

"Punch somebody?" She chuckled at the thought.

"If I were King of the World, the Gellers would have their parenting licenses revoked on the spot—for the safety of the townsfolk."

"Really?" Oh, how she'd missed this man! "I don't know, Fig. Kids do hurtful things without their parents' encouragement. I had very good parents, but I was no angel."

"I don't believe that."

"Oh, trust me."

"Is there a confession coming?"

"Absolutely not."

"Hmm. You'll feel better if you tell me, and I'll take all your secrets to my grave."

She sighed. "I haven't missed your twisted sense of humor."

"But you've missed some of the rest?"

"No comment."

The trees along the road looked like paper cut-outs against a navy-blue sky. A shooting star fell and they gasped and pointed in unison. A trio of bats dove for insects above the river.

They talked of inconsequential things.

Finally, he said, "Are you ready to tell me about your devilish deeds? Or, do you need another glass of wine to loosen your tongue, because I'm really curious."

After two glasses anything seemed possible, even casual intimacy with a man who had rejected her.

He was waiting. "How long has it been since your last confession, my child?"

"It's not a funny story. Certainly not youthful high jinx."

"Unless it involves body parts in your freezer, I won't judge. Go ahead. Try and shock me."

She looked down into her glass and said softly. "I've never told anyone."

When she looked up, Fig's face was serious. "Then, I would be honored."

"I was 'the good daughter,' you know? I slept through the night and smiled at everyone. I walked and talked ahead of schedule. Blah, blah. I brought my teachers fistfuls of daffodils and turned my homework in on time." She rolled her eyes. "Boring, I know. Anyway, my parents thought they were parental rock stars and I knew from an early age it was my job to make them happy."

Fig nodded. "We all play our part in family dramas."

"In our case, a Greek tragedy, because four years later, along came Lauren. Colicky, sleepless and generally pissed off. Bratty and reckless from the start. She spent her school days in the principal's office and her vacations in the ER. My dad says they felt like they had a comet by the tail.

"When I was in fifth grade and Lauren was in first, my dad built us a treehouse in one of the old apple trees in the backyard. It had a retractable ladder and a trap door and a fire pole for quick escapes from pirates, or aliens or boys, depending on our age. It was a monument to fatherly love."

"Sounds idyllic."

"It was. At first. My mom covered a bunch of pillows for the floor. God, I loved everything about that place except that I had to share it with my little sister. That first summer, we played Little Orphan Annie a lot. My friend Patti and I made Lauren play Annie. I was Miss Hannigan, of course so I could order her to bring us peanut butter sandwiches and steal bags of marshmallows or chips from the kitchen. Of course, she wasn't allowed to eat with us because she was just an orphan. God, Fig, I was so mean to her and mostly she just took it—I don't really know why."

"She wanted to be included."

She sighed. "In middle school the orphanage became a Hobbit house and I let a neighbor boy kiss me because he had a Hobbit face and big Hobbit ears. But I digress."

"So far, I see no indictable offences."

"I'm getting to that. Then, in my sophomore year I had a brief, unfortunate crush on a junior named Justin. I realize now he was a narcissistic, early-stage alcoholic. But to my addled adolescent brain his access to beer, cigarettes and weed looked a lot like maturity."

Fig nodded his approval of her analysis.

"Anyway, Justin started coming over after school to smoke weed in the treehouse. I won't say I didn't join him sometimes, but I never liked it much. For the rest of that fall, he hid his stash inside a pillow. Then, one day when Lauren was about eleven she caught us."

"What did she do?"

"I'll never forget her look of wild-eyed fascination. She demanded to try it and threatened to tell our parents if I didn't let her. She looked at me with such contempt. I rattled off a whole list of her recent transgressions that I'd tell our parents if she told on me. But she didn't care."

"So, you acquiesced?"

"Sadly. I wish I could blame the weed, but it wasn't that. She was threatening my good daughter status and I couldn't have that. My parents' approval was more important to me than my — " She couldn't continue. She shrugged, finally. "After that, Lauren spun out of control. I tried to break up with Justin, but I couldn't get rid of him. Then one day I came home from school and he was sharing a joint with Laur—."

Her face contorted and she had to stop.

"I remember screaming at him. 'What are you doing? She's only eleven!' He blew smoke in my face and said, 'Really? 'Cause she looks a lot older.' Lauren just laughed. I didn't know what to do, so I said, 'Lauren, so help me God, if you don't leave this treehouse in the next ten seconds I will tell your entire class that you wet the bed.' She scooted slowly toward the ladder, and said, 'Fuck you, Charlotte.' At that point, I have to say, she really did seem older.

"I'm proud of one thing though. I dumped Justin's bag of weed over the railing. He swore at me too, but at least he stopped coming over.

"But that wasn't the end of it. Lauren found other friends who partied on the roof of the middle school and God knows where else. And you know the rest."

"And you've been holding on to this guilt since—?

"Since my sister became a full-blown coke addict at sixteen and died of a drug overdose at nineteen? It's the least I can do for her memory. Don't you think?" she said bitterly. Then after a pause, "Sorry."

After a longer pause, he said. "I'm no shrink, but I know what the law says." He shifted so he was facing her. "In civilized society we don't hold adolescents to the same standard of moral behavior as adults. Our judges and juries—with admittedly many notable and tragic exceptions—recognize the limits of an immature person to foresee consequences. Kids just aren't very good at making complex moral judgments and anticipating what is obvious to a mature adult. They don't have the life experience or the brain development yet. So, we isolate them for most of the year in schools and basically keep them under strict surveillance and almost complete isolation from adults—which only makes things worse, in my opinion. We treat teens like completely useless creatures. Too old to be cute and too young to be valuable. If the Geller girl and her gang were 20 instead of 12, they'd be in police custody tonight. But, despite what I said earlier, I suspect by the time she's your age she'll be a decent enough human being."

"I hope she at least feels guilty for what she did today."

"She probably will eventually, but should this incident ruin her life?" His sideways glance was full of meaning.

"No. But my life isn't ruined, if that's what you're getting at." She felt defensive.

"Is that why you're so devoted to Mazie?"

"You think I'm driven by guilt?"

"I'm asking."

"I don't know. Maybe some. I want to help my parents. That's part of it."

"Whatever it is, I think it's admirable."

"And do I really seem devoted? Mazie's never given much in return." A knot tightened in her throat. "But tonight—. When—I thought she had—" She shook her head.

"When you almost lost her."

A tear rolled down her cheek before she could catch it.

"When I realized she hadn't made it to the island and then saw your kayak at the top of the spillway—. I've never been so scared. Not since the day my dad found Lauren in the basement. I realized I would've—" Her voice rose to a squeak.

"—gone over the dam to save her?" he prompted.

She nodded.

"God, Charlotte. I felt the same way. It's miraculous, don't you think? I never wanted kids. I had no idea I could feel this was about a child. I couldn't love her more if she was my own daughter."

She had no response to give. This declaration made no sense, considering he didn't want them in his life.

A moment passed.

Fig said, "I'm glad you told me about Lauren."

A great-horned owl hooted across the river, bringing Charlotte back into the present. She wiped her face on her sleeve. "I've been wanting to ask. How did your meeting with my WILHA friends go?"

"Pretty well. I've been meaning to thank you for arranging it." He paused. "I took them on a tour of the island. I'm sure I missed a lot of detail, but they were quite impressed. I can tell they respect you. And by the way, Nicky is a yes. Katie and Portia are thinking it over, but I'm optimistic." His voice trailed off.

They fell into silence again. There was nothing more to say.

She looked down at her hands.

The awkwardness grew until it was excruciating.

Finally, he said, "Do we really need to keep avoiding each other, Charlotte? We've worked so well together this whole summer." He leaned forward on his elbows, trying to get her to look at him. "I could really use your help."

She got to her feet. "No. I—I can't do this." She stepped toward the door and saw him reach for her. She stepped back.

"Please, Charlotte, don't leave."

She shook her head. "I can't be in this limbo with you." She looked up at the porch rafters, trying to maintain control, but this day had been so long and she was so tired.

"It's just too hard," she said.

She needed to get off this island. But how would she explain her puffy eyes to her niece who was already so upset and wanted so much to be here.

"Charlotte, I did my best to explain—."

"Stop, dammit." She spat the words at him. "I heard you! You don't have to tell me twice." She ran down the steps and down the path. All her anger was back and more with it. She heard him call to her, sounding so desperately tired, but she didn't stop until she reached the thinkin' log—the farthest she could get from him on his blasted island, which felt like a prison now.

Ahead, the river slipped quietly away. She sat down and wept uncontrollably. Keeping him at arm's length was impossible. And pretending to be just colleagues? How could she, when he had so little time left? How could he ask that of her?

She pressed her thumbs into her aching temples. She needed to get off this island and never come back. She got up to splash water on her swollen face, but tripped over a boulder, jamming her toe as she fell. She hopped on one foot, saying, "Damn rock. Damn island." She picked it up then and heaved it into the river, drenching her clothes all over again.

She threw back her head. "Damn you, Fig!"

She sank onto the damp ground, rubbing her toe and whimpering.

Fig wasn't any kind of bastard. He was selfless and noble—which was making this impossible. Try as she might, she couldn't think of one good reason not to love him. Seeing him tonight—seeing him risk his life for Mazie—and knowing she couldn't be in his life was the worst kind of torture.

She needed to think this through logically. That's what Fig and Mazie would do. She hobbled over to the thinkin' log and sat down.

It was clear she had just two options: walk away and be lonely and love-sick, or be his colleague and be frustrated and love-sick. She didn't like either choice. Logic was getting her nowhere.

She squinted into the dark. Dilemmas like this caused some people to throw themselves into rivers. But she was too good a swimmer to drown in the Hawthorne River and throwing herself over the dam sounded way too gruesome.

If she was going to throw herself anywhere, she thought, it should be into building her business. She'd take out some ads in local publications, maybe register for another business class at the community college. Some spite-fueled rebound dating might be therapeutic although she pitied the poor sap who swiped right on her profile. Despite his words to the contrary, Fig didn't really need her when he had Portia, Nicky and Katie to be his plaintiffs.

Just go, was sounding like pretty good advice.

She wiped her face on her sleeve for the umpteenth time and limped toward the house to wake Mazie and leave—really leave this time. Mazie would just have to understand.

But her toe hurt like hell and with every step her anger grew like a mushroom in wet leaves. By the time she reached the house, she was cursing Fig and her whole stupid life again.

He was sitting on the top step with his head in his hands. He looked up when he heard her footsteps. He was blocking her way.

She stopped at the bottom of the steps, her fists thrust deep into her pockets, her shoulders drawn up to her ears.

"Charlotte," he exhaled her name with profound sadness. "Again, I'm so sorry. I-I—."

She raised her palms. "Don't." She closed her eyes, waiting for calm to return. "I won't do this—whatever we did here tonight—ever again. I swear. Never, ever again."

He reached toward her, offering something invisible. "But I think we could—?"

"Well, we can't."

He started again, "I was hoping we might—."

"Well, it's not going to happen. Excuse me, I'm leaving now."

He flinched as if she'd slapped him.

She sputtered on. "But before I go, I just need to ask one question. Do you—? Do you— ?" She lowered her voice, remembering Mazie. "Do you really think you have anything—anything at all to say about when and how and how much I need to be with you? How much . . ." She couldn't say it. "How much I *care* about you? Why do *you* get to decide everything? Why?"

Fig raised his hands as if she were throwing darts at him. She could see his jaw grinding. She could only guess what emotions were at war.

He shook his head slowly. "You had a future with Harp. Why did you throw that away?"

Charlotte shook her head slowly. "Harp is a good man. Better than I deserved. But I didn't want that future. I probably deserved to have my own heart broken. But you! You should not push me away."

He looked away.

"Look at me, Fig! Look at me and tell me that you don't want me and I'll leave." She put her fists on her hips. "I'll wake Mazie and we'll leave. Right now. Say it. I can't be your landscaper or your plaintiff and nothing more. I can't. Not when—"

"Of course, I want you, Charlotte. That's never been the problem."

"Yes, that's *exactly* the problem. I'm a grown woman. We may not have much of a future together, but we have *now*, Fig. I want now! With you. Don't deny me that. Don't deny *yourself* that. You say I shouldn't throw my life away, but what about yours? You, of all people, know how precious life is. Please share yours with me. That's all I ask."

Fig's head sank further into his hands. "God, Charlotte! You make this so hard."

"Me? *I'm* making this hard? *You're* the one who wanted to do this lawsuit together. Was that so we could keep seeing each other, but without any—any complications?"

"No. I don't know. Maybe."

"Well, I'm done with only having a piece of you."

He shook his head. "I should never have let it get this far."

"Listen to me!" She started in with no idea what she was going to say. "You sh-should've thought of that sooner. Before you swept me off my feet with—with your weird take on motel coat hangers and the little prince and his baobabs and Mickey's dancing mops and tribbles and sweet Nanette and our fuckingly brilliant lawsuit and your . . . your big fat wine glasses and your big, fat *mind*. You totally, completely fascinate me, Fig Newton Ellery Bigelow. You're curious and clever and funny and you love plants and insects and everything I love and care about. Especially M—" Her voice gave out.

"Mazie," he said quietly.

She looked up at the dark sky and took a deep breath. "It's way too late to stop this now.""

"I—I'm sorry. I can't—"

"Oh, God. Is that all you can say?" She dragged her hand across her wet cheeks and bit her lip. "Do you know what I almost said right before lightning struck the cottonwood a month ago? I almost said, 'I think I'm falling in love with you.'"

She let that sink in. "I know our timing is crap, Fig. But let's not torture each other now because we didn't meet sooner." She let her arms hang limply at her sides. She was out of ammunition. Out of arguments. "If you die tomorrow or next week or next year, I want be there. I don't want to be anywhere except by your side."

The light of the rising moon reflected off the tears on Fig's cheeks. For once, he had nothing to say.

"Wouldn't you want to be with me if it I were sick?" She sighed. "Despite every logical reason not to, I love you, Fig! I can't stop loving you just because you tell me to. If you send me away again, I'll still love you and when the end comes, I'll feel worse for not being there."

He reached for the railing and pulled himself to a stand. He was going to walk into the house and shut her out of his life.

"Fig, please."

He took one step toward her and stopped. "And I, sweet Charlotte, find myself hopelessly in love with you." He opened his arms and she fell into them. "May God have mercy on us both."

They swayed together in the silvery moon shadows for a moment and an eternity, until his shoulders shook and he began to cough. She led him up the porch steps and then up the stairs, stopping on the landing to let him rest.

"I'm wrung out," he said, not letting go of her.

"It's been a long day."

"Yes," he said. "The worst and the best."

"But the best after all," she said.

In Fig's study, Prince had tunneled under the covers and Mazie had one arm over him, just as she used to do with White Bear.

Charlotte unplugged the oxygen machine next to the desk and carried it upstairs. She peeked around the door frame and knocked. Fig was propped against the headboard with his eyes closed. Even in the dim light she could see his lips were still blue. He was wearing the same red plaid boxers he wore the day they met. She wouldn't be surprised if all his boxers were red plaid.

She plugged in the machine and handed him the tubing.

"Thank you," he said, reaching for her. "Can you stay?"

She nodded. "For a while. But there's a thirteen-year-old downstairs so, I'll sleep on the couch. But after that, I'd rather not go anywhere—" Ever, she almost added, then—what the heck—she added, "—ever."

He patted the bed next to him. "Don't worry, I'm perfectly harmless tonight. Most nights actually, or possibly all of them, I'm not sure. We'll find out soon enough if you're curious."

"Shhh." She slid in next him then, resting her head lightly on his chest and listening to the oxygen fill his weary lungs.

"Full disclosure. I'm going to be a terrible boyfriend." He looked truly worried.

"Well, I have a checkered history with men, so we're made for each other."

"I'm serious, Charlotte. What I'm trying to say, with some delicacy, is that while the spirit is willing, the flesh, and various other important gear, may be weak or possibly out-of-commission. Basically, the doctors say sex could kill me."

"Then it's a good thing it's your spirit—not your 'gear'—that I love."

He chuckled. "I have no idea what you see in me, Charlotte Adair."

"Shhh. Don't make me start ranting again."

"Which rant? Invasive species, plastic packaging, pants with tiny pockets?"

She ran her hand up his arm. "I am passionate about many things."

"I'm happy to hear that." He drew her closer. "How about some heavy cuddling? I'm incapable of doing more but won't be able to sleep with anything less."

She turned off the light. "When you put it that way—"

He removed the tube from his nose and slid his hand under her hair. He kissed her earlobe and neck, making a trail to her lips.

She was smiling so hard, she could barely return the kiss.

He opened his eyes. "Why are you laughing? Do I kiss funny?"

"No. I just can't stop smiling."

"Concentrate," he whispered, kissing her upper lip, then the lower one. "This is some serious business I'm up to."

Blissful minutes passed, but soon he started to wheeze. She rolled over and sat up.

"Have I worn you . . . out . . . already?" he asked, starting to cough.

"I'm beat," she whispered, rolling on her side. She unhooked her bra and guided his hand.

"Eureka and God be praised," he mumbled into her neck. Soon his breathing came in long, easy waves.

She slipped away to sleep on the couch.

She awoke to Prince's tongue on her face.

"Morning, my little superhero." She kissed his velvety ear. "Did you like sleeping with Mazie?"

He backed up and sat down, waiting for her to get up.

She let him outside and filled his dish with kibble topped with a dollop of canned dog food. She was starting the coffee when Mazie yawned loudly from the study door and shuffled into the kitchen still wearing Fig's tee shirt and sweat pants.

"Do we have to go home right away?" she asked, slipping onto a stool. "I like it here."

"Good morning to you, too."

Mazie rubbed her eyes. "Sorry. Good morning." Then she added, "It's just that I can't face the Big People. They'll absolutely freak when they hear about yesterday." She clasped her hands to her chest and made a horrified face to demonstrate what freaking looked like.

"They'll be glad you're all right though."

"Nana worries when I get a pimple. She thinks it'll infect my brain or something. And Pop'll get all huggie and won't let me out of his sight for a month. I don't need the drama. The whole thing was so stupid and embarrassing. And it's not like I'm ever going to take a one-oared boat down a river again—or go to another slumber party with *that* crew." She gagged as if she was about to throw up.

Charlotte pushed a curl behind Mazie's ear. "How about a hug?"

Without any hesitation or eye-rolling Mazie laid her head on Charlotte's shoulder. And when Charlotte pulled her closer, she felt Mazie's arms tighten around her.

"I love you, Madelyn McDougal Adair. Don't ever forget that."

Then she held Mazie by her shoulders and gave her a hard look. "So, are you really thirteen?"

"You were at my birthday party." The eye roll was back.

"I remember." She sighed. "And I'm thinking that at thirteen you're entitled to a private life. I guess we don't need to upset Nana and Pop needlessly."

"Really?" Mazie hugged her again. "I love you too, Charlotte Anne Adair."

There were footsteps overhead and the sound of water running in the bathroom. Charlotte filled a mug with coffee and headed up the stairs.

"Where are you going?" Mazie asked, her eyes widening. "That's Fig's bedroom."

Charlotte smiled. "Private lives, Maze."

If the rest of that day was enjoyable for Mazie, it was positively blissful for Charlotte and Fig. He insisted they stay for homemade blueberry waffles. Afterwards while he dozed on the couch Charlotte puttered around the kitchen and Mazie stalked the island's insect population.

Fig gave her a casual kiss when she brought him iced tea on the porch and she dabbed mayonnaise off his cheek at lunch. Charlotte knew that Mazie—Mazie the watcher—took note of these things. But she kept silent, when only a few weeks ago she would have bombarded them with impertinent questions.

Charlotte ordered pizza delivered to the landing and sent Mazie over to wait for it.

At sundown, they brought pillows and blankets to the raft and pulled themselves into to the middle of the river to watch Labor Day fireworks burst above the river.

When the wind kicked up and the sky darkened and Fig's hand grew cold in hers, Charlotte announced, "It's time for the Adair girls to return to the world before the Big People send out a search party."

When they were alone, Fig said, "Do you have to leave?"

"I need a bath and clean clothes."

"Can you come back then?" He interlaced his fingers with hers. "When?"

"ASAP. *Tempest fugits* and *carpe diem*." He kissed her temple and propped his chin on her head. "I don't want you out of my sight."

"That sounded borderline creepy. But I know what you mean. We need to make up for lost time."

Fig's chest relaxed with a long shudder. "So much lost time."

In the truck, Mazie asked, "When did Fig become your boyfriend?"

"The exact moment is hard to pinpoint."

"Cool," she said, nodding her approval. "I wonder what the Big People will say. Can I tell them?" Then she added quickly, "Unless you want to."

"Go ahead, but they won't be surprised." She squeezed Mazie's knee. "I'm glad you approve. That means a lot to me and to Fig, too."

"Fig's great. A lot better than—never mind."

They drove on in silence.

Finally, Mazie said, "When I was really upset after the party, it wasn't just about the girls and what happened on the river. I was afraid that now that you're done working on the island, I'd never see Fig again."

"I was too. But we'll be seeing him a lot more now."

Ted and Mally met them in the driveway and began pumping Mazie for details about the sleepover.

"It was okay," she shrugged, aiming a warning death ray at Charlotte.

Charlotte rolled down her window. "I believe you said the party was 'enlightening.' Right, Maze?"

"Basically. Yeah."

Mally seemed satisfied. "Well it'll be nice to have some new mates to start the school year."

Mazie walked backward toward the porch, grinning now. "Auntie Charlotte's has a new mate, too."

30

CHARLOTTE'S CROSSING

It was past ten by the time Charlotte got to the farm. While the tub filled, she tossed her clothes into the hamper and packed several changes of clothes into a duffel. Then she stepped into the tub and sank slowly into the steaming water, grateful for this time after such a long and emotional two days. She closed her eyes and listened to the familiar pings of the old pipes, waiting for serenity to come.

But her parents' anxious faces wouldn't let go of her.

Twenty minutes earlier, after the light in Mazie's bedroom came on, Charlotte told her parents that she would be staying at Fig's from now on.

From the look on her mother's face, she might have said she was leaving for Mars.

"Come inside, honey," Ted had said, patting her hand. "Let's talk about this."

"I can't, Dad. Not tonight. There's so much to do—and not much t–time–." She cursed her runaway emotions.

He brushed a tear from her cheek.

"Don't worry, please. It's been, um, a really hard decision for us, but it's the right one. Right now we need to be together. I'll come by soon, I promise. I want you to meet him."

As she backed out of the driveway, her father took Mally's hand and led her into the house.

Charlotte sank deeper into the tub and let the water envelope her. She hated to add to her parents' worries, but she had no regrets either. None whatsoever. It was a new, exhilarating feeling.

She pulled the plug with her toes, sat up, toweled off, slipped into a t-shirt, jeans and flipflops, closed windows, watered her houseplants and was back in her truck fifteen minutes later.

Fig had left the porch light on for her. She tiptoed upstairs, slipped off her jeans and slid in beside him.

He stirred and chuckled in his sleep. The oxegen machine whirred at his bedside.

She kissed his shoulder and whispered, "Honey, I'm home."

She woke to the smell of coffee and Fig standing over her with a ridiculously wide grin.

"Imagine my surprise to find a gorgeous woman in my bed last night."

Charlotte sat up, wiped drool from her cheek and yawned. "Yeah, I passed her on the stairs when I came in."

He laughed, handed her a hot mug and slipped back into bed with a cool ease she found remarkable. How could he be so relaxed?

She wiggled her toes and admired the lopsided tent their feet made under the covers. Prince hopped up and curled between them as if this was his daily routine. She stroked his ears and sighed contentedly.

"Thank you for coming back last night," Fig said. "I still can't believe my good fortune. This is a shocking turn of events, don't you think?"

"How so?"

"I thought when you got home you'd come to your senses."

"Me? Never."

He lifted the back of her hand to his lips. "You've got grit, m'lady"

"Grit?" She considered this. "Remember how you said that going after Mazie in the kayak wasn't bravery, but 'just needed doing?' Well, you and I—we need doing. Loving you was—is—unavoidable."

He nodded. "I fought it all summer."

"Me too." she said, and after a moment, "My parents are afraid for me."

"I am too."

"But not Mazie. She's over the moon. Bless her. A few months ago, she wouldn't have noticed or cared." She took another sip of coffee. "So, tell me what's happening with the lawsuit."

She felt him shrug. "I was considering calling it off."

"Really? Why?"

"The idea lost its luster after you left."

"You *sent* me away. Remember? Besides, Portia's email is so compelling. And Nicky's. And Katie's too, in its own quirky way."

His eyebrows rose in amusement.

She grimaced. "I may have seen the emails when you were at the Gellers. But in my defense, I was bored and still pissed off."

"That's your defense? Anger?" He chuckled.

"Temporary insanity then." She rubbed her eyes. "I've felt a little crazy all summer, but this—" She pointing at their toe tent, then smiled up at him. "—this feels perfectly sensible." She rested her cheek against his shoulder. "But, back to the case. You aren't really going to drop it now, are you?"

Fig drew a long breath. "To be honest, it was partly an excuse to be near you and partly a pathetic attempt to leave my mark on this world." He looked into his coffee. "I was in pretty bad shape after you left."

"Again, you *sent* me away."

"I know I did. I wanted to protect you. I still do, but have thrown caution to the wind." He kissed her temple. "I regret the time we've lost."

"Not entirely lost. I loved this summer. And I'm here now. All-in. Both feet." She rubbed her toes against his. "So, should we reopen your *pro bono, magnum opus, raison d'etre* lawsuit so you can leave your mark on the world? *Tempest fugits* and *carpe diem*."

"You'd join the other plaintiffs?"

"Sure. Just add it to the list of 'things that need doing.'"

Fig frowned. "Even if it saps my strength and shortens my already truncated life? Even if we don't win?"

She pulled back the sheet and got up to stand at the window where he couldn't see her face.

"I'd like to encase you in bubble wrap and never let you out of my sight. I don't know how I'll feel if–when–our time runs out. I want to be stoic and philosophical and attentive and grateful for every day we have together, but I can't promise I won't be a big fat crybaby if you just get sicker and . . . and . . ." She raised her arms. "See? I can't even *say* it and don't you dare make me." She came back to the bed and sat to face him. "But, here's what I know. Whenever you talk about the case, you radiate heat and light. The law and fighting the good fight are oxygen to you. The work might ultimately kill you, but I know it will also bring you unadulterated, bad-ass joy. So, I vote yes." She put a hand on his cheek. "Just know that my greatest fear isn't that we might lose the case, but that you'll feel you've wasted the time you had left."

Fig nodded slowly. "There's a chance we won't get our TRO. But if we make some noise, raise the alarm, others will join the fight. Susan B. Anthony never lived to cast a vote, but she led the way for other women. We – or you and your compatriots after I'm gone—can sue any of several state agencies, the growers, big consumers or the MHA. If we push the first domino over, the rest will fall."

"So, where do we start? I have a lot I want to tell that judge."

He wrapped his arms around her and held her.

"It's such a relief to look down the road and see something ahead besides my own demise. At the very least, working on this case together will be a hell of a good time. We'll get those plants banned, or die trying."

She groaned. "Please, no gallows humor before breakfast."

Neither of them spoke for a while.

Finally, he said, "'If a man hasn't found something he will die for, he isn't fit to live.'"

"Well said, Mr. Bigelow."

"Nope. Martin Luther King, Jr." After a pause, he added, "The day you see death at your door is the day you ask whether you deserved the life you were given."

"Dr. King again?"

"Nope, Mr. Bigelow."

A few days later, Charlotte received a hand-written letter from Heather Geller referencing the "unfortunate incident at the sleepover" and stating that she and her husband had been "unaware that Mazie was in danger" or the "role" that their daughter and her friends had "apparently played." But after "getting professional advice," they were sending Alison to counseling "to address her aggressive behavior."

She enclosed the business card of the counselor, apparently as proof. Charlotte did not reply.

When Kiza, Martin and Hector had arranged the last of the boulders along the riverbank just so, and when Charlotte had tucked cardinal flower, sensitive fern and Virginia waterleaf into the gaps between them, she declared the work of Adair Natural Landscaping for Mr. Newton E. Bigelow to be complete.

On the crew's final day, she bought apple-cinnamon scones from the Farmer's Daughter and Fig served coffee on the porch. As rain began to fall, Charlotte handed out small bonus checks with glowing letters of reference from both herself and Fig. She promised she'd contact each of them as soon as she found more work.

She helped them load the wheelbarrow, shovels and rakes onto the raft and accompanied them to the landing. The three men had been smiling and casting meaningful glances at each other all afternoon.

What are you all grinning about?" she asked.

Hector elbowed Martin who was working the rope. "We think you and Fig are not *complicado* no more."

Kiza's grinned widened. "Will you be marry now?"

She wished she knew how to say, none of your business (politely) and in Spanish, French or Swahili.

Hector was tapping his temple. "It is love. We see this."

Martin looked serious. "You are happy, so we are happy too."

Charlotte shook her head and smiled. "Nothing escapes you guys."

Martin frowned. "What is 'scapes.'"

"You're astute, perceptive, and observant men. Smart."

"No big words," Hector said. "We see *amor*. In de eyes."

At the landing they quickly loaded the truck.

When they were done, Martin extended his hand. "I want to say thank you, Charlotte Adair, for this work and for what you teach me about the plants of America." He looked past her across the river. "What we do on the island, it is important. Very good for the earth."

"Thank you, Martin. I hope we can work together again. I wish you success."

Before she returned to the island, she addressed the final task of the day.

"Hi, Harp," she said into her cell.

"Hey Char. What's up?" he asked, sounding oh-so casual.

"I'm calling to find out where to send your check—and, um, to find out how you're doing."

"I'm at Mike's for now. I'll text the address."

"Are you okay?"

"Never better. I'm back at TipTop. VanSlee offered me a sweet deal."

"Great. Great."

"Yeah, it is."

She bit her lip. "Look Harp. I'm—I'm really sorry about the way—."

"Don't worry. It was never meant to be."

"But the way it ended. I never wanted to hurt you. It's just—."

He interrupted her. "I'm dating Mike's niece, Amanda. She's doing an internship at the credit union this semester. You'd like her."

Charlotte frowned. She had always admired Harp's minimalist inner life and certainly didn't want him pining for her, but she suddenly felt like the perfectly good snowboard he'd left in her barn. He'd already replaced her with a shinier, newer model.

"Well, congratulations to you and Amanda," she said with sarcasm that would be lost on him. "And oh, by the way, next time you're in the neighborhood, can you clear your stuff out of my barn. Please?"

"Sure. No problem."

She knew he wouldn't.

"Well, take care, Harp."

"You too, Char."

When she stepped onto the raft again the sky had cleared except for a few white puffs scattering to the east. In front of her, the island floated between blue sky and bluer water.

She stepped onto the raft and crossed to Fig, leaving behind every last sliver of doubt.

As thunder rumbled again in the distance and a cold front brought the first breath of autumn, Fig built a fire in the fireplace. This fire,

Charlotte noted, was not a mere pile of sticks, but an engineered py-ro-teepee of tinder and kindling sized incrementally, and surrounded by a palisade of split logs.

He held up a match. "Watch now. I'm going to light this fire with one match."

"Is there a match shortage, or are you just into competitive fire starting?"

"The latter," he said, striking the match and letting it burn for a few seconds before touching it to the dry tinder. He puffed on the fire, which led to a spasm of coughing.

A curl of smoke rose into the flue.

Charlotte applauded from the kitchen. "Wow. Jack London could have learned a thing or two from you."

He sank into the couch and patted the seat beside him. "Fire starting should be an Olympic sport, don't you think?"

She sat down next to him, curling her legs under her. "Would the event be timed, like a race, or would there be points for style and creativity, like gymnastics? And how would you judge when the fire starting is complete?"

Fig waved his hand. "Details. Details."

"Maybe the first Olympian to hard boil an egg gets the gold."

"There you go," he said, laughing, which brought on more coughing. The fire crackled, radiating warmth into the room.

"What a beautiful fireplace," she said, following the split fieldstones upward to the rafters. "Your chimney was the first thing I saw on that foggy day back in March."

He followed her gaze upward. "I spent . . . a small fortune. . . . getting it tuck-pointed." He coughed several more times. "Sorry. They capped the chimney and cleaned out the flue. I want to get my . . . my money's worth."

"Can I bring you some water?"

"I'm fine now." Fig wrapped his arm around her shoulders. "So, you like living here so far? Any regrets?"

"None. I've never been happier."

"But you were frowning just now." His voice was raspy.

"That's not regret, it's worry. You're coughing a lot and you look exhausted."

"No more than usual."

He didn't want to talk about it. She shouldn't have said anything.

"So, are *you* happy?" she asked, nudging him.

He looked surprised at the question. "Why wouldn't I be?" He watched the fire for a minute. "But, to be honest, I'm worried, too. Worried you're getting the short end of the stick. Worried I can't give you everything you deserve in a relationship. Everything you need."

She squinted up at him and grinned. "Are you talking about sex again?"

"Is that funny?"

"No, no. But—" She interlaced her fingers with his. "I loved you way before I ever thought about anything physical between us."

He laughed. "Is that meant to make me feel better? Am I like the jolly fat boy in sixth grade? If you tell me you want to be 'just friends'—." His voice trailed off into a low chuckle and more coughing.

"Not at all. I'm totally in love with you. But—" she paused, choosing her next words carefully. "But you have to tell me how—how to be with you without all the benefits. God!" she said, grinning up at the ceiling. "I feel like I'm back in high school."

"Not my high school, but I know what you mean."

"Well, I'm not suggesting we make out in your car or under bleachers or at the gravel pit or over-looking the lake or in the attic of your frat house, or . . . " Her voice trailed off into a giggle. "Never mind."

"Just as I suspected. You were one of those cool girls who ignored pale, late-blooming boys with stupid nicknames."

"No. I was as insecure as everybody else."

He was studying her, imagining, she imagined, what she was like at sixteen.

"Insecure? Somehow, I can't believe that," he said.

She waved a hand. "Never mind. Just remember, I'm here because I want to be. When it comes to sex, I'm flexible."

Fig slapped his forehead and moaned. "Flexible too? You're killin' me now."

She gave him a playful nudge. "I mean, if we never actually, technically consummate this lovely, beautiful liaison, it's okay." She let her head fall on his shoulder. "But only because you're a world-class kisser and the best cuddler ever."

"Promise me that if at any point it's not enough, you'll tell me."

"And what? You'll call a male escort?"

"If that's what it takes to make you happy."

"I'm already happy." She paused for effect. "What I need from you is what you've given me since last spring—this deep connection. This easy, peaceful bond we've finally acknowledged. You listen when I talk—I mean, really listen. You care about what I care about. Sex is something I never expected would be part of this—although when I started to find you sexy, I knew my engagement was doomed—or I should have. I'm so attracted to you, Fig."

"Hmm," he said, which she interpreted as skepticism.

She lifted her face to kiss him. "How can you doubt that? What I'm trying to say is that I can live without sex, but not without your love, which you already give so generously." She kissed him again. "And lots and lots of nuzzling."

"Nuzzling? Really? Where exactly?"

She lifted her hair and pointed to a spot about an inch below her hairline, behind her ear. "There."

Fig ran his hand through her hair to the back of her neck. She felt the moist warmth of his lips. He unbuttoned her shirt and slipped his hand inside. "And what about here?"

"That's good too. Your hands have secret powers."

"So you've said." He turned his free hand over several times. "I still don't see it."

"I have wanted these hands to touch me ever since—" she stopped.

He drew back to smile at her. "Since when? Tell me."

"You first. When was the first time you lusted after me?"

"That's easy. After we went to VanderLee Gardens, at the coffee shop."

She smiled. "Way back in May? Really. Wow."

"You?"

She laughed. "Same."

Fig pinched the bridge of his nose. "Holy mother of God, we've wasted a shitload of precious time. And now I can't even give you a normal love life."

"Then we will be courtly lovers. Dulcinea and Don Quixote—but with kissing and other stuff."

He tucked a lock of hair behind her ear. "Petrarch to your Laura. Dante to your Beatrice."

"Who?"

"Petrarch was a poet of the Italian Renaissance who—"

She put a finger to his lips and kissed him slowly. "Let's not waste another minute."

"Yes," he breathed. "Good point."

"And if you steal another base, I'll look the other way."

He found the soft, bare skin under her waistband.

She kissed him again—demonstrating her skill with lips and tongue until she felt him pull back.

"Too much?"

"Not at all," he said, inhaling hard, "but keep in mind my need for air."

She winced. "Ah yes, air. I will definitely keep that in mind."

That night, as Charlotte was drifting off to sleep Fig pressed his forehead to hers.

"I feel rooted," he said.

"Mmm," she said, her eyelids fluttering.

"I've been looking for you my whole life."

"Mmm. Yes, me too."

"You and I, we are an eco-system. We meet each other's needs." He chuckled. "Or do the best we can."

"Uh-uh," she murmured, drifting off.

"I love you, Charlotte."

"Love you, too, Fig," she mumbled, rolling over and wiggling backward until she felt his body against her back.

"Let's spoon," she said. "I love to spoon."

"Okay," he said with a sigh, "But for the record, I'd rather fork."

31

HONEYMOON

There was much coming and going on Fig's island that September. The ruby-throated hummingbird who had so fiercely defended the red beebalm was on her way to Mexico. Cedar waxwings and robins had descended upon the dogwoods and hawthorns, stripped them of their red berries and moved on. Downy milkweed parachutes carrying a single seed lifted off from Fig's meadow to colonize new meadows elsewhere. Mazie arrived at the island each Friday after school and stayed till Sunday night. But Charlotte came to Fig's island to stay.

Indian summer arrived that month too, bringing golden days and unseasonably warm nights. Fig and Charlotte watched the evening sky turn from blue to orange from the front porch, just as they had done on those few precious evenings that summer. But without discussion, they abandoned the pair of matching Adirondack chairs for the double glider where they wrapped themselves in blankets and each other's arms.

After a brief trip to the farm, Charlotte returned with three sweaters and her grandmother's crocheted afghan which was now warming their knees.

"Cozy, right?" she said to Fig, tucking the orange and brown granny squares around him. "We can have coffee and happy hour on the glider and let the snow cover us."

He fingered the yarn and picked off several wooly pills.

"It's warm, I'll grant you that," he said. "Just promise me you won't get any funny ideas about redecorating the rest of the house."

She laughed. "So, I should cancel the pink throw pillows I ordered?"

Fig laughed softly and propped his chin on the top of her head, which was her new favorite thing about him.

Charlotte found solace in their daily routine. After coffee and breakfast at the kitchen counter, they moved to the dining room table to compose their request for a temporary restraining order.

Charlotte fleshed out each argument with examples as Fig typed her words into his laptop. Sometimes he'd ask for clarification, listening intently as he folded and unfolded his reading glasses. Sometimes he'd ask her to read what he'd written out loud while he made a fresh pot of coffee.

Each afternoon, Fig rested on the couch connected to his oxygen machine. Despite her fears for his health, he seemed to draw strength from the work and perhaps, she hoped, from her presence.

Charlotte spent her afternoons wandering the curved paths of the island. She watched goldfinches harvesting the seeds of the coreopsis she'd planted. She'd looked up to see a noisy flock of sandhill cranes following the river south to join others of their kind near the little town of Bellevue before their mass migration. This daily communion with the island's wildlife was her own kind of rest.

Each day with Fig brought Charlotte more peace and quietude than she had ever known. If she lived to one hundred, she thought, nothing could come close to the happiness of that September.

"The meeting of the Saskawan Five will come to order," Charlotte said, tapping her coffee mug with a spoon and smiling.

On a Tuesday morning, Fig, Charlotte, Portia, Nicky, Katie, Barb and Mazie were crowned into the big corner booth at The Farmer's Daughter. Fig had finished the Heart-Healthy Breakfast but was reaching for a second apple-cinnamon-pecan scone.

Katie was to blame for the name—the Saskawan Five—which Nicky pointed out sounded as if *they*, not the city and the county, were the ones on trial. But, when Katie handed out baseball caps imprinted with the name," Nicky was the first to put hers on.

Technically, there were only four plaintiffs, since Barb had argued that VanderLee Garden's history of selling invasive species made her a liability. But she wanted to help with strategy and had even offered privately to help pay Fig, which he flatly refused.

Mazie was seated next to Fig taking notes. Her middle school was having a teacher in-service day and she was writing a report about the lawsuit for her social studies class.

Fig put down his scone. "By now, both the city and the county should have received your individual written requests to postpone the Plant-a-Palooza or revise their plant lists to exclude invasives. This will demonstrate to the judge that you've done all you can on your own to stop the event. Has anyone had a response?"

Katie made a face and shook her head. "Nope."

"No one has heard a thing," Portia said.

Fig continued. "Good. This strengthens our case."

"They've got *some* nerve," Katie said "If you need someone to chain herself to a Bobcat, I'm your girl."

Fig smiled. "We'll keep that in mind."

"Okay," Charlotte continued. "I've emailed a draft of the TRO to each of you. Please look it over carefully and send questions or comments this week."

"And to review for Mazie," Fig said, "we're asking the judge for a Temporary Restraining Order to stop the city and county from planting four species: Bradford pear, barberry, non-native honeysuckle and Norway maple in the Cross-County Linear Park. If the judge agrees, the Plant-a-Palooza cannot take place until a full hearing is held."

Charlotte said, "And a postponement will probably delay planting until spring. That'll give us time to raise public concern."

Mazie's brow furrowed with concentration as she took this down.

Fig continued. "Remember, the judge will rule on our document alone. No one is going to appear in court at this point."

Mazie raised her hand. "Wait. So, there's no a trial?"

Fig said, "Not at this point. If the judge rejects our TRO, we can file a regular lawsuit. But if he grants it, he'll set a date to hear from both sides in court. I expect that will be soon after the new year."

Nicky made a face. "Will you call Elena to the stand, Fig? I mean they are donating the invasives for the project. I'd love to see you rip her limb from limb."

"Let's hope it doesn't come to that," he said, "but the MHA will certainly see this lawsuit as a threat to the horticultural industry."

"They'll start throwing their weight around," Katie said, rolling her eyes. "Count on that."

Fig nodded. "I expect so, but remember a TRO is just the first step."

On the drive home Fig said, "We still need a statement from you, Charlotte."

"I know. But I'm stuck. I haven't been in business long enough to sustain damages like Nicky and Katie have. Besides, I've had the ideal client, so it's really your fault when I think about it."

Mazie leaned forward from the back seat, pencil at-the-ready. "What kind of statement?"

Charlotte said, "All plaintiffs must explain why they will personally be harmed if these species are planted."

"Isn't that obvious?" Mazie asked.

"Not to the court," Fig said. "The judge wants to know why each plaintiff needs the court to help them. It's called 'standing.'"

Mazie shrugged. "But what happens to the environment harms everybody. I mean, the whole planet will be screwed if people keep planting invasive plants."

"That's true," Fig said, "but everybody on the whole planet can't ask the court for damages."

"Well, that's just wrong!" Mazie said.

Every year on the 21st of September for as long as either Charlotte or Mazie could remember, the Adair family gathered at the farm to celebrate Great-grandpa Adair's birthday. On this, his 105th, he hadn't been physically present for many years, but the birthday remained a perfect excuse for a bonfire, hotdogs and s'mores—and this year the perfect excuse for Mally and Ted to meet Fig.

Charlotte spent the morning power-cleaning the neglected farm-house. This included sweeping mouse droppings off the kitchen counter, hiding the leak buckets on the back porch in the bushes at the side of the house, scrubbing the rusting harvest-gold stove top, polishing the oak kitchen table and vacuuming the entire downstairs.

In the afternoon, she mowed a circle around the ring of stones already piled high with scrap lumber and sticks. Later her father would douse it with gasoline, toss in a match and stand back, looking half-crazed and extremely happy. Fig would be horrified and baffled by her father's fire building methods. Charlotte smiled at the thought.

At 4:00 Mally, Ted and Mazie arrived with a cooler of hotdogs, potato salad, and baked beans. At 5:10, the family was milling around the fire, poking and prodding the flames, when Fig's old Mercedes bounced down the drive looking comically out-of-place. The vintage car got an appreciative whistle from Ted.

Fig's outfit (#2 -Preppy Weekender) looked equally incongruous, although he'd traded his Panama hat for a brown trilby. He had a carefully folded fleece jacket draped over his arm.

"Hey, Ficus!" Mazie greeted him with a rare, spontaneous hug.

Prince leaped out of the car toward Mazie, only to turn a back flip at the end of his leash.

"Whoa there, buddy," Fig said. "He hasn't quite mastered the leash yet."

"Poor guy," Mazie said, kneeling to let Prince cover her face with kisses. She led him off on the pee-and-sniff tour of the farm while Charlotte made introductions.

Fig took in the scene. "So, this is where Charlotte disappears to every now and then. Very picturesque."

Ted draped a beefy arm around Mally's shoulders. "It's a bit ramshackle, but we're glad to have an Adair back on the premises—even if it's only now and then."

Charlotte reached for the six-pack of Bell's Two-Hearted Ale Fig was carrying. "I'll put these in the cooler."

"I hope you like beer," Fig said. "I couldn't find a wine that pairs well with hotdogs and marshmallows," he said, grinning.

Charlotte rolled her eyes. "We Adairs prefer moonshine. Ain't that right, Paw?"

Ted laughed. "I reckon, but not since the still blew up last Christmas."

Fig rocked on his heels with laughter.

"Would you like a tour?" Charlotte asked.

He lifted his hat. "Why, yes, ma'am, I surely would."

"Victuals'll be ready whenever you get back," Mally called out.

She led Fig toward the barn. It really did look pretty ramshackle when she saw it through his eyes.

"I plan to put a workshop in the barn," she said, "but it needs a new roof first. I'm going to put a greenhouse on the south side, too, but I need to get that door fixed and the windows re-glazed. Someday I'll plant natives around the house, but you know—the shoemaker's children and all." She shrugged apologetically.

By the time they reached the leaky enclosed back porch, she couldn't stop talking. "I use this as a makeshift greenhouse to get a few things started. It's not nearly big enough, but . . ." She was momentarily distracted by the old house smell she'd never noticed before. She nodded toward the kitchen's bay window and a half-sheet of plywood on a pair of sawhorses. "My office—if you can call it that."

He nodded. "Good work comes from there."

She stood with her back to the refrigerator to cover the spot where the linoleum had worn through.

They stepped into the front room. "This is it. Your basic farmhouse. There are three bedrooms upstairs, but I can't really use them in the winter until I get a new furnace and better storm windows. That's the plan anyway."

Apparently, all she had in all the world were plans.

She shoved her hands into the back pockets of her jeans. "My parents have been so generous and I've promised to take care of this place, but . . ." Her voice trailed off. "Sometimes it's overwhelming."

"But full of charm and possibilities."

She glanced at him sideways. "That's one way of putting it."

He crossed the room to take a closer look at the family photos on the sideboard, causing the floor to creak. He rocked back and forth smiling. "House music."

"House music?"

"I have house music on the fifth and ninth steps of my stairs. Have you noticed?"

She smiled glumly. "At least no one can sneak up on me in this house."

She caught him glancing at the cracked ceiling.

"I need to get a plasterer in here too."

"How old is the house?"

"Great-grandpa Adair built it after the first World War, so more than a hundred, I think. He'd only ever built fences before. My dad says that if you dropped a marble in here it would never stop rolling."

She led him toward the front entryway with its long flight of stairs leading to the second floor. "We don't need to go up. It's a long climb and the house music becomes death metal when you get to the top. But my bed is made, I'll have you know."

He touched her shoulder and frowned. "I'm not judging, Charlotte."

"I know. It's just—." She yanked the sticky front door open and stifled the desire to explain her plans for rehanging it. Who was she kidding? For the next fifty years she'd watch helplessly as this place fell down around her.

Fig was still frowning. He went down the porch steps into the yard and looked back at the house. "Here's what I see. I see a charming old house with love baked into every creak and crack."

"But compared to your house –."

"Mine looked a lot like this not long ago. And I loved it even then. For years, all I had was plans and ideas. That was the fun, creative part."

"Your house has history."

"And so does this one."

She couldn't help thinking that Fig always knew he'd have the money to repair his home one day. Her own future was much less secure.

"I do love this house," she admitted. "It's like an old dog that can't help piddling on the kitchen floor. No more apologies." She sighed. "I guess I'm a bit stressed about you meeting my parents. Aren't you?"

"Should I be?" He so obviously wasn't.

She let her gaze drop. "No. But they're feeling protective. But they like you, I can tell already."

"I'm glad they're nearby and that they'll be there to support you when I'm gone."

She absolutely did not want to talk about that right now.

"Anyway," she said, pointing to the field in front of the house, "if you think this is just an ordinary tangle of invasive weeds, you would be wrong."

Fig smiled again. "I would?"

She swept her arm in a wide arch over the pasture. "Imagine, if you will, a row of oak seedlings there. Dogwood and red-bud there and maybe a few dozen shadblow there, at the edge of the woods. And up near the road, rows of native shrubs—viburnum, buttonbush, red-twig dogwood. And here, where I can reach them with the hose, rows and rows and rows of prairie wildflowers in pots." She clasped her hands together and smiled. "Cars will screech to a halt and back up for a second look. I might open for retail sales on Memorial Day and Labor Day." She laughed. "But mostly, I'll sell my imaginary plants to my imaginary clients. Cut out the middle man and make heaps and heaps of imaginary money."

Fig reached an arm around her waist. "When's the groundbreaking?"

Charlotte shook her head. "This pasture is choked with honeysuckle—the invasive kind and about a million Norway maples. I need to cut it all to the ground, then treat each stump with herbicide."

Fig's eyebrows shot up with interest. "Show me more."

"Wouldn't you rather have a beer with my parents?"

"Yes, but this won't take long."

They waded into the waist-high brush.

"My dad cut all this down about three years ago and I planted a row of acorns. They came up fine, but none of them survived because they got shaded out by this." She snapped off a leaf from a three-foot maple sapling. "See this milky sap? This is a Norway maple, not our native species."

"Where did they come from?"

She laughed. "I'm guessing Norway."

"No, I mean how did they get into this pasture."

She pointed toward the road. "Norway maples were planted all along the roadsides around here."

"By Saskawan County?"

She shrugged. "I suppose. They're the most common street tree in the United States."

Fig lifted his arms. "There you go! There's your legal standing. Your business has been compromised by the same tree the county is proposing for the Cross-County Linear Park."

Charlotte scowled. "Of course, I should have thought of that. If these maple seedlings weren't here—"

"You'd have a row of three-year-old oaks to sell to clients. Add up the profit you would have made on the sales and—"

Charlotte brushed her hands together. "—Bob's-yer-uncle. Ticketyboo!"

Fig laughed. "Sure. Whatever you say."

"I'll write that up tomorrow and we can add that to the TRO."

He offered his arm with a chivalrous nod. "And now, my darling, I'm ready to be your charming boyfriend."

"Well, it's about time."

Five lawn chairs were arranged up-wind of the bonfire.

"What a charming place," Fig said, sitting down. "I visited a farm once when I was at camp. But a bonfire is something new."

Mazie, who was looking particularly content with Prince on her lap, announced, "After dinner Pop said we can go pick some marshmallows for s'mores. In the marsh."

Ted gave Charlotte a wink.

"I can run to the store and get some," Fig offered.

"The fresh ones are tastier," Mazie said. "Isn't that right Aunt Charlotte?"

"Exactly right. We have a great crop this year."

"Of marshmallows?" Fig asked, looking from Charlotte to Mazie. "I didn't know they were a . . . vegetable? A fruit?" He gave Charlotte a quizzical look. "Are they native?"

"*Althaea officinalis*? No, but I make exceptions for deliciousness," Charlotte said.

Ted chuckled. "My girls are pulling your leg, Fig."

"I knew that," he said, pointing a finger at Mazie.

Charlotte said, "But marshmallows really were made from the candied roots of the plant at one time."

Mally pulled out a plastic bag of marshmallows from a basket by her chair. "Lookie here. I found some!" She read the label and frowned. "These days, they're made from sugar, corn syrup and gelatin."

Fig grinned. "This is some sort of Adair family hazing, right?" He pinched Mazie's cheek. "You country bumpkins are so adorable."

Mazie buried her face in Prince's fur and giggled.

Ted handed Fig a beer. "When it gets dark, you and me can go snipe huntin'."

Fig took a swig and grinned. "I'm not falling for that one. I was a boy scout once."

"Take a seat, Ted," Mally said sternly. Then she turned to Fig. "So, tell us about this lawsuit."

"Well," he said, shifting gears. "Charlotte and I are about to stir up a nest of hornets here in Michigan. You should be proud of her. She's got guts."

"Grit," Charlotte corrected. "And now guts to go with my grit, besides being an adorable country bumpkin. A few weeks ago, he was telling me this would be a piece of cake. But honestly, a lawsuit is way overdue in this state."

When the coals were hot, they roasted hotdogs on sticks followed by store-bought marshmallows.

As the sun set, swallows flew out of the barn and Mazie went to the house to finish her homework. Charlotte sat between Fig and Mally poking at the coals and sending orange missiles spiraling toward the darkening sky. Their faces were flushed with the fire's warmth and the effects of the beer. Charlotte watched the Big Dipper rise above the barn and pour its magic over her little farm, with its many, many promises, and this new chapter of her life.

A gust of wind caused the barn to creak.

"Barn music!" Fig and Charlotte said in unison. He reached for her hand as a deep, contented sigh escaped. Despite his claims to the contrary, Charlotte knew the evening had been stressful for him.

"We have a court filing coming up," she announced. "Shall we call it a night?"

Fig nodded. "Yes, though I hate to leave the party." He rose slowly to his feet, tucking Prince under his arm like a football. "It was a great honor to be included in this family tradition. Now I see where Charlotte and Mazie get their brains and good looks."

Mally smiled broadly. "Why, thank you, Fig. Though I've never figured out what they got from my husband."

Charlotte started to walk Fig toward his car, but Ted touched her shoulder.

"If you've got a minute, Fig, I'd like a closer look at that ride of yours. Do you mind?" He shot Charlotte a look that said, I got this.

Fig tipped his hat. "Good night, Mally and thank you. Please tell Mazie I'll see her on Friday."

Charlotte kissed Fig's cheek. "I'll be a while. Don't wait up for me."

Ted patted Fig's back as they walked together toward the Mercedes. "How 'bout you show me what's under that hood."

Fig hiked up his pants and answered in a low, gravelly voice. "Under m'hood's where I keep m'motor and underneath m'motor she's got four rubber wheels. Five, if yer countin' 'er steerin' wheel. Six with the spare. I souped 'er up with a seat cover. Gen-u-wine sheepskin. And when I go to fuel up, I fill the tank m'self . . . ."

Then he gave Ted a return pat on the back.

It was almost dark by the time Charlotte took a bag of trash toward the house. Her father and Fig were still leaning against the fender of the Mercedes, legs and arms crossed left-to-right and right-to-left like bookends. Prince was seated in the driver's seat.

She ducked behind a bush to listen.

She overheard her father. ". . . grown woman . . . respect her choices . . . ." And then, "Mazie. . . hangs on your every word. . . what it will do to her . . . She needs to know."

Fig nodded soberly and ran his hand over his face.

Ted went on, ". . . lost her mom. . . . no dad . . . just us old farts. . . . shattered. . . betrayed . . . Don't wait."

Fig nodded slowly. ". . . inflict pain . . ." He looked beyond Ted into the darkening sky. ". . . to protect her . . . " He nodded again and pushed away from the car. ". . . you're right, Ted. . . . can't leave it to you or Charlotte . . . It's time."

He offered his hand and Ted shook it, gripping Fig's shoulder in a gesture just short of a hug. ". . . upright guy, Fig. You'll do what's right."

When Mazie saw Fig's retreating taillights she ran out of the house.

"I wanted to show him my constellation chart."

Charlotte wrapped a arm around Mazie's shoulder. "Bring it this weekend."

"I know, but I wanted to say goodbye, too."

When the sun sank below the horizon, Mally and Charlotte moved their chairs closer to the fire.

"Well, he's as charming as you said he would be. Despite that daft name of his."

"But it fits somehow. Don't you think?"

"I don't know about that, but he's a proper gentleman. Bigelow's a good English name, you know." She gave Charlotte's wrist a good squeeze.

"I knew you'd like him."

Mally sighed then. "But he's so thin, love."

Charlotte nodded. "It takes a lot of effort just to breathe."

"Is he getting worse?"

"It's hard to know. He tries so hard to hide it."

"But you're happy, in spite of everything?"

"Fig's the wisest, most interesting and generous person I've ever known. Every day's a gift."

"Well, Mazie seems to agree. I think she's a little in love with him herself." Mally turned to face her daughter. "So, when this is behind you, no regrets?"

"I don't think so, but I can't even imagine what that day—and all those days and years afterward will be like without him. And I keep making the same damn mistake."

"Of?"

"Being optimistic. Of expecting a miracle. If he wakes up early from a nap, coughs a little less one day or takes a short walk with me, I take it as a sign. I'm constantly imagining silver linings and new clinical trials. But Fig's cardinal rule is 'no false hope.'"

Mally nodded. "When someone we love is hurting our instincts take over. We'll do anything to relieve their pain. Hope is a natural part of our need to make things right." After a long silence, she asked. "There's no chance the doctors are wrong?"

Charlotte laughed. "Now you're doing it too. It's hard to accept. So he hates talking about it."

"I can't blame him. It's humiliating to be the object of pity." Mally threw a paper napkin into the flames. "When we lost Lauren, I worked so hard to get past it, but a couple of friends just wouldn't let me. They were forever asking how I *was*, and how I *felt*. Sympathizing. Pitying. So after a while, I avoided them."

Charlotte recall the feel of Heather Geller's partonizing looks and clutching fingers and did a slow burn.

"So I agree with Fig," Mally said. "He needs to enjoy life as much as he can for as long as he can. Focus on living."

"Yes, but it's hard to know how to help him do that."

"Looks like you're doing a brilliant job." Mally pressed Charlotte's hand against her warm face. "The most powerful act of love is your presence."

"That doesn't feel like nearly enough."

Mally sighed. "We hug children when they cry, even though it doesn't fix their skinned knee or banish the boogie man. We do it to show them we're there when they're scared and hurting. You can't heal Fig's damaged heart or erase his fear of death, but you can help him find his own strength."

Charlotte nodded, but couldn't form words.

"You know how to do this, honey. Remember after Lauren died," Mally went on, "you drove home from State almost every weekend to babysit and give Dad and me a break. That meant so much to us."

"I'd forgotten that."

Mally's brow creased with indecision. "There's another thing that concerns me, love. Does your decision to stay with Fig have anything to do with Lauren?"

"Why? Why would it?"

"I know you have regrets. We all do."

Charlotte looked down at her knotted fingers.

"Are you staying with Fig to the end because you couldn't save Lauren?"

"Couldn't? I could have tried harder. But when she pushed me away, I let her. I left. It was easier and less painful that way. At least I thought it would be." Charlotte drew her legs to her chest.

Mally sighed. "You were both so young, Charlotte, and she was so difficult."

"There's something I never told you, Mum." She fought to keep her voice steady. "Do you remember that guy Justin I dated in high school?"

"No, should I?"

Charlotte described their afternoons smoking pot in the treehouse and Lauren's threats to tell if they didn't let her try it.

"That was the start of everything. I introduced my little sister to drugs! What a selfish idiot I was."

Mally sighed deeply. "Charlotte, listen to me. When we first found out that Lauren was using, Dad and I talked to every one of her teachers. I think she was in eighth grade by then. And honey, our little Lauren was anything but naïve about drugs when she threatened you in the treehouse. There were signs she was experimenting with alcohol and probably pot just after fifth grade." She rubbed her eyes. "I still find that hard to believe. But kids get it at school and from older kids and even at camp these days. There wasn't one incident that triggered her addiction—certainly not the one you just described. Your sister was a thrill-seeker. Life was always all about the next high."

"Do you think her overdose was inevitable?"

"Lauren was a restless soul, an adventurer. In another century she might have gone to California to pan for gold or sailed the high seas. Ordinary life didn't interest our Lauren." Her voice grew husky. "She was born with a hunger our culture can't satisfy—at least not for a teenage girl. It wasn't just the drugs, but the adventure, the risk she craved. Drugs were how she coped with our quiet lives." She shook Charlotte's wrist for emphasis. "What I'm saying, darling, is that it wasn't your fault. Or mine and your Dad's, for that matter."

"Thanks, but—"

"Stop blaming yourself, Charlotte. You were both just kids. Kids incapable of appreciating how fragile life is. No one saw the danger she was in until it was too late. No one. Put that behind you."

"I don't want to put it behind me. I want to learn from it."

After a long silence, Mally asked, "Why didn't you tell me about this before?"

Charlotte chuckled. "Because I knew you'd forgive me. But I accept that what I did was wrong. I didn't stand by my little sister, but I'm going to stand by Fig."

"As some kind of penance? I know you've stayed in Saskawan partly to help us raise Mazie and we appreciate it, but you don't owe us anything."

"Maybe not, but I'd still like a do-over. To leave Fig now would be impossible. Either I see this through and make the most of the time we have together, or I'll be full of regrets for the rest of my life."

Charlotte tipped her head back, fighting tears she didn't want confused with doubt.

Mally said, "I guess Lauren wasn't the only adventurer in this family. She'd be so proud of Adair Natural Landscaping, and she'd think your love affair with Fig is so bloody romantic."

Charlotte smiled. "Yeah, and she'd be right."

They watched the fire for the longest time.

"I guess you'll let Dad and me know how we can help." She stood up then and offered her hand to Charlotte. "Come on, let's clean up."

When they had doused the fire and put the lawn chairs back in the barn, Charlotte walked her parents to their car.

Ted tooted the horn for Mazie.

"She's grown up so much this summer," he said. "She looks forward to visiting the island, and you and Fig, every weekend."

"Fig's crazy about her," Charlotte said. "She follows him everywhere and Prince follows them both."

As Mazie ran toward them, Ted said, "We were wrong, Mal. Our little alien turned out to be an Earthling after all."

"Bye, Aunt Charlotte," Mazie said, giving her a quick hug. "I'll see you Friday."

Mally leaned toward Charlotte . "If you want a miracle, there you have it."

"What miracle?" Mazie asked, getting into the car.

Charlotte tousled Mazie's curls. "You kiddo. You. Have a good week."

As they drove away, Mazie shouted out the window, "Happy Birthday, Grandpa!"

<u>32</u>

TELLING MAZIE

O n Friday, Charlotte was chopping onions for a pot of navy bean soup while Fig helped Mazie study for her algebra test. His oxygen hummed under the table as they worked. Charlotte dabbed at her smarting eyes, wondering what portion of her tears were in anticipation of Fig's talk with Mazie. A load of dread felt like a boulder strapped to her back. She knew he was waiting for the right moment. She understood better now why he had been so reluctant to share his prognosis.

Fig said, "And three X plus five is?"

"Twenty-three?"

"Right. And twenty-three plus four X minus two?"

"Um. Forty-seven?"

"Try again."

"I caaaan't," Mazie moaned. "Maybe if I breathed pure oxygen I'd understand this stuff better. Is that what makes you so smart?"

"I was smart before," he said, nudging her playfully. "Besides, you're plenty smart to get this—with the benefit of my tutoring, of course."

They worked for the next half hour, bent together over the textbook, shoulders nearly touching. Mazie grunted and fussed, but Fig spoke in low, even tones that kept her from storming off.

"So, X here is 16. See?"

"How did you get that?"

"Because we already know three X plus Y plus two equals forty-six, right?"

"Yeah."

"So, we can substitute Y in the next equation. See?"

"Uhhhh. Maybe. Yeah."

"Go ahead. Take us through the next one."

Halfway through Mazie slapped her forehead. "Wait! X equals negative three. I get it." She looked up at him, amazed at herself. "Why can't my teacher explain it like that?"

They went through two more.

"So, do you think you can do the rest by yourself?"

"No problemo—after I get some brain food." She got up to stand beside Charlotte. "What's for dinner?"

She reached for an apple slice that was meant for their Waldorf salad and leaned against the counter, her legs crossed at the ankles. Fig junior, Charlotte thought.

Charlotte nudged Mazie and mouthed, Thank you.

"What?"

Charlotte frowned. "My niece here is grateful for your help, Fig, even though she sometimes forgets to say so."

Mazie was unfazed. "My gratitude was expressed non-verbally, but just to cover all the bases—" She clasped her hands and bowed. "I am deeply grateful, Professor Ficus E. Bigelow."

Fig stood up and stretched. "An A on your test will be the most appropriate expression of gratitude."

"Your wish is my command, kind sir."

Mazie lifted the lid of the soup pot and made a face. "What's this?"

"Navy bean soup."

"I only like—"

"Chicken noodle. So I've heard a million gazillion times." Charlotte nudged her out of the way. "There's always PB and J."

"I'm getting sort of tired of peanut butter."

Charlotte lowered her chin. "Maybe that's a sign that it's time to expand your horizons, food-wise." Charlotte spooned out a piece of ham and fed it to Mazie. "Taste."

Mazie stuck out her bottom lip and nodded. "Hmm. I might try a little." She reached for another slice of apple. "Aunt Charlotte, do Nana and Pop have a college fund for me?"

"I'm not sure. Why?"

"Because if they don't, I'd like to know now so I can stop taking algebra and start acquiring barista skills. I'm going to ask them." She took several of Prince's treats out of the drawer. "Where's Prince?"

And with that, she wandered into the yard. Through the kitchen window, Charlotte watched her trying to teach Prince to row over, but he responded to every command with only a yip.

Fig came to stand behind Charlotte at the sink. She leaned into his arms and felt his chin propped on her head.

"The soup needs to simmer a while," she said. "You've got time to lie down."

She felt his shoulders lift and fall in a long sigh. "She's going to ace that test. God, she's got such a keen, analytical mind. She reminds me so much of myself."

"Wow, that sounded conceited."

He laughed. "An unfortunate juxtaposition. I just meant that I can read her, you know?"

"As she does you."

"I suppose. Yes."

She turned around to face him. "She's smart enough to know you aren't using oxygen to make yourself smarter."

He sagged. "I know. It's time. Your dad—"

"—is right." She tilted her head back until he kissed her. "Do you want me to tell her?"

"No. It's best coming from me, but I'd like you there."

She had to turn away. "Of course. And thanks for helping her with algebra. If you and Mazie were any smarter or more alike, it would be frightening."

It was a glorious end-of-summer day that Sunday. The dogwood leaves were tinged with pink and the spice bushes radiated golden light.

Charlotte and Fig packed a basket of tuna sandwiches for themselves and peanut butter and grape jelly for Mazie and set off for the thinkin' log. Mazie squatted near a boulder at the river's edge with her sandwich in one hand and her bug net in the other.

"Hey, Maze?" Fig said. "Come join us on the thinkin' log."

Charlotte moved aside to make room for Mazie, feeling a sickening heat in her gut.

Mazie sat down, wiping her hands on her jeans. "This is just a dead old tree. You do know that, don't you?"

"Maybe to you," Fig said, "but it helps me gather my thoughts. There's nothing more conducive to lucid contemplation than a fine seat in full view of water. See that squirrel over there? She's burying an acorn. I bet she has a thinkin' twig somewhere up high in that tree." He looked into the tree canopy. "She was probably tempted to eat that delicious acorn for lunch, but after some serious contemplation on her thinkin' twig, she's decided to save it for a winter day. A much wiser move." He grinned down at Mazie.

She eyed him with a wry half-smile. "So, you absorb wisdom through your butt?"

Fig laughed. "I get it wherever I can."

Charlotte opened a bag of cookies. "Oatmeal cranberry or Oreo?"

"Oreo," Mazie said, adding, "Please and thank you."

The three of them watched a robin bathe between two half-submerged boulders. It flew up to preen its feathers on the lowest branch of a redbud. Charlotte reached behind Mazie to touch Fig's hand.

"Mazie," Fig said, "I know how you don't like surprises."

"Like birthday parties?"

"Or, oatmeal bars with cranberries," Charlotte offered. "Or any cereal other than Cheerios. Any soup other than chicken noodle."

Fig added. "Or pop quizzes or changes of plans."

Mazie gave a so-what shrug. "So what's the surprise?"

Fig continued. "You know my lungs don't function as they should."

"Because you got pneumonia when you are younger."

"Right."

When he didn't continue, Mazie looked up at him. "Do you have pneumonia again?"

"No, Mazie, but my lungs are damaged. You've known me a while and you're a keen observer. What are you seeing?"

Mazie looked away quickly and Charlotte saw her expression darken. She dug a pebble out of the dirt with her heel and flung it hard into the water. "You're coughing more. You need your oxygen more." She bit her lower lip and began blinking. "You're not getting better."

"Yes, that's true."

"Are you getting a transplant?"

Fig looked at Charlotte. "No, Mazie, I'm—I'm not. I can't."

Mazie looked steadily into his eyes, not with her death ray, but something new. Something alert and open. "You can't get better?"

"No. The doctors have tried everything."

"So, are you—Are you going to die?"

Fig nodded.

"Soon." She said it for him. "That's what this is about. How soon?"

Fig dropped his gaze. "I don't know the answer. A few months. Maybe a year."

Mazie considered this. "But at least you know, so it won't be as big of a shock when it happens. That helps a little, doesn't it?" She glanced at Charlotte for confirmation. Charlotte nodded and rubbed Mazie's back. This seemed to be Mazie's idea of a silver lining.

He kissed the top of her head and rested his chin there. "You know me well, Maze."

Mazie stayed in Fig's embrace for a long time.

Charlotte asked, "Do you have any questions, sweetie?"

"About a million," she said, straightening her back and standing up suddenly. "But there's no room in my head for any more answers right now."

Then she turned and ran down toward the house. A minute later she heard the rhymthic creak of the swing in the oak clearing.

Charlotte and Fig both let go of the tears they'd been holding back and helding each other for the longest time.

"God, that was hard," she said, finally. "I thought I'd feel relieved somehow, but I just feel worse."

Charlotte had been carrying Fig's pain with her own—and now she would carry Mazie's too, because even at thirteen, her niece had already lost too much. Fig interlaced his fingers with hers.

"Truth's a bitch," he said. "It has the power to split time into before and after. I hate doing that to people—especially those I love."

Fig pushed a handkerchief into Charlotte's hand.

She wondered if he had enough strength held in reserve for what lay ahead. She wondered if he had enough handkerchiefs.

A great blue heron landed at the water's edge and stood like a lawn ornament in the reeds, unaware of its audience.

"I'd like to sit here with you forever, Charlotte Anne, just watching this river slip by. Its steadfastness is reassuring, don't you think? It will endure, no matter what."

"Yes," she said. "No matter what."

That evening when Mazie was leaving for home, she looked up at Fig. "You said I could ask more questions, right?"

"I did," he said, lifting her backpack to her shoulder.

She fiddled with the strap. "Well, I sort of want to know why, um, you didn't tell me sooner?"

Fig sighed. "I guess because I knew it would hurt you. And I was afraid knowing might frighten you so you wouldn't want to visit anymore."

She drew back. "That would never happen. I wish I could spend every minute here."

Fig nodded slowly. "Well clearly, I underestimated you. I'm sorry, Maze." He opened his arms and with no hesitation, she stepped into them. He smoothed her hair and kissed her forehead. "I'll never make that mistake again."

Mazie was quiet on the ride home and made no move to get out when they reached Mally and Ted's.

"I have another question, but I couldn't ask him."

"You can ask me."

Mazie turned her face toward the passenger window. "I'm not a child, you know. You can be honest."

"Okay."

She heard Mazie swallow hard. "Um, is Fig getting sicker because of me?"

"What? No! Why would you think that?"

Her chin was thrust forward. "He almost died trying to save me in the rowboat."

"No. No, he—."

"Yes. Yes, he did." Her voice rose.

She gripped Mazie by her shoulders. "Listen to me now. Fig was sick long before either of us met him. Not you, or anyone else, caused this or made it worse." Mazie's wet cheeks glistened under the streetlights. "And you know what else I think? I think rescuing you made him stronger."

"Why?"

"Being sick all the time makes him feel useless sometimes, but that day he jumped into the kayak to save you. He forgot all about his sick body and did something really brave. Superman to the rescue!"

Mazie smiled.

"That night, after you were asleep, he told me he loves you like you were his own child. I mean, I know you're not really a *child*—"

"I can be a child a little longer for him." Then, Mazie covered her face and wept. "It's just so unfair!"

"I know."

After a long silence, Mazie asked, "So, you really like him now? I mean, like-like him?"

"I'm in love with him, sweetie."

Mazie nodded. "I thought so. So, you must be extra sad, right?"

"Extra, extra. You probably understand that better than anyone."

The porch light came on and Ted and Mally came out to wait on the top step.

"Do they know?" Mazie asked.

"Yes."

"Do they know I know?"

"I expect so." Charlotte smiled. "Go get some hugs."

Mazie sighed before opening her door. Then she walked slowly toward the house and into her grandparents' arms.

OCTOBER

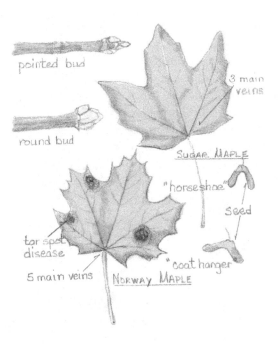

pointed bud

round bud

3 main veins

SUGAR MAPLE

"horseshoe"

seed

tar spot disease

5 main veins

NORWAY MAPLE

"coat hanger"

33

REALITY

To survive in the wild, a plant must adapt quickly to change. During dry spells, its roots pump harder to draw water in. After a heavy rain, its roots reverse the process and pump water out. This constant activity makes the plant stronger. Conversely, when a plant is grown under ideal conditions—say, in a planter box on a sunny deck with just the right amount of water and fertilizer—it can become weak and needy. A gardener returning from a short vacation may find that her prized beauty has turned leggy and brown.

Fig was stretched out on the couch next to his oxygen machine, dictating to Charlotte as she typed changes to the TRO sent by Portia and Barb. It was ten o'clock and except for lunch and a brief siesta, they'd been working all day.

Charlotte closed her laptop and stretched. "Okay, I'm calling it a day. Let's finish in the morning."

She pulled Fig to a stand and they walked up the stairs together. When they reached the creaky step Fig said, "My house music is now a chord. Have you noticed? Perfect harmony."

She woke to the sound of Fig moving around in the kitchen.

"Morning," she said, yawning from the stairs.

"What would you like for lunch?"

She yawned again. "What about breakfast?"

He pointed to the clock above the sink which said eleven ten.

The dining table which had been littered with books and papers the night before was neatly rearranged in stacks and at ninety-degree angles.

"Have you been working all morning? You should have gotten me up."

He handed her a cup of coffee. "The rest was just legal minutiae."

"So, we're done?" She tipped her face up for a kiss. "That makes me incredibly happy."

She sat on the stool facing him. Gray circles rimmed his eyes.

"Can you take it easy this week?"

He nodded.

She opened her phone and read a text from Mally.

"Ooo, good timing. My parents are having their annual jumble sale—that's 'garage sale' to us Yanks. They want to know if I can help. I get free stuff for my trouble and I'll be out of your hair."

He nodded. "Enjoy. But I rather like you in my hair."

She scrolled the message. "She also says they'd like to do a color tour up north next week and wondered if Mazie could stay here."

"Of course."

"Good. They'll love it. Everybody will love it." She texted back and yawned again. "I can't believe I slept so long." She propped her chin on her hand and sighed. "Man, telling Mazie knocked me flat." She watched him over the rim of her mug. "You?"

Fig nodded. "It'll be good to have some extra time with her."

On the way to Mally and Ted's, Charlotte stopped at the farm to pick up her mail and some warmer clothes. She stood at the kitchen table sorting it into piles and humming to herself. Then she opened her bank statement and stared at the bottom line and went silent. She had $378.45 left in her checking account and $276.52 in her business account. She dropped into a kitchen chair with a hand over her mouth.

Fig had compensated her generously, but after she paid the crew, VanderLee Gardens, her summer taxes, four truck payments and monthly loan payments, she was nearly broke. Ahead lay six months of winter with no income.

She looked at her abandoned kitchen in her abandoned house. Clearly, she'd taken her eye off the ball. Fig, the lawsuit and Mazie had distracted her from the management of Adair Natural Landscaping.

Big mistake.

Fig had made her feel secure. So secure that for the first time in her adult life she stopped worrying about money. And except for a few bags of groceries, he had rebuffed all of her offers to contribute financially.

She had allowed herself to be lulled into a comfortable stupor. A love-struck stupor. She caught her reflection in the kitchen window. "Charlotte Anne, you are a kept woman."

How could she have been so stupid and shortsighted?

She got up wearily and turned the thermostat down a few more degrees. She locked all the downstairs windows and closed the blinds against the cooling weather. Then she trudged up the stairs and emptied her sweater drawer into her duffel. The bedroom window she'd left open was stuck. She got a hammer from the kitchen and tapped it until it fell into place.

Back in the kitchen, she unplugged the refrigerator and emptied its contents.

Then she went outside to retrieve the drip buckets she'd hidden in the bushes before the bonfire. A loud crack overhead and a crash behind her made her jump. On the ground were the splintered remains of her bedroom window. She looked up.

"Damn house!" she yelled. "Are you trying to kill me?"

She picked wood and splinters from the grass and dropped them into a bucket and emptied it into the garbage bin. Upstairs, she stapled two garbage bags over the window frame and sealed the edges with duct tape. How much were new windows these days? Too much at any price.

She looked at her handiwork. She wouldn't be able to use this room all winter. For Fig, their current domestic arrangement was permanent, but it could never be that for her. Her own life on the island with Fig was destined to be a brief interlude, an ephemeral thing, a mirage. A honeymoon in Camelot.

This old house and this unproductive farm was her world, her reality—not Fig's island kingdom. This was where she came from and where she would return after their one brief shining moment.

At Mally and Ted's that afternoon she carried boxes up from the basement, set up tables in the garage and tacked signs to utility poles around the subdivision. When she told her father about her vanishing bank account, he loaded up her truck with a toaster oven, Mazie's old bike, a vintage wine rack, an antique rocker and a set of bunk beds.

"You can get good money for these," he said.

She planted a kiss on his grizzled cheek. "Thanks, Dad. This'll really help."

Late that afternoon, she returned to the farm and sorted through the stuff Harp had left behind. There was the snowboard, a set of dumbbells, two baseball gloves and a rusting pinball machine he was going to restore. Then, she cleaned out her grandmother's collection of carnival glass from the sideboard and brought down an old steamer trunk from the attic full of vintages bedspreads and quilts.

She stood back and tried not to feel nostalgic or guilty. Then she took photos and posted everything on Craig's List. With any luck, proceeds would cover the cost of getting Adair Natural Landscaping back on its feet.

After Fig fell asleep that night, she slipped out of bed to work at the dining room table. She uploaded new photos of the island to her website and went back to bed about three.

On Tuesday, she helped at the garage sale until noon, then slipped off to make sales calls on nurseries and greenhouses—pausing only to check the progress of her Internet sales and replace her holey brown sweater with another from Goodwill. At midnight she sneaked downstairs to the dining room table again where she reserved a booth at the Saskawan Home Expo for next March and scheduled several Craig's List customers for their pick-ups.

On Wednesday and Thursday, she fired up the tractor and mowed the front pasture, stopping at the end of each pass to daub shoots of Norway maples and honeysuckle with herbicide. She took breaks to help her customers load their purchases. Her pile of cash was growing. Before leaving for Fig's, she gathered a bucketful of white oak acorns in Grandpa Adair's woodlot to plant later. And after Fig went to bed that night and the next, she revised her business brochure.

By Friday noon, she had sold everything except Mazie's old bike and the toaster oven. She deposited $1,040 in her account, sent her revised brochure to the printer and ordered two dozen seedlings each of dogwood, redbud, shadblow and native honeysuckle from the Saskawan

County Conservation District. By the end of the month, she'd have five rows of trees in the ground, as well as a whole row of white oak acorns that would sprout next spring.

Adair Natural Landscaping was back in business.

When she returned to the island that evening, Fig was seated on the glider next to a stack of boxes.

"Your dad dropped them off this morning. He thought you might want to sell the contents." He paused. "He also said he hadn't seen you since Tuesday."

She collapsed into the glider next to him, rubbing her eyes. She puffed her cheeks and exhaled.

"I thought you'd been at their garage sale all week. Are you okay?"

She shook her head. How do you describe poverty to someone who has probably never wanted for anything?

"If you're having an affair, you can tell me."

"What?" She flushed red with anger, but Fig's eyes were twinkling.

"Sorry. That wasn't funny." He reached for her hand. "Never mind. You don't have to account for your time, Charlotte."

Fig run his thumb over a deep scratch on her forearm. "I just worry you're not happy. You've had a far-away look all week and I know you've been up half the night."

Charlotte lifted her arms and dropped them. "I was trying to save my business." She gave a review of her finances and the activities of her week, ending with, "Basically I'm broke. I can't afford an island vacation right now."

He let his head drop back to look at the porch ceiling. "God, I've been a royal nincompoop."

"Why? No. This is *my* doing."

"I wanted you to have some time off, but I have missed the point by a mile, haven't I?"

"I did too."

He shook his head in disgust. "The ill and infirm can descend into selfishness, you know. And being terminally ill has made me short-sighted as well. Just because *I* don't have a future to worry about doesn't mean you don't. I've been thoughtless. I apologize."

"No, the mistake was all mine."

"May I offer a bit of a bailout? It's the least I can do."

"Thanks, but I have things in hand now."

"Okay. But just out of curiosity, when's your birthday again?"

"Not till March."

"Then how about a festive greenhouse for Christmas or a jolly red barn?"

She laughed. "No bailouts, thank you, but if anyone admires your landscaping, you are duty-bound to tell them who designed it."

"I promise."

"I didn't mean to mislead you, by the way. I was going to tell you tonight, but first I needed to prove to myself that I could handle things on my own."

"It puts my mind at ease to know you'll live a full life A.F."

"A.F? Ah, 'After Fig.'" She shook her head. "No, not full. I expect there will be a great deal of emptiness, but it will be a good life—eventually. Wait until you see my updated brochure and all the pictures of the island on my website. And my new tree nursery. It's all good." She rested her head on his shoulder and as soon as he began pumping the glider, she dozed off.

She felt him stir.

"It's time to pick up Mazie," he said. "If you don't mind, I'd like to rest before she gets here."

She stood up and stretched. "I'll pick up dinner on the way back." She held out her hand. "Come on. I'll walk you upstairs."

When Charlotte arrived at her parents', the camper was parked in the driveway with the door opened. Ted was carrying a box down the porch steps.

"Mom and I are really looking forward to this getaway." He glanced up at Mazie's window and lowered his voice. "She's been awfully stoic about Fig. Hasn't wanted to talk at all."

"She's still processing it, Dad. We need to give her time."

Mazie appeared then, dragging a duffel bag behind her and letting it thump down the steps.

"You won't believe the homework I have," she called out.

"Greetings to you, too, miss," Charlotte said. "Give Pop a big hug and let's go. We'll talk about it over dinner."

Fig was waiting for them in the open doorway.

"You won't believe my homework!" Mazie grumbled as she dropped her backpack and duffel on the floor.

"Wait. Before you tell me, what about your Algebra test?"

"Aced it. Well, A-minused anyway. One dumb mistake."

"Do you know what you did wrong?"

"Yup. Forty-two squared is not seventeen hundred sixty." She smacked her forehead. "Duh!"

Charlotte put two grocery bags on the counter and lowered her chin at Mazie.

"Oh," Mazie said, stepping forward to give him a hug. "Thanks a million times X plus forty-two squared for helping me study, Professor Ficus."

"My pleasure," said Fig, bending over her. "So, what is this homework we won't believe?"

She reached deep into her backpack and slapped a sheet of green paper on the counter. "This! This is crap."

"Can you be more precise?" he asked.

She threw her head back and groaned. "I have to write a *poem* about *autumn*, and it has to *rhyme*. And it has to be at least twenty-five stupid words. What a way to ruin a perfectly good weekend! I bet Emily Dickenshiemer and Eddie Poe never had to cough up a poem just because their English teacher assigned it."

Fig drummed his fingers on the counter top, considering this. "Well, I suspect *someone* suggested they write poetry or encouraged them to try."

Mazie sat down across from him and propped her chin on her hands. "But I'm no good at poetry."

"You weren't much good at algebra last week either," Fig pointed out.

Mazie sniffed dismissively.

"Besides, I don't think being *good* at poetry is the point of this assignment, Mazie. The process of creation is its own reward. Proficiency rewards the reader, but the *doing*—the very act of writing a poem or creating any work of art—that's your reward."

"Not if I hate doing it."

"Think of it this way. The more new things we try, the more interesting and complex we become."

That got her attention.

He patted her shoulder and got up. "What you need is a little inspiration. Accompany me now, my child, and I will introduce you to a dear old friend."

Mazie rolled her eyes and shuffled behind him into the study.

Charlotte had just put the pasta on to boil when Fig returned.

"All sorted?" she asked.

"We'll see."

A few minutes later Charlotte called Mazie for dinner.

Mazie called out from the study, "Eat without me. I can't stop now or I'll lose my train of thoughts."

Charlotte shook her head at Fig. "Nice work, Professor Ficus."

Fig smiled. "I think she's found her muse."

"Who?"

"Ogden Nash. A Harvard-educated poet. He wrote hundreds of wonderful poems."

"Would I know any of them?"

Fig cleared his throat. "The cow is of the bovine ilk. One end is moo, the other, milk."

"Seriously? No wonder I haven't heard of him."

"I'm shocked by your ignorance, Charlotte Anne. Surely you've heard, 'Candy is dandy, but liquor is quicker.'"

She rolled her eyes. "That's what he's remembered for?"

"Here's another:

A panther is like a leopard
Except it hasn't been peppered.
Should you behold a panther crouch,
Prepare to say ouch.
Better yet, if called by a panther,

Don't anther."

"Okay," she laughed. "That one's pretty good."

Mazie reappeared as Charlotte and Fig were cleaning up.

"Are you ready to hear my poem?" She lifted her chin and stood very straight. 'Autumn Leaves,' by Madelyn McDougal Adair.

> Leaves are lovely on their branches
> But on the ground, they're avalanches!
> I wouldn't mind raking the valleys and hills
> If autumn leaves were dollar bills.

Charlotte clapped, Fig whooped and Mazie took a deep bow.

"Wonderful, Mazie," Charlotte said. "Really clever."

"Good old Ogden," Fig said. "He'd be so proud."

That night Fig sat on Charlotte's side of the bed massaging her shoulders. "You've had a tough week—all that mowing and fixing and burning the midnight oil."

She sighed heavily. "I came close to losing my business. It was stupid."

He waited for more, but she was too tired.

She stretched her neck. "Did you know that brain scans of people in love show a marked decline in cognitive ability? Surges of dopamine produce euphoria, even hallucinations—in my case, that I didn't need to earn a living. Basically, love makes people stupid and a little crazy." She closed her eyes. "I don't know what I was thinking."

Fig was working on a knot behind her scapula, making her moan.

"I do," he said. "You were putting my needs above yours, which—as a fellow love-sick dopamine fiend—I let you do. I'm so sorry."

"Well things are back on track now," she said, turning over to face him. "Seeing the sorry state of my farm and my bank statement was a honkin' big dose of reality."

"But you're still in love with me, right?"

She cupped his face in her hands and kissed him. "Crazy in love."

He wrapped his arms around her. "For an hallucination, you feel remarkably real."

On Monday, Mazie handed in her poem to her English teacher and her report on the TRO to her Social Studies teacher.

Mazie Adair
8th Grade Social Studies
Mr. Hogarth, 2nd Hour

PROJECT REPORT
BEWARE! INSECTS ARE PICKY EATERS

I'm a pretty picky eater, but nothing compared to some insects I know. Everybody knows monarch caterpillars eat only milkweed. But hardly anyone knows that lots of other insects only eat or pollinate certain plants. It's like some plants are made only for them.

For example, only bumblebees are strong enough to open the closed petals of a bottle gentian or the turtlehead flower. Only bees with long tongues or really tiny bees can reach the nectar inside the narrow tube of a columbine flower. Only hovering bees or humming-birds can get nectar from hanging bell-shaped flowers. The great spangled fritillary caterpillar eats only violet leaves.

Most gardeners love bees and butterflies, but they hurt them by filling their yards with plants insects can't eat. Many don't realize that some of these plants will spread all over the place until there are no milkweeds or violets or bottle gentians or turtleheads anywhere. These dangerous plants are called invasive because they were brought to North America from other continents and just take over.

The reason they spread so fast is because the insects or animals or diseases that eat them didn't come to America. Also, some of them have really pretty flowers so a lot of places sell them. I think that's wrong and so does my Aunt Charlotte.

She is the owner of Adair Natural Landscaping. She and four other women are asking the city and the county not to plant invasive species in the new Cross-County Linear Park, like barberry, honey-suckle, Bradford pear and Norway maple. They are asking a judge for a temporary restraining order, also called a TRO.

My aunt even met with a man from the county parks department and told him why he shouldn't plant invasives. She wrote out a list of native plants he could use instead, but he didn't listen!

Did you know that the Bradford pear trees in front of our school have spread into the woods behind the ballfield? They are so thorny that we can't use the woods anymore for nature study like they did when my mom went here. No one should buy invasive plants!

What's really weird is that most of the invasive plants I've named are illegal to sell or grow in other states. So I wonder why they are still legal in Michigan.

From now on we should plant only native plants instead, like oaks, dogwoods, sugar maples, redbuds and spice bushes and native wildflowers because they are good food for our pollinators. Insects need all the help they can get. Trust me, I've been studying them all summer.

In closing, I would say that in my opinion, invasive species are a plant pandemic. They are killing American plants and bees and butterflies every day. Invasive plants should be outlawed from Saskawan and Michigan and all of North America.

In the halcyon days of early autumn, hours slipped by when Charlotte didn't think about Fig's illness. Like the blurred hum of crickets and katydids, Fig's health was background noise she held at bay. But then, a bout of sudden coughing or a longer nap on the couch could conjure up a fearsome presence, a screaming noise, a crushing weight that could knock her flat.

Charlotte inched her truck forward in the pick-up line at South Saskawan Middle School. It was Friday afternoon and she looked for Mazie standing alone or reading a book under one of the school's now-infamous Bradford pear trees. But today, Mazie was nowhere in sight. A security guard waved her on.

"If you can't find your student, you'll have to move to the parking lot to wait."

She nodded, pulled into an empty spot and called Mazie's cell.

She heard her niece laughing before she said, "Oh, Aunt Charlotte. Is it that late? Sorry. I'm coming now." More laughter and a male voice said, "I'll text you–" before Mazie hung up. Two minutes later Mazie tossed her backpack onto the floor and climbed—or more accurately, jumped —into the truck.

"I lost track of time." She was pink-cheeked and out of breath.

"Was it a good day?"

"Yeah," she said without a hint of a shrug.

Charlotte pulled into traffic. "So, who's going to text you?"

"Huh? You were eavesdropping?"

She grinned. "You should have hung up sooner."

"Nate." Now she shrugged.

"Nate?"

"Captain of the junior debate team."

"So, how do you know this 'Nate?'"

"Because I'm on the team—duh."

"Since when?"

"Since Mr. Hogarth ask me to read my report about the TRO to the whole class this week. It was soooo embarrassing. After that, Nate asked me to join the team. We're having a special practice tomorrow morning at school. Can you drive me?"

"Sure. Sounds fun."

Mazie frowned. "It's not supposed to be fun, like volleyball or glee club, although those wouldn't be fun for me. But so far, I like it. And guess what we're going to debate?"

She waited for Charlotte to ask, "What?"

Mazie grinned. "Resolved: Invasive species should be banned."

"No way!" Charlotte hit the brake harder than she intended at the stop sign. "That's amazing, Maze. In fact. I'm going to call you A-Mazie from now on."

"Try to restrain yourself," Mazie said, flushing pink.

Just as they turned onto River Road, Charlotte's phone rang. She reached for it, but Mazie grabbed it first.

"You shouldn't talk while you're driving. Hey, Ficus. We're almost there." She paused. "Yeah. Bye. He wants us to pick up dinner at that Greek place at the plaza. He already ordered it."

"Oh good," she said, braking for a U-turn.

"Wait. Could you drop me off first? I want to start my homework."

Charlotte pulled into the landing. "Set the table first, please."

Mazie nodded and slammed the door.

"And hang up your coat and don't leave your backpack by the door. I'll be back in twenty minutes."

She returned with two bags of take-out and was locking the truck when she heard Mazie shout at her from the island dock.

"*Char*lotte! Hurry! Come quick!" she screamed, waving her arms wildly. Prince was circling her legs and yelping. She searched the shore for any sign of Fig.

Bottle Gentian *Gentiana andrewsii*

He must be in the house, clutching his chest and gasping for breath, on the kitchen floor or passed out in his study or at the bottom of the stairs. Oh God, save him!

She ran toward the raft but slipped on wet leaves and fell hard onto her hip. She scrambled to her feet and leaped onto the raft, yanking the rope so hard she pitched backward and almost fell into the river.

Call 911, she thought. She patted her ribs where her bag should be, but she'd dropped it and their dinner on the ground next to the truck.

She screamed at Mazie, "Call 911!"

Mazie stopped jumping and froze.

"911! Mazie!" Charlotte screamed again, frantically yanking the rope. "Help him!"

But Mazie didn't move. Why was she just standing there?

Please, God. Please, God. I'm not ready to lose him. Not now. Not today. It's too soon.

Then slowly, Mazie clasped her hands on the top of her head and sank to her knees.

It was too late, Charlotte thought. Fig was gone.

This wasn't the way it was supposed to end. Without warning. Without one last goodbye. She was supposed to be with him. To be there for him.

She was halfway across but was shaking so hard the rope went limp in her hands.

Mazie rose to her knees and cupped her hands around her mouth. "He's okay! Fig's okay! I'm sorry, I—Oh, I'm sooooo sorry."

"Did you call 911?" She looked back at the landing, hoping to see an ambulance pulling in.

"No. He's fine!"

Before the raft hit the dock, Charlotte was halfway up the walk with Mazie running behind. "Aunt Charlotte. He's f-fine. I was just—. I didn't m-mean –"

The screened door opened and Fig came out with a dishtowel in his hand. "Did they lose my order?" he asked, seeing her empty hands which were now clapped over her cheeks.

"Oh, thank God!" She ran up the steps, grabbed his forearms and doubled over. "Are you okay?"

"I'm fine. What is going on?" He looked at Mazie. "Did you tell her?"

Charlotte swung around to glare at Mazie. "Tell me what?"

Mazie started to cry. "I-I just wanted you to hurry. F-Fig said I c-could tell you first, so I came to the d-dock to. . . " She shook her head. "I didn't know you'd think—. I'm so, so sorry I scared you."

Charlotte looked from Mazie to Fig. Fig looked from Charlotte to Mazie.

"I sent Mazie out to tell you the news."

"The TRO was granted today," she said, "But I really, really messed that up. I'm sorry."

"Oh Maze," Charlotte said laughing weakly and sinking onto the porch steps. A tsunami of relief swept over her.

Fig reached into his pocket and handed her a handkerchief. "You'll have to share." Then he went back into the house, shaking his head.

Mazie offered to retrieve their dinner from the landing while Charlotte went upstairs to change out of her muddy pants and do some deep breathing. The bruise on her bum would heal in a week or so, but the PTSD would stick around much longer.

Downstairs, Fig was opening a bottle of sparkling wine. "What Mazie was trying to tell you is that Judge Roberta J. Gould has granted our TRO."

"That's wonderful!" She rose to her tiptoes to meet his lips. "Did she set a hearing date?"

"January 15. We have a lot of work to do before then. I've called a breakfast meeting of the Saskawan Five at the Farmer's Daughter tomorrow morning. My treat."

"That's good. Really good."

They stood at the window and watched Mazie returning with their dinner.

"Do you want to tell me what just happened between you two?" Fig asked.

She gave a wry smile. "No. But be sure to ask her about Nate. All about Nate. Lots and lots of probing and impertinent questions about Nate."

"I was a debater in high school, you know," Fig said at dinner. "Resolved: Capital punishment should be abolished," he said. "Will you invite me to your debate?"

Mazie eyed him shyly and wrinkled her nose. "Maybe."

"Maybe you can help us build our case," he said.

"Really?" Mazie said, sitting up taller.

Dinner was followed by two rounds of *Scrabble* at the dining table. While Mazie got ready for bed, Charlotte and Fig played a third.

Mazie watched the board over Fig's shoulder as she chewed on her toothbrush. "Swain? That isn't a word."

"It means boyfriend or suitor," Fig said.

"An alternate spelling is N-A-T-E," Charlotte said.

"Ha-ha," Mazie said, retreating to the bathroom to spit.

Charlotte moved her pieces onto the board. "Take that, my lovelorn swain! Q-U-I-D. And a double-word score. You're in double trouble now, mister."

Mazie called out, "That's a pound in English money."

"Almost as obscure as 'SKIVE,'" Fig said. "What does that mean again?"

"Skip school," Mazie said. "In England you 'skive off' school."

"Maze and I are practically bi-lingual," Charlotte said. "We're aces at obscure British vernacular. Mum's chuffed to bits to hear us use it."

Mazie came out again drying her face. "Nana watches the BBC and talks to her sister back in Bristol all the time. I think she takes notes." She mimicked Mally's accent. "'Aunt Fi finally stopped whinging and gave that shirty old gov'nor a right old bollocking. Just walked in and demanded a pay rise.' Brits say pay rise not 'raise."

"And Bob's-yer-uncle, ticketyboo," Charlotte added with a grin.

Fig put down four tiles. "I haven't a clue what either of you said, but I'm sure it wasn't English. But never you mind, I'm aces at legalese."

"L-I-E-N? It's L-E-A-N," Mazie protested.

"A lien is the legal right to keep possession of something owned by someone who owes you a debt."

Mazie headed for bed on the couch in the study. "You two are such nerds. And, I still say LOL is a word."

34

ACT III : SCENE 3

Roadsides and riverbanks in the upper Midwest are a riot of reds, golds and oranges in October. But it's inaccurate to say that leaves "turn." Young leaves contain a variety of pigments, but green chlorophyll dominates in spring and summer because of its role in making food from sunlight. But when autumn nights cool and days grow shorter, plants absorb their green pigment. Reds, yellows and oranges seem to appear overnight, but in truth, they've been there all along.

On Saturday morning Mazie showered without prompting and stayed way too long in the bathroom. She emerged wearing a pair of skinny jeans, an oversized sweater with a bulky scarf and red high-top All-Stars. Her hair was scrunched into shiny brown curls.

"Wow. You look nice," Charlotte said. She was even wearing mascara.

Mazie shrugged. "Nana took me shopping."

A silver chain with an acorn charm glinted at her neck. "Pretty. Did she buy you that?"

"This? No, it's just a good luck thing for debate. Acorns are a symbol of luck and wisdom in Scandinavian culture."

"From Captain Nate?"

She shrugged again. "Yeah."

Charlotte lifted her eyebrows. "So, he gives a 'good luck thing' to everyone on the team?"

Mazie stuffed a notebook into her backpack and sucked in an exasperated breath. "No. Just *me*. He likes *me*, if that's what you're trying to pry out of me."

Charlotte smiled with satisfaction.

"When do we get to meet your young swain?" Fig asked coming down the stairs in his robe and slippers.

"Uh, never. Would that be soon enough?" She couldn't quite hide the smile.

Fig gave her a peck on the cheek and lifted her backpack to her shoulder. "You look especially lovely this morning, Madelyn McDougal Adair. Truly. Although you're going to throw poor Nate off his game, you know. Let's hope he's on the other side of the debate today."

He draped an arm over Charlotte's shoulder and said in a stage whisper. "Maybe it's time for 'the talk.'"

"Ah yes, the talk. She already knows everything about the bees, so we'll start with the birds."

"Oh *my God*, you guys! I already know all that. I'm not seven!"

Charlotte smiled up at Fig. "Yes, 'birds' would definitely be the best starting point."

"LOL!" Mazie jerked the front door open and stomped across the porch toward the raft. "Come on, Aunt Charlotte! We'll be late."

Charlotte turned to Fig. "I'll meet you at the restaurant in forty-five minutes," she said, noticing his robe and slippers. "You feel okay?"

He nodded. "Go on. I'll catch up."

"We won't start without you."

Fig held her coat open and watched Mazie pacing on the raft. "She's grown at least three inches this summer, don't you think?"

"Yes—and another this week. A giant among nieces."

He let out a long, satisfied sigh. "She's a treasure."

Because of Mazie's extended time in the bathroom, she was ten minutes late for practice and Charlotte was ten minutes late to the Farmer's Daughter. As she entered the back room, she expected Fig would be halfway through his first scone. Instead, Katie started clapping and Nicky, Barb and Portia joined in. The mood was electric, but Fig hadn't arrived.

"We did it!" Katie said, throwing her arms around Charlotte.

Nicky was eying the door. "And where is the man of the hour?"

"I had to take Mazie to debate practice at the middle school this morning, so we drove separately."

"We took the liberty of ordering scones," Katie said. "We know how much Fig likes them. Pumpkin spice this month."

Barb poured her a cup of coffee.

"Thanks," Charlotte said. "As soon as Fig gets here he'll go over all the details."

Katie turned to Portia. "Tell Charlotte what you told us."

"I got a call from the *Evening Star* this morning. They heard about the TRO and want to do a feature. We're meeting at my office at 11:00. I hope some of you can be there."

"And Channel 13 contacted me," Nicky said. "They're planning a story too."

"I'm so proud of us!" Katie said.

Portia said, "I hope Fig can be at the interviews too."

"I hope he gets here before the check does," Katie said. "I have about fifty cents in my wallet."

Charlotte glanced at her phone. He was twenty minutes late. It was more like him to be twenty minutes early. She texted him, "Saving you a scone. ETA?"

Her phone rang before she hit send. The caller ID said Saskawan General Hospital. Her heart banged into her ribs.

She stood up and went into the hallway. "Hello?"

Words uttered by an unfamiliar voice pitched her backward and buckled her knees. She slid slowly down the wall to the floor. Barb was next to her, speaking to the phone. Yes, okay. I understand. I'm a friend. I'll see that she gets there.

Someone pulled her gently to a stand and gripped her by the shoulders. She heard Nicky. What's the matter? And Barb: Fig was admitted to the hospital. I'm going to take Charlotte to him now.

Someone helped her into her coat and lifted her bag to her shoulder.

"He'll be fine, Charlotte." Katie's voice, muffled. "I just know it."

Searching her pockets. "My keys. Where are my . . . ?"

Barb: "I have them, honey. I'm driving you there."

Charlotte felt the firm warmth of Barb's arm around her waist as they stood before the lobby elevator.

"This is a great institution, Charlotte. Fig's in the best hands."

Charlotte turned to face her. "Fig's been sick for a long time. We both knew this day would come."

"Oh, honey, I'm so sorry."

Her eyelids fluttered as her voice rose. "I don't know if I can do this, Barb, but . . ." Her voice trailed off.

Barb brushed a tear from Charlotte's cheek. "Oh, honey. Yes you can! You can because he needs you."

"Thank you, Barb for being so kind . . . and so right." Charlotte took a step back. "I-I have to go the rest of the way alone. If I lean on you, I won't be able to stay upright. Please understand."

Barb shook her head, then nodded. "Okay. Of course. If you're sure."

"After this is over, I'll need all the support you can give me. But now—"

The elevator door opened with a ping. Barb hugged Charlotte tightly. "If you change your mind, call me. Three a.m. Six a.m. Ten minutes from now. I'll come back."

In ICU bed fourteen, he lay motionless. His eyes were closed. A tangle of wires and tubes disappeared under the blanket. Monitors blinked and beeped. In a bed designed for much heavier patients, he looked even further diminished. She felt her anger rise.

His face was ashen, his lips purple-gray. She watched his chest heave with Herculean effort, pause for a long, frightening interval and collapse into his chest. She held her own breath until his lungs made their next draw.

His pale hair fell over one eyebrow. She brushed her lips against his cheekbone and brushed it aside. She reached for his hand, but when she saw how her own shook, she pulled back.

This wasn't the way she'd rehearsed it. Her role was to be a rock of support. She backed up until she hit the wall. She looked at the ceiling and chanted, "Please, please, please, please. . ."

"Can I get you some water?" A petite nurse in green scrubs and a short Afro was smiling. "Juice maybe?"

"No. Thank you. Unless courage comes in cans."

She glanced at the chart. "You're his wife?"

"No, but—" She knew her rights. "He doesn't have any family, but I'm his—I'm his—" Her voice sounded shrill.

She pointed at the chart again. "I bet you're Charlotte. See here? It says you're his medical advocate."

"Oh. Yes." She remembered signing the papers.

"Mr. Bigelow chose you. You're his voice, his protector."

Charlotte nodded weakly, but couldn't speak.

"Has Dr. Bryant talked to you yet?"

She shook her head.

"I'll let him know you're here."

"How did Fi—Newton—get here? Did he come by ambulance?"

"He drove himself to the ER less than an hour ago. He had you as his emergency contact. He's sedated now, so it would be a good time for you to talk to Dr. Bryant. Meanwhile, I'll get you that courage juice — a double shot. I'm Verna, by the way."

Charlotte looked around the room. The furniture was metal and the only chair was upholstered in tan vinyl. Fig would hate the decor. His clothing had been stuffed into a yellow plastic bag that hung from a hook behind the door. He would hate that too. She hung his blue Oxford shirt on a hanger attached to the closet rod. He would hate that too. She folded his pants and removed the handkerchief from the back pocket.

Then she sat down next to the bed to dab her eyes and focus on Fig's hands. Her love for him began there and worked its way through the whole rest of him. They lay open at his sides like matching crescent moons. Dancer's hands, she thought, or a magician's or a symphony conductor's. She wondered if anyone in the ER or the ICU had noticed.

She touched them lightly. They were like ice. She rubbed her palms together until friction turned to heat and laid them over his. He didn't move.

She unfolded a blanket at the bottom of the bed and tucked it around him. She combed through his hair with her fingers.

"Fig?" she whispered. "It's me. I'm here and I love you."

She wanted to slip beneath the blanket and warm him with her body. She wanted to breathe her own breath into his tired lungs. She wanted to rest her cheek on his shoulder.

"Don't leave me, Fig. Please, please don't leave me. Not yet," she pleaded. "I'm not ready."

Behind her, Verna spoke softly. "Here's your juice, honey."

She turned. "Thank you."

"Dr. Bryant is ready to see you. Can you follow me, please?"

Charlotte hesitated.

"He's heavily sedated. He won't wake up for a while."

Reluctantly, Charlotte followed Verna to a door labeled Family Room. The nurse opened the door and stepped aside. "Ask for me if you need anything at all. I'll be here till 3:00."

The Family Room was the interior design equivalent of comfort food. Queen Ann chairs upholstered in a muted paisley print appeared to be having their own conversation around a glass-topped coffee table equipped with a box of Kleenex, a Bible and a pot of yellow and orange chrysanthemums. A grandfather clock in the corner ticked softly next to tasteful watercolors of Lake Michigan dunes and fruit trees in bloom.

A compact man with silver hair came in. "Hello Charlotte. I'm Dan, Dan Bryant. I'm Fig's doctor." He shook her hand and smiled warmly. "Fig has told me a lot about you. Let's sit, shall we?"

She nodded because she didn't trust her voice.

"I understand that Fig has no family and that he appointed you as his medical advocate. Is that –?"

She raised her palm. "Please. I need to know what happened this morning."

"Of course. I'm sorry. Let me back up." He leaned his forearms on his knees and lace his fingers. "Fig drove himself to the ER this morning just before 9:00. He was having difficulty breathing and was experiencing considerable pain in his chest. We got him stabilized and I've sedated him for now so he can rest." He paused before continuing. "As his advocate I expect you know his wishes. There are to be no heroic measures taken to extend his life." He let that sink in before continuing. "That means if his heart stops, we won't try to restart it. If he stops breathing, we won't intervene. I believe he has shared all this with you—"

She nodded.

"I've been treating Fig for over ten years and count him as a friend as well as a patient. But by law, I must respect his wishes—as difficult as that will be."

He paused to let this sink in too.

"I'm afraid there are signs that things are coming to the end. You should prepare yourself, Charlotte."

She brushed a tear away and nodded.

"He has told me what a big difference you've made in the quality of his life these last few months. I hope it helps to hear that."

She nodded again.

She had imagined this day a hundred times, a thousand ways. His silent, still-warm body beside her. His motionless body on the couch. Clutching his chest and keeling over during his closing remarks at the hearing.

She'd even cradled him on his thinkin' log as he professed eternal love and took his last breath.

"Can I take him home?"

"That was his wish, but when we talked recently, he realized it would be impossible for us—or you—to care for him on the island. Hospice care here made the most sense to him. And Charlotte, we are going to move him there this afternoon."

She opened Fig's handkerchief and buried her face in it..

"Losing the use of your lungs is difficult, Charlotte. But we'll keep him comfortable. He'll tell us when it becomes too much and we'll sedate him fully. It will be much easier for both of you."

"How long?" She choked out the words.

He hesitated at the threshold of saying something momentous and unspeakable.

"When patients get to this point, it usually means a few days at most. As his doctor and his friend, I can't wish him to continue like this. I'm so sorry, Charlotte. He's a wonderful human being—a gentleman in the truest sense of the word and one of the best men I've ever known."

An hour later, when Dr. Bryant pressed a stethoscope to Fig's chest his eyes fluttered open.

"Sorry, to wake you."

". . . was . . .dreaming." Fig said drawing shallow, wheezing gulps of air between words. His voice was weak and gravelly. "I was . . . in a . . . balloon . . . with—"

He smiled at Charlotte who was at the foot of the bed with her hand on his foot.

"—with her. Thank God . . . Jesus . . . the Buddha . . . Rah . . ." His voice trailed off and he mouthed, "Charlotte."

Dr. Bryant looked at Fig's chart and nodded. "You've slept well. That's good. The drugs are doing their thing. How's the pain?"

"Better, but . . . I need something . . . to . . . stay awake."

The doctor frowned. "Rest is what you need."

Fig looked at Charlotte. "I . . . need to talk to . . . her. Now."

Dr. Bryant hesitated before pressing the call button. "I'll order something, but it'll wear off quickly, so keep that in mind. Thirty minutes or so." He patted Fig's shoulder and smiled at Charlotte. "I'll check back later."

Fig gave a thumbs up and his eyes closed again.

Verna came in with a syringe on a tray. "In a minute or two he'll be pretty alert, but not for long. This would be the time to tell him whatever he needs to hear and listen to what he has to say." Her attention darted from the monitor to Charlotte. "Talking is hard work in his condition, so give him time. I'll leave you alone, but use that button if you need me."

Charlotte nodded. "Thank you, Verna."

She wished she'd made a list of talking points, a multi-media PowerPoint, covering every little thing she needed to ask him and a notebook for his answers. She wanted to remember everything. Every little thing, overlooking nothing that would be cause for later regret.

But all she wanted to say was, Don't leave me, Fig. Please, please, please, don't die.

Fig's eyes opened halfway and his lips moved but produced only wheezing. She kissed his cheek.

"I'm glad . . . you're here," he whispered finally.

"How do you feel? Are you in pain?"

He shook his head. "Except for the truck... parked... on my chest."

"Don't talk. Just let me hold your hand."

"We ... need to talk... Should have ... sooner." He closed his eyes again.

Outside, the clouds parted, flooding the room with sunlight. She adjusted the curtain.

"It's going to be sunny today," she said. "Is that too much light?"

Someone had bumped the clothes hanger again. She crossed the room to smooth the wrinkles. He followed her with his eyes.

"Come ... sit." He reached for the row of buttons by the bed.

"Do you want to sit up?" she asked.

He nodded. She raised the head of the bed, plumped his pillow and smoothed a wrinkle in the blanket.

"You're ... making me dizzy." He patted the mattress. "Sit. Please?"

She sat on the bed, one leg folded under her so she could face him. "I'm here." She tried to think of a topic of conversation. "So, everyone was at the Farmer's Daughter this morning. They were so excited about the TRO. And so grateful to you."

He nodded. "But ...so much ... I want ... to say... Please."

"You don't need to talk." All she wanted to hear was his steady breathing. "So, everyone's optimistic about the hearing, too," she went on although she didn't know if that was true anymore. "Portia's doing an interview for the paper and the TV station will be doing a story soon. So it is all happening. The public is going to hear about invasive plants, just like you predicted."

He closed his eyes again. "Shhh."

"Sorry." She squeezed his hand. "I'll let you sleep."

"No," he said, opening them again. "I have ... a proposal ... but ... so hard to talk... Please .. hush."

"Okay."

"Come ... closer."

Somehow, she managed to nestle against his shoulder without dislodging any wires or tubes.

"I'm going ... soon. They won't resus ... resuscitate me. When I can't breathe ... anymore ... they'll ... put me out ... Those are ... my wishes and ... they have to ... abide... Understand?"

"Yes, Dr. Bryant told me that." This had all seemed reasonable and necessary when she'd signed the papers, but now it seemed barbaric and so wrong.

"I don't have . . . much time."

She ran her hand up his arm. "I know. Are you afraid, Fig?"

"Of dying? . . . No . . . I'm more afraid of . . . going on . . . like this."

If he said this just to make it easier for her, it helped a little. Of course, she didn't want him to suffer.

"But it . . . won't be heaven . . . if you're not there. I'm angry about that. Maybe . . . I could sue . . . my Sunday school teachers if they're there."

The drugs were taking effect.

"That sounds like your kind of heaven," she said.

They lay side by side until she thought he was asleep again.

"I'm afraid of one thing though."

"Hmm?"

"That . . . when I'm gone . . . no one will know what you meant to me . . . what we had and how much . . . how very much I loved you. I want everyone . . . to know." He took a long, raspy breath and held it before his shoulders shook with coughing. Charlotte started to sit up, but he held her with surprising strength.

"I don't . . . want you . . . to be . . . just the girlfriend . . . of a dead guy. You're . . . so much more to me."

"Mazie knows. My parents. The Saskawan Five. They all know."

"But I want . . . the world to know."

"I'll tell them. I'll tell everyone."

He stirred. "Look at me. I want to see your face."

She sat up to face him again. He reached for her hand, smiling.

"What?"

"Close your eyes," he said. "We're on the back patio. . . I've just grilled . . . marinated steaks and shrimp . . . and we've shared . . . that bottle . . . of premium chardonnay . . . because we're celebrating . . . the TRO . . . I'm wearing . . . my best navy suit."

"While you're grilling?"

"Shhh."

"What am I wearing?"

"Brown . . . cargo pants. Burrs in your hair. Hat hair. Dirt under your nails." He kissed her fingertips. "Ravishing."

She laughed. "I don't know what you see in me. Do I have pee in my hair, too?"

He smiled. "You're ruining . . . my special moment."

"Sorry. Go on."

"After dinner, I pull out a bottle . . . of chilled Champagne—the real thing . . . that I've hidden behind. . . that big boulder."

"Pink?"

"The Champagne?"

"No, the boulder under the dogwood."

"Yes, that one. Anyway, I pour your glass . . . and then . . ."

She waited.

"I get down on one knee."

Charlotte blinked.

"I look into your eyes . . . like I'm doing now, and . . . I ask, 'Charlotte Anne Adair, will you marry me?'" He was pinching an invisible ring between his thumb and index finger and holding it up for her to see.

Verna stood in the doorway with a vase of flowers. "I'm sorry, but I couldn't help but hear." She set the flowers on the bedside table and pulled a ring from her finger. She pushed it into Fig's hand and tiptoed quickly out of the room.

Fig managed a laugh, but his shoulders sagged from the effort. "Marry me . . . Charlotte."

Charlotte frowned. "Wait. Are we still on the patio?"

"What do you say?"

"Really? You mean here? Now?" Mental images clicked by—a chaplain, witnesses, Verna coming in and out, Mazie, her parents, music, beeping, wires and tubes. And Fig dying.

"ASAP. I love you." Fig closed his eyes then.

She kissed him softly. "I love you, Fig. I love you so much."

She also wanted to ask, how? And why? How could she pull off a wedding now?

His eyelids opened. "I'm so tired, Charlotte. Please say yes." His eyes closed again, the ring still in his hand. When she stroked his cheek, he didn't stir.

"Yes! Yes, Fig. Of course, I will. I'll marry you!" She opened his fingers, slipped the ring onto her finger and kissed his lips again as long as she dared. Then, she laid her head on his shoulder and wept.

The man she loved was dying before her eyes and his last wish was for a wedding? It was so romantic, unbelievable and completely ridiculous. Was he delirious?

Verna came in to check the monitor. She glanced at Charlotte's hand. "Congratulations."

"I think he fell asleep before I said yes." She turned to Verna feeling panicked. "I don't think he *heard* me! Oh God, what if he—?"

"Just look at that face, honey." Fig was smiling. "He heard you all right."

She took a syringe out of a tray and busied herself with his IV. "He'll sleep for the next few hours now. Meanwhile, we'll move him downstairs to the hospice wing. It's all about comfort down there, but I bet they haven't seen many weddings." She stopped what she was doing. "Now would be a good time for you to make that wedding happen. You're getting married, girl! It's okay to smile."

Charlotte made a brave attempt, looking down at the ring. It was silver with a row of small turquoise stones. She slipped it off and handed it back to Verna. "Thank you for the loan. Your timing was perfect."

Verna backed up. "It's just a little souvenir from the Badlands and not worth much, but it's priceless now. You keep it, honey."

"I don't know how to thank you, Verna."

"If you make that wedding happen it'll make my day. My whole week even. Go on now."

Charlotte scratched out a note and left it under his water glass.

Yes! Yes! A million yeses!
I love you, Fig Newton.

Your fiancée and future wife, Charlotte

P.S. Back soon.

On the way to the elevator, she called Mally and Ted who were still touring northern Michigan. She sobbed the news into her phone.

"Oh, my love." Mally breathed out the words with great effort. "We're so, so sorry, honey. Dad's on speaker."

"Hi, Dad. Mazie's at debate practice, but please don't call her. I'll tell her when I pick her up. This will be so hard for her."

"We're leaving now and be there about 2:00."

"Okay, but Mum, Dad, I need . . ." She paused to choose her words. "I'll need you afterward and I know you'll be there for me, but now, right now, I need every minute with Fig. Please don't be hurt. But Fig and I need this time to be together and say our goodbyes."

There was a short silence, followed by Mally's broken voice. "Of course. We understand."

She heard Ted say, "But if it gets too much, just call. We'll sit with him. Bring food. Anything."

"Thanks, Dad. Mum. I love you both so much."

"And we love our girl," Ted said.

She hung up. She should have told them about Fig's proposal. They would support her—of course, they would, but they wouldn't understand. She wasn't even sure she did. The fierceness of Fig's love could be overwhelming. Somehow she needed to make a wedding happen. ASAP.

She pressed the down button.

The elevator doors opened to the sound of Mazie's strident voice. She was leaning over the information desk in the lobby.

"What difference does that make? I'm mature for my age and he's like an uncle. You *have* to let me see him!"

The receptionist said something softly.

"That's just it, I don't *have* a mom, or a dad. I'm an orphan. It's just me and my almost-Uncle Newton and my Aunt Charlotte. She's up there now. Just call her!"

"Mazie!" Charlotte called out.

"Aunt Charlotte! I texted you about a million times!" She aimed her death ray at the flustered volunteer and turned on her heel.

"How'd you get here? I was about to call you."

"Barb." She pointed to Barb who was walking toward them. "She found me at debate practice."

"Hi Charlotte. I thought I'd take her to your parents but she said they aren't home. I invited her to come home with me, but—"

"I made Barb bring me here. It's not her fault."

Charlotte hugged Mazie and mouthed 'thank you' over her shoulder. Barb blew a kiss and turned back toward the lobby doors.

"How is he? I want to see him," Mazie said.

Charlotte pushed Mazie toward the revolving doors. "Mazie, listen to me. You can see him later. He's sedated now."

"But—"

"Walk with me."

Charlotte led Mazie to a small park across the street with a bench that overlooked the city.

She took Mazie's hands. "Fig had a heart attack on the way to the restaurant. But he was able to drive himself to the hospital." She let this sink in.

"Is he okay though? What does that mean?"

"It means, Mazie, that we need to prepare ourselves for the possibility that he's not going to come home."

"Not coming—? You mean he's going to die? Is that the prognosis?" It was so like Mazie to need the correct medical terms.

Charlotte nodded.

Mazie got to her feet. "But this morning he was *fine*. We were joking around about the birds and the bees." She lifted her hand to her forehead and turned in a circle. "He was fine. *More* than fine. "

Charlotte pulled Mazie onto the bench beside her.

"This morning and every other morning we've known him, Fig has not been fine. He told us this. He tried to prepare us—for this day."

Mazie began chewing her thumbnail. "I know, but—"

"His doctors have taken very good care of him, but they've done all they can do—all Fig *wants* them to do. Now he wants to be free from pain."

"Palliative care," Mazie said bitterly. "That's the last thing."

"When we see him later today, he'll be in hospice care."

Mazie pulled on a lock of hair.

Charlotte said, "You can stay at the hospital with me as long as you want. But Nana and Pop will take you home whenever you need to go. Right now, Maze, I could really use your help. But first, I need a major hug."

Mazie leaned forward and laid her head on Charlotte's shoulder. They clung together until a brown and white spaniel poked his muzzle into Charlotte's knee.

"Buckie, leave the ladies be," said a man at the other end of the leash. "Sorry, he loves people."

"That's okay," Mazie said, stroking the dog's head. She turned to Charlotte looking stricken. "What will happen to Prince now?"

"We're not going to give him up, that's for sure." She dug through her bag for a Kleenex.

"Really? But before, you said—"

"Everything's different now." Everything, she thought. She pushed a Kleenex into Mazie's hand.

"Who's going to feed him tonight?"

"We'll figure that out later. But Mazie, I have something important to tell you. Fig asked me to marry him."

Mazie frowned. "You're joking, right?"

"It's what he wants."

"Why?"

"It's important to him. He asked; I said yes. Bob's-yer-uncle. Ticketyboo." Mazie didn't smile. "But I can't pull it off by myself. I need you to be your logical, practical self and help me get a marriage license at city hall. We'll have plenty of time later to cry and feel sorry for ourselves."

"I'm a bridesmaid?"

"Maid of honor and maybe Fig's best man, too. Come on." She took Mazie's arm and they walked down the hill.

"I'll wear ruffles and heels if you want me to."

She looked down at Mazie's fashionable ensemble and thought how lovely she looked. "You're perfect just the way you are."

The city clerk's office was off the main lobby. Charlotte took a numbered slip and sat with Mazie on a long bench next to two young couples holding hands. Their presence made Charlotte instantly resentful. There should be an express line for emergency deathbed weddings.

After several minutes a clerk called out, "Sixty-seven?"

Mazie sprang to her feet. "That's us!"

The middle-aged woman with a name badge that said Teresa, looked at them over a pair of half-glasses. "May I help you?"

"We need a marriage license," Mazie said.

Teresa's eyes narrowed. "How old are you?"

"Ew! No! It's not for me. It's for my aunt. She needs one ASAP. Today." Then she added a perfunctory, "Please."

The woman took a closer look at Charlotte. "Where's the groom?"

"He's unavailable," Charlotte said.

"Both parties must be present. And you said today? Michigan doesn't do quickie marriages and we're only open until noon today, so you'll have to get him here or come back Monday."

Mazie stood on her tiptoes and leaned over the counter. "The groom is ill and in the hospital."

"Oh," Teresa frowned. "I'm very sorry, but the law says that both parties must be present. Perhaps when he gets out—"

Mazie leaned even closer. "He's not getting 'out.' Ev-ver."

The woman backed up. "I don't know what to tell you."

"This wedding is my uncle's dying wish!" Mazie said, louder than necessary.

Clerks behind the counter stopped typing and looked up.

A man came out of a glassed-in office at the back and approached the desk. "How can I help you ladies?"

Charlotte repeated her appeal.

"You have my deepest sympathy. But there is a three-day waiting period after the application before a license can be issued. I'm afraid the law doesn't make exceptions."

Charlotte turned to leave, but Mazie pulled herself up to her full height. "You look like thinking human beings, but you're acting like drones. I'm sorry for your powerlessness. Come on, Aunt Charlotte." She grabbed Charlotte's wrist and pulled her into the lobby.

Charlotte sank onto a bench and dabbed at her eyes with Fig's handkerchief.

Mazie began pacing and gnawing her thumb. "A quickie wedding would solve all our problems. Well, some of them."

If Fig were here, Charlotte thought, he'd explain to Mazie the power of diplomacy, but he wasn't, and she didn't have the time or energy, because he was on his deathbed, demanding the impossible of her while she was experiencing the first symptoms of panic, partly because she was relying on a hormonal thirteen-year-old who expected the world to bow to her superior sense of fairness and logic.

Mazie was still pacing. "Las Vegas is too far away. There must be a better way."

Charlotte looked at the clock above the brass elevator doors. They'd been away from Fig for a half hour and had accomplished nothing.

She opened her bag and handed Mazie a twenty-dollar bill.

"Go get us something to eat. I haven't had breakfast and you'll need lunch. There's a deli around the corner. I'm going to go talk to the judge who handled our TRO. Maybe she'll officiate. Let's meet back here."

An army marches on its stomach.

On the third floor, she knocked on the door of the chambers of Judge Roberta J. Gould. Inside, a young man wearing a skinny black tie sat at a reception desk typing. He nodded toward one of two chairs. Charlotte didn't move.

"I need to speak to Judge Gould. It's urgent."

"She doesn't come in on Saturdays," he said without looking up. "You can make an appointment, but not until at least next –." He clicked his mouse twice and looked at the screen. "Thursday. Afternoon," he added.

"As I said, it's urgent. Can you call her?"

"Do you have a case before her?"

"Yes. She'll know my name. Charlotte Adair. Adair vs –"

"Adair," he repeated, clicking the mouse again.

"She just granted our TRO."

"You can't have any contact with a judge when–."

"I told you. It's not about my case. It's a private matter concerning my attorney, who—."

"If you have a complaint about your attorney you can call his firm or the Bar Association. Besides, like I told you, the judge isn't here."

The phone rang. He turned his back and picked it up.

She ran into the stairwell and filled Fig's handkerchief with hot, sloppy tears.

"You look awful," Mazie said, handing her a sandwich and sitting down next to her on the lobby bench.

Charlotte sniffed. "Plans A and B have both failed and I don't have a Plan C."

"But there're twenty-four more letters in the alphabet, right?"

"I can't tell him I've failed."

"But *I'm* the maid of honor. *I'm* the one who's failed."

Charlotte rubbed Mazie's knee. "Thanks for trying, sweetie, but wedding or no wedding I need to be with him now. We both do."

"This just sucks," Mazie said. "We need to find someone who's got some *power around here*." She said the last part loud enough that a clerk rushing by with an armful of files frowned in their direction.

"Shhh. I shouldn't have promised him." Charlotte said, twisting her ring. She felt in her pocket for a dry Kleenex but came up empty. She was too angry to cry anyway. She stood up quickly. "Just forget it. This is a ridiculous waste of time. I'm going back to the hospital."

She was gathering up their lunch wrappings when she heard her name.

"Charlotte, right? How are you?" A tall man in a gray coat was smiling down at her. "Any news about your TRO?" His smile faded when he saw her red eyes. "Ah. I take it things didn't go as you hoped. Where's Fig?"

Mazie stood up. "You know Fig?"

The man laughed. "Forgive me. I have you at a disadvantage. Picture me in a fishing hat and waders. And a fishing pole?"

"Oh, of course," Charlotte said, offering her hand with a wan smile.

"I'm Bill. Bill Daley. Fig has told me about you and the lawsuit. Very interesting, by the way."

Mazie cocked her head. "I thought your name was Ronner?"

"Ronner?" He scratched his head. "People call me many names, some quite unpleasant, but never Ronner."

"Yes, they do," Mazie protested. "Fig always touches his hat and says, 'Morning, Ronner. Anything biting?'"

He rocked on his heels, laughing heartily. "Ah! I see. Well, around here, that's sort of a nickname, but Fig is saying, 'Your Honor.' I guess that sounds a lot like Ronner. I'm a circuit judge."

His smile faded when he saw Charlotte's face. "I'm sorry. I'm sure Fig's disappointed too. Please give him my best and tell him I'll be over soon with some smoked trout."

He gave Charlotte a sympathetic nod and continued across the lobby.

Mazie nudged Charlotte. "We need to tell him. They're friends."

"Not now, Mazie." She was too tired for more conversation.

"Wait, Ronner! Judge Daley!" Mazie ran across the lobby and caught up with him as he stepped into the elevator. "Hold the doors!" She skidded to a stop and pushed through the opening.

"Fig's in the hospital. He and my aunt want to get married more than anything. But it *has* to be *today*! Because . . . because he's . . ." She swallowed hard and whispered something.

The judge stepped out of the elevator and strode toward Charlotte with Mazie at his elbow, still talking.

"Those wankers in the clerk's office say Fig needs to be here to get a license and then they have to wait like three days and a bunch of other crap that shouldn't count in this case. How is that justice? You're the only person who can help us."

He nodded, not taking his eyes off Charlotte.

"Please," Mazie added. "You're our only hope."

The judge sat down next to Charlotte, running his hand along his jaw and drawing a long breath.

"I'm so very sorry, Charlotte. I knew Fig was in poor health but had no idea."

"Thank you."

"So, you need an officiant? And today I hear?"

Charlotte closed her eyes and nodded. The effort of holding back tears had given her a raging headache.

"Well," he said, nodding. "Justice may be blind, but she's not heartless." He put a hand lightly on Charlotte's shoulder and stood up. "Go do whatever you need to do and I'll meet you in the hospital." He looked at the lobby clock. "Will 3:00 work?"

She nodded again, unable to form meaningful sound.

<u>35</u>

LONG LIVE THE KING

1824: A nut from a shagbark hickory is buried by a fox squirrel on an island in a West Michigan river. In this iso-lation, the young tree escapes the lumberjack's ax and grows tall. 1924: The tree is in the prime of life. Its trunk is three feet thick. Its loose, shaggy bark provides shelter for the over-wintering Eastern comma butterfly and other in-sects. But like all healthy trees, it is ninety-percent dead. Only its leaves, root tips and the thin, outer ring of sapwood contain living cells, while its sturdy heartwood is dead. 1956: A bolt of lightning splits the trunk, exposing the heartwood to fungi and bacteria. Gradually, the trunk rots, turns to sawdust and collapses downward. 1975: The trunk is hollow, but the tree lives on. Its healthy sapwood ring still feeds the leafy canopy. A pair of great-horned owls nest in a cavity. One by one, the oldest branches dry up and fall to the ground. 2015: The roots of the old tree fail to send sap. The branches remain bare. But in one of nature's dearest ironies, the old tree still teems with life. Swifts, woodpeckers, flying squirrels and bats take up residence inside. 2017: A windstorm topples the hollow trunk, and chipmunks, mice, mason bees and even an American marten move in. In its entire existence, the old tree has never been so full of life. The king of the forest is dead. Long live the king.

A white-haired volunteer named Alan met Charlotte and Mazie at the information desk and escorted them toward a pair of elaborately carved wooden doors hung with wreaths of silk chry-santhemums. A brass plaque read Margery H. Walsh Memorial Hospice. When Charlotte hesitated, Mazie pushed her gently though.

A quiet, carpeted hallway curved to the right around a circular courtyard with a white gazebo in the middle. Somewhere, someone played guitar and sang softly. A toddler ran out of a room chased by a boy about Mazie's age.

Alan stopped at an open door. "This is Mr. Bigelow's room," he said.

Charlotte took Mazie's hand and they stepped inside. Fig's eyes were closed. Only his chest moved, searching for oxygen.

The bed had un-hospital striped sheets and an un-hospital oak veneer headboard that Fig would think overly fussy. The heart monitor with its countdown to his final heartbeat, was gone, but its absence amplified the sound of his tortured breathing. Each pause, each hesitation between one breath and the next brought her closer to panic.

She slipped her hand under his.

Alan's voice was white noise barely heard. He was saying something about cafeteria hours and take-out food. He pointed to a slider leading to the courtyard, then to a set of drawers across from the bed.

". . . more blankets . . . stay the night . . . get your rest . . . eat on schedule." He smiled warmly and turned to leave.

"Thank you," she remembered to say. She had forgotten his name.

He smiled and backed toward the door. "I'll tell the staff you're here, but mostly they'll leave you alone unless you ask for them." He pointed at a discreet button on the bedstand. "Press that button if you need anything. Anything at all."

A miracle? she thought. Could she have one of those, please?

"Thanks," she said again, but her eyes stayed on Fig as the door clicked shut. She placed her palm on his cheek and pressed her lips to his temple. His eyelids fluttered. "Mazie's here," she whispered.

His lips curved upward, but his eyes remained closed.

Mazie stepped forward and slipped her palm under his other hand.

"Hey, Uncle Ficus," she said a little too loudly. "My side won our debate today. At least I thought so, but it was just practice." Then, "Nate brought me a brownie this morning. I guess he likes to bake, or whatever. You wouldn't believe how smart he is."

When he didn't respond she whispered to Charlotte. "What if he isn't awake for the wedding?"

"We'll ask the doctor to give him something to wake him up before the ceremony. So, he should sleep now."

Mazie's lashes were wet with tears. "I would have thrown you the best bridal shower ever, with fun games, Fig Newtons on a fancy plate and a cake with your names on it. I would have been an awesome maid of honor." She lowered her head and rubbed her eyes.

"You are already. We got us a judge. That was truly A-Mazing." She ran her fingers through Mazie's curls. "You've saved this day already."

She left Mazie hovering over Fig and went into the bathroom.

The swollen-faced woman in the mirror looked more like a widow than a bride. She didn't want to be that woman.

She sank onto her elbows at the edge of the sink and closed her eyes. She breathed in and out slowly.

In . . . out. In . . . out.

If she didn't get control of her emotions she would rob Fig of the peaceful, meaningful death he wanted and so deserved.

She turned on the faucet till the water ran cold and let it run over her face.

In . . . out.

The joy he'd asked for was in very short supply today.

In . . . out.

She dried her face. But if joy was what he wanted, then joy was what he would get.

Just then, a little prayer sprang up from nowhere and surprised her. She offered it up to whomever might be listening.

"Give us this day.

This one day.

And let joy be part of it.

That's all I ask.

Amen"

Mazie rose from her chair when she saw Charlotte. "I'm going to get more chairs and something for us to drink."

"Thank you, Maze."

Charlotte slipped off her shoes and crawled under the sheet. Her hand found the soft pillow of Fig's shoulder and her forehead came to rest in the curve of his neck.

She awoke to whispered voices and a cup of cold coffee on the night-stand. Charlotte glanced at the clock. She'd slept almost an hour.

Mazie came in from the hallway. "While you were sleeping, I got some wedding stuff together. Come look."

Next to her, Fig hadn't moved, but his chest still rose and fell. She got up and followed Mazie into the hallway.

Mally and Ted were waiting there, looking distraught.

"We aren't staying," Mally said. "We just—" Her chin quivered.

"I asked them to bring some things for the wedding," Mazie explained.

They stepped closer to hug her.

Mally blinked hard. "A wedding! What a beautiful, beautiful thing, Charlotte."

"But we're not staying," Ted emphasized.

"Look!" Mazie said, opening a zippered bag to reveal a tea-length dress in peach silk. She held up a pair of matching pumps. "They match."

Charlotte gasped. "It's beau-tiful. Whose is it?"

"Mine," Mally said, looking sheepish. "I know I said I hadn't bought a mother-of-the-bride dress, but—. Anyway, it might fit you."

"It's gorgeous." She wrapped her arms around her mother. "I

don't know what I was thinking before. I need you both to be here. I'm getting married!"

"In half an hour!" Mazie said, bouncing on her heels. "Come on. I need to get you dressed and do something about your face."

"We need to wake Fig soon," Charlotte said. "Dr. Bryant said–"

"I just talked to him," Ted said. "He'll be down in twenty minutes to give him something."

Mally and Ted tiptoed into Fig's room and sat on each side of him while Mazie pulled Charlotte into the bathroom.

Twenty minutes later Charlotte stood in her mother's slip, looking at a new and improved version of the mirror woman. "When did you learn to do make-up, Mazie?"

"A girl on the debate team," she said, unzipping the dress. "She says it makes us look older and more credible."

Charlotte stepped into it and felt the zipper tighten around her waist. It was a perfect fit. Mazie held a pair of pearl earrings in her palm. "Nana says you can borrow them."

Charlotte knew them well. They were a gift from Ted to Mally on the day Charlotte was born in this same hospital.

"And this is from Pop." Mazie opened Charlotte's hand and pressed a plain gold band into her palm. "It was Grandpa Adair's, but he wants Fig to have it."

Charlotte bit her lip and nodded.

Mazie stepped back, her hands on her hips and smiled. "You look awesome, Aunt Charlotte. Really awesome."

There was a light tap at the door. Mazie opened it a crack.

Mally whispered, "A woman named Katie dropped these off. She pushed a bouquet of purple asters and yellow goldenrod through the opening. "And the doctor came by. Fig's awake now."

"We'll be out in a sec," Mazie said, closing the door again. "Ready?"

Charlotte shuffled backward until she hit the sink, flapping her hands at the wrists, her face crumpling. "I can't do this. I *can't!*"

Mazie gripped Charlotte's elbows. "Yes. Yes, you can. You absolutely can—for Fig's sake. Besides, I put a ton of make-up on you, so if you cry you'll look like a zombie. Sorry, but I'm not kidding."

Charlotte lowered her face into the center of the bouquet and inhaled the sweet anise scent. "Okay. I'm ready."

Mazie opened the door and stepped aside.

Charlotte stepped into Fig's smiling gaze. Somewhere in the background, a string quartet played *Ode to Joy*. Fig reached for her hand as his eyes swept down and up the length of her body. He swallowed hard.

"Your the woman . . . of . . . my dreams."

Judge Daley stood at the foot of the bed with her parents to one side. She felt Mazie at her elbow.

Fig removed his oxygen mask and nodded to the judge.

Judge Daley said, "Welcome to the marriage ceremony of Fig and Charlotte. Marriage is a union between two people founded upon mutual respect and affection—and in this case, faith and a great deal of courage. From my favorite fishing spot across from Fig's island, I've had the pleasure of witnessing Fig and Charlotte's business relationship become a friendship, a legal collaboration and then, apparently, a great deal more. I have also watched as Mazie and Prince joined Fig's island family. Their special bond was demonstrated to me again this morning when Mazie cornered me in an elevator at city hall. And so, dearly beloved, today we gather —"

Fig stirred the air with his hand. "Haven't . . . got . . . all day, Bill."

The judge smiled. "Okay, just the Cliffs notes. Charlotte Anne Adair, do you take Newton Ellery Bigelow, to be your husband, to have and to hold, from this day forward, in sick–"

Fig's gestured again. "Let's not . . . put too fine . . . a point on it."

The judge skimmed through the text. "—as long as you both shall live?"

"I do." Charlotte said, squeezing his hand. "Forever and ever."

"And so . . . do I," Fig said. "And so do I."

"Are you exchanging rings?" he asked.

Charlotte lifted her hand to show her band of turquoise. "I have mine."

"Then, by the power vested in me—"

"Wait," Charlotte said, looking at Ted. "My Grandmother gave this ring to my Grandfather on their wedding day in 1952. My father gave it to me today so I could give it to my husband. Thanks, Dad."

Ted rubbed his eyes with the back of his hand as she slipped the ring onto Fig's finger.

"Then, by the power vested in me by the State of Michigan, I pronounce this couple husband and wife."

Charlotte kissed Fig softly to a round of applause.

There was a tap on the sliding door. Barb VanderLee stood outside holding a white box. Mally slid the door open.

"Congratulations, Charlotte and Fig. This is from the Saskawan Five." She pointed to the center of the courtyard. Katie, Portia and Nicky were waving at them.

Fig lifted a hand.

Mazie opened the box. "It's a wedding cake."

Barb said, "And tell Fig, we went ahead with the interviews today. We aren't giving up on this lawsuit."

Fig raised a thumb and smiled.

Barb touched Charlotte's cheek and whispered. "We're all praying really hard for you. We love you, honey. You're not alone."

Charlotte nodded and waved to the others. "You're the best, Barb."

When she turned back, Fig handed her a pen.

"Our . . . marriage license."

The judge said, "A bit unorthodox, but it'll be legal when I'm done with it."

Fig nodded. "Thanks, your honor."

Mazie brightened. "See? It sounds like he's saying Ronner!"

The judge laughed. "Well, this wedding has been *my* honor."

"Thank you," Fig said again.

"Don't thank me. Thank this fierce young woman," he said, looking at Mazie.

Mally handed out chocolate cake on paper plates. Charlotte fed Fig a small bite as Ted snapped photos. When she looked up again Mazie had disappeared and Mally and Ted were getting ready to leave.

"Should we take Mazie with us?" Mally asked.

"Not yet, Mum. She's been so busy, she hasn't had time to just sit."

"Okay," Ted nodded. "We'll be nearby. Just ring us.

Then they were alone.

"It was . . . perfect, Charlotte." His eyes swept over her again. "You are . . . a wonder. Queen Charlotte . . . of the World." He closed his eyes and opened them again. "Where's Mazie?"

"I don't know where she went. Doing something useful, I'm sure. She's taking her maid of honor and best person duties very seriously."

Right on cue, the patio door slid open and Mazie stumbled in, flushed and out of breath.

Fig smiled. "Maze . . . I'm glad . . . you're here."

"Just a minute." She opened the hall door and looked left and right before closing it again. Then she exited to the courtyard, calling over her shoulder. "Be right back!"

They watched as she ran to the gazebo and lifted up a duffel bag as if it contained a bomb on a hair trigger and walked it slowly toward them.

"Here's one surprise you'll like, Fig," she said, coming in. She lifted the bag onto the bed and unzipped the top. Prince's head pushed through and he scrambled out to lick Fig's face, wiggling in every direction.

"Hey there, boy. How'd you get here?"

Mazie grinned. "No one was there to feed him, so I called Martin and Kiza and they called Hector and they all went to the island to feed him. They were arguing who should take him home when Martin said they should bring him here. So they did." She looked into the bag. "They put about a gazillion treats in here to keep him quiet. Anyway, they all say hi and *felicitations*. Oh, and they told me to tell you that they are going to stop at Hector's church to light candles for you."

"Good men," Fig said.

Prince turned in circles before lowering himself into the bend of Fig's arm. Fig's lids began to droop and finally closed, but his smile remained for a long time.

Meanwhile, Mazie was chewing on her thumbnail again.

Charlotte tucked a curl behind Mazie's ear. "Bringing Prince was really thoughtful. You're the best best-person and maid of honor ever."

Mazie shot a sideways glance. "You think so? I did everything I could think of."

"It was more than I ever expected."

Mazie shrugged. "But now what?" Her eyes darted around the room. "What can I do *now*?"

Charlotte cupped Mazie's face with her hands. "It's been a very long, very hard day. But your work here is done. It's time for you to go home and let Nana and Pop take care of you." She reached for her phone.

"Can I take Prince with me?"

Charlotte nodded.

Mazie looked down at Fig's closed eyes. "Can he hear me?"

"Yes, I think so. Would you like to say goodbye?"

Mazie took a step closer and put her hand on Fig's. "Uncle Ficus? Hey. It's me, your niece Mazie. Prince and I have to go now, but we want to say goodbye." She drew her breath in and held it for a long time. "If Prince could talk, he'd tell you that he had the best summer a dog could ever, ever have. He made lots of new friends. He got to run around the island and be free. But best of all, he got to spend all that time with you."

She leaned over and pressed her face into Prince's neck. "And even though he maybe can't live on the island anymore, he knows I'll take really good care of him and love him as much as you do. We won't let him forget you either and how you tamed him and taught him to be a good dog and be part of a family."

She wiped her cheek on her shirt sleeve and sniffed.

"Well, I guess that covers just about everything, except to say that pretty much goes double for me. And one more thing. I know I'm not very good at thank yous, . . . so, I just want to say it. Thank you . . . a lot. . . for saving me . . . and I don't mean just that one time on the river either."

She touched her lips to his cheek and pressed her face into his shoulder.

When she stood up again, Mally was in the doorway. "Okay, love. It's time to come home."

When they are gone, Charlotte stepped out of her dress and crawled into bed next to Fig in her slip. She traced the lines of his face with her fingertips.

He drifted in and out. Eyes fluttering open sometimes. Sometimes speaking. Sometimes just squeezing her hand.

"Hector . . . Martin . . . Kiza. . . . Don't forget them."

"I won't. I promise."

"No one knows . . . where . . . you go . . . when you die. . . Don't let anyone . . . tell you otherwise. . . I'll. . . find out . . . soon."

"We all will. Someday."

"I'm a little curious though. More questions . . . than . . ." He coughed.

"Than answers?" She pressed his hand to her lips and held it against her cheek. "You like it that way."

"No memorial, please . . . No ceremonies. Today was . . . everything."

"Yes. Thank you for being my husband."

"But if *you* want one . . . a mem . . . orial . . . or need one . . . okay."

"Shhh."

"You . . . did it, Char."

"What did I do?"

"Radical . . . ba . . ."

"Bad-ass joy?"

He nodded.

She said, "Yeah. We both did. These last months were the best fun I ever had."

"Really?"

"Really truly."

"Me too."

"You're a champion. You . . . stood up . . . for yourself . . . and . . . what you know is true . . . You're . . . a woman . . . of substance.

"You'd make . . . a great monarch, . . . Queen Charlotte the Great."

"My happiest memories . . . include you. . . and Mazie. . . Tell her."
    "I will.
    "Don't forget."
    "I won't forget. I promise. She loves you so, so much."
    "I love her too."

Dr. Bryant and a nurse came in. Fig rallied.
    "Ladies and gentlemen. I'd like . . . to present . . . my wife . . . Charlotte Anne . . . Adair."
    "We heard the good news. Congratulations to both of you."
    "On our first date . . . I peed on her."
    "You did? Why?"
    "To claim her as my own."

"Rememb . . . wha . . . we had, . . . Charl . . ."
    "I will. I'll remember everything."

"Charl . . ."
"I'm here."
"Don't worry about . . . anything . . . I've arranged . . . everyth—"
    "I'll be fine. I promise."

When he thought she wasn't watching, he winced in pain.

"I love you, Fig."

"I love . . . you too."
"I love you three."

Legs cycling. His hand grasping. Lungs desperate for air.
"Can't . . . breathe." Eyes wide, pleading. "Sor . . . So sorry. Please."
"Fig? Fig! Do you want me to call Dr. Bryant? Is that what you want me to do, Fig? Tell me what you want."
Eyes squeezed shut. Tears escaping. "Please . . . sorry. . . . so sorry. . . so . . . sor . . ."
"Tell me. Is it's time? Just tell me."
"Yes. . . . . Time."

A syringe in a tray.
He: Have you said all you need to say to him, Charlotte?
She: (Nodding. Lying) Yes.
A syringe on a tray. A syringe on a tray.
He: . . . heavy sedative . . . ease his discomfort . . . (Hand lightly on her shoulder) I don't expect he'll wake up again. I'm so sorry, Charlotte."
The door clicking shut.

Her face pressed to his shoulder.
"Goodbye, Fig. I will always love you. Always, always, always, always, always, always . . . "

In time, his breath slowed.
In time, he drifted away.
And in time, he didn't return.

<u>36</u>

DAYS OF GRIEF

Bumblebees have their favorite flower patches. They make the same orderly circuit from blossom to blossom each day. But if one flower is removed, a bumblebee will search for it again and again.

Warm hands. Time to go home, love. Come on now.
Mally's minivan floating behind red taillights.
Black tree fingers splayed against a moonless sky.
An empty bedroom of a dead sister.
A quilted floral tent. Shivering.
Dead silence.
Dead silence.

DAY ONE.
   Mally, bearer of tea and warm hands.
   Bacon.
   The doorbell. Muffled voices rising.
   Somewhere, a siren. Somewhere, a fire. Lives up in smoke.
   Where is Fig today? She covers her ears.

DAY TWO.
   Cars passing. A basketball bouncing. Flouting the first law of
her buckled world: Don't move. Nobody move.

   The mattress listing under her father's weight.
   Comfort food. Prince against her belly.

Sleeping without rest. Waking on the dark side of the moon.
Beyond reach: Sleep. Fig.

DAY THREE.
    Disbelief vs despair:
    He can't be gone. He's gone.
    He's gone. He can't be gone.
    Repeat. Repeat. Repeat.
    A senseless ceaseless mantra.
    Words fail. Repeatrepeatrepeat.
    Why didn't she keep his forelock?

DAY FOUR.
    Mazie's face, feather-lashes against her shoulder.
    "The Big People made blueberry pancakes. Come down?"
    Slow breath pushing out.
    I . . . can't . . . move.

DAY FIVE.
    Mazie. A vase of mums.
    "You'll be okay. Won't you, Aunt Charlotte?"
    "With time. Yes. I promise."

DAY SIX.
    Mally's unhurried ascent. Cold rushing her quilt-tent.
    "Morning, love. Portia's sending over her massage therapist. She'll be here in an hour. Come on. Up you go."
    Mally pushing Charlotte into the bathroom, pulling off her musty t-shirt and sweatpants and pushing her forward.
    Knees-to-chest till the water runs cold.

Tears and snot dripping through the face cradle leaving a dark spot on the bedroom carpet.

Question: If a widow merits sympathy proportionate to the length of the marriage, what is owed a widow of a marriage lasting nine hours and twenty-six minutes?

DAY SEVEN.

Migration to the couch. Baby steps.

Ted stands in the archway offering a phone. "For you, honey."

"Hey, Char. It's Katie. Do you know what today is? It's Saturday, October 8, and guess what's *not* happening? The Plant-a-Palooza! Hundreds of invasive plants are *not* being planted along the river today. Yay you! Yay Fig! Yay us! Something to smile about, right?"

"Yes. Thanks."

"Hey, the Saskawan Five are meeting for coffee and scones at the Farmer's Daughter Monday morning. Pumpkin spice or apple walnut scones this month. Nine o'clock. I'll swing by and pick you up."

"Thanks, Katie. But just—just tell everyone that the wedding cake was beautiful and so kind. We were really touched. And, thanks for calling."

There was a voice message from Katie later. "Sorry to bug you. I forgot to say there's a new lawyer taking our case. Fig arranged everything. He'll be there on Monday too . . . the new guy, not Fig . . . Oh God, sorry. Forget I said that. Just *call* me!"

DAY EIGHT.

Ted stood in her bedroom doorway holding a bakery box. "A woman named Nicky stopped by with this." It was a box of scones. "There's a note with it."

> Dear Charlotte,
> We're all just devastated about Fig. He was a cracker-jack lawyer and true friend. That you got married was epic and you looked beautiful.

I hate to bother you, but I can't wait to tell you about the lawyer that came to the Farmer's Daughter this morning. His name is Brewster McCall and Fig arranged for him to represent us, and pro bono, too. Your awesome husband thought of everything, didn't he?

There's so much to tell when you're ready. But just so you know, things are moving forward. We owe that and so much more, to you and Fig.

Love from the Saskawan Five,
Nicky

She folded the note and looked up. "Thanks, Dad. Want a scone? Pumpkin spice or apple-walnut?"

"After our walk." He whistled. "Prince? Walkies!"

Prince bounded up the stairs and onto the bed.

Ted chuckled. "Did someone say 'Walkies'? That's his new favorite word. It's almost sixty out there, honey. The maples have turned. Prince wants you to see them. Don't you, boy?"

"Thanks, but I was just . . ." She scratched her matted hair and brushed crumbs off the sheet. She pointed vaguely at the room as if it would be obvious what she needed to do. But there was only her unmade bed, clothes draped over the chair and a pile of unopened mail on the nightstand.

Prince glared at her and barked.

Ted laughed. "I'm afraid he's not taking no for an answer."

Prince towed her through the neighborhood like a tenacious little tug-boat, while Ted prodded from behind.

"Ah, sweetheart, I know it doesn't seem like it now, but it will get easier. I speak from experience."

"I know you do, Dad. I just need to wallow a little longer."

"I know that, too."

She raised her arms and let them drop to her sides. "I mean, it's like I've been dumped in the wilderness with a bobby pin, a cake tin and, I don't know, a list of the kings of England. I need an instruction manual. *The Life of Charlotte, 2.0* or *Widowhood for Dummies*. I'm so unprepared for this. It's not that I don't want to go on living. I just don't know *how*. Not without him."

"You have a home, family and friends who love you and a business to run. You'll get through."

"I know, Dad. I just need time."

"You have that too, but don't wait too long."

DAY NINE.

Mally stood at the sink waiting for their tea to brew.

Charlotte said, "I think I kind of believe in reincarnation."

Mally turned, her hand on her hip. "I knew we should have sent you to Sunday school."

"Seriously, how else could the world let go of a soul like Fig's? It's not like nature to be wasteful."

"So, when will he be back?"

"I'm not sure."

"What will he look like? I'll watch for him."

She shrugged. "I'll know him when I see him."

Mally looked into the backyard. "You-who, Fig! Oh, look there, a giraffe!"

Charlotte laughed, surprising herself.

DAY TEN.

Mally was dividing the contents of a half dozen casseroles into freezer containers when Charlotte came into the kitchen. A pile of empty Pyrex and Corning Ware pans were submerged in the sink.

"I need to return the pans, but we can't eat them fast enough."

"Where did they come from?" Charlotte asked.

Mally pointed to a list on the fridge. "Mrs. Grosnickle, your friends Barb and Katie, two women in my book club and our new neighbors. Nice people."

"Yes, very thoughtful," Charlotte said. "I'll write notes in a few days." What a strange convention, she thought, bringing food to people whose loved ones and appetites have entirely left them.

Mally knelt in front of the freezer, rearranging things. "Oh, and this," she said, holding up a long package wrapped in white paper. "Smoked trout from the Hawthorn River. It's from that nice judge. He dropped it off yesterday. What's his name?"

"Ronner," Charlotte said, with a hint of a smile and surprising herself again. She ran her finger across her lips to make sure it was real.

Mally twisted around to look at her daughter. "Everyone keeps saying how brave you were to stay with Fig until the end."

"Really?"

Charlotte shuffled back upstairs and thought about this for the rest of the day.

DAY ELEVEN.

"It wasn't bravery that made me stay."

She was folding Mazie's clean tee shirts at the dining room table. "I was in denial or paralyzed with fear most of the time. But the need to be with him was greater."

"So it was love more than bravery," Mally mused. And four t-shirts later, she added, "Love is powerful, isn't it? What other emotion gives us the courage to stay when running would be so much easier?"

On the third load, Mally said, "Your dad and I won't ever put Lauren's death behind us, but as hard as it was, and still is, it hasn't ruined our lives. We have happy times. You will too."

The doorbell rang and Mally come up the stairs.

"There is a young man at the door who says he works for you." She lowered her chin and frowned when Charlotte didn't move. "I'm not sending him away."

"Hello, Martin," she said, coming down.

He offered his hand. "I am very, very sorry for coming here now. I am very, very sad about Fig. He was a very good man. I hope—I don't have words . . ." He looked desolate.

"Thank you, Martin." She gestured toward the couch. "Please, sit."

Mally set two cups of tea on the coffee table.

Martin began to speak very slowly, considering each word.

"I have good news to tell, Charlotte. My wife, she work for a family, the Dunhams. They have build—*built*—a big, new house with many, many trees all around. She hear—*heard*—Mrs. Dunham talk to her husband that she want a landscape designer. My wife said, 'My husband knows a person like that.' She showed to them to your website and the pictures of the island. Mrs. Dunham liked it. She wrote emails to you and I made a message in your phone also, but—" He looked down at his hands.

"I'm sorry, Martin. I haven't been checking them."

"I understand. But—" He paused. "But I think it is a very good business opportunity for you. So today, I go—*went*—to that house for you. I tell—*told*—her the names of the trees—oak, redbud, hickory, hemlock. I show to her a sunny place to grow coneflowers and asters and milkweed."

"You did all that?"

"Yes. Then I tell—telled, no *told* her, sorry, you will make her house look like it grew from the earth."

"Thank you, Martin."

"I hope you make a call to her very soon. Your business, it needs more people to buy. What is the word?"

"Clients. Yes, you're right, Martin."

"Kiza and I go to the community college to study botany and business now. We study our English, too."

"I can tell. You have improved."

"Thank you." He smiled before speaking again. "But there are many books to buy and Hector and his wife have another baby coming. We want to work and your business will grow with our help I think."

He handed her a slip of paper with a name and phone number. "Can you make a call to Mrs. Dunham soon?"

She gave a small sigh and nodded. "Thank you, Martin. I will. Soon. I promise."

He sighed in relief. "I am so glad."

DAY TWELVE.

Charlotte was watching *Sesame Street* with Prince when her father came into the living room.

"Fig's attorney called. His name is Brewster McCall. He says you haven't returned his calls so he tried our number."

Charlotte picked at the dog hair on her sweater.

Ted said, "You need to call him back, honey."

She sighed. "Dad, we were married less than a day! At the hospital, they called me Mrs. Bigelow and I didn't even know they meant me."

She headed for the stairs. "Why does he keep calling?"

"Because you're Fig's wife."

DAY THIRTEEN.

"Good morning, Mrs. Dunham? My name is Charlotte Adair from Adair Natural Landscaping. I believe you've met one of my employees? . . . Yes, Martin. He told me you're looking for some advice about land-scaping your new home? . . . . Of course. I'd love to come by. . . . All right, Wednesday would work . . ."

She pulled the covers over her head and slept for the rest of the afternoon.

DAY FOURTEEN.

Mally stood over Charlotte's bed with a phone in one hand, a cup of tea in the other and an odd look on her face.

"We had another message from that attorney, Brewster McCall today." She tapped the screen.

I'm terribly sorry to keep leaving messages, Mr. and Mrs. Adair, but I know your daughter will want to hear what I have to say. I'm sending a messenger to your home today with two letters, tell her one is from Fig. He left it with me to give to Charlotte. After she has read it, it's important that she contact me. Thank you. I am so sorry for you loss.

Mally held out an envelope, her eyes bright and glistening. "This came a few minutes ago." She set the tea on the nightstand, kissed her daughter's forehead and tiptoed out.

The letter was typed on Fig's legal stationery.

My Beloved Charlotte,

As I write, I am trying to summon the courage to ask for your hand—and every other part of you—in marriage. That's quite a move for a confirmed bachelor, but it was easy once you insisted that we should be a couple. Just the idea of popping the question makes my heart beat so fast I may not live to finish this letter.

But, if you are reading this, sweet Charlotte, I asked and, wonder of wonders, you said yes!! Thank you, my dear, incomparable wife. You made me the happiest Earthling on the planet.

Sadly, if you are reading this, you are a widow now. I'm so, so sorry I couldn't stick around. It wasn't for lack of trying.

You have a right to feel disappointed and resentful. You must have questioned my sanity for asking and maybe even your own for saying yes. I can't blame you. I can't blame you at all. You did it for me, more than for yourself, I know that. It must have seemed a silly request on my part.

I hope you'll change your mind about that after reading this.

Charlotte, please know that I loved you more in our time to-gether—however short it might have been—than I could have loved anyone else for a full three score and ten.

If I could have been King Fig the Benevolent, I would have decreed so many things for you, fair Queen Charlotte. Every day would be filled with whimsy, meaningful endeavors and ecstatic madness. And for balance, there'd be lazy Sundays left for meditative wanderings in flower-filled meadows with Mazie and Prince. I would also decree for you free and unfettered access to dirt because you love it so.

I never subscribed to the idea that the vicissitudes of life—dying in one's forties, for example—happen for a reason. If that were the case, the daily headlines would make a lot more sense. But I do believe that you will thrive after I am gone. I couldn't stand it if entangling my life with yours left you too scarred to go on. I won't rest peacefully until you have happily moved on with your life—Please remember that.

You and the Saskawan Five are moving a mountain. That takes guts (and grit) and I'm so proud of you. I was honored beyond words to play a supporting role. Old Brew (Brewster McCall) is your guy now. You can trust him completely.

You, my darling, were put on this earth to be a messenger and a prophet—a voice for all things living and green. You are a restorer of the land, of overgrown islands and of a man whose fighting spirit had just about left him six months ago. Sometimes I think that if we had met sooner, the heat and light you radiate might have cured me. You were so good for me.

Now back to the subject of making you glad you married me.

There is money—a shocking amount of money—coming to you from my estate. Lest you think yourself undeserving, remember it came to me in much the same way. I didn't earn most of it and never felt entitled to any of it, but I tried to use it wisely and generously. And, I never thought it gave me an excuse to sit on my ass either. I am happy to pass it along to you because once you get over the shock of being an heiress, I know you'll put it to good use. (Not a bad substitute for being Queen of the World, right?)

I've also asked Old Brew, to advise you about finances, because when you come into a lot of money all at once, it can ruin you. It can take the wind out of your sails and pretty soon you're just sitting on a deck chair sipping piña coladas and never leaving port. The trick is to keep sailing in the same direction as before—but faster and with more power. And never, ever give up the helm.

I hope that new roof and working furnace can take solid form now and that your tree nursery and greenhouse will materialize ASAP, as Mazie loves to say. I hope too, that you'll put the American dream within reach of Hector and Martin and Kiza—or people as deserving as they are.

I hope you continue to take an interest in our case, but I have arranged for Old Brew to see it through if you choose not to. You have a business to run and you've already launched our case so beautifully.

I hope you take time to rest from your labors. Read some fine books—or perhaps write one—"Charlotte's Nature Fables, The Ant and the Bloodroot, The Bumblebee and the Turtlehead, and more." It would be a bestseller.

Watch over Mazie for me. Help her take flight and find her place in the world. If she really wants the house, I'm happy for her to have it, but I've put it in your name for you to decide when the time is right. I truly regret that I won't read her college essay or her Ph.D. thesis or sit in the front row when she wins all those awards.

I never expected to love a child. She is a revelation to me. Tell her that for me. She might not believe you, so keep telling her until she does.

I insist you fall in love again, Charlotte. You're so good at it. I insist that you kiss at least three new men each year until you find one who loves (and kisses) you as well and as deeply as I did. Fall hard, Charlotte. Remember the magical power of radical bad-ass joy, and don't hold back on my account. It will be the best balm for the pain I've inflicted.

I probably I left this life still harboring hopes for reincarnation. (Life cannot be denied.) So keep your eyes peeled. That frog with the long legs calling to you from the water's edge might be me. Or that trout leaping from the river could be me hoping for a glimpse of you. The tallest oak seedling in your nursery could be me, too. Someday, my leaves and acorns will feed a new forest you planted.

And finally, Charlotte Anne, live so that life makes you shout "Wow!" at least once a day. Surprise yourself—just as you surprised me by becoming my wife. Wow! Just wow!

With my undying love,

I am your husband, King Fig the Benevolent

P.S. Old Brew's letter is attached. It will make a lot more sense than this one.

Dear Ms. Adair,

I want to express my very deepest sympathy. Fig was a dear friend as well as a highly respected colleague who was in possession of a brilliant legal mind.

I was Fig's attorney for over a decade and am now the executor of his estate. Before he passed, we met on several occasions to get his affairs in order.

Because he had no heirs and you were not yet married, he asked me to prepare two wills. The first named you as a beneficiary and the second, as his wife. Please know his marriage proposal was not a fevered, deathbed plea, nor was it merely a legal maneuver. (He wanted me to emphasize that to you.) It was a thoughtfully conceived plan to express his deep affection and fulfill his obligations to you as your husband.

Before going into detail, I would like to give you some background on the Bigelow family. Fig's maternal grandfather was Dr. Newton Ellery. He was born in 1925 and was drafted into the Army Medical Corps while a medical student during World War II. He served in Europe. As a young medic, he had a knack for improvising medical devices in the field. He was decorated for saving many lives. After the war, he patented some of his ideas and founded the Ellery Medical Equipment Company. Today, there are manufacturing sites in four US states, France and China.

Fig's mother, Jean, was Dr. Ellery's only child, just as Fig was hers, so when his parents died the majority shares of the company passed to Fig. That's why he was able to work for Legal Aid, which he did so passionately for many years, taking only a modest salary.

Fig thought long and hard about how to manage his inheritance. When he realized he had little time left, he and I began consolidating his assets with the idea of creating a charitable fund. We kicked around several ideas for a mission for this entity but none was a clear winner. Then he met you. Your interest in protecting native ecosystems found an enthusiastic disciple.

So, here's what Fig directed me to do.

First, on the matter of *Adair, et al vs the City of Saskawan and the County of Saskawan*, it was Fig's intention that if his death occurred before the case was resolved, the lawsuit would go forward with my firm representing you. As you know, the TRO was granted and the Plant-a-Palooza did not take place. But perhaps you haven't heard that last week, both the City and the County agreed to revise their list of allowable plants to exclude the invasive species you named in the TRO. This applies not only to Cross-County Park but throughout their jurisdictions.

So congratulations, Ms. Adair. Victory is yours, and of course, Fig's. Your co-plaintiffs and I are now discussing the feasibility of adding the Michigan Horticultural Association to our list of defendants. We'd like to know your thoughts.

Second, about a month ago, Fig ask me to begin the process of creating the Newton E. Bigelow and Charlotte A. Adair Fund for Land Restoration. It will have a board of directors with seats for yourself and others you may appoint. The Fund will be managed by a professional staff of the board's choosing.

The Bigelow-Adair Fund will be endowed in the amount of $23.2 million from the estate. This will allow the distribution of roughly a million dollars annually in the form of grants to qualified organizations. Fig wanted you to have this tool to continue "fighting the good fight" as he said, but he insisted that it be your choice to stay involved. You may decline or resign all involvement at any time, but know that the Fund's work will continue.

He has also set up a trust fund for your niece, Madelyn McDougal Adair, that should be more than sufficient for her college and post-graduate education, with you as the trustee.

And to you personally, he leaves the remainder of his estate, including the house and the island, with no strings or restrictions of any kind. He hopes only that you will never again have to build another "raised-bed rose garden." (He said you would know what that means.) The current value of your share of the estate is $5.2 million.

As I believe he explained in his letter to you, I can act as your legal and financial advisor as long as you want me. Please call my office at your earliest convenience, as I'm sure you have many questions.

Again, I am terribly sorry for your loss. Fig was a dear friend and a true gentleman. You just can't get a better combination than that.

Yours sincerely,

Brewster A. McCall
Attorney at Law

DECEMBER

Michigan Holly/Winterberry   Ilex verticillata

37

LIFE A.F.

After a drought or infestation, trees may drop their injured leaves, but they can also grow a new set in the same season. A lima bean plant infested with mites can release a chemical to attract a cannibalistic mite to come over for dinner. When the purple blossom of a coneflower is picked, the plant refocuses its energy and grows stronger roots. A tomato plant that becomes pot-bound sets extra buds to increase its odds of survival.

As the winter solstice approached, Saskawan, Michigan's first snowfall came and went leaving a black and white patchwork over the landscape. The pale sun barely managed a shallow arc across the southern horizon.

At the sound of Charlotte's truck leaving her gravel driveway, a flock of goldfinches rose up from the pasture in an undulating wave and settled back down on the tips of the dogwoods, redbuds and shadblow saplings in her new tree nursery. They were planted the day after Thanksgiving by the Saskawan Five who arrived at the farm unannounced bearing shovels, a big thermos of coffee and a bag of scones.

"We're your private Plant-a-Palooza!" Katie announced.

They worked all day then gathered around Charlotte's kitchen table for pizza and beer.

Now, two weeks later, Charlotte looked over at her silent passenger. "Have you thought about what you want from the island?"

Mazie shrugged. "I'll look around and see."

"You can have anything that fits on the raft without swamping it."

That didn't even get a smile.

Mazie had been begging to go to the island for weeks but now seemed to be having second thoughts.

"Fig would want you to have some of his things," Charlotte said.

Mazie was silent.

At the landing, Mazie leaned against the truck's bumper, watching the island but not moving. Charlotte came to stand beside her. The lines of the house were blurred by a wintry haze rising up from the river.

"I wish Prince could've come."

"He would just search for Fig. That wouldn't be fair."

"I just wish I could explain everything to him." She dug her heel into the gravel. "Do you think he'll forget Fig?"

"Dogs have long memories. But I know he's happy living with you and Nana and Pop. And he loves coming to the farm on the weekends. One day we'll bring him here."

Mazie lifted her chin. "One day I'll come here and never leave. Ever. But right now, I don't know. It's weird how good memories can make you feel so awful." She kicked at a stone, sending it down the slope toward the dock.

"There's a word for that, you know. Bittersweet."

"How can anything be bitter and sweet? That's an oxymoron."

Charlotte shrugged. "I don't know, but it can. I'm bitter about losing Fig sometimes, but knowing him was the sweetest thing."

"Yeah. I guess."

A pair of cardinals flew to the island and landed on Fig's roof.

Mazie sighed. "When do the renters move in?"

"This weekend. The cleaning crew comes tomorrow."

Charlotte knew it made no sense to keep a house for a child barely in her teens, but her parents had kept the farm for her. After meeting with Brewster McCall, she had decided to rent out the property until Mazie was older.

"I bet I could find a new species of beetle or dragonfly here," Mazie said. "One one knows about. I could write my thesis here."

"Or, you might become a lawyer or an economist or a chemist or you might marry Nate, move to New York City and have Nate babies. You're young. You'll change your mind a dozen times." She gave Mazie a playful nudge.

"Well, Nate babies aren't happening. We broke up weeks ago and I'd shrivel up if I had to live in New York City. But I might go to law school. Insects will always be a serious interest though. And I'll live here. That's for sure."

"Just keep your options open, Maze. When I was your age no one knew much about invasive plants or even native plants."

"Really?"

"Really."

"Maybe I'll invent my own job."

"Sounds like something you'd do." She threaded her arm though Mazie's. "Come on, kiddo. Let's go."

Mazie piloted the raft into the river, but stopped in the middle.

"Fig stopped here," she said. "Because he was out of breath, I think."

"And to enjoy the view too," Charlotte added.

She watched the Hawthorn River move past the island. This was not the same river she crossed on that March day nine months ago. Where was called now? Lake Michigan? Lake Huron? Niagara Falls? The Gulf stream?

Mazie pulled on the rope again and the raft moved toward Fig's island, so steadfast and unmoving.

They walked the paths first, stopping at each vantage point to recall some memory of Fig.

"Will the thinkin' log be here in ten years?" she asked.

"In one form or another. Insects will love it."

They stopped in the oak grove.

"And my swing? Will it be here?"

"Of course," Charlotte said, brushing a coating of slush off the wooden seat with her glove. "Shall we?"

Maze shook her head.

"For old time's sake. We'll do it together."

Charlotte coaxed Mazie up the ladder with one hand, pulling the rope behind them.

"At least I'm not blindfolded this time," Mazie said, starting to giggle. "Oh, God! This is higher than I remembered."

They wedged their hips into the wooden seat, arms wrapping each other's waists and fingers clamped around the thick ropes.

"No screaming," Mazie ordered. "I'm serious. I'll freak out."

"Ready?" Charlotte said. "One . . . two . . . three!" They dropped toward the earth, skimming above it and rising into the bare canopy. Their screams echoed off the water.

Reverse. Repeat. Reverse. Repeat. Finally, their feet dragged the ground. Drunk with laughter and vertigo, they weaved toward the house and stumbled up the steps. While Charlotte rooted through her bag for the house key, Mazie sank into an Adirondack chair to catch her breath.

"Do you think Alison Geller's parents heard us?" Mazie asked, her eyes bright with mischief. She fluttered her eyelashes and raised a pinky finger. "I say, daaaaaling, did you hear that unGAWD-ly shrieking coming from the island? You know, I heard that old hermit kicked the bucket. They say his ghost haunts the island. Oh, poor me, poor me! My nerves." She fanned herself theatrically.

Charlotte played along. "Ah yes, my love. I heard he was the uncle of that *peculiar* girl who came to Alison's party last summer. What was her name?"

Mazie grinned. "Midgie. No, Miniver. Or was it Muzzly? Anyway, she wasn't half as peculiar as that aunt of hers."

Charlotte pushed the door open and stepped inside, their laughter swallowed up by the emptiness.

Behind her, Mazie whispered, "Do you think he's here?"

"Wherever I am, he's with me. I can feel him."

"I think I sort of get that."

Charlotte inhaled the lingering scent of coffee, leather and pine. Masculine things. And other things too with no words to attach to them. If she had been alone, she might have sunk to her knees on the entry mat.

This wasn't the first time she'd been to the house since Fig died. Weeks ago, Portia and Barb helped her gather up Fig's files and deliver them to Brewster McCall's office. Since then, the Saskawan Five had spent many hours briefing him.

After the city and county capitulated, they were dropped from the suit. But on Brewster's advice, the state's three regulatory agencies—the Departments of Agriculture, Natural Resources and Environmental Quality were added as defendants.

And when VanderLee Garden's annual order for five hundred poinsettias was "misplaced" by Oosterbaan Wholesale Greenhouses, Barb and Hal joined the list of plaintiffs. Michigan Public Radio aired stories about the lawsuit, the epidemic of invasive species and the state's failure to ban them. Meanwhile, Saskawan's own state representative was promising to push through reforms in Lansing.

And when Elena Scott, alias Elena Lewis, announced that her organization was mobilizing its legal team (and "digging in for a long fight") the Saskawan Five voted unanimously to add the Michigan Horticultural Association to its list of defendants. A sapoena was on its way to Elena.

Thanks to Fig's largess (He really was King Fig the Benevolent) life had taken other astonishing turns. When she decided to rent out Fig's house, the property manager she hired advised her to leave it furnished. The only exception was the porch glider, which Martin, Kiza and Hector tied to the raft and ferried across the river. It now sat on her front porch where she planned to spend many evenings watching her tree babies outgrow their nursery.

The new tenants, two young professors from Saskawan State University, seemed thrilled with the house, the furniture and the isolation of the island. They listened with interest when she told them about the former owner, the house renovations and her work to restore the island's ecosystem. She cringed now to think how she'd gone on about her late husband.

Mally and Ted helped her clean out the house. Fig's sheets and striped duvet were now on her bed at the farm. "They don't call them comforters for nothing," Mally had said. Charlotte had kept several blue oxford shirts, with their lovely, full-length sleeves, to wear around the house. The rest of his clothes went to a homeless shelter.

Money may not buy happiness—and she had many, many tearful moments—but Fig's bequest gave Charlotte a powerful boost. She was working harder than ever but more confidently because she was no longer teetering on the brink of bankruptcy. She even changed the name of her business to Adair Native Landscaping.

The farmhouse had a new roof, a high-efficiency furnace and a lovely new double-paned window in her bedroom. In the corner of Charlotte's kitchen was an antique roll-top desk. Her designs for the Dunham's woodland path, small prairie and rain garden were nearly finished. Meanwhile, Hector was studying how to build a greenhouse next to the barn. Martin would oversee the nursery and a new crop of perennials while Kiza was proving to be a skilled bookkeeper.

Mazie followed close behind as Charlotte ran her hand along the sofa where she and Fig had so often fallen asleep in front of the fire. Mazie shadowed her as she touched the polished surface of the dining table where she and Fig had composed the TRO.

At the bottom of the stairs, Mazie stopped. "Um. I'll just let you…" Her voice trailed off. "I'll be in the study if you need anything."

Charlotte sank into the mattress and curled into the place where their bodies met. His possessions were gone, but the room was still so full of him—of the two of them. There were more good days than bad now, but little things, like finding his reading glasses in a coat pocket, could still knock her flat.

"Aunt Charlotte?" Mazie called from the landing. "I found something."

She got up slowly. "Coming."

Mazie was holding something. "I found this on the bookshelf. I thought it was a book, but look."

It was a framed photograph of a lanky boy of perhaps eighteen wearing white tennis shorts and a Polo shirt. He was holding a tennis racket in the ready position and smiling at the camera. A white-blond forelock fell over one eyebrow.

"He was pretty cute," Mazie said. "I figured you'd want it."

Charlotte touched his face through the glass—her beautiful golden boy and whispered. "Thank you."

"I laid a fire." Mazie pointed to a neat Fig-esque teepee of wood in the fireplace. "Can I light it? It's kind of cold in here."

"Sure. I'll put a kettle on."

Mazie lit the tinder and the two of them drank tea and watched the fire take hold.

Mazie said, "I *hate* that strangers will be sitting on this couch and sleeping in Fig's bed and sitting on his thinkin' log." She got up and poked angrily at the fire, making one side of the teepee collapse. "Now look what I did!"

"It wouldn't be good to let the house sit empty."

"But *you* could live here. I could come on the weekends, just like always. I could catch insects, watch fireflies . . ." Her voice faded into silence.

'Always' for Mazie meant just a few weekends last fall, but Charlotte knew what she meant.

"There are lots of insects at the farm, Maze," she offered. "Fireflies, too, and just as many stars. Besides, Maze, I have a business to run."

"Did he leave you a lot of money too? More than in my college fund?" Mazie had already decided that the Ivy League, U of M or Kalamazoo College was in her future.

"He was generous enough that I don't have to worry about money all the time. Or, discuss it all the time." She gave Mazie a look.

"Why is money such a taboo subject with grown-ups?"

"Why are taboo subjects such interesting subjects to children?"

"I'm not a child."

"If you were a grown-up, you'd know the answer."

Mazie grunted and went to stand in the doorway of Fig's study. "If I write my dissertation here I'll be, like, channeling him." She laughed. "Okay, that sounded weird and stupid."

"People who inspire us don't have to be physically present, I've learned that."

"Do you think Fig would want me to have his office chair or his pencil holder?"

"I think he'd want you to have both."

"How about this silver pen? It looks expensive, but I'd never sell it. And some of his books? It'd like the Ogden Nash collection. 'God in his wisdom made the fly, and then forgot to tell us why.' Classic, eh? Granted, Nash should have known that flies actually *clean up* the world's messes. If they didn't lay their eggs in poop so their larvae could eat it, we'd all be wading through mountains of shit right now. There's your 'why', Mr. Nash. But it's still a really funny poem."

Mazie put the volumes in the box and the box on the seat of the chair. "I'm going to memorize a bunch of Nash poems because they're so hilarious. I might even write some more poems. Fig would like that."

She fingered the book bindings, looking away. "Did I tell you that my autumn poem got an A-minus? It would have gotten an A if my English teacher had a decent sense of humor. The class loved it." She let her hands drop to her sides. "I-I never got a chance to tell him that."

When the fire had burned to embers, they rolled Fig's chair onto the porch, carried it down the steps, pushed it onto the raft and secured it with a length of rope.

Charlotte locked the front door behind her and paused on the porch. So many important conversations took place here, she thought.

"I'll be back," she whispered to the Adirondack chairs, the gazebo, then to the redbuds, the oaks, the swing, the sleeping frogs and turtles and perhaps, she thought, to Fig himself who might already have a robust new body.

Or, perhaps he was still resting. He was so tired at the end. Perhaps he would wait for the first warm days of spring to reappear. The thought cheered her. She would come back then to sit on the thinkin' log and watch for him.

She'd recognize him anywhere.

When the raft reached the landing and the truck was loaded, Mazie unzipped her backpack.

"I almost forgot. I found these in Fig's desk." She held out a stack of carefully folded handkerchiefs.

Charlotte traced the raised monogram, N.E.B, with her thumb.

"They'll come in handy sometimes, right Aunt Charlotte?"

"Sometimes, yes." She took one and pressed it back into Mazie's palm. "For you, whenever you need it."

Mazie closed her eyes and nodded. "Thank you."

As they drove to the farm, fog descended like a gauzy curtain over Fig's dock, his house, the big stone chimney, and finally, the island itself.

NOTES AND ACKNOWLEDGMENTS

In 2017, a suburb near my home announced plans to landscape a major street with Bradford pear trees. With some alarm, I composed a letter to city officials describing in detail the damage caused by this species. No one responded to my letter, but the experience got me wondering why these trees are still legal in Michigan.

I asked several environmental professionals to explain. I got an earful about Michigan's unwillingness to control the importation, propagation, marketing and sale of millions of invasive plants to municipalities, school districts, businesses and home gardeners. Plants that will end up in our woodlands, wetlands, dunes and lake shores. It defies logic until you follow the money. Michigan isn't the only state to drop the ball. Check out your state's list of banned plant species.

But there's plenty you can do, dear read, to protect the ecosystem you live in. To get started, pick up a copy of Doug Tallamy's *Bringing Nature Home*. I can't overstate this book's impact on American gardeners' burgeoning interest in native plants. Next, consider joining a chapter of Wild Ones (www.WildOnes.org) near you. This national, volunteer-driven organization is a great resource for home gardeners.

Let this be the year that you replace part of your lawn and *all* of your invasive plants with beautiful, life-giving North American native plants. Then, sit back and watch the wildlife return.

No one can write a book without help. The knowledge I needed to write *Charlotte's Crossing* came from many sources, including the Kalamazoo Nature Center, the Land Conservancy of West Michigan at The Highlands, Michigan's (sadly defunct) Master Naturalist Program, the Kent Conservation District and especially Wild Ones and *most* especially my beloved River City Chapter.

I'm grateful to Thom Clay who years ago invited me to a Fourth of July picnic on his enchanted island. His raft, his Adirondack-style home and sky-high rope swing were just begging for a story to unfold.

I must acknowledge some real "WILHA women"—Amy Heilman, Deb Montgomery, Tammy Lundeen and Esther Durnwald, who are so generous with their time and professional knowledge of native landscapes. They provide vital resources and information to native gardeners, including one gardener/novelist. The world needs more professionals like them.

The story of the TRO would have been impossible to write without the *pro bono* advice of Ann Nowak, Amy Preston, Jan Mann, Bob Kullgren, Adam Arnold, Kirk Halbertson and Lori Jacobs. Any inaccuracies are due to my own ignorance or wishful thinking.

I am blessed to have generous and literate friends and family. My super-sister and linguist, Shirley Thompson, patiently read and reread every sentence of every draft. (Remaining typos are my own late creations.) Lydia Mosher, Flossie Bode, Julie Stivers and my daughter, Leah Arnold graciously shared their wisdom at critical moments. Their observations were spot on and their encouragement was like rocket fuel.

I'm so lucky to have my own one-man, in-house book design department. And Paul Arnold is just that—my one man. How wise I was fifty years ago to marry such a lovable and useful individual.

Writing Lauren's story was painful, but cathartic. Addiction and overdose happens in the very best of families, including my own. If love conquered all, young people like Lauren, would be living long, productive lives. My heartfelt gratitude goes to those who shared their painful stories.

The love story of Charlotte and Fig is not entirely fictional. It belongs to Debbie and to Bruce. She loved her "Fig" fiercely, selflessly and to the end which came way too soon. I will always miss him.

Finally, I'm grateful to those who read my first novel, *Raised in Captivity* and asked for another. Here you go. And, thanks for asking.